SEDUCTION'S SWEET FIRE

Emily drew back a handful of Rob's hair and very gently pulled the comb through it. Wet, it was the color of walnut boards, dark with reddish highlights. A few gray hairs softened the color at his temples, and her fingers gently stroked them.

"God's blood, Em, do you know what you're doing to me?" Rob's lip beaded with sweat as the image of Emily climbing into his bed assaulted his mind. Giant pulses of energy throbbed through his body, and he bit his lip to bring himself under a familiar icy control. It didn't work. Emily Gorton, a mere slip of a woman, shattered his composure merely by touching him. . . .

"I cannot take anymore," whispered Rob, as he turned her to face him. "I've been so damn patient it astonishes even me. . . ." His big hands framed her face, and he looked deeply into her eyes. Then he brought his mouth to hers in a blazing kiss that stoked fires deep within them both.

"Rob, are we going too far?"

"Ah, Em, we haven't gone far enough," he said as he scooped her into his arms and carried her across to the bed. . . .

DANA RANSOM'S RED-HOT HEARTFIRES!

ALEXANDRA'S ECSTASY (2773, $3.75)

Alexandra had known Tucker for all her seventeen years, but all at once she realized her childhood friend was the man capable of tempting her to leave innocence behind!

LIAR'S PROMISE (2881, $4.25)

Kathryn Mallory's sincere questions about her father's ship to the disreputable Captain Brady Rogan were met with mocking indifference. Then he noticed her trim waist, angelic face and Kathryn won the wrong kind of attention!

LOVE'S GLORIOUS GAMBLE (2497, $3.75)

Nothing could match the true thrill that coursed through Gloria Daniels when she first spotted the gambler, Sterling Caulder. Experiencing his embrace, feeling his lips against hers would be a risk, but she was willing to chance it all!

WILD, SAVAGE LOVE (3055, $4.25)

Evangeline, set free from Indians, discovered liberty had its price to pay when her uncle sold her into marriage to Royce Tanner. Dreaming of her return to the people she loved, she vowed never to submit to her husband's caress.

WILD WYOMING LOVE (3427, $4.25)

Lucille Blessing had no time for the new marshal Sam Zachary. His mocking and arrogant manner grated her nerves, yet she longed to ease the tension she knew he held inside. She knew that if he wanted her, she could never say no!

Available wherever paperbacks are sold, or order direct from the Publisher. Send cover price plus 50¢ per copy for mailing and handling to Zebra Books, Dept. 3609, 475 Park Avenue South, New York, N.Y. 10016. Residents of New York, New Jersey and Pennsylvania must include sales tax. DO NOT SEND CASH.

BARBARA CUMMINGS

BLAZING PASSION

ZEBRA BOOKS
KENSINGTON PUBLISHING CORP.

To the men in my life. Especially my husband, my father and father-in-law, my grandfathers, my son and son-in-law, my brother, and all my uncles—those who are here and those who have died. Your love, devotion, and dedication to Wife and Family are remarkable in this day of throw-away relationships. You are the true heroes, everything men should be, everything women hope to find.

Thank you for your encouragement, love, and support.

For us in the Galli and Cummings families, you are truly the wind beneath our wings.

ZEBRA BOOKS

are published by

Kensington Publishing Corp.
475 Park Avenue South
New York, NY 10016

First printing: December, 1991

Printed in the United States of America

Chapter One

Lord, we know what we are, but
know not what we may be.

William Shakespeare
Hamlet, Act IV, Scene V

1772—Block Island—June 10

Boom!

Emily Gorton sat up in bed. There it was again.

Boom!

Cannon? Yes, cannon. What had some damn fool done now to irritate the damned British?

"Wilt they be puttin' into port, Misuz?"

Emily smiled at the sleepy Manissee Indian girl, her servant and friend, who stood at the door with a lighted candle in her hands. As was typical of Tab, her muslin nightslip was tattered and torn in places, yet white from many washings. The beaded deerskin and fox fur vest she wore over the nightslip for warmth was lovingly beaded. Rags or riches, it made no difference to Tab. What she was, she was. And Emily loved her because of, rather than in spite of, her oddities.

The young Manissee maiden rubbed her eyes and,

as usual, tried without success to control her unruly black hair from covering her entire face. A huge yawn billowed out—all the way from her bare toes, it seemed to Emily.

"Go back to bed, Tab. If they need us they know where to find us."

"Huh! Half the blinkin' sea full o' ships knows *that.*"

"Like as not. But I'd rather get a full night's sleep before finding out what's causing this new rumpus off shore."

Tab slipped back to her room, muttering under her breath about cold nights, calamities, and cannon fodder.

Regardless of what she'd told the girl, however, Emily was far from being relaxed and ready for sleep again. Tension kept her head slightly elevated from her pillow and cocked to one side as she listened intently until the cannon stopped and an eery quiet took over. With the booms silenced, the harsh sounds of a young person's snore filled the upstairs in the small cottage.

In moments Tab had managed to fall fast asleep again.

So why this unease?

"You've heard sea battles before, woman," she chided herself. "And no doubt you will again. Get some sleep! If there are wounded, you'll be needed."

She punched her hard chicken and duck feather pillow into a hollow shape. As she sunk her head into it, the beam in the ceiling above her bed caught her eye. Yellow and orange light danced across it.

Cursing like Island fishermen who plied their double-ended boats, Emily flung aside her summer quilt. Two steps and she pressed her head to the window pane. Fires on the horizon. There was a ship ablaze offshore, between the island and the mainland. "Damn your eyes!"

The waste of it all! England couldn't be content to rule the colonies. She had to lord it over them with those damned import taxes, knowing full well the settlers needed the goods, even though they were unable, or unwilling, to pay. But recently more and more of her neighbors and their families and friends had been willing to run the revenue cutter blockades, just to get their produce to market and get some supplies in. She knew several merchants who had ships out that week, and captains—one in particular—who were willing to face death rather than bow to hated taxes.

War was coming. Jeremiah Davies, their aging itinerant minister, had so declared it and she no longer doubted him. Too often these days she'd fallen asleep to sea fires. Too often there'd been cannon shot for lullabies.

Her beloved Block Island was vulnerable. Stuck out there in the middle of British and French patriots, privateers, and pirates. The small porkchop-shaped land knew them all and tried to keep neutral. But the island accommodated gently rolling hills, a game-filled hollow she could see from her window, craggy mussel-loaded rocks at Lookout Point, a protected salty pond with dozens of eating fish and clams, and tidy farms and fisheries. Each was a bounty and a lure to all the old and new enemies. Foraging parties had stripped the islanders more than once. They would again. Perhaps this night. Perhaps another.

She sighed. Tomorrow, she and Tab would like as not be called upon to do what they could to help the survivors of tonight's mayhem. Now, however, it was wasteful to worry. Sleep was a precious gift which renewed both body and spirit. She'd best get on with it.

So Emily trudged back to bed, turned to her side to avoid the glow on the beam and fell asleep watching dark, wispy clouds feather themselves across a sickle-shaped moon.

This time it wasn't a cannon that wakened her, but the crash of a door against the wall in the hall belowstairs. In the time it took to sit up, footsteps reached the top landing. She heard great, heaving, out-of-breath gasps coming closer, down the short hall to her room. Her fingers fumbled to light the candle on her bedside table, then scrabbled for the breechloader under her bed.

She was too late for both.

A man-shape darker than the room loomed over her bed. She surprised herself by cowering away. *Emily Gorton, the woman who was always so brave in the face of danger, cowering away?* But she remembered other women—Rose Hall and Rebecca Pines, and Patience Sands, her great-cousin—who had been snatched in the night by pirates or French and never seen again.

The shadowy man-shape drew in a deep breath and pulled the covers off her. "Need you!" he gasped, his voice raspy from running. When she pushed away at him, he pulled her to her feet. "Now! Get . . . things together."

"No!"

She could see that it was taking a super human effort for him to control his breathing and get his words out. Strained, harsh, hoarse . . . he had the kind of voice she'd heard many times from men of the sea, men used to giving orders.

"Em . . . no time. Don't argue."

So he knew her. That was as may be; but it mattered little. As Tab had said, half the blinking sea knew her. She couldn't let him take her. She would end up in some pirate's haven, mistress to him or whore to all the others. God's blood, she would die rather than face a fate such as that!

She scrambled off the bed and ran around the small room, grabbing up whatever was to hand. She threw her great-aunt Bella's badger brush, then grabbed up books more precious to Emily than gold sovereigns. Her dog-eared Shakespeare and the new translation of *Don Quixote* went sailing toward his head, followed by pitcher and washbasin, as she tried to duck under his outstretched arms and out the door to freedom. Despite his apparent weariness, however, he was still quick. He batted away the books and dodged the shattering crockery. Before she knew what had happened, he had her in a locked grip, pulled tight against his hard, sweaty, powder-smoky body.

She kicked, screamed, wriggled. All it did was pull up her long night chemise. She didn't waste time trying to cover herself with the fool thing. If she couldn't get away this man-thing would clap eyes on far more than a little leg and thigh, of that she was sure. Her hands were useless and she was barefoot but she had her knee. If she could just. . . .

"No, Em . . ."

He caught her under the upraised knee and lifted

her easily. All she saw was a glint of white teeth as he plucked her up.

"Explain later," he said. "Sorry."

"Sorry? I'll make you sorry, you scurvy bag of potage. Put me down!"

But he slung her over his shoulder and out to the hall. She saw Tab huddled in her own doorway, her eyes round as chowder quahogs, her bedslip bunched in her hand and held to her mouth.

"God's love, don't just stand there like a ninny! Shoot him."

"Oh, lordy, Misuz, I couldn't!"

"Then hit him with a poker! Trip him! Do something!"

The man grunted and shifted her weight and she said, peevishly but hopefully, "Right you are! Since I'm so heavy, put me down."

His short caw made her realize that the grunt, too, had held a note of triumph mixed with laughter. She beat at his shoulders and head, boxing his ears the way her father had boxed all seven of her brothers's. He merely shrugged her blows away as if she were no more than a pesky sand flea.

His chest was heaving by then and she realized he must have run all the way from the docks, or wherever he'd beached his skiff. She couldn't have told why or how, but she had a feeling he was one of the men involved in the battle that had wakened her earlier. Doubtless one of the pirates who plied his wicked trade along the coast and the islands. Her island. Her beautiful Block Island. And he was taking her away from it. Away from her work and her family and the people who depended on her.

"Damn. Damn. *Damn!*"

They were at the front door now. A few more steps and everything she had worked for, every sacrifice she had made, would have been done for nothing. Damn the man's eyes! She grabbed for the lintel above her head and held tight. Her new handmade beggar's lace curtain that Nancy Martin had draped over the door "for luck" ripped straight down when he pried her hands away.

"Give in, Emily!" he growled. Choked on the words. Coughed.

One small triumph, at least. "Never!"

She flayed at him, then bent low and clutched the large, black, forged door latch. For a moment he lost control and her legs locked around the left doorpost the way she locked them on the back of a horse. Countering, he gave one mighty heave and tore her away. They both began to topple.

He swore. She cried out.

Heading straight for the edge of the oak door, she felt a tremor of what her brothers' porkers might feel as the blunt end of an axe swooped down on them. She put out her hands to ward off the blow but knew, before she hit, it was no use. The pain was excruciating. She screamed, moaned, then a blessed darkness enveloped her.

Chapter Two

1772—Atlantic Ocean—June 11

The sharp-hulled schooner *Patriot* lurched from the force of the waves crashing into its starboard side. From his perch on the equipment chest in his steward's tiny box of a cabin, Captain Robert Sears braced himself on the solid timber above his head. Had he stood, his six-foot length would have been doubled over. No cabin, including his own, could handle the height of men such as he, so he spent most of his time on deck, only coming below in an emergency or to sleep.

This time he wasn't there to sleep, however. Although, God's blood, if he were to get back to his normal self he needed at least twelve hours of uninterrupted slumber. Like as not, that would come much later, if it came at all.

Rob shook the fuzziness out of his head, ignoring the aches in his body, trying to block out the screams and moans coming from below and forward. The brig and mess had been turned into temporary sick bays following the last British foray and were filled with mortally wounded men. Their agony and the possibility of additional attacks preyed heavy on his mind.

He looked steadily into the hammock that was slung from corner to corner. He frowned at the raggedy mass of dirty homespun that had been dumped there.

It had been folly, stopping at Block Island in the dead of night, when he knew the British were mere leagues behind him. Folly, to lower a boat into those damnable counter-current waves off Black Rock. He'd lost a hand to those waves. Old Jack. A hand he couldn't afford to lose. A good hand. A better man. One who'd been with him on seven blockade runs through British revenue cutters, who'd fought valiantly in this last skirmish.

Folly! Damned folly!

Yet, he needed this . . .

He began to smile and felt his body harden and heat. By a supreme act of will he snapped it back into icy, coiled attention. Yes, he needed this bundle of rags. This infernal bundle of rags.

But he didn't need the problems it brought. Ah, the devil take it, no, he surely didn't need them!

He snorted and his boot kicked at a large, torn strip of linen that was smeared with mud and blood. It was finely woven and lace edged. So he knew it hadn't come from his captive's spindle. Not much she wore did. She could sew, of that he'd had ample evidence during his cousin Jason's accident three years ago. But she couldn't weave to save her soul. Her half-hearted attempts usually ended up in the lambing room, to be used to wipe off the afterbirth. Though once she'd been forced to wear her work, she now had better days. Cranberry-dyed pieces no longer graced her body; they were too coarse and holey. *Not* the spiritual holy, he amended, remembering the string of curses that had snapped like saber clashes from her mouth right after he'd slung her over his shoulder. He almost laughed aloud, but luckily was interrupted before he forgot himself.

"Rob?"

Without turning, he answered his third mate, Jason Broadbent, his cousin and only one of three men on board who dared call him by his first name. "Aye, Jason."

"Mr. Peters needs you at the wheel. Two British gunboats coming fast."

Rob grunted. "Not surprising, that."

"No, sir."

Rob should have gone to his first mate right away but he was caught up in remembrance of times past, where guns and the sweet-acrid smell of burning flesh had no home. A time when he'd run in the meadow with a golden-haired girl, with eyes as brown as a beaver's pelt. A time when privateering had been honorable and necessary and he couldn't wait to get his first berth. It hadn't been much. Just cabin boy to One-eyed Jack Saunders, at that time a fine privateer, now a finer pirate. There was some irony in that, considering his present circumstances.

He shook his head to clear it of the memories, took a moment (after all, the damnably tenacious British would still be there when he went up on deck), bent, and laid a work-calloused hand on the homespun. Tugging, he exposed the figure under the torn nightwear. Much as he'd fought it—*And damn me, I have fought it!*—that wheat-blond hair and fine, lovely face had been burned into his memory, into his very flesh, for more years than he cared to count. Regardless, he ran his eyes over her, as if looking for something he didn't already know.

There was a flush in her cheeks, a small bluish bump on her forehead. She'd smashed into the edge of that door. God, the sound of it! The force! He'd thought her dead. But when her breathing steadied quickly, his heart had managed the giant leap back into his chest where it belonged.

He felt a twinge of pride mixed with regret when he remembered how she'd fought as bravely and fiercely as his men always did. And like his men, sustained injuries because of her fierce bravery. Besides the bump on her head she had bruises on the inside of her thighs where she'd clung so tight to the door post. But he'd best not tell her he knew *that*. If she knew he knew, she'd like as not take a cutlass to him first chance she got.

The little devil! She had a grip like a lobster. No wonder the heavy lace curtain had torn, and the door post's wood given way. When it had, her shoulder had been gouged by splinters. After they got her aboard, he and Jason had spent five minutes picking out bits and pieces from her torn and bleeding flesh.

He touched a nasty cut, visible through one of the rips in her nightdress. It had bled heavily, staining the white linen. He was sorry for that. But not sorry he'd taken her captive. He sighed and shook his head. So. He was a kidnapper, now. With this final, desperate act, the British could honestly label him *Pirate*, adding one more sin to his growing list of crimes against the Crown.

"Rob."

"Aye, Jason. I'm going."

He checked both pair of pistols, tucking one pair into his waistband, the other into chest-slung holsters. He tested the sharpness of his cutlass and sword. If they were attacked and boarded, he'd need them all and more besides.

"Keep an eye on her, Jason."

"I will, sir."

"Poultice that knot on her head."

"Aye."

"But *don't* untie her bonds."

Jason glared at his cousin and ship's master but resignedly answered, "Aye." He, too, knew the spitfire Emily Gorton could be. He'd witnessed it many times before, as well as that night. And he knew better than to argue with Rob, Captain of the *Patriot*. In truth, by all rules of the sea Rob's word was law. More important, however, his temper was on a short fuse these harrowing days.

They had *not* been involved in the burning of the hated British revenue cutter *Gaspee* in the port of Providence only eleven hours before. They'd been docked in Newport, taking on their final stores before putting out to sea. But a fair lot of good it did them. Because of the attack every manjack on the bay—ships, crews, and all—were suspected revolutionists or sympathizers. Gunboats were everywhere and they'd been warned by friends in the Newport Sons of Liberty to stay out of harm's way. Thanks to the expert seamanship of Rob and their navigator, Orrin Mayotte, they'd slipped through the easternmost tip of one British blockade. But it had taken three times as long to shake Narragansett Bay behind and finally get under full sail.

Jason swore he'd heard the collective sigh as the entire crew breathed easier as soon as they were out into open water. Yet only a scant league had been covered before their lookout spotted the ensign of a merchant vessel returning to Newport. Its captain must have had Loyalist leanings. Like as not he had alerted British authorities in the harbor as soon as he'd docked. A cutter and gunboat had come after them. In the dead of night, under grey and black clouds, they'd been engaged in a stiff battle. Skillfully, Rob and Orrin had once again maneuvered carefully and craftily in the shadows and dark. They'd sunk the cutter, left it burning, and gotten a good head start while the gunboat picked up the survivors. But the fighting had been ceaseless, worse than any they'd ever experienced this close to home. Men had been maimed, killed. One of them had been Cutter Hobbs, their ship's doctor.

So Rob had had no choice. Men died quickly at sea if they got no doctoring. There were men dying right now. Rob had had to get Emily Gorton!

The only problem was, how long before *she* saw it that way?

Emily fought to come out of the darkness where she'd been drifting. Each time she tried to open her eyes, however, splinters of light shattered straight to the pain center in her brain. She groaned and lifted her right hand. Her left came with it, tied to its twin with a dirty neckcloth. Raw and pulsing pain at her wrists and shoulder joined a dull, throbbing ache in her head. Luckily, her hands were bound in front so she had more ease of movement.

Huh! Luck. That black shadow who had stolen her had best pray for all the luck in Ireland because she planned to strangle him the first time he came to her bed.

"Yes, and hell is paved with good intentions, as Mr. Johnson says," she muttered, remembering the strength of the giant who'd plucked her so easily into his arms and pitched her over his shoulder. She wondered if he'd . . . well, if he'd done *that* to her already. Her thighs *were* aching. But with some eery womanly knowledge that came from God knew where, she was certain he hadn't. So she still had *that* to look forward to. Humbuggery!

Gingerly, opening her eyes only a slit because the slightest bit of light hurt like hell, she lifted both hands and felt her forehead. A lump the size of a turnip met her groping fingers. And just below her shoulder, a crusted scab meandered down almost six inches.

"Damn and tarnation!"

"I have a soft cloth, Em. And a basin of water laced with vinegared wine and powdered hyssop, like you always said."

She brought her hands up to shade her eyes and looked across the tiny quarters. "Jason? Is that you?"

"Aye. But lie still and I'll tend to you."

"Who did this to me? You aren't captive, too?"

"No, I'm not captive." Gently and playfully, he batted her prying, curious fingers away from his ministrations. "I can manage."

"Do you have tansy and mustard?"

"Aye. I brought the herb case, your carpet bag, and the traveling chest."

Despite the pain, her eyes widened as she took in the horrifying knowledge that a friend had aided in her capture. "You were there? You helped that monster?"

"Rob needs you, Em. He wouldn't have done it, otherwise."

"Rob? Oh, my God!"

She held perfectly still, making Jason's job easier, but not because of that. She was conjuring up the images, the giant shadow, the words, the smells. After a time, she sniffed, but not from sorrow. "We're on *Patriot.*"

"Aye."

"And that scurvy bag of potage who took me was Robert Sears." It was no question but a statement filled with fury, holding dire consequences when she got the answer she expected.

"Aye."

"All right, then. Untie me, Jason."

"Rob gave me strict orders."

"I don't care if King George gave you orders. I said untie me!"

"If King George gave the orders I probably *would* untie you. But Rob has his reasons."

"He knows I'll scratch his eyes out."

"That he does," came a deep, chuckling voice from across the room.

Although it hurt like blazes, Emily turned her

throbbing head toward the sound of Robert Sears's voice. The small, square, glass-encased brass candle holders on the wall of the cabin cast enough light so she could see her gaoler. He lounged against the doorjamb, his arms resting on pistols he wore on his chest. His legs were nonchalantly crossed at the ankles as if he had no worries in the world, when she could hear the guns over her head! The devil take the man, he was impossible to understand.

His head was slightly cocked to one side and there was a hint of a smile lifting the corners of his mouth.

But the fastidious captain, a man she'd known for more than fifteen years, was gone. In his place was a weary man. His usually straight, strong back slumped forward. His brown hair was black with soot, trailing over his shoulders rather than caught with a riband into his usual neat rat tail at the nape of his neck. His eyes—she remembered them as that indeterminate shade called hazel, not quite any color but most times green as bottle glass—were hooded, so she couldn't see what they held. It didn't matter. The worry lines at their edges and on his forehead gave enough of the story. The rest was filled in by his once white linen and green breeches which were dark with pitch and soaked with blood.

She held up her bound hands. "You didn't have to do this."

"As you said, you would have gouged out my eyes."

"I still may. You scared me to death. You had no right to do that."

"I needed you and there was no time for explanations. As you can hear, the British have arrived, with reinforcements, too."

Reluctantly, she said, "I hear other things, too."

He nodded and pushed himself away from his support. His step was sure but slow as he approached the hammock. "Have you finished?" he asked Jason.

"The cut is clean and bandaged. But I've not had time to poultice her head."

"It will have to wait, I'm afraid."

Rob hadn't taken his eyes off Emily. She was quiet now but he knew if he weren't careful she could erupt into a force worse than a hurricane. There was only one way to tame her. No, two. But she wouldn't be a party to the one that would be the most interesting, the one he had awaited all these years. He put that behind him, as he'd had to do too many times, and said what he knew would pique her interest.

"I lost Cutter Hobbs."

"Oh."

"The British were at my back."

"Oh."

"I had to move quickly."

"Yes."

"But you're still furious."

"Yes."

"You'll lose that when you get below and get to work."

"I don't think so."

"I will have to risk it. The same way I've risked everything else this night."

He whipped out his shortened cutlass—the one he used for close-in fighting—and with one quick slice cut through her bonds. Her hands were free, but the neckcloth she'd been bound with still cut into her wrists. Motioning for Jason to bring him the water laced with hyssop and wine vinegar, gently Rob unwound the two pieces. Just as gently he sluiced them, holding the basin under to catch the vile smelling liquid.

Emily winced as the vinegar bit into raw places; but she held her tongue. She was watching Rob's eyes. They were as gentle as his hands. Gentle and contrite. Her anger went from boil to simmer. He'd had a job to do and done it. But he hadn't had to scare her half to death. If he'd explained . . .

"I'd have come. . . ."

"No, Em. You wouldn't."

He stood back and his eyes bored into hers in such a way that she had the feeling he knew her better than she knew herself.

"There was no way in hell you would have left your precious island willingly, Em."

Aye, there was the rub, as Mister Shakespeare knew. God himself would have had to order her off. And what would happen now? The British were formidable foes. They could sink *Patriot* or be sunk by Rob's crew. Regardless, Rob and Jason and she were nomads now. She might never see her beloved island again.

And Rob had done it.

"I hate you, *Captain Sears.*"

"I hope it doesn't last," he said affectionately. "We've a mighty lot to do and close quarters to do it in. Enmity is best left to real enemies, *Miss Gorton.* You won't find any enemies, among my crew. Only men. Some of them desperately wounded."

She swung her legs over the sides of the hammock and noticed for the first time that she was still in her night chemise. She clutched it round her throat. "I can't go like this."

"Jason only had time to gather two dresses and a few personal items. But he's hunted up some things from the crew that will fit."

"We hope," Jason muttered, appending a quick prayer that Emily's anger would soon dissipate. Though it might be best if it continued. Hadn't she once told him that anger fueled her skillful fingers? Astern, she'd need all the skill she could muster.

He scurried to a scarred oak chest in the corner and plucked up a bundle. "The cabin boy is about your size."

"Men's breeches? Oh, wouldn't the women on the island love this!"

As she took in the man's clothing she was expected to wear, pain lodged in her breast. A deep, abiding pain she'd thought long gone. Man's clothing. Fitting, that, since she was without doubt an *unwomanly* woman.

Such had the island women labeled her for twenty years, since her seventh birthday when they'd brought her her first tiny spinning wheel. Like the girl in the fairy tale—she never could remember her stupid name—she'd pricked her fingers eleven times on the cursed thing and bled like a stuck pig. Weeks later, she had red, blue and purple fingers. They were permanently puckered from all the vinegar water Hopeful Rose, the Manissee Indian woman who sometimes worked for her father, had soaked them in. The island women had been patient—make that dogged—in their attempts to teach her to spin. But it had been impossible! God must not have meant her fingers for the spindle, but destined them from birth for something else. And when she and everyone else found out what her destiny was, the island women declared it something *unwomanly.* Detestable, they said. The work of the Devil.

Yet, she gloried in it. So what did it matter that she had to wear men's breeches? She did a man's job and loved it.

Bitter gall rose in her throat and she swallowed, hard. Oh, how she wished it truly didn't matter. But she knew better. Even Rob had laughed at her those many years ago. And last night he'd laughed again when he'd slung her over his shoulder like some sack of meal from the gristmill. Well, she'd show him. She'd show them all. She hadn't given in to the pain which had, it seemed, lodged forever in her breast at the women's derision. She wouldn't give in to the pain now. No matter how hard they laughed, they had to admit she was valuable. Why else had Rob taken *her* instead of someone else?

Rob watched emotions change Emily's face. When she got to grim determination, and a little pride snapped in her eyes, he nodded and hoped for the best. "Since you may be on this ship for weeks we thought we should save your dresses for a more *appropriate* time."

But that was wonderful! "Only weeks?"

"At best. Months, at worse." At her instantly stricken look and the fierce anger in her eyes, he backed toward the door. "I'm sorry, Miss Gorton. But I can't chance putting into port—any port—lest I'm sure it's safe. Now, just get changed and Jason will take you astern."

He bowed slightly before he left but Emily wasn't mollified. She glared at Jason and waved him from the room. He went, clomping harder on his wooden leg than usual—to let her know his own anger and disappointment, she'd wager.

Well, she decided, as she struggled into the coarse, heavy indigo breeches, *her* anger and disappointment was more acute. And they weren't being helped by the clothes Jason had laid out for her to wear. The breeches almost fit at the hips but the waist was too large by several inches.

Huh! Unwomanly she might be in household matters but her body belied that hateful label. More than belied it, if men's glances could be credited. Her waist was smaller, her breasts heavier, hips gently sloped but her backside rounder than her cousin Rachel's. Rachel was the only woman in her family Emily had to compare herself to; her mother had died when Emily was five, she had no sisters, and her great-aunt Bella was already old and fat when she came to care for the motherless child. Over the years Bella had made many comparisons of Emily to Rachel. None had been flattering. Now, however, Emily wasn't so sure those comparisons were just.

Ah, well, best to put it out of her mind when there was so much else to do.

She struggled into the shirt, wincing when she had to move her shoulder. Damn his eyes, Rob had much to answer for!

She tried to loop a black, oily neckcloth—Jason had once called it a sweat cloth and she could easily see why—around her waist to hold up the breeches but it was a mite small. She knotted it as tightly as she could. But when she sat down to pull on the cabin boy's smelly stockings and boots—Had the stockings never seen lye soap?—the small knot in the neckcloth strained and pulled, then finally gave. The breeches slithered to the floor as soon as she regained her feet. Jason had provided no belt and there were no loops in the infernal belled trousers. Probably because belts were precious things on a vessel and needed by the crew to hold everything from grease horns to rigger's knives to cutlasses and flintlock pistols.

Humbuggery! If she didn't want them to fall down every two seconds there was nothing for it but to sew the damned breeches to the shirt! After all, her bag was there by the door and her needles and threads in it.

The front was easy. But her shoulder ached when she turned to stitch up the back. She struggled, and with a few well chosen oaths she managed.

A hesitant knock came at the door. "Emily?"

"Leave off, Jason! I'm almost ready." She bit through the thread and tugged at the breeches. Not her best work, but they held. "All right, come in."

"I brought a cap for you to tuck your hair . . ." he began, then choked with laughter when he saw what she'd done. "How will you get out?"

"Scissors, you ninny."

"But what if you have to . . . uh . . . you know . . ."

She saw his eyes flick to the tin thunder jug in the corner. It had never occurred to her. And she'd called *him* a ninny. How had Cervantes put it in *Don Quixote?* Ah, yes, like the pot calling the kettle black. Apt, that.

"Oh, humbuggery. If I do have to use the cursed thing, I'll have to sew everything back again! What did I do to deserve this punishment?"

"We could cut holes in the breeches. And I'll get some rope to weave through. That should do it."

It did.

"I'm sorry I called you a ninny," Emily said, as they made their way below decks to the heart-wrenching sounds that even thunderous cannon couldn't obscure.

Jason grinned. "I've been called worse."

"So have I."

Far worse and far more often. The names had hurt, still did. The taunts had seared through to her soul. She had tried to escape them but wondered if she ever would.

They came from *this*. The easy way she shouldered aside a strapping, heavy-set lad and took her place at the crew's board, a rough hewn plank hinged to the vessel's larboard side and hung from the timbers by rope. There were ten of the boards, five on each side of the crew's quarters. Usually, they were used for everything from sleeping, to mending barrels and nets, to eating meals. But now they were all filled with wounded men.

The smells were awful but Emily paid them no mind. "Jason, have the lads bring me rum and hot water."

"Aye."

"And I'll need spoiled ale or wine."

"Aye."

"And lye soap and a good bristle brush."

"Aye. All to hand."

Emily looked where he pointed and nodded, pleased that he had remembered, when it had been so long ago. Yet, it seemed like yesterday when he had first been brought to the island, wounded, near death. And destined for the corpse pile behind Matthew Cox's surgery if she hadn't pulled him aside, ignoring the angry curses of the islanders because she dared question the decision of their doctor. It had been confoundedly hard and tiring taking care of him—touch and go, for weeks. And Jason had been given up as hopeless, on his last legs, by more than one villager. Yet here he stood, a little crookedly on his wooden leg as the ship rocked in the waves, but healthy, alive.

She would do all she could to insure that these poor men would have half the chance Jason had had.

She gave orders to the cabin boys that as soon as she finished with each man they were to scrub the boards down with the lye soap and hot water. When they nodded their understanding, she began to work on the first casualty. She cleaned the man's wounds with a solution made from heartleaf plant, to hinder infection, just as Hopeful Rose had taught her years ago. She rubbed yarrow salve on those wounds that would heal but were bleeding badly. The bleeding slowed, satisfying her that there was enough of the herb in the pig's fat she had used to make the salve. She then went on to sew the deep-seated wounds with catgut, surface ones with strong cotton thread, and left the rest to heal alone. Done, she stationed herself beside the next patient.

She had no time to distinguish one man from another. She merely took them in rotation. Clean.

Drain. Sew. Smear with salve. Bandage. When bullets had to be removed, she bit her lower lip, gave a quick prayer, and removed them. Amputations took four crewmen to hold the patient in place and she was thankful there was only one arm to come off, which she left until there was naught else to do.

Quickly and efficiently she worked, giving orders for fragrant healing teas to be made, salves to be concocted from her herb case, and poultices to be applied. Jason worked just as quickly and efficiently at her side.

"You'd be a good ship's doctor," she said, when he'd anticipated a trillium solution to clean gun powder out of a man's eye.

"I reckon. But my father aspires me to better things," he said bitterly. "Lace and cutlass and a first mate's berth. Than on to captain my own ship."

She cleaned her hands in the strong hyssop and vinegar water before going on to the next patient. "You must do what will make you happy."

"As you did."

"Yes."

And no. She sighed, partly from fatigue, partly from the knowledge that while she loved her work, there was something left undone, unsaid, unexperienced.

Her hands did what they knew from instinct to do. But her mind lifted and traveled far from the smells and moans, far from the red stained linen, far from the guns booming over her head. She floated back to the beginning, to the dark stall in her father's barn and the oily scent of new washed wool, to the meadow above her father's farmhouse and the sweet scent of new mown hay and nose tingling mint, to the gold and black of butterflies flitting from daisy to wild onion to saint's truth, and the high-low throb of the robin, trill of the bluebird, and bark of the loon.

But then, as now, there'd been smells and moans, red-stained linen and guns. And too soon the meadow had been left far behind.

Chapter Three

1754—Block Island—May 7

God rot it. God rot it. God rot it!!! There had to be a birthday devil. There had to be.

Emily Gorton sat on a three-legged stool in the gloom of the barn. From one of a dozen baskets filled to overflowing, she plucked up a handful of her brothers' newly shorn and thoroughly washed wool. The grotesque mountain of the lot seemed to leer at her out of the shadows. She stared at it then dropped her eyes to what lay nestled in her hands.

A set of combing boards! For her ninth birthday! Aye, there was surely a birthday devil.

She had been hoping for a gathering basket filled with herb seeds. Or special seamen's sewing needles (she didn't dare tell her father why she wanted them). Or a set of tiny knives. Oh, how she had pined and prayed for those knives. She'd even spent hours drawing the plans for them and had left copies all over the house: In every nook of her brothers's loft room. Propped against her father's shaving tin in the kitchen. Tucked behind his long, curved clay pipe on the mantle in the gathering room. Slipped between the pages of his ha'penny newspaper in his study. Why, she'd even rolled up one set and shoved it into his Sunday-go-to-meeting shoes in his bedroom. Papa and her brothers must have seen them. How could they have missed them? And the plans disappeared as quickly as she produced them.

But she knew her family. Carefully planted plans might go for naught if she weren't persistent. So, she'd dropped hints seven or eight times a day for the last two weeks. God's blood, she might as well have wished for silver bells and cockle shells! No gathering basket nor herb seeds nor needles nor knives had appeared in her pile of presents last night.

Instead, from great-aunt Bella she had gotten a bolt of dimity for a new dress. Dimity and dresses. Humbuggery! Billy's gift, a reed basket, was good only for gathering robin eggs, it was so small. Four different colored ribbons from the four youngest of her seven brothers—Davey and Ned and John and Carter—were pretty but she needed them about as much as she needed a new dress. The most useless of all was the tiny tea set from her oldest brother, Henry, made from acorns and carved and bent willow twigs. Only Jasper's gift would come in handy: a reed-thin whistle which he'd carved from a knot in a maple branch. Perhaps she could tame it to the tunes of the island's birds.

Suddenly, she felt shame wash through her. Henry, Billy, and Jasper surely had spent hours working on their presents. Even great-aunt Bella and the other boys had chosen the fabric and ribbons with love and attention to the colors Emily preferred: sky blue, ocean green, orchard peach, and strawberry red. But why, oh why were they still trying to mold her into something she was not and never possibly could be? Dainty dresses with dozens of tucks and gathers made her skin itch. She hadn't had a tea party with her dolls in three years! And as for gathering eggs . . . she'd rather patch up robins's wings than reach into their vermin-filled nests.

Her family didn't understand her. Not a one of them. Most of all Papa.

He had grinned broadly when he presented her with these infernally clumsy paddles! And she had had to look happy. Surprised had come easily, she had been so shocked. Had he forgotten so soon the purple and blue and black fingers she'd had when Bella and other island women had tried to teach her to spin and weave? Three years went by before her production had graced the backs of any of them! Except, of course, for the ewes as they birthed their lambs. Now here she sat, expected to perform still another task her hands were unsuited for.

Why did he do it? Why did he keep on pushing her?

Tears dammed up behind her lids but she clenched her jaw to chase them away. A fair lot of good crying would do!

Kicking at the ornery basket of wool at her feet, she fumed. If naught else, Papa could have given her the same present he had bought last year—a giant bag of horehound and peppermint drops, brought all the way from London on a merchant vessel.

If naught else.

But she had truly wanted those knives.

Emily stamped her foot—which only relieved her of a wee bit of her anger—and jammed the wool between the combing boards. It was so hot inside the closed-in barn that beads of sweat stood out on her forehead. Yanking on the neckline of her green and white striped homespun linen dress to pull it down and give her some air, she took a few moments to cool off and reflect upon the instructions great-aunt Bella had given: *Try to think of the wool as someone else's hair and gently comb it to get all the snarls out.*

Hair! Humbuggery!

Hair wasn't wool! She supposed it was close, however. As close as anything she'd likely see that day. *Damn your eyes, birthday devils, you've done it again.*

She stretched out her legs, then decided it was no use to dawdle or complain. She had to do something. The awful piles wouldn't comb themselves out.

So Emily hooked her feet around the stool legs for balance and glared at the mountain of clean wool in front of her. She shrugged her shoulders, trying to ease the ache that had developed between her shoulder blades, and thought hard. She had often enough scrutinized her reflection in the mirror as Bella combed out unruly snarls that had taken residence in Emily's hair after a long day of household duties, school lessons, and gathering times in the woods with her Indian friend, Hopeful Rose. Great-aunt Bella used two brushes, one on top and one on the bottom, to get right through the clumps and straighten them out. It had never looked difficult when she did it. There was a rhythm to it, Bella had assured Emily. Emily had but to put her mind to it, imitate great-aunt Bella's movements and she'd be able to comb the wool just as perfectly as Bella combed her hair.

Thank goodness the paddles were at least shaped like brushes. Now, if they only worked like them.

So, she sucked in her breath, tucked her tongue in the corner of her mouth and concentrated, drawing the scratchy sides of the boards together in a quarter circular motion that went: *One, two, three . . . hesitate . . . four, five. One, two three, hesitate . . . four, five. One, two, three, hesitate . . . four, five.* And there it should be!

Emily stared at the mass of whateveritwas that trailed out of all sides of the combing boards. She knew it wasn't right. There should have been a nice, smooth sheet hanging from one side of the boards. Instead, she had tiny clumps and trailing strands everywhere! As she stared, they detached themselves and floated in the air, like puffy cat-o-nine-tails which every autumn sent forth their seeds to find a likely spot, take root, and produce a whole new crop the next year.

For this wool, Emily herself appeared to be the likely spot to take root and reproduce. She owned that it felt as if there were more wool now than there had been in that tiny handful when she'd started this beastly business.

She blew at a sticky piece that danced on an air pocket right up to her nose, where it clung stubbornly. When it wouldn't dislodge, she ran the back of the combing boards across it, and ended up with a long woolen trail from her nose to the mass between the boards. It was worse than running through the woods into a hundred giant spider webs!

Reaching up, she tried to pull the strands back to the blob where they belonged. But she hadn't counted on the scratchy side of the paddles catching in the hair at her forehead. When she snatched the paddles away, she screeched. Some of her hair pulled right out of her scalp, still intertwined with the wool. Worse, more woolly strands had attached themselves and refused to let go of her sweat-sticky hair. They hung there in front of her face like an unwelcome shroud.

"God rot it. God rot it. God rot it!" she boomed, cringing when she heard the side door open with a screech on its rusty hinges.

"That you, Davey?" a boy's voice—not one of her brothers's—called out.

"Oh, no!" she moaned, and scrabbled, pulled, jerked. But her hair and the wool continued to keep company.

If she were the kind of girl who cried, she'd be in worse trouble than she already was. But ever since the day she'd watched her mother struggle futilely to hold onto life as she gave birth to Carter, Emily had refused to cry.

Ever.

Because if tears could change anything her mother would still be there, patiently and lovingly helping her with this horror. But Emily's buckets of tears had not held back her mother's last breath, nor stopped her pine box from being lowered into the ground. So it was. So it be.

She was on her own with a boy bearing down on her and her face dripping woolen sweat. Just one more tug . . . one more tug . . . one more tug!

But it didn't work. She was prisoned fast by the damned boards and the temperamental wool.

"Oh, no. No. NO!"

"Not Davey, then? Must be Jasper . . ."

As Rob Sears, cabin boy on the merchant vessel *Nancy,* rounded the stall looking for one of the Gorton boys to go clamming with him, he jolted to a halt at the sight that greeted his eyes.

Gossamer white hair fluttering in the breeze. Hands and arms draped with stuff that looked like withered moss. Moans and groans and swishes of web-like skirts.

A ghost!

No, an oriental houri!

He'd heard tales about them from the crew. They crept up on an unsuspecting soul and tried to take his breath away!

"Yiiiey!" Rob yelled.

"Get away with you!" Emily screamed, diving away from a Bedlam-bound boy who had drawn a short sword out of his belt and was advancing in a mad dash toward her. But she was unable to get her feet unwound from the legs of the stool quickly enough and she pitched sideways, yelling, "God rot it! Somebody help!"

Robert skidded on the straw to a halt. He stared. Two legs encased in blue and white striped stockings kicked wildly in the air. Those were no spirit legs. And that nice rounded pink bottom just above them was as real and as beautiful as ever he had imagined a girl's bottom would be.

In all his fourteen years it was the first glimpse he'd had beneath a female's skirts. The times he'd seen his baby sister being swaddled was hardly of any note because she couldn't be described as a girl. Course, if he had gone with the other seamen from the *Nancy* to the small house tucked into the hollow around the bend from the dock he might have actually touched a girl's nether regions. But he had been to sea for sixteen months. Long enough to know that seamen came away with more than they bargained for when they frequented a "friendly house." And he'd be damned if he'd shorten his life or go insane simply because his mates expected him to be a man.

He would gain his manhood soon enough. As soon as possible, judging by the way his body felt as he watched this lass wiggle and struggle to cover herself.

His hand shook as he tucked his short sword back in his belt. "Damn me, that is a sight!"

"Then damned you be," Emily declared, still squirming, wool stuck to her from head to toe. She sneezed, shot a wicked glance over her shoulder and ordered, "Don't stand there like a Jack-a-Lent. Help me up!"

"Your legs are caught in the rungs of the stool." He put his palm on her bottom and pushed down. "Stay still a minute and I'll untangle you."

Emily gasped at the contact of his hand on a part of her body it shouldn't be. She batted it away. He grunted and put it back.

"Still as stone, I said!"

Two twists of the stool and she was free. She scrambled to her feet and tugged down her skirt, glaring at him all the while.

His eyes twinkled with merriment, flashing green and brown and gold. His right hand came out and plucked away one of the clinging clumps of wool. "Did you win or lose the battle?"

She kicked at the closest basket and heard one of the combing boards clunk against the stall. "I lost. As usual." Sighing, she bent down to retrieve her unwanted birthday gifts. It took a few minutes to locate them. When she did, she picked at the wool that was left between the paddles, trying to clean them. She shot a glance at the young man and was surprised to see him leaning casually against the stall, watching her every move. "Go away."

"Haven't any place to go. My mates won't be rowing back to the *Nancy* for some time yet. Besides, I like watching you. This is the best time I've had in weeks."

"Then you must lead a very boring life."

"Aboard the *Nancy?* Riding the waves to exotic islands and far away lands? Oh, aye, very boring, that," he said sarcastically.

"Then why is this the best time you've had in weeks?"

"I met me a houri who turned into a girl. A girl with pretty legs, umber eyes, and maize silk hair who has the softest, nicest, pinkest, roundest bot . . ."

"Finish it and you'll eat dung," Emily warned.

"Won't be the first time."

"Judging from how quick you are to put your hand to sword, it won't be the last, either."

"Aye. So One-eyed Jack has told me. It's the Sears's curse, to be blessed with a short-fused temper."

"Sears? You must be Robert, then."

"Rob, they call me."

"And I'm Emily."

"Ah . . . the only lass in the Gorton family."

"If you don't count great-aunt Bella."

She held up the fluff she'd taken from the combing boards and examined it in a sunbeam. Short hairs instead of long strands. Clots and clumps and clusters. Could they be twisted into thread? Using her fingers, she tried twisting a bit to the right. When that unraveled, she tried again, twisting to the left.

"Don't you need a spindle for that?" Rob asked.

"I have one. But only to test what I've done. Great-aunt Bella said if the strands don't stick together or can't be made into hanks, they won't be fit for spindle or loom." She put a little spit on the end of the wool and tried again. "If it would only stick together, then I might be able to save some of what I've ruined." She worked at it and managed finally to keep the strands from separating. But when she tried twisting it onto her portable spindle, it unraveled again. "Humbuggery!" She was hot, sticky, and tired. "If it takes this long, I'll be here until harvest getting this lot combed. And Papa said it must be done by Sunday, week."

Rob took one look at the heaped baskets and shook his head. "How long have you been working?"

"Since midday meal."

"Half the afternoon has gone and that's all you've got done?"

She put her hands on her hips and glared at the young man in his black belled breeches, dirty tan homespun shirt and red neckcloth. "You have a fine gentlemen's way about you, Robert Sears. You know just what to do to put a girl at her ease." She sat the stool back on its legs and slammed the combing boards down on it. "I've never done this before! If you think it's so easy, you do it."

Rob grinned. "A challenge, is it?"

"Aye."

"And what do I get if I pass?"

"What do you want?"

"I came to ask your brothers to go clamming with me. I'll settle for the sister. But I take all the clams."

"You take your clams and a tenth of what I dig and it's a deal."

"Half of what you dig."

"A quarter . . . and I'll not go more than that."

"I accept the challenge."

Before he could take his place on the stool she shot out an arm. "Stay a bit! What if you don't pass the challenge? What do I get?"

"What do you want?"

Had her prayers been answered? Had the birthday devils turned into birthday angels? "Can you whittle?"

"Course! I'm an able seaman."

"And hone steel to a razor's edge?"

"Aye. I've helped the ship's smithy many a time."

"A set of knives is what I want. Seven small knives with maple or cherry handles, small enough to fit my hands but large enough so I won't grow out of them, and made to the plans I've drawn."

"That's a curious request."

"Mayhap. But that's what I want if you lose."

Rob settled himself on the stool and hefted the combing boards. No wonder she'd been so clumsy with them. They fit into his hands perfectly. Whoever had made them had forgotten they were meant for a little girl.

Little girl, hell!

He grinned, remembering that luscious bottom and decided that in some places she was *not* a little girl.

"Hand me that wool," he commanded, in a voice he'd heard One-eyed Jack use to get the entire crew to hop to his tune. But this lass was having none of it.

"Get it yourself," she snapped, with a toss of her head and a shake of her green and white striped homespun skirts. "I'll sweep out the stalls and put in new straw. Three ewes are set to lamb and we'll have to clean a new place for them."

"Late for lambing . . ."

"This strain seems to come in late every year. Doesn't matter when Flower, Pearl, or Daisy gets mated, they always drop their lambs two months after the others. And hard births they are, too. Almost lost Pearl's last set of twins to fever. Clean stalls, that's the solution—or so my Manissee Indian friend Hopeful Rose says."

"Hopeful, is it? It's hope you'll need if you're to win our challenge."

"We'll see."

He stuck the wool between the boards and set to it, trying to match the way Privey Jones combed out the hemp they used to make rope for splicing. It was stickier, this wool. And stubborn.

Emily kept a close watch out of the corner of her eye. He struggled at first; but damned if he didn't soon get the hang of it! By the time she had two stalls swept and washed, he had several nice unbroken hanks of wool in a neat pile beside him. She wouldn't give him the satisfaction of seeing her startled expression. She didn't dare. So, she whipped into the next stall and began sweeping the rough planked floor.

But Rob had seen. He chuckled to himself when Emily shot a puzzled and amazed glance at the growing pile next to him, then flounced away to wrestle a bale of straw into the barn and untie it. It was hot, sweaty work. And he supposed he should help her. But he reasoned it would be more help to finish at least one basket of wool for her than to heap straw. Anyone could do barn work; but not everyone could card or comb wool. Except every woman he knew, including his baby sister, who was now eight.

Funny, that. Here he was doing a girl's chore and there she was doing a boy's chore. And he didn't feel any the less manly for it.

He looked at his hands and marveled at what he was doing. A man's hands, they were. Used to doing a man's day of work. Hauling in lines, climbing shrouds to the crow's nest, scrubbing the deck, helping the smithy or baker or sail maker. He had sewed up torn canvas. Nailed and pegged smashed barrels. Gutted and cleaned fish. But, too, he'd had to sew up his own clothes when they tore; and make a whole new shirt, the one he had on. He'd also cooked several meals for the forenoon watch, six men who—if they weren't satisfied with the fare—would not hesitate to take a slice from his ear. So far he had both ears intact.

Rob went back to the *Nancy* with three baskets of clams and a set of plans for the strangest knives he'd ever seen. Since he had won the challenge, Emily had been reluctant to give the plans to him but when he insisted he only wanted to see what all the fuss was about, she shrugged and handed him a set of drawings that were both intricate and beautiful.

"You're an artist," Rob said, awed at the way she could show two sides in a sketch where the blade curved down from the handle.

"Huh! Those are naught but chicken scratches. But some day, when I have those knives I'll make the kind of art they never imag . . ."

She broke off, embarrassed and, Rob suspected, a little anxious she had said too much. There was fear in her dark brown eyes when she raised them to smile at him.

"Thank you," she said, reluctantly.

"What for?"

"You didn't have to finish the whole basket to show me you'd won the challenge. The first few inches were enough."

"One basket of wool. Three baskets of clams. Seems a right bargain to me."

"If I'd won, I would not have given you any of my clams."

"Ah, but I knew you wouldn't win." He laughed when she glared, with her bottom lip pouted out in anger. "I've had sixteen months of combing hemp, twisting it, and using it to splice small lines and larger rope. The difference is only in the size of the fibers. You'll learn to comb and card. All girls do."

A lot you know, Rob Sears, Emily admitted sadly, as she trudged back up the hill from the docks. Rob wasn't a part of their island. He didn't know the kind of girl she was, unless he'd heard it from her brothers. But they would never tell; they were too burdened with embarrassment. A sister who couldn't sew or cook? Whose needlework looked like it came from the fingers of a girl of five years? No. They wouldn't discuss it with a boy who risked his life on the open seas. It was enough they suffered the islanders' taunts.

But she had a whole basket of wool to give to Bella! And a supper's worth of clams to put on the keeping board. She'd not have ridicule that night. Course, to avoid it she'd have to omit telling about Rob's help.

She skipped up the stone slab stairs and into the side door of her father's large white-washed farmhouse. She'd risk it. She'd risk just about anything to have peace at table.

But through the meal and her family's congratulations at getting her chores done, she cringed. She had nothing of which to be proud. While Rob was still near, she could be found out. And if she was . . . She shuddered to think about the consequences. Already, she was worried about how she was going to finish the rest of the wool without Rob's help. If it was left to her skills, it would take a month of Sundays to complete the job. But if she could work something out with Rob . . .

"When does the *Nancy* leave?" she asked her father.

Thomas Gorton broke his cracker into his chowder and thought a minute. Emily waited patiently. Even if he knew the answer immediately, her father would take time to get his words right. He was a slow and methodical man. A trait, he always pointed out, that she hadn't inherited.

"Seems I heard the *Nancy* is to stay moored off shore until Wednesday, week," Thomas said.

". . . for repairs, Captain Jack said," her eldest

brother Henry interrupted, not without a frown from his father. Old enough at eighteen to ignore their papa, he laughed. "The old buzzard said they needed time to dry out. Can you imagine? Dried out sailors!" He and the other boys snickered—for, after all, they were fishermen and whenever they put on their fishing gear it was always still clammy damp from sea drenching.

Their father rubbed his chin, looked up to the ceiling and said, "I expect the captain has more in mind than repairs."

"Oh, aye, Papa," Henry said. He nudged seventeen-year-old Davey. "He has in mind to visit the friendly house!"

"That, Henry, is enough! You have a young sister at this board."

Although Emily pretended she didn't know what her brothers and father were talking about, she did. Every islander knew. The friendly house had been there ever since she could remember. Rooms were let to Indian women or halfbreeds, mostly. But a few mainland women, who had been stranded by shipwreck and had naught but the clothes on their back, so couldn't afford the passage to Newport or Norwich, also lived there. A couple were women abandoned by their husbands to fend for themselves and who had no skills with which to do it. All of the women resided in the large barn-like structure that was left to weather to a dull grey-black. It mattered little what ship put into Block Island. French, British, Hessian, Spanish, privateer or pirate owned, sooner or later the crew would find their way to the friendly house. When they left, the women who lived there scurried happily to the stores to stock up on supplies they badly needed to survive. Though Emily didn't know exactly what went on in the house, she felt sorry for the women, yet knew enough to keep away from them and their place of residence.

"Rob said they were staying so the crew could get over their last battle with the French and get ready for their next one." *Humbuggery! What had she said?*

"You saw Rob Sears today?" Jasper asked.

"Aye," she all but whispered. "When he couldn't find you or Ned it was Rob who went clamming with me."

Thomas Gorton's brood was large but he knew each person in it. Only Emily gave him pause, and cause for alarm. Thus, when she kept her eyes on her plate as she described her day with Robert Sears, when she squirmed uncomfortably in her seat, he knew there was more to the telling than she let on. So he determined to discover what it was that lay behind her words, what was making her so anxious that she couldn't look him in the eyes.

He found it without searching. While Bella and Emily cleaned the supper trenchers and tidied the gathering board, he and the boys led Pearl, Flower, and Daisy into the birthing stalls. He was pleased to see that Emily had set everything to order. Thanks to her the lambing would take place in clean stalls and, hopefully, they wouldn't have the problems they'd had last spring.

He was less pleased when he found a clump of matted wool shoved under the stool in the back of the barn. He examined it closely, recognizing that this was nothing like the fluffy balls Emily had brought into the house. Course, it might have been her first try. But where, then, were her second and third and fourth? No, he knew instinctively there was something wrong. The combed wool she'd given Bella was as good as any he'd seen. Nothing like what he held in his hands. He knew from past mishaps that *this* was Emily's work. He wondered about the other.

Shoving the matted wool into his breeches pocket, he said naught to the boys. They were busy enough, deciding who was to take first watch and who was to take the others. Naturally, Henry and Billy would stand them all with him, as they always did. The other boys were too young to stay up all night. But he let them pretend they were helping. It didn't hurt. And he never admonished them for falling asleep. He'd done it himself when he was their age.

He did, however, put Henry in charge while he went back to the house. "Emily," he called as he shut the door, "bring me a hot mug of ale. I'll take it in my study."

His study wasn't large, but it served his purpose, giving him a retreat when his family got too loud or boisterous. Six feet wide and twelve feet long, with doors which bisected it, it had been partitioned off from both the front drawing room and his bedroom, taking three feet away from both. It held only two slipper chairs, upholstered in brightly colored turkey work, and his desk and chair, which he'd had made in Newport. Since the double fireplace which heated both the bedroom and drawing room was the left hand wall of the study, the room was warm in winter and cool in summer. He often stayed there long into the night, reluctant to enter a bedroom he could no longer share with his beloved wife, Sarah.

While he waited for the girl who looked so much like Sarah but wasn't like her at all, he took out the wool he'd found and put it conspicuously on a book which took up space squarely in the center of his desk. He took a clay pipe from his drawer, tamped tobacco into it, and lit it. He was puffing gently when Emily brought him his ale.

"Sit down, Emily," he said, taking up the mug. He lay his pipe right next to the matted wool and took a sip of his homemade brew, all the while watching the girl. When her eyes followed his hand, caught sight of the wool, and widened, he felt vindicated for his previous thoughts, unflattering as they were to his daughter. Thus, he took time to formulate what he wanted to say. He had no desire to hurt this copy of his dead wife. But before this hour was out he intended to know all there was to the mystery of how Emily had suddenly developed skills that produced a full basket of carded wool.

"Have ye naught to say for yourself, daughter?"

Chapter Four

1758—Block Island—October 10

Emily had had little to say for herself that night four and a half years ago. Her father had been disappointed in her—again. It hadn't been the first time. It wasn't to be the last. Yet, she had learned to comb wool. Oh, she couldn't do it as well as any of the other women on the island. And most eight-year-olds were still better than she. But she managed to produce enough rough spun for great-aunt Bella to make her father's and younger brothers's shirts and breeches, her own work clothes, and some of the shawls and blankets they used in the house. Because time and time again she pricked her fingers on the spindles and loom, the wool was blood spotted. So, she spent hours over a bubbling hot dye pot, stirring the fabric in boiling cranberry juice until the dye blended with the blood. Consequently, most of their homespun was some shade of red.

Yet, as she trudged up a path leading to her favorite hill and her skirts swished against her legs, Emily had to admit she liked the color. For some reason, she looked good in it. Perhaps it was because it gave a glow to her cheeks, or brought out red highlights in hair that was otherwise so blond it was almost white.

Emily squinted up at the blaze of the hot sun. Indian summer, Hopeful Rose called it. At a time when the days should have been getting cooler, they were, instead, almost as hot as those in June.

She sighed. It wasn't going to cool down for hours, so she might as well rest. Slipping the strap of a damp burlap bag off her shoulder, she let it plop to the ground with a soft thud. The willow and chestnut trug which her brother Ned had fashioned (it looked like a scooped out watermelon instead of the berry basket he'd been planning to make) soon followed. After a morning of gathering, the two containers were heavy as anchors. The sack was filled with fresh clams dug out of the squishy mud flats in the cove; and the trug jammed with cress, chestnuts, salsify, marigolds, thistles, and wild radishes.

She stretched, then bent from the waist to touch her fingers to the ground. Immediately, her back spasmed, yet soon relaxed, getting used to the weightlessness. Brushing the sweat from her brow, she held her arms out, as if to catch and hold the intermittent breezes which wafted up from the shore to the top of the hill she had staked out as her own picking grounds.

Below her, scurrying back and forth in a disorderly fashion in a field full of maize were her brothers—five of them. The other two were out with her father in their double-ended fishing boat to bring in the week's catch of cod or haddock or, please God, a swordfish.

As her brothers walked through the neat rows of maize, they reached out and tested one ear after the other. Those that were ready, they pulled off the stalk and dropped into canvas bags much like the one Emily had just dropped—except theirs were so big, they dragged along the ground. This was their third crop of maize—the best—bound for the dinner table and the miller's wheel. It seemed to Emily that every time one of her brothers picked an ear of maize he would laugh, jostle another, hop over the pumpkins and squash planted beneath, and later pop out further down the row, making a funny face meant to frighten the others.

As she tucked her unruly, sweat-drenched hair up into her mobcap, she fumed at their unrestricted movements. "Don't know why boys can run free and girls have to be weighted down with pounds of dad bursted gingham!"

Looking around to be sure she wasn't being observed, she smiled mischievously and tugged the back hem of her long skirt up between her legs and jammed it into the front of her waistband. She kicked into the air and ran in a circle, her arms outstretched like a gull's wings. Wasn't as good as having breeches, but she felt less constricted—though the heat which rapidly built around her nether regions was pure misery.

An amused, yet warning snort stopped Emily's jubilation. She turned to see her Indian friend, Hopeful Rose, the Manissee's medicine woman, emerge from a small stand of pear trees that started halfway down the other side of the hill.

Shaking a head furrowed with worry, though a gaped toothed grin softened her dark features, Hopeful tut-tut-tutted, "Let Bella catch ya like that and ya'll be housebound for a month."

"I'm hot!"

"So's the gaggle o' goodwives coming up the hill behind me. Best behave yourself or we'll both suffer for it."

They had suffered before. Hopeful, banished from the town last summer for a fortnight because she'd allowed Emily to strip down to her chemise and underskirt and paddle in the cool waters of the cove. Emily, confined to her room and her loom—such torture!—for the same amount of time, for *"forgetting she was the child of a true, and long dead, God-fearing English lady, not trashy spawn of a godless Manissee Indian witch."*

The words weren't great-aunt Bella's but Mistress Delia Davies's, wife to Jeremiah Davies, one of the itinerant ministers who had accepted a permanent call from the inhabitants of Block Island. Delia's words had the bite of a recluse spider in them, meant to sting, even kill. And they had. They were also meant to separate the two friends, Emily and Hopeful. But they hadn't. Great-aunt Bella was too old and too fat and too tired to watch Emily every minute. Hopeful Rose was too clever and too independent and too respected among her own people.

Even today, after banishments and other *lessons,* Hopeful Rose never worried—much—about what white women said.

But as she watched Emily leaping like a doe, Hopeful frowned. She had long ago decided that she would act no fool for the island woman; because she *was* no fool. She knew her place and she knew Emily's.

Emily—lonely, neglected, and aching for friendly female companionship as she was—wasn't an Indian squaw, never would be. So even if Emily hadn't taken that first lesson to heart, Hopeful, at least, had. She had gently led her very young friend into behavior that would lessen the blows of Emily's maturing into her own society. Now, if Hopeful could only direct Emily's interest in other things . . . broken and half dead birds and animals high on the list. She wanted to direct Emily in such a way that the girl would be satisfied and the island women wouldn't be scandalized.

For a while.

Hopeful shook her head ruefully as she watched her young friend angrily jerk her skirt back into place. No direction of Emily Gorton would last forever less'n Emily wished it to.

The child was willful, but gifted. Why did none but the Manissee understand?

Shame on the whites! They wasted a precious gift from the Great God. If Emily were part of the Manissee tribe, her healing touch would be revered and honored, as Hopeful's was. But Emily was a white girl—fast becoming a white woman. Perhaps no one else saw it but Hopeful's eyes detected slight hills and hollows where none had been before. So in order to fit in, Emily had to be turned to wifely arts: cooking and spinning and weaving and needlework. The messes she whipped up now were not good enough. Whatever she did or made had to look or taste as good or better than that made by the other women on the island.

And how was *that* to be accomplished?

With Emily's father and seven brothers to care for,

Bella was too busy *doing.* She had no time to teach an impatient, wistful, stubborn woman-child. And Hopeful had learned no white woman's chores, few Manissee ones. She was a medicine woman. She had her totems, her herbs and her potions. And she performed a valuable service among her people. Thus, her meals were cooked for her and served to her from the communal pot. If she tore her moccasins or they wore through, John Connor would make her a new pair. And each year, at the change of the seasons, fresh, sweet-smelling muslin or gingham or dimity or deerskin shifts were presented to her by the Chief, Watson Connor. Unlike Emily she didn't have to learn complicated skills except medicine.

As the sound of high-pitched chattering voices got louder, Hopeful Rose sighed. The women were getting closer. They'd be here soon, as would Emily's maturity. She wondered what future Emily had with women like these. They little understood her. They valued only those girls who observed the proprieties of the small, yet fast growing, community. And Emily was certainly not one of those.

The great god Manitou would need powerful medicine to help this poor white girl. Which was why Manitou had directed her steps. Why Hopeful had befriended the poor girl in the first place. And why she suffered silently the scorn the island women heaped on her. She was Emily's buttress against the headwinds that threatened to topple Emily's independence or undermine it little by little, as the waves undermined the clay cliffs on the southeast side of Manissee—or Block Island, as the fool whites called it.

Had Hopeful been a divining woman, she would have long despaired for the motherless child. But she was a medicine woman. So she had no other choice. It would bring Emily more hardship. But in the end it might make her a better woman than the others. She had begun almost at once to teach her arts to Emily, to help her prepare a way for herself. It was a risk . . . one that could get her and Emily thrown into the pits of the hollow or . . .

No use dwelling on that right now, since the fool women approached.

"Spread ya skirts and sit like a lady," Hopeful hissed to Emily, then stepped back several paces before squatting on the ground. Near enough if Emily needed her. Far enough away to show respect to the island women, although none had been earned.

At Hopeful's two warnings, Emily's first thought was to grab up her sack and trug and light out for home. But she had no time to blink before the goodwives were on her. So she sidled a glance at Hopeful, who nodded encouragement. Emily dropped a curtsy to the quartet and smiled grimly before sinking slowly to the ground, remembering to smooth out her skirts the way "ladies" did.

The next half hour was torture. In the heat of the day, Emily half listened to descriptions of the latest fashions from Delia Davies who had just gotten back from Newport where she'd been entertained by the stately and "correct" Goddards and Adams. As the others droned on, Emily totally blocked out recipes for chowder and stew and pumpkin pie. How did the women keep all of it in their heads? It sounded like gibberish. A dash of this . . . a peck of that . . . two turns with the grater . . . sixteen knobs of sugar . . . ginger, nutmeg, laurel leaves. . . . It *was* gibberish. If you put all that together you'd have . . . well, you'd have what usually happened to Emily's kitchen concoctions, an inedible, grey mass fit for neither man nor hogs. Emily's interest perked only when the women began a litany of nervous gossip about French ships being sighted in the fishing lanes.

"French regiments have seized the whole of the New Connecticut Valley, are already in New York, and are moving Eastward," Polly Gibbs said. She glanced around nervously as if Frenchmen or pirates were hiding in the brush. Emily stifled a giggle.

"And King Louis has put a bounty on all British vessels. You know what that means," Delia warned.

Lotta Stubbs nodded. "Pirates will lie right off shore, just waiting for a ship with the British Jack. And they'll attack, they will . . . just for the booty."

Polly almost squeaked, she was so upset. "Oh, dear. Next, Crown officials will issue new letters of marque to more privateers to fight them off. *Crown* privateers! Huh! No better than pirates, themselves. Last year three ships came to the Island to raid our storehouses, strip the fields, steal chickens and lambs and pigs. We're isolated, out there on Settler's Point . . ."

"As are we all," Lotta pointed out. "So far from the mainland that the Governor refuses to send any militia because it's too expensive and too far away if there's trouble! We have only our own men and their little double-ended fishing boats, a few ketches, and one sloop. We're vulnerable to attack from anyone!"

"Which is why you must not be out here alone, Emily," Delia said, with a determined glare at Hopeful.

"Pirates have raided more than livestock before. Your own cousin . . ."

"I know," Emily said, in a sing-song way that children have when repeating a story they'd heard over and over and over again. "Patience Sands was dragged right out of her bed . . . down to the docks. There she was thrown into a boat, rowed out to a tall square-rigged brigantine, and never, ever, seen again."

"The same could happen to you," Polly admonished. "Alone out here or on the bluffs. We've seen you. God's love, child, you've only that *squaw* to protect you if trouble strikes."

"I'm pleased that you worry about me," Emily said, gritting her teeth all the while, since she was *not* pleased to have these infernal women spying on her. "But listen to what you say. Tell me the sense of it. Cousin Patience was taken from her own bed, with her husband right there, his musket to hand. What does it matter if I'm out gathering or tucked in the garret?"

"That's as may be. But thou shalt not question your elders, Miss Pris," Delia snapped. "I see I've a duty to inform your father about your recalcitrant attitude." She stood and shook out her skirts. "You need a man's hand where it does the most good. *Spare the rod and spoil the child.* The Good Book knows." When she jerked her head the other women made a single file behind her and marched straight down the hill.

Emily tried to control herself but that Mistress Delia made her so mad sometimes! She called softly to their backs, "The Good Book also says, *A little child will lead them* and *Suffer the children to come unto me* and *Blessed are the peacemakers for they shall be called children of God."* Thank goodness the wind carried her words to Hopeful, rather than to the harrowing horde. "God's blood! And these are Christian women!" She pulled up dirty clumps of old, pungent wild carrots and threw them after the "good" wives of the Island as Hopeful got up from her squat and came closer. "Humbuggery! As Rob Sears says, *right daft they be!* If I'm to choose, I choose to believe in Jesus' teachings. Did you ever wonder why Delia never spouts anything but the old prophets, Hopeful?"

"Cause your Jesus doesn't quite fit into eyes for eyes and tooths for tooths."

Emily laughed. "Teeth, Hopeful."

"Huh! English is one dumb language. Sometimes using a *S* and sometimes using a whole nother word to count more than one something. Indians are smarter. Our words are simpler. Our endings are always the same." She bent to pick up the burlap sack. "Best get these into the pot. Heat like this can change their juices into stomach turning poison." Her head jerked up as terns and gulls bolted from their nesting places in the brush and screeched off towards the incoming tide.

Emily watched them glide and swoop in almost a straight line. "Must be ships coming round the point, with nice tasty leavings for the birds. Yep, there they are!"

Two tall square riggers—a brig with a black hull and white water line and a brigantine with a barn red hull and yellow ochre water line—had caught the gusts that whipped across the point. Both were traveling fast. Faster than a double-ended island fishing boat, with its two ends shaped like the point of an Indian canoe, that was close by.

As Hopeful and Emily watched, the double-ender crested a huge wave, coming into port low in the water from a good day's fishing. Its course was right across the bow of the square riggers. By rights, the great ships should have tacked off and given him precedence because the counter current waves near the point were heaving almost into the little boat. For the double-ender's captain to tack and give way to the overpowering square rigged ships would surely swamp him; and the water was deep, the current treacherous. By rights, the great ships should have tacked. . . .

But the tall black-hulled square rigger was too tall. Too powerful. Too fast. It was on the little boat in the time it took for Emily to croak, "God's blood!"

The double-ended fishing boat, its men and all, were flung high in the air. On their way down they crashed against the black hull. Emily had seen rag dolls tossed into the air like that. Never men. She waited a heartbeat for the square rigger's bo'sun's pipe to bellow, giving a warning that there'd been an accident. But no bellow came.

"They don't know! They don't know! We may be the only ones who saw it!"

Both she and Hopeful picked up their skirts and dashed down the hill, an unladylike action that would surely bring the wrath of Delia. But they had to alert someone to ring the island bell, calling all hands out of the fields to rescue the men in the double-ender.

"Let it not be Papa! Let it not!"

* * *

Not many islanders ate supper that night. When the rescue work was finished, three men lay dead under salt water stained blankets. Polly Gibbs's screams could be heard for miles around the minister's house, where she'd taken refuge. She and the islanders mourned her husband Nathan and their second son, Will.

The other lump under the blankets was a newcomer to the island, a man they called Burley, hired by Nathan for a few weeks' work. But was Burley his first name or his last? They didn't know He'd merely showed up one day when the Point Judith merchant ship docked, bedded down in a lean-to in the woods, taken on a few odd jobs here and there, and mostly kept to himself. Emily wondered what he had been running from, for surely to live like that meant he had a past that haunted him. With naught but Burley to go by, what would the mason put on the stone over his grave or would there be a stone at all? Didn't seem fitting not to have something above his head. These were hard times, however, and likely to get harder, what with the French and Indian Wars to contend with.

And if truth be told, Emily wasn't really interested in the bodies under the blankets. She was more piqued by the one in Matthew Cox's back room, on a table, being readied for surgery.

While Polly Gibbs moaned and cried her mourning chant in Delia's front parlor, her oldest son, Benjamin, lay unconscious as Dr. Cox examined what was left of Benjamin's battered body and tried to put the pieces back, to mend him in the best way Dr. Cox could.

All around Polly, adults bustled about, trying to help out the widow and her two little girls. Emily gave a hand for a while, then she hung back until she knew she wouldn't be missed. Rushing home to an empty house, she took her stoutest boot box and sneaked through the back garden to the end of her father's farm.

Keeping to the brush beside the lanes or the copses of trees where shadows mingled so she didn't stand out in the dark, she crisscrossed the fields until she came to the back yard of Dr. Cox's house. She recognized island men's voices coming from the front yard, angry at the wanton loss of life. Likely, the contrite voices which were unknown to her belonged to One-eyed Jack Saunders's crew, the ones from the black-hulled brig. Just as she was about to dash across the yard to the house, a privateer from the crew rounded the corner to relieve himself and Emily ducked behind a mulberry bush. When he left, she skirted the yard, keeping to the dark of trees and bushes, and then edged over to the window which gave onto Dr. Cox's back room. She found the right window, dropped her boot box into position and hopped up onto it so she could see into the candle-lit interior.

God's blood!

This was nothing like the little lean-to room behind her father's barn where she nursed back to health all her injured robins and chipmunks and island family pets. There, the animals were in reed cages, sleeping. Only the birds made sounds; plaintive when the pain was bad, joyful, when their wounds had healed. Here, there were blood and moans and nerve-tingling screams. And once Dr.

Cox slipped in the muck on the floor.

Emily averted her eyes, blinked them hard.

She had to be strong. Strong like cousin Sarah.

But how had Sarah Sands done it? Sarah, the legendary Block Island woman who had been the community's very first doctor way back in the 1650s! One hundred years ago, Sarah, a "gentlewoman of remarkable sobriety and piety," as her grandson, Samuel, had once described her in his journal, "was for many years the only midwife and . . . doctor on the Island." Sarah had dug out bullets, sewed up wounds, given draughts and potions, birthed babies, cured rattlesnake bites, brought a woman back from death who had been struck twice by lightning. She had married Captain James Sands, one of the first settlers of the Island and bore him five children.

Sarah Sands.

Emily's great-great—oh, so many greats! cousin, who was a shining light to the Sands and Niles and Raymonds and Gortons. Sarah, who had passed on her healing skills to her Negro slave, Hannah Rose, the great-great—oh, so many greats! grandmother of Hopeful Rose, the half-breed squaw who was Emily's friend. Sarah, who had freed Hannah Rose and all her other slaves, long before anyone else on the island had done so.

Emily couldn't imagine Sarah Sands being chastised for anything.

Her mother—another Sarah, named for their ancestor—had first told Emily the story when Emily was three years old. It eclipsed the stories about wolves and fairies and leprechauns, or angels and saints. It was real where the others were fantasy. It was the best story Sarah Gorton ever told her daughter and Emily requested the tale be told every night before she fell asleep. So, even though her mother was weakening in the last days of her pregnancy with Carter, she told the Sarah Sands story. And Emily listened in awe and admiration about this extraordinary woman.

Since Sarah Gorton had died so soon after she'd heard about Sarah Sands, Emily always pictured them as one person. If that person was more Sarah Sands than Sarah Gorton, it was understandable. Sarah Sands was, to Emily, a beacon of what a female could be, might be, should be.

Emily was sure she had inherited Sarah's skills. The healing mission burned in her as brightly as she imagined it had burned in Sarah. But she was just as certain that that mission was the only thing she had inherited. Sarah Sands and Sarah Gorton had been wives and mothers, as skilled in household duties as Sarah Sands was in a surgery. Emily could but barely hold a stupid spindle! She hated cooking. Despised needlework. And swaddling a baby was a complete mystery.

Ah, but bandaging . . . now that was different. She could set a splint—only on a crow's wing or a rabbit's hind leg, so far; but she had a feeling the procedure wasn't much different from a human arm or a leg. She made potions and salves and concoctions and teas, which she fed to sick animals to make them well. And she had even stitched up one long gash on Blinkers, tiny Tab Rose's dog.

She pressed her nose against the speckled, wavy glass in Dr. Cox's house and held tight to the window ledge. What was Dr. Cox doing with that saw?

"God's blood!"

As she averted her eyes from what she saw, something poked into her waist, unbalancing her, sending her toppling off the boot box. The box skittered across the damp grass, Emily hit her shoulder on the house, her legs went out from under her and she hit the ground, screeching. A hard body covered hers and a hand clamped itself across her mouth.

"Damn it, Emily, don't be a fool! Shut yourself up!" said a deep, husky, and amused man's voice.

"What's goin' on back there?" a loud voice called out.

Emily had heard it before: One-eyed Jack. One of his men had her! Had to be. She knew every voice and smell of each man, woman and child on the Island. Was she to be taken just like cousin Patience?! No . . . this pirate wouldn't have to fight a husband to get a woman out of bed. Here she was, Emily Gorton, fully dressed and ready to hand.

Humbuggery!

Emily squirmed and tried to bite the callused hand. It only clamped harder.

"Hush up!"

"What in thunder be ye doin', Rob?" One-eyed Jack demanded.

Even Emily trembled. So did the ground, as Jack Saunders threw his considerable three hundred pounds into each step he took closer to Emily and . . . and . . . Rob? Oh, no. Not again!

"Mmmph . . . nnnng!" she said into Robert Sears's hand. But Rob held fast.

"Well, now, what 'ave we got 'ere? So ye've found yerself a young gazelle, eh, Rob, me boy?"

The earth stopped shaking as One-eyed Jack fixed his unpatched smoldering blue eye on Emily. As she peeked out from under Rob's body, One-eyed Jack stood tall and solid as a great oak. His boots were black and buckled with silver. His legs, encased in scarlet breeches, were spread wide. His huge hands curved over two cutlasses, which were tucked into a wide brown belt which also held three long barrelled pistols. A white shirt and multi-hued waistcoat looked as if it had been patched and embroidered by a hundred hands. And the neck cloth he wore was green and soft, not the usual dirty white, blue, or black band most able seamen wore. Long hair slicked back into a queue was black as the patch over his eye. And a striped red headband that covered his forehead down to his eyebrows gave him a hooded look like a badger or great brown bear.

No wonder he was a feared privateer. If she had been a member of the crew of a ship that Saunders Jack boarded, she'd take one look and give up her arms without a fight.

"A mite skinny, don't ye think? Little more meat makes for a better handful." Jack winked broadly, then let his eyes roam over the little bit of Emily showing beyond Rob's body. "But she moit be t'only kind ye kin 'andle roit yet, Rob. So go to it, boy. Just don't let 'er menfolk ketch ye!"

As if he could read her horrified thoughts, his expression was mocking and terrifying all at once. For the first time in a long time Emily had no bravado to spare. She buried her head in the crook of Rob's neck and shook it as Jack shook the earth once more, this time in the opposite direction.

Rob loosened his hand and Emily saw her opportunity. She beat at his shoulders until he eased back enough to let her scurry out from under him. But he kept a hand on her wrist and pulled her to his side.

"Robert Sears, you Jack-a-Lent! Let me go!" she hissed.

"Hush. You want people to know you were peeking into the doctor's window? With a half-naked man on the table?"

She looked up and only then noticed that Rob had a grin the likes of which could melt snow. Gently he let go her wrist.

"Not *half*-naked," she said, and felt embarrassment creep unwilling and unwanted over her. "I didn't expect him to be . . . Well, go ahead . . . you're aching to find out what made me jump. Look for yourself."

Rob didn't have to crane his neck to see over the sill; but what he saw made him gasp. *"I'm* a Jack-a-Lent? God's blood, Emily, you can see . . ." He shook her once, hard. "What kind of girl are you?"

"A regular girl."

"No regular girl sneaks peeks at a full-naked wounded man who's getting his arm cut off."

"I didn't expect that, either."

Rob studied the sad-faced, stubborn girl he had never forgotten since that day four years ago. She had grown almost as many inches as had he, which still brought her head to his chin. But where his body had hardened and filled out in his shoulders and arms, hers was still slender yet had begun to form into soft curves. He imagined if he were given another peek under her skirts her bottom would be a wonder. The child's face was gone. The woman's, just beginning. It was a lovely face, bathed in moonlight. Her brows arched delicately over eyes round and dark as the center of black-eyed daisies. Her nose was still slightly turned up at the bottom, but it topped lips which were full and sensuous—though God and he knew that this child-woman had no idea what sensuality was.

"Ah, Emily Gorton, what am I to do with you?"

Chapter Five

"*Do* with me? What do you mean, *do* with me? I can take care of myself, thank you!"

"If you could do that I wouldn't have to keep rescuing you." He picked at a brown-specked red maple leaf that had drifted onto her hair and flicked it away. "Remember that day in the barn and you with wool all over your hair and trailing into your face?"

"I remember three weeks of torture over those combing boards because Papa made me do every last bit that was left after you did one tiny basket. And I remember that you and Davey spent every day of your shore leave fishing or clamming in the cool air, while I sat in the heat of a dark, dank barn, sweating and listening to the plaintive bleats of new born lambs. Baa, baa, baa . . . all the day long. I almost purely lost my mind."

Rob laughed. "I dared not come near the house. Davey said your father was ready to tar me."

"Although he *was* angrier than a swatted wasp, it was at me he was angry. He wouldn't have done anything to you," she admitted . . . reluctantly; because she dearly wanted to put the fear of God into this boy who always caused her so much trouble!

But he was right. He *was* always rescuing her. Why didn't that make her annoyed and angry? What was it about him that she held back the full bite of her tongue?

Humbuggery! It was too much to think about.

She picked up her boot box and started off across the yard. Half way she called back, "Well? Are you coming with me, or not?"

"Not. I have to get back to the ship. I'll call on you tomorrow, if that's all right."

"Call if you want. We won't be there. We've men to bury."

"Aye. Me and my mates are sorry about that."

"We know. Don't worry. We're islanders, used to the treachery of the sea. These aren't the first men we've buried this year and like as not they won't be the last."

He watched as she disappeared through the hedges, into the dark. A proud, stubborn, puzzling woman, who, he was ghastly afraid, had stolen his heart that day in the barn when she was naught but a babe, and he just growing into a man. To this day he hadn't yet frequented a friendly house, and didn't intend to. But his gait, stature, and body now attracted women, commoner and aristocrat alike. And contrary to what One-eyed Jack thought, Robert Sears was no longer an untried boy. He liked British women for their aloofness. American, for their spirit and fire. And French . . . ah! French women were delectable, one young mademoiselle in particular. Yet, when he sunk into his hammock at night it was not perfumed and powdered flesh he dreamed about but a grimy, turned-up nose with a smattering of freckles. It was not murmured French love words he heard but *Finish it and you'll eat dung.* Not silks and satins and laces and chemises but dirty black shoes, blue and white striped stockings and a pink bottom that was but two hands wide. Not kohl-lined lids outlining flirtatious and audacious glances but bright brown snapping eyes full of life and fire.

"Ah, Emily Gorton," he whispered into the night, "what am I going to do with you while you take your time growing up? Nay, what am I going to do with myself?"

Rain, the first they'd had in two weeks, had begun after midnight and continued all morning. When it had come, the heat of Indian summer had blasted away. Now the island was blanketed with mist and fog and bitter breezes; and at midafternoon it looked as if the rain was fixing to stay, an unwelcome visitor. Its bite soaked the outer garments and capes of almost every islander as they left their wagons on the rutted road and climbed the steepest hill to the cemetery.

From that vantage point Emily could usually see the hollow, where winding paths, broken through in the distant past by Manissee Indians, led to caves and gullies and hedgerows where wild things nested. It was good hunting there, as it was in the maze along the cliffs. The maze and cliffs—North, South, East, and West—were also usually visible from the heights of the cemetery. As was Black Rock, where the currents had sent the brig into the double-ender. Or Settler's Point, where the Gibbs's family had their farm.

On clear, cloudless, sunny days when she came to lay flowers on her mother's grave, Emily could see all the way to the mainland. But not that day. That day it seemed that as three men's lives had been cut off by the vagaries of the sea, even God had cut Block Island off from the rest of mankind. Isolated by sea and mist and rain, she and her neighbors buried three men, two of them the best liked men who had walked for too few years on the small green oasis they had called home.

The service was brief, the minister probably as chilled to the bone as she was. After Thomas Gorton and the other elders lowered the plain pine boxes into the ground and shoveled on dirt to cover them, Emily looked away, mumbling her prayers by rote. She didn't want to be there. She dreaded the dozens, hundreds more times she would come to this hill, say these same prayers, until she, herself, would be lowered into the earth. Her thoughts were only brought back to the service when Jeremiah Davies, the minister, intoned, "And we commend their souls unto Your care, oh Lord God. May they rest in peace."

"Amen," she said, along with her neighbors.

Others cried. She remained dry eyed, surprised that she almost envied the men in the ground. They were at peace. But she knew there would be naught but restlessness for her until she could . . .

What? Perform miracles? Not even Matthew Cox, their doctor and a surgeon of note all the way to the mainland, could do that.

Rob caught up with the Gortons as Emily mounted the wagon seat. Jasper gave Rob a hand up and he settled in with the brothers, but he kept his eyes on the back of Emily's head, where her blond hair broke out of her woolen mob cap and spread across her cranberry colored cape. Thomas Gorton clicked to his horse and the wagon jolted forward. Because of the narrow, uneven, wheel-rutted road, the jolting didn't stop until he pulled up the reins in front of his barn.

"Ye are welcome to sup with us, Robert," Thomas said. "It's simple fare."

"Thank you, sir. I'd like that."

Although he preferred to spend some time with Emily, Rob followed the boys into the barn to help them put the wagon and horse away. Davey mumbled something about dinner with Ellen van Wyke and took some good natured ribbing from his brothers about being hog-tied. But he merely grinned, saddled his horse and cantered down the trail toward the center of town. Later, when they all trooped into the keeping room, Emily was crouched in front of the fireplace, stirring a large iron pot which hung on a hook over the fire. Rob sniffed but couldn't identify the contents of the pot.

She snapped, "Fish stew."

"If you can call it that," Jasper said.

When the boys laughed, Emily pretended she didn't hear them. But she fumed inside. No, it was more than that. She was nervous. It was the first time Rob had been to table with them. The first time he would taste her cooking. Humbuggery! Would naught go right?

"Jason," she ordered, "set the table."

Jason quit pushing Carter closer to the fire. He pulled worn wooden trenchers from pantry shelves built into the corner near the fireplace and plunked them down on the rough hewn pine table top. Each member of the family took a trencher and sat on pine benches to either side of the table. Two-tined forks and knives and spoons were tossed in a heap in the middle. Thomas and the boys reached for the cutlery. Jasper took two of each and gave one set to Rob, who waited for Emily to sit down; but when she didn't he found a place next to Jasper.

Surprised that Emily was working in the kitchen by herself, Rob asked Jasper, "Is your aunt sick?"

Jasper shook his head. "She died last February right after Henry married Jenny Niles and right before Billy took Purity Rawlings to wife."

Ned scowled. "And we've had to endure Emily's wifery ever since."

"It can't be that bad."

The boys exchanged knowing glances and not a few chuckles. Even Thomas looked slightly askance. He winked at Jasper and tapped one finger on the side of his nose. Rob had seen that gesture made by other islanders and some pirates. It signified many things, one of which was, *Don't say anything. Let him find out for himself.*

When Emily ladled out the fish stew she looked at the rim of the pot, the table top, the floor, her father's neck cloth. Anywhere and everywhere but into Rob's eyes.

One mouthful of the brew and Rob understood the boys' eager anticipation and her nervousness. Red and black pepper bit into his tongue and the roof of his mouth. A fish bone—at least he hoped it was the bone and not the hook—stuck halfway down his throat. He choked. He coughed. He clutched at the spot where the bone sent spasms of pain clear to his fingertips and up to his scalp. Jasper thrust a water pitcher at Rob and he drank two mugs. Still the bone scratched murderously at the inside of his throat. He could not talk. He could only gesture.

Emily gave a strangled cry and rushed into the kitchen, to return with a large grey lump of bread and a pilot biscuit. "Eat this. It might help," she said, her voice quavering with embarrassment.

Too much salt, or soda, or . . . good Lord, had the girl put *mint* into the bread? . . . made Rob gag. Tears came to his eyes, the first in years.

Emily wanted to crawl under the floorboards and die right there. John and Ned leaned against each other, each mimicking the horror-stricken, distressful faces Rob made. Carter laughed so much he rolled on the floor. Even Emily's father was finding it difficult to keep a straight face. If he pursed his mouth together any harder like as not he'd pull his jaw out of joint! Only Jasper seemed to sense what she already knew because he jerked his head to the right and raised his eyes to the ceiling.

She threw her father a stricken glare and bolted up the center stairs for her room. When she returned Jasper had Rob in a chair in the middle of the floor. He stood behind Rob, using his strong, muscular arms to pinion him against the chair's wooden back. She nodded, relieved that he, at least, had sense.

"Hold him steady, Jase," she said, as she opened a small box and pulled out a pair of scissors whose ends had been blunted by a hammer and anvil.

Rob took one look, his eyes went wide and he strained to get out of the seat. Emily pushed him back and stamped her foot. "Damn your eyes, Robert Sears. Sit back there and mind you don't act like a wee babe."

When she brought the instrument close to his mouth, he shut it tight.

"Open your mouth!"

He shook his head vehemently.

"Open it, I said!"

Jasper smiled mischievously. "Might's well do as she says, Rob, or she'll bedevil ye to death."

Rob was sure she'd almost done that already. He wasn't going to give her another chance. Pester or pepper. Bone or bedeviled. It was all the same. He'd be dead, whatever method Emily chose.

But he was in agony trying to hold her at bay. By keeping his mouth shut, the bone scraped against the sides of his throat each time he breathed. He tried to swallow and it scratched another spot. The damn thing smarted more than a saber cut! What was worse, he couldn't stop a stream of salty tears from coursing down his cheeks.

Damn. Damn. Damn!!!

"Hold his head, Papa," Emily commanded, yet with a softness that Rob was surprised to hear.

When her father didn't immediately jump to her instructions, Emily stamped her foot. "Humbuggery! I won't kill him! You're the strongest man here and I need him still as stone. Now, do it." She gulped at the anger in her father's eyes. "Please, Papa. I know what I'm doing."

I hope.

From her frequent perch on her favorite boot box outside Dr. Cox's window, Emily had seen him remove teeth and extract bullets. He had several instruments such as the one she held in her hand. . . . Or as close to it as dozens of whacks on the anvil could fashion from her sewing scissors. *A fine waste,* Mistress Davies would say. But if they worked. . . .

Thomas Gorton glared at his daughter, but did as she bid.

"Don't lose your grip, Jasper," Emily warned.

"Best have the boys hold down his feet," Jasper said to his father. "We don't want him to kick out and bruise our stones . . ."

Thomas harrumphed but jerked his head to Ned and John. They took hold of Rob's legs while Carter watched with his eyes wide as moonstones.

"Open your mouth wide and stick out your tongue, Rob," Emily pleaded. "I can pluck the bone out if you give me enough room to see. But if we wait much longer your throat might swell up and then I don't know if I can do anything."

It sounded reasonable. But Rob could find naught about this night that had been reasonable so far. How did it happen? Did trouble follow as close to Emily Gorton's heels as a puppy? Was she bewitched? Her dark brown eyes had bewitched him before and were bewitching him now. He studied their delicate shading: from chocolate to nut brown to soft amber. They were beguiling. Without knowing he'd given in, his mouth opened. Emily smiled once and her smile blotted out the pain.

With her left hand, she pressed down on his tongue and up on his top row of teeth. With her right she guided the scissors inside. He felt the cold metal and his throat convulsed. Before he could gag, however, she made a clipping motion with the scissors and the pain went away.

She pulled out the scissors and held them in front of his face. Jasper immediately released his hold. Rob pushed her hand back so he could focus on what the scissors held. The fish bone was nigh as big as the middle joint on his middle finger. Blood and a little pink skin coated one end of it. Shuddering to think what torture he would have endured had the bone gotten into his innards, he plucked it out of the scissors and tucked it into his waistcoat pocket.

Jasper snickered. "A fair lot o good that will do."

"Have you never heard of a talisman?"

Jasper and the other boys shook their heads.

"Well, it's a charm, like an arrow or a bullet that

almost kills you. But once it's dug out of you, it holds a spell that keeps evil spirits away. A fish bone is a good talisman for a seaman. Sure and it will ward off sea devils," Rob said. He patted his pocket and watched Emily out of the corner of his eye. She skittered into the kitchen as quickly as a squirrel skittered up a tree. He heard the side door bang shut.

"Might's well sit and finish the stew," Thomas Gorton said. "It's cold as ice but that might settle the sting of the pepper."

Rob tried but because of his sore throat he couldn't swallow the deadly dish. Thomas must have seen his discomfort because he went into the kitchen and fetched a large mug of buttermilk. Rob let it roll slowly down his throat, soothing it as it went. He passed up the grey bread and crumbling pilot biscuits. If there was mint in the bread he wouldn't put it past Emily to dump skunk cabbage in the biscuits.

After a quick card game of Chase the Fox, Rob bid good night to the boys and went in search of Emily. Following a flickering light, he found her in the barn, in the back stall. The candle she'd lit in a sconce on the wall showed her sitting on a stool, her head leaning against the warm belly of a brown and white cow. At first he thought she might have dozed off but a huge sigh alerted him to her wakefulness.

"Emily?"

"Go away, Robert Sears."

"In this very spot four years ago you said the same thing. . . . I didn't obey then. I'll not do it now, either."

"Then right daft you be. Can't you see I'm cursed?"

"Clumsy, sometimes, surely. Unschooled in housewifery, certainly. But *cursed?* You just removed a weapon near as deadly as a bullet, lass. And you did it without batting an eye."

"Nay! I was scared to death. My stomach was clenched into a knot so tight it hasn't yet stopped trembling."

"You're not saying this was the first time you drew something out of a man's throat?"

"Aye."

"God's blood!" He sank onto the straw at Emily's feet. "If you had slipped and the scissors had cut through the sides or slipped down my throat . . . God's blood!"

"Aye." She took a deep breath and finally faced him. "There's something terrible wrong with me, Rob. Something terrible wrong. And I don't know what to do about it. Papa is naught but . . . Papa . . . no help at all. Great-aunt Bella never was. And the island women . . . they cluck their tongues and chastise me but it does no good. I'm fit for nothing around the house. Can't cook worth a damn unless someone's looking to take poison! And my homespun! Well, you see it. Red. Always red!"

"Looks mighty good on you, Emily."

". . . Red because it's the only way to hide the blood."

"Blood?"

"I prick my fingers. Always." She thrust her hands under his nose. "Look at them!"

When he saw the cut and bruised fingers—one had an ugly blister on it the size of a sovereign piece—his heart felt torn in two. These were not the pampered hands of Lily, the French mademoiselle he'd been seeing whenever he got into Marseilles. They were not the hands of ladies Jane or Margaret Hobbs, sisters to his friend Jonathan Hobbs. Those women creamed their hands night and day with perfumed unguents, used their fingers only to pick up food, never prepare it. Rob's temples throbbed with fury that this girl's . . . this lovely young girl's hands should be as torn and bleeding as a twelve-year-old seaman's, new to the rigors of work aboard ship. God's blood! Emily did not deserve this! She deserved rose water and violets. Exotic almond salves and sweet perfumes. She deserved everything!

Reaching across the short space between them, he took her hands and brought them to his lips. "Ah, Emily . . ."

He kissed the blister first. "To make the pain go away . . ."

Then each fingertip received his attention. By the time he reached her fourth finger his heart was racing, blood pounding furiously through every part of his body. He looked into her big brown eyes and saw wonder. Her mouth opened involuntarily and her hands began to tremble in his.

"Emily . . ."

From his bruised throat the sound of her name was like music and Emily lost sight of the rough plank barn walls and the brown and white cow's sides. She was caught in the deep depths of Rob's eyes, the candle light flickering across them—green and gold and brown. She saw him swallow and her heart constricted, knowing what pain he'd endured. Because of her. Because of her inexperience, her helplessness.

Helpless to stop herself, for her mind and body mysteriously moved to a tenderness she hadn't known existed, she reached out with both bruised hands and stroked Rob's neck, felt him swallow, felt a strong, erratic pounding at the sides, just below his jaw.

His hands came to rest against her neck as hers were against his; and she felt what he must be feeling, the tickling sensation, the heat. But his fingers went further, higher and higher into her mobcap, which fell to the ground and released her hair. He gave a slight tug and she slipped easily off the stool into the circle of his arms.

"Rob?"

"Shhh. Let me . . ."

He kissed her. And, oh, God, something was terrible wrong . . . and terrible right.

His lips were hard and soft at the same time. Was that possible? He opened his mouth slightly and she took that moment to draw in a breath. He chuckled and drew her closer to him, until she was sprawled against him. She felt his body shudder as his . . . God's love! Was that his tongue? . . . Aye. It brushed back and forth against her lips.

And she liked it.

Without thinking about what she was doing, she touched the tip of her tongue to his lips. So that's what he felt! Rough and soft. Dry and wet. And warm . . . so warm . . .

This time, when his lips touched hers, they captured her tongue and drew it into his mouth. She started to protest at this unusual, strange sensation, but his mouth opened and his kiss lulled her into a dream world. His scent overpowered the smells of the barn. His skin gave off the aroma of soap and precious oranges and spices, with the tang of salty sea and maple smoke. Right then, at that very moment, if she was given the chance to choose, she'd choose to remain there, with him . . . forever.

Rob's mind muddled. Here was the stuff of his dreams. Emily in his arms, lying against him, her breasts rising and falling with his. His body responded to her and he moved against her. The ache she . . . no, *he,* damn his soul! . . . had created was now a demand that tightened every muscle and every sinew.

He wanted her. He wanted this girl. And he didn't know if he could stop himself from taking her.

She was so young. And so trusting. Damn his eyes, had he no sense? This was no friendly house. She was no strumpet. He was not in France, where kisses and bodies were joined easily, with joy and little regard for "proprieties" that argued against natural urges. He was here, in America, where proprieties were disregarded at his peril. Damn his eyes. Damn, damn his eyes!

"Damn. Damn . . ." He lifted Emily. And like the will-o-the-wisp she was, it was easy—and the hardest damned thing he'd ever done—to move himself out from under her and set her back on her stool. "Em, I'm sorry."

"Why?"

"For almost . . ."

"Almost what?" she asked in such innocence that Rob clenched his teeth.

"Emily, isn't there any woman on this whole damn island who can tell you about what happens between men and women?"

She looked at the anguished anger in his face and was confused. "Between men and women? But you're not a man and I'm not . . ."

She gasped, realizing for the first time what he meant . . . what they had been doing. For there *was* one woman who had told her. The day Emily had first discovered the stain on her sheet and thought herself bleeding to death, she had run into the woods and down to the Manissee huts. There had been none other to tell her except Hopeful Rose. None in whom she had dared confide. And Hopeful had explained, calmly and lovingly, about a woman's body and a man's body and how they fit together. But Hopeful had also warned her about the laws of the community and how much trouble she would bring down on herself if she *anticipated the wedding night*. Until now Emily had had naught but words to describe that act. But, thanks to Robert Sears, this night she had experienced the feelings, the forces about which Hopeful had cautioned.

Horror and shame washed over her. She jumped to her feet, kicking over the stool. Her hand came up to slap his face; but two inches from her target, she stopped.

"A fair lot of good that would do," she muttered.

"I own myself an ass, Emily."

"Aye, Rob. As do I."

"It was my fault."

"Oh, aye. I'll not argue on that point. But I will ask you to keep it to yourself, Rob. I wouldn't want the island women to get wind of what happened. I've nothing but my pride to keep me from buckling under to their scorn. If they knew that I let you . . ."

"Never will they hear it from me. On my honor, Emily."

"And your mates? Will you brag about a free and easy Emily Gorton?"

"Free and easy? You, Em?" Rob laughed, caught Emily up and whirled her around. "The furies of hell in your peppered fish stew? Cutlass fish bones in my throat? Nay, there's nothing free and *easy* about you, girl."

He set her back on her feet, gave her a quick kiss on the forehead and winked at her. She followed him from the barn and watched as he sauntered down the hill toward the dock, whistling all the way.

Three days later her father told her that One-eyed Jack had hoisted anchor in the middle of the night, to get back to combat with the French. Relieved, yet sad that Rob hadn't come to say good-bye, she went about her chores praying that One-eyed Jack and his crew would see nothing but waves until the damned war was over. She didn't want to admit that she feared for Rob's life. But there it was, in the back of her mind.

After she cleaned up the breakfast mess—burned corn gruel stuck to an iron pot!—she went down to the barn to milk the cow. On the stool, she found a rolled up leather pouch with a note attached. *For Emily,* it said. *On my honor.*

Inside, nestled against soft brown suede were a hand-carved set of knives. She recognized them. They were exactly as she had drawn them four years ago.

Rob had remembered.

Amazed at the intricacy of the workmanship, she picked up one after the other, examining them, feeling them fit into her hands. Four years ago they would have been too big, hard to work with. Now, they were just right. And she felt such overwhelming joy! These were what she was meant to hold. Not wooden spoons and spindles. Not candle molds and muslin. Not butter churns and chinaware.

If for no one else, I will use these for you, Rob. With honor. It was time she got on with it.

Chapter Six

1761—Block Island—March 14

His pristine shirt with a lace jabot, colorfully embroidered waist coat and soft brown brushed woolen breeches were meant to soften the hardest heart and bring warmth to a frightened body. But when a nervous Emily finished her prepared speech, the blustery old man's ruddy Scottish face paled and his sky blue eyes turned flinty cold. "No! Confound it, lass, no!"

"But I've learned all Hopeful can teach me, Dr. Cox. And that's a right heap, you know."

"That's as might be. But, Emily Gorton, I wilna be a party ta wha' yer seekin'!"

He made as if to shoo her from the room, the front parlor of his house, where his patients usually waited to be admitted to the surgery behind it. It was empty now, since she had waited behind the old oak in his back yard until she'd heard his usual Scots grunt of a good-bye and seen the last patient's flickering lantern disappear down the hill.

"I said git away wi' ye, now, lest ye beach us on a lee shore and noo but bad come o' it!" He turned on his heels and went into the back room, muttering to himself.

Emily knew he expected her to obey him. Because of his bluster almost everyone on the island did. But she had been finished with obeying two years past. She was as fixed on her course as Robert Sears and One-eyed Jack were fixed on theirs. So she followed her North Star, Dr. Matthew Cox, into his surgery. Without examining the room, she knew where everything was—she had seen it often enough through the back window, standing atop her boot box.

"A young lass . . . menfolks's bodies . . . daft, she must be . . ."

"Not I, Doctor."

He whirled. "Are ye still 'ere, lass?" He made as if to block the surgical table, where a coarse linen sheet lay bunched over something unmoving. "I doona want ye 'ere! An' if yer papa knew, 'e'd tan yer 'ide."

"Papa has long stopped tanning anyone's hide, Doctor Cox."

"Aye, lass. An' tis sorry, I be, that 'e's ailin'. But there's noo more I kin do for 'im. The ague's got 'im an tis old 'e be."

"He's younger than you!"

"But 'e's been ta sea, fishin' in thay cold salt air. It eats inta thay bones an' sets them shakin'. An' 'is lungs fill with water laden salt an' kin noo longer work. So if thay ague does na get 'im, thay cough will."

"And still you bleed him. When you know he's already weakened."

"For ta get oot thay bad blood what's in 'im, lass. Tis accepted medical practice."

She wanted to say, *It's foolishness.* Which it was, Hopeful said. But Emily knew the good doctor resented the Indian medicine woman and her "superstitious nonsense." Dr. Cox could amputate and his patients recovered. But he could not and would not admit that bloodletting made his patients succumb to ailments they could have resisted had they been given soothing teas or herbal curatives.

And her father . . . her own father . . . was one of Dr. Cox's patients. About that, she was still angry enough to tie a hog!

Thomas Gorton had taken to bed after a storm at sea had settled in his lungs. Emily and Hopeful had almost had him cured. Almost had him ready to take to the Manissee hot house, where the heat of the stones could sweat the ague out of him. Then he'd regained enough zest to insist a *real* doctor be brought in. Now, he was teetering between days when he felt good—the times she and Hopeful filled him with lungwort broth and sassafras tea—and those days when he could hardly raise his head from off his pillow—the times when Matthew Cox arrived with his many-bladed fleam and lancets.

Angry enough to tie a hog? She was angry enough to gut and roast it!

But she held her tongue. She had to. Matthew Cox was the only man on the island who could teach her about surgery. He didn't know she had been operating on every village cat and dog for the past two years—since Rob had given her those wonderful knives, her scalpels. Not one of her "patients" had died. Truth, a few were hobbling about on only three legs and some had lost an infected ear or eye. But she'd cured them all, including two exotic yellow songbirds and one gaudy parrot that belonged to One-eyed Jack's friend, Dover Quince.

Though she couldn't tell that to Matthew Cox. He'd like as not have her drawn and quartered—or throw her to the mercy of the island women, which was one and the same thing.

"I'm not leaving until you hear me out, Dr. Cox. I can't! Don't you see? I want to be a doctor every bit as much as you did when you began." She held up her hand when his face turned red and his lips spluttered. "I know I'm a mere lass," she conceded. "But too soon I'll be a woman and I'll be left on my own. Papa will be dead, lying beside Mama on top of the hill. The boys will be married and raising their own families."

"Carter's a mere runt!"

"He's fifteen. In three more years he can take a wife."

"Bide a while, lass. When thay time comes for Carter ta take a wife ye'll be puttin' yer third child to yer breast."

"The only thing I'll ever put to my breast is a woolen shift, and you know it!"

The old man and the young woman glared at each other. He dropped his eyes first. Sighing, he shook his head. "Tis because of wha' yer askin' that thay island men stay away, ye knoo."

"They stay away because their mothers think me unfit for a wife to their sons," she said with bitterness, but also a quiet dignity and pride. "My hands were meant for something other than housewifery, Dr. Cox. Like Sarah Sands . . ."

"Lore, lass . . . de ye believe those tall tales?"

"They aren't tall tales. I have letters and journals from Sarah's son and grandson to prove it. She was who she was. She did what she did. And I've inherited her skills. You can't slam the door in God's face, Matthew Cox. He gave me the fire and skills. I'm merely asking you to be my guardian angel on earth, to help me use them."

"An angel, is it? This old man? A devil, more like it, if'n I do as ye ask. Delia Davies will skin me, sure as thay's clouds in 'ta sky."

"There's clouds one day and none the next." Emily cocked her head and assessed her possibilities. Leastwise, he wasn't ordering her out of his surgery, nor out of his house. If she could show him . . .

Opening a glass-fronted cupboard door to her left, she drew out a box and handed it to him. "Opium," she said. "An anodyne for lessening pain." Another box, almost exactly like the first; but she knew the difference, not merely by the label but also because, while she'd been spying on him, she had seen Matthew give it to dozens of women patients. "Laudanum . . . a mixture of opium and saffron. When you mix it with wine from the Canary Isles, it's an effi . . . efficacious pain reliever." Next, she picked up an earthen vessel. Without looking at the label, she held it out to him. "Chinchona . . . you use that with quinine for ague."

She pointed to one medicine after the other, naming off ipecac, asthmatica, potassium carbonate, febrifuges and emetics, Dover's powder, juniper berries, mercury suspended in oil, magnesium sulfate, pilular extract of cassia. She described how she and Hopeful had made infusions by boiling dried herbs for ten minutes over the fire and straining them before using as a medicine. She told him how decoction was used when boiling would destroy the herb or chemical, so it must be simmered gently. Or that tinctures were oils dissolved in alcohol. Or that insoluble substances could be made palatable when mixed in a sweet tasting food like honey or maple syrup. Or that she could make pills from beeswax, some as small as a pea—just right for children; others as large as an acorn—perfect for cattle. She could mix salves and unguents and liniment and ointments, their variety only achieved by the oil or wax content of the spreading vehicle.

By the time she finished, Matthew Cox had his large linen handkerchief out and was patting off the sweat from his forehead.

"And still I can't cook or sew or spin. And I've never finished one sample of needlework. But I know what a mortar and pestle are. I've seen illustrations of trepanning but haven't had the courage to cut into the skull of an animal. I also know the difference between surgical scissors and bullet forceps. Or probes and retractors. I know that tendons are different from muscles, and muscles different from cartilage. But I don't know how to do surgery on a human being. And I must learn more if I'm to get better. I must learn from you, sir. Oh, don't say *no*. You can't!"

"Lore bless me! Where did ye learn all this, lass?"

"Books. One-eyed Jack and Dover Quince and Robert Sears brought me doctoring books by the box full. I've read them all." She gulped, but with faith took the last argument she had. "And I've practiced."

"Practiced!?"

"On animals."

"Those three-legged beasties roamin' thay fields! *Your* work they be?"

"Aye."

"I need a drink."

He edged past her as if she were some kind of beastie herself and headed for his office. Whether he expected her to follow or no, she wasn't letting him off so easily. When she caught up with him, he was pouring two glasses of port. He handed one to her and pulled out a blue damask covered armless slipper chair, bowing her into it. He sank into its twin opposite her, looked at her carefully, drained his glass, then filled it again. He said not a word but stared into the fire and the minutes stretched out.

"Sir . . ."

"If ye knoo what's good fer ye, lass, ye'll say naught fer a bit. Tis thinkin', I am."

So it was that at sixteen years of age Emily Gorton became Matthew Cox's medical assistant.

And how the fur did fly!

Delia Davies stormed into Matthew Cox's office and confronted the pair as they were dissecting a piglet that had died the night before. After one look at Emily, her hands thrust deep into the pig's body, Delia tore at her hair and screeched. Her hand shook as she pointed towards Emily. "This is the Devil's work!"

"It's *my* work," Emily said, stubbornly.

"Well, of course it's *your* work. Because it's man's work. Because you can't be a woman if your life depended on it. Mark my words, Emily Gorton, you will rue this day! There won't be a man on this island who will take you to wife after this."

"I didn't know there was one who would take me to wife *before* this!"

Matthew chuckled. "She's got ye, there, Mistress Davies. Tis the one good reason she gave what convinced me to take 'er on."

"Don't you laugh at me, Matthew Cox. You and your heathen ways!"

"Now, bide a bit, woman. Just because I do na tend yer husband's church do na make me a heathen, Delia. I tend services on thay mainland, an' ye know it."

"Once or twice a year does not a Christian make."

"Noor does twice on Sunday! Tis what ya feel in yer 'eart, woman. Tis lovin' ya neighbor, for who knows when that neighbor wilt be the Christ 'imself? Who knows when ye moight be called on ta do somethin' fer the least o' is brethren, eh?"

"You needn't quote scripture to me, Matthew Cox! I know every verse."

"Aye, but ye practice 'em little enough, Delia. Give the lass a chance. This island 'as seen a few female doctors. They'll like as not see more."

"You've like as not seen the last of your patients, Matthew."

"An' where wilt ye go, Delia? When yer monthlies 'ave ye screamin' with thay pain, wilt ye 'op in a boat an' ride thay waves for four hours to Jerusalem or six hours to Newport to get yer laudanum? When Jeremiah 'as pleurisy, wilt ye risk 'is life 'cause Emily will be standin' beside me when I dispense 'is medicine? Think on it, woman. Tis a big mistake ye'll be makin', if ye stop comin' ter me surgery, simply because I took on a good assistant who just 'appens ta be female. Think on it, I say. Think long an' 'ard."

Delia's mouth and eyes screwed tight until her whole face looked like one big prune. Emily's sides hurt, she was trying so hard to keep the laughter in.

Or was it the pain of knowing that the door to the mysterious world of husbands and wives had finally and forever been closed off to her?

The islanders did hold off for a few weeks, as Delia had predicted. But Matthew had said prophetic words in that confrontation. One by one they drifted back to the surgery. It was, after all, a long, hard boat ride to the mainland and bones must be set, monthlies made pain free, children birthed, ague cured. And when each islander discovered that Emily was not to touch the men's bodies in the middle third, nor the women's unless they gave permission, they were satisfied to allow her to observe Dr. Cox's ministrations.

But Emily, too, had been prophetic.

As if they had to rub in her isolation, she was invited to every wedding on the island. Dutifully, she took a piece of cake home to put under her pillow. And she watched as silently as she did in the surgery as each newly wed young woman tossed her head with a smile that held so many secrets. Secrets Emily would never know, the smiles seemed to say.

And the morning following each wedding, before she tossed the wedding cake in with the hog slops, Emily burned with unshed tears and withheld fury.

Yet, still she went to the weddings.

She wore bright or pale muslin—never again cranberry red—which had been purchased from her small salary. She wore dresses cut down from her mother's old clothes and adapted for her to the fashions of the day by the women in the friendly house, her own patients. Earbobs and brooches handed down from her great-aunt Bella sparked her outfits. Her eyes sparkled. Her shoulders held her head high.

More than once she caught a young man's assessing eye or heard high praise about her sun-kissed hair and delicate features. But fiddles fiddled and drums drummed and except for her brothers or Matthew Cox she danced not one dance with an eligible partner. She probably knew more about men and what happened in marriage than most of the blushing brides. But with each invitation to their festivities her neighbors cut a new wound and added new salt to it. Thanks to them and their narrow point of view, she would know what she knew only from books about anatomy, Hopeful Rose, and a haltingly embarrassed Matthew Cox, never from the physical union that produced the many babies she watched Matthew birth.

Thomas Gorton died quietly in his sleep a year to the day after Emily began her apprenticeship with Matthew Cox. Once again wagons parked below the hill, the islanders donned their dull greys and blacks, and Jeremiah Davies consigned a good man into his mortal resting place on earth. This time, however, Rob was not there to ease Emily's sorrow. The only comfort she took was in knowing that she could now afford to hire Tab Rose, Hopeful's niece, to be housekeeper for her and her younger brothers. Jasper and Ned married and moved into small cabins on the farm, as their older brothers had done. They pooled their resources and bought more land and another double-ender fishing boat. The farm prospered. Their fish brought good solid silver and gold from Newport merchants. While the family was not wealthy, Emily did not worry that they'd founder.

But she did worry—in fact, fretted—because Matthew would never let her take on difficult surgery. Five times they'd had cases that seemed more than Matthew could handle; but each he'd struggled through, gruffly brushing aside her offer—sometimes her plea—to help.

"I'm noo so old I canna do this meself, woman!"

"I did not say you were old, Matthew. But how am I to learn if you will not . . ."

"Ye'll larn in time, as I did. That's how. Now pass me that spanner. . . ."

He did allow her to clean up after him, however. And, for the first time Emily didn't mind doing household chores. If it advanced her skills or the practice of medicine, she would have walked on her hands. Besides, Matthew left his surgery a mess! From Hopeful, she had learned how important it was to keep everything clean if a patient was to have a chance. In truth, most of what she did in the surgery was not taught to her by Matthew. It was Hopeful's advice, and the Manissee medicine woman's bags of herbs and roots and wild plants, that Emily clung to. Gradually, Matthew added some of Emily's own concoctions or tinctures to his supply, not once admitting he was giving in to her advice; but heeding it, nonetheless.

Finally, as a gift for her eighteenth birthday in 1763 Matthew grudgingly allowed her to begin suturing cuts and helping to set and splint broken bones. One afternoon, around three o'clock, she even worked on Joshua Davies's fourth trip to the surgery with a broken arm, naught a one of which had been broken in the same place, but all nasty, compound things. It was delicate work and while Delia wrung her hands and moaned in the front parlor about her nephew, Emily and Matthew sweated in the surgery to get the small bones back into place while Joshua lay sleeping under a strong dose of laudanum.

They were almost finished when the door banged open and Jasper rushed in. "Came to give you a hand with the shutters, Matthew."

"Busy now, laddy. Come back later."

"Later may be too late. A hurricane's coming. Fast!"

"Lore, an' thay two o' us as tired as a bull in season." Matthew gave the last tug on the leather strap to hold Joshua's arm in place and patted Emily's shoulder. "Finish up, lass. I'll give an 'and to yer brother. Then we'll see to yer own 'ouse."

"Ned and John and Carter will take care of that," Jasper said. "We've enough to do here."

As they rushed out the door, Emily heard Matthew ask, " 'ow many boats still out, laddy?"

"Six. Including the *Mary-lou.*"

Emily gasped. Her bothers' double-ender! Henry and Billy were out in the storm. And she could do naught about it.

Emily cleaned up Joshua. While she struggled to pull on his shirt and warm sweater, Delia paced beside her, urging her to hurry.

Emily snapped, "Help me, then!"

"But that's your job."

Emily glared daggers at the blithering woman until Delia leaned over the surgical table to lift her nephew. With her help Emily soon had him dressed warmly, his arm cradled in a sling Emily had fashioned from coarse homespun. By the time they carried Joshua out to Delia's wagon, the sky was cloudless, a pewter grey with a bright, white horizon that always put Emily in mind of the pallor of the dead.

Although she was worried to death about her brothers, she had no time to dwell on it. The wind was blowing so hard the trees in Matthew's yard were bent almost to the ground. Barrels and old fence posts tumbled down hills. Anything that hadn't been secured was a deadly projectile. Matthew and Jasper were busy enough getting the solid wooden shutters nailed down across the windows, since the islanders had learned the stout wooden bar they usually used might be fine for normal storms but would never hold against a hurricane.

It was her responsibility to settle the animals in Matthew's barn and batten down whatever she could.

The wind whipped her long skirts about her, entangling her legs and she pulled them up to tuck them in her waist as she'd done that afternoon on the hill. Harem pants, Dover Quince had called them when once she'd done the same to come aboard his ship to tend to his men. Well, if it was good enough for exotic foreign women, it was good enough for her. And it did stop the damned things from tripping up her feet or blowing in her face!

She was exhausted by the time Matthew and Jasper were finished. Everything that she couldn't tie down she'd dragged into the barn. Her final act was to nail the two barn doors shut. She looked at the dozen long nails, bent double in some places, all of them crooked, and knew they'd have a hell of a time getting them out when the hurricane was over. *If* the doors were still there. *If* the barn was still standing. Matthew was not the handyman her brothers were. His barn harbored more holes than she could have boarded over. She had to trust that what she'd done would hold, although she doubted it.

"Ye should go 'ome, lass," Matthew yelled against the rising whine of the wind, as the three gathered in the front yard to survey their work.

"Not when you might need me, Matthew!"

Jasper caught sight of a boat trying to breach waves that had reached twelve feet, and were still rising. "I'm going down to the docks! There'll be men and women to ferry up to you."

"Aye, laddy. Our thanks, we give ye."

Inside Matthew's house Emily hurried to stir the stew Tab Rose had brought them that morning. There wasn't much in the pot and it was unlikely they'd get more until the hurricane blew itself out—which could be hours, or days. Emily ladled enough for their next two meals into cracked tin plates that she set next to the hob to keep warm. Then she washed and cut up potatoes, carrots, celery, salsify, onions, salted beef and parsley. She added a handful of dill, a pinch of red pepper and plenty of water, set the cover on the pot and swung it back to the simmering spot in the corner of the fireplace. It wouldn't be as tasty as Tab's—and it might burn if she became too busy to keep an eye on it—but they'd have enough for a few meals.

Emily was used to the sounds of hurricanes. She'd seen four already in her eighteen years, and too many steady, deadly nor'easters. The wind howled plaintively, rushing in from the sea to the south, cutting across hollow and hill, uprooting trees, smashing small buildings, whipping crops out of their beds. Each act had its own distinctive sound. Each sound was eery and furious, as if the hurricane had built up all the anger in the world and was spewing it out all at once on their small rocky island, to let each settler know that they were puny things compared to Nature.

Should take Delia down a peg or two, Emily thought; but then decided only God himself could do that.

Emily and Matthew ate a cold and hurried supper that night. Matthew's parlor was filled to overflowing with islanders who had been injured in the hurricane. She set two broken arms, cleaned out dozens of lacerations, poulticed as many head wounds. She was putting away a trillium solution after cleaning dirt out of her brother Henry's eye—both he and Billy got in safe, although cut from flying flotsam—when a young negro slave knocked on the door and handed Matthew a note.

"Jack Donahue's sloop *Calumet* . . . tis comin' 'round Black Rock, 'er sails an' masts gone. Lookout says thays bandaged bodies aboard."

Emily groaned. Her back and shoulders felt permanently twisted and sloped forward like the mark at the end of a question. Because she'd been standing for almost ten hours—all through the night—her feet had swollen so much she'd long ago kicked off her boots and now wore soft wool slippers. And a pounding in her head resembled the sounds usually coming from the blacksmith's shop. She avoided a mirror, knowing she must look like a hound from hell.

"How long before they get here?" she asked.

"Ah, lass . . ." Matthew shrugged.

She saw then the exhaustion in *his* body, which was fifty years older than hers. After pouring Matthew a good mugful of his favorite Scotch whiskey—which he drank with a grateful sigh—she filled a ewer with hot water from the black cast iron kettle on the hob and dropped a heavy Turkish towel into it. "Sit in the tilt back chair, sir."

"I'd best prepare thay surgery."

"I'll tend that. You rest."

It was a mark of how tired he was that Matthew Cox didn't argue. As soon as he sat in the chair, Emily tilted the back a few degrees and settled a pillow behind his head. When his eyes closed, she wrung out the hot towel and draped it gently on his face. At the first touch, he sighed. Soon, raspy snores filled the room.

As Matthew slept, Emily surveyed the surgery. "First things first, girl."

She scrubbed down the table, slopped water on the wide plank floorboards and washed up the worst of the dirt and body grime that had accumulated during the past six hours. She had to struggle to get Matthew's apron off without waking him; but she managed. It and her own apron went into a hog's head barrel filled with vinegar water that they kept on the large rock to the right of the back door. Already the barrel was half filled with other aprons, waiting Tab's thrice weekly washing.

Emily was jolted to find the sun had already risen and the horizon was tinted a pale yellow-gold, which meant the hurricane and its aftermath must be far to the north of them—or out to sea, since its death pallor had been replaced by wisps of clouds. From Matthew's vantage point on the top of the hill, she could see the destruction around and below her. Contrary to what she'd thought, Matthew's barn had survived the howling winds and pounding rains. There were a few more holes bored through the sides, but it still stood. Not so the old oak that she'd hidden behind that night when she'd seen her first naked body. It lay with its knotted roots reaching to the sky in useless supplication.

"At least Matthew will have enough firewood for winter," she said aloud.

"Most of the island will, too."

Emily spun. "Hopeful!"

"None other. How are you, child? You look tired."

"So do you."

In fact, Hopeful looked better than Matthew. Her black hair hung in two neat plaits on her shoulders and down the front of her plain woolen shift. And her eyes sparkled as they had often done when she and Emily got into one scrape or another.

"Your people?" Emily asked.

"Fared better than yours, since we're settled into the hollows and caves. Lost a few gardens but we can forage for a time."

"What are you doing here?"

"*Calumet*. Thought you might need a hand, what with Dr. Cox being so old and all."

Emily snickered. "Aren't you only six years younger?"

"That's centuries difference for a Manissee, don't you know that?" When Emily smiled and opened the back door, Hopeful shook her head. "You're a mess, child. Let me help you wash by the well."

"I can do it myself."

"All right. Then I'll comb and plait your hair."

"I'll just push it up into my mobcap."

"Your mobcap is as dirty as a hog pen. And your hair isn't much better."

"All right. You win. Why do you always win?"

"Because I've the wisdom of the ages in my blood; and you can't argue with that."

By the time Emily had washed her face and sluiced the parts of her torso she could reach with a piece of soapy cotton toweling, Hopeful had combed her hair and plaited it with rawhide and ribbons. It hung down her back almost to her waist. Emily had to admit it was lots easier than constantly having to shove unruly curls back under a hot, ill-fitting mobcap. Why hadn't she worn it like this before?

Because it was one more reason for the island women to mock her. That was why.

Well, let them mock. It didn't matter if she went to church thrice on Sunday, twice on Wednesday and never broke any commandments—God's or Delia's. She could be given a halo and wings and it wouldn't matter. Mockery was chiseled into her relationships with the islanders as deep as the inscriptions on gravestones.

Matthew woke as soon as Hopeful and Emily made a steaming pot of tea. He peeled the towel off his face, sighed and sat up. "Is't tea I smell?"

"It is," Hopeful said, bringing him a steaming mug.

He took it from her but frowned. "Why are ye 'ere, squaw?"

"She's come to help if we need it," Emily said. "And don't argue! If there are wounded men on that sloop, we're both going to need every hand we can find."

"She kin clean up . . . but tha's all she kin do," Matthew said. "I'll no 'ave contention from crew nor neighbor!"

"Fine," Hopeful agreed as the front door banged open and *Calumet*'s wounded began to arrive.

Chapter Seven

Hopeful did more than clean floors. She bandaged those who were not badly hurt. She closed the eyes of those who had died in their comrades' arms as they were being carried to the surgery. And she prepared those who needed expert care from Matthew.

If the relegation to an assistant lower in status than Emily grated on her pride, she did naught to show it. Instead, she brought in a steady stream of hot mugs of tea to Emily and Matthew. That she sneaked into it bits of her herbs to give them both strength and endurance—and Matthew didn't notice . . . or did and said nothing—was just fine with her. She hadn't anticipated a fond welcome or *thank you*. So when it didn't come, she wasn't disappointed.

But she was horrified that many of the patients hadn't been hurt by the winds or waves of the hurricane but by an accidental fire on board *Calumet* which had set off a portion of the sloop's store of ammunition. The number of wounded! And the ghastly mess cannon shot and grape clusters could make in a man's body!

Indian wounds were neater. Tomahawks gouged; they didn't explode. Of course, some animals—bears and rutting bucks, especially—could cause terrible problems. But none like what came in from *Calumet.*

White men! Pah! They thought themselves so civilized. But this . . . this *accident* was only an example of what they brought on themselves. Barbarism! It saddened Hopeful.

Her people were dying out. Already the once proud Manissee—which had numbered close to five hundred when the first white settlers had dropped anchor on their precious island—were reduced to a scant half hundred. No longer could the tall, strong, peaceful Manissee roam the land free and unfettered; the whites had taken most into slavery. Those that were in Hopeful's small settlement had been set free, not left free. No longer could the tribe sit undisturbed around their summer fires; the white men owned the land the Manissee had once called theirs. No longer could they eat the succotash or hominy they had grown themselves; the best farming land lay well above their scrabby soil. No longer could they smoke unlimited supplies of wild game; most of the land was marked off by the stone walls of the whites, and Indians were not allowed to traipse it. No longer could they paint their faces and beat their drums and dance their victory over their enemies; their worst enemy had nearly wiped out their parent tribe, the Narragansetts, as well as the Mohegans, Montauks, and most of the Pequots. No, they could do naught save sit around their fires, braiding mats and baskets to bring in a few pence, their only defense against starvation. Do naught save tell their history about a time when a proud, strong, hardy remnant of the Narragansetts had set their canoes out to sea in search of the gods knew what and found this beautiful tree covered rock. It had been waiting for them, their history said. Waiting for the Manissee to live there in harmony with the gods who ruled the rock, which was why they had named it Manisses, little god's island.

But harmony was no longer to be found.

Not even for the white man.

Pah! Never for the white man. War was his favorite game. Sometimes, it seemed to be his only reason for living. And dying.

She wanted to scream out at the waste of it. Hurricanes weren't dangerous and destructive enough? Young men—boys, mostly—had to have their lives blasted away by accident simply because white men could not live in peace with each other? Pah! She was sick of it.

And there was other sickness. Not too many seasons were left to her, she knew. Already a burning heaviness in her gut told her her Manissee medicines were not strong enough to cure herself. She had seen it in her mother and her aunt and her sister. The day was coming when she could put it off no longer. The day when, as they had, she would take a strong dose of her special medicine, lie down on her rush palette, turn over on her side, and slip into the land of dreams.

But not yet. She still had much to teach Emily. Although her tribe was dying, the ways of the Manissee would live on in a troublesome, strong, lovely white woman who valued the heart of life—even if she didn't yet know what it was.

Where Hopeful was horrified by the injured seamen, Emily was disgusted. She wanted to shake the captain who had allowed such wanton destruction. Jack Donahue! A pox on him! Why, he hadn't even had a ship's doctor aboard. Though some of the men had told her their First Mate had hastily applied tourniquets to stop the bleeding—thereby staving off sure death—Emily saw too many who had had nothing save wet cloths applied to their wounds.

Matthew couldn't clean and suture fast enough. Two men died on the table. Another, soon after he'd been taken out onto the front grounds. The corpse pile in the back yard got bigger. There were so many wounds, Matthew finally—and grudgingly—allowed Emily to do more than pass him supplies. Weak from sleep, his usually steady hand had slipped five times as he tried to sew up a gaping hole in a seaman's side.

He stood away from the table and wiped his brow. " 'ow good are ye at stitchin', lass?"

Emily was so shocked, her heart beat faster than a robin's. Her mouth opened but no words came out.

"Very good," Hopeful said, quickly.

"Lass?"

Emily gulped. "I can do it, squire. Truly."

"Go to it, then. I'll assist."

As Emily and Matthew changed places, she asked Hopeful to bring her a basin of vinegared water.

"Whate'er for, lass?"

"To wash my hands, Dr. Cox. I've dirt and other . . . *things* on them and I don't want to get any of it in the wound."

"I suppose 'tis more damned Manissee doin'?"

"It is," Emily said. "But it makes sense, doesn't it?"

"We'll see, lass. We'll see."

As Emily began her first real surgery, a pounding on the door startled them. Hopeful rushed to open it and a young man hurried in, a small boy slung over his shoulder.

"He's hurt bad!"

The familiar voice sent a wave of heat coursing through Emily. It surprised the breath out of her. *Now, why in the world had that happened,* she wondered. When she could, she called, "Robert Sears! Is that you?"

"Aye." Rob helped Hopeful ease his burden down on the floor, then crossed the room to peek into the surgery. What he saw made his heart skip a beat. "God's blood! Emily Gorton, what are you doing?"

Emily smiled without looking up. "Surgery, Rob. Finally."

"Will this awful night never end?!" Rob went back and bent over the silent form on the floor. When the boy made a strangled cry, Rob swore both in English and French. He grabbed Hopeful's sleeve as if it were a lifeline and explained, "We were just cleaning up the deck. Just cleaning up the deck, that was all. It was a simple job, so I let Jason give the crew a hand. Damn my eyes! He should have been below deck when that mast let go. He's just a cabin boy, a lad. He should have been below deck, not having that weakened mast come crashing down on his leg, mashing it to bits. Damn my eyes! Damn, damn, damn my eyes!" He looked toward the surgery and swore again. "Dr. Cox, can you not lend a hand here?"

"Go ahead," Emily said, trying to soothe and bolster the old man who had reluctantly given up his pride of place to her. "You know more about these things than Hopeful. I've only a few more stitches here and I'll be ready for the next patient."

Matthew took a careful look at what Emily had done. "Niver thought I'd see the day . . . but ye've larned a gra'deal from me it seems, lass."

"Yes, Doctor. That I have."

Emily and Hopeful exchanged knowing smiles, remembering Hopeful's supervision of the days and weeks and months of practice stitching on the pets and wounded animals of the island—and, for the past three years, the careful doctoring Hopeful had allowed Emily to do to the Manissee.

When Matthew went to the stricken boy, Hopeful took his place on the opposite side of the table from Emily. She dipped her hands in the vinegared water, shook them out and waited for Emily to indicate what she wanted. They worked quickly, closing the layers of skin. While Emily put in the last few stitches, Hopeful began to prepare a salve of yarrow and pig fat, to keep the dreadful wound from bleeding.

"Nay. There's naught to be done, I tell ye!"

"But he'll die!"

Emily's head jerked up. "Finish up here, Hopeful."

"Aye."

As Hopeful bandaged, Emily quickly dipped her hands in the basin and grabbed up a towel to dry them. Three steps and she was beside Robert, looking down on his anguished face as he knelt beside a young boy.

"What's wrong?" she asked.

"Ta lad's leg is crushed below the knee," Matthew said. "I kinna save it."

"Amputation?"

"Nay, lass. 'e's lost too much blood. 'e'll niver make it. Tis best ta take 'im ta the corpse pile in the back yard."

Rob reared back with his fist and almost struck the old man. "Not my cousin! Not while he's breathing!"

Emily knelt and examined the young boy. His skin was clammy cold, grey with the pallor of creeping death. When she lifted one of his eyelids, he seemed to be staring straight ahead, oblivious to the world and the pain he must be suffering. She put her ear to his chest and had to strain to hear a fluttering sound that stopped and started too often to be mistaken.

"He's in a very bad way, Rob," she said, reluctantly. "Shouldn't you accept the decision of Dr. Cox?"

"Never! At the very least, Jason deserves a try." He appealed to Dr. Cox. "Try. What can it hurt to try?"

"Thay's others waitin', Mr. Sears. An' they've bin waitin' longer an' 'ave more chance o' survivin' than yer cousin. Nay, I kinna put 'im ahead o' them. I kinna an' I willna!"

Emily had never seen despair in Rob's face. Never seen defeat in his body. She never wanted to see it again.

"We've only two more patients, and one of them only has superficial wounds," Emily said. "Hopeful can take care of him. You and I can finish the last of the surgery. Then we can amputate Jason's leg together."

"Nay! Aye, Hopeful kin do wha needs ta be done fer t'other man. An' we kin work together. But do'na hold out hope where no hope is. 'e'll likely be dead afore we kin git t'im."

"But if he isn't," Emily insisted, "can't we try?" Matthew leaned against the wall and Emily knew it was more for support than ease, he was that tired. "Or, if Rob will let me, I'll do the amputation myself. Hopeful can assist."

Matthew sighed and motioned to Hopeful to bring in the next man. He shuffled into the surgery, waving back his decision. "Do wha' ye want."

Emily turned to Rob to explain, "Dr. Cox has been at this for over twenty hours, first with the islanders and now with *Calumet*'s crew. He's not being unfeeling, Rob. He simply cannot take the strain of hours more work to amputate Jason's leg."

Rob brushed back the light brown hair from the face of his cousin. "I promised my mother and aunt I'd take care of him. I gave my word!"

He pushed unsteady fingers through his own unruly brown hair, hunkered back on his heels and faced Emily. His normally sparkling green flecked hazel eyes were darkened by pain and worry . . . and fear. Yet there were still the pride she'd come to know of his character. He would never lose that, she was sure, because he had worked hard to achieve the place he had. Here was the man the crew credited with saving their lives, she judged. Rob . . . her Rob . . . was Jack Donahue's First Mate. Why else the lace on his sleeves, the careful cut of his blue waistcoat and breeches and the black soutache braid that trimmed them, his clocked stockings, black leather shoes—no more boots for him unless the weather demanded it—and the shiny silver of his buckles? Blood-stained though they might be, they were still the mark of a hard working, proud, and steady man.

Could she disappoint him as she had disappointed him too many times already? As Rob would say, *Never!*

"Will you let me try my hand on him, Rob?"

Rob's head jerked up. From those books he and his friends had sent to Block Island he knew Emily had decided to be a doctor. Hell, he had even brought his own cat, Dragon, to her when he'd had one of his legs almost shot off by a musket. He couldn't watch while Emily had amputated Dragon's leg. He had sat outside, fashioning a crude peg leg for a cat he *knew* wouldn't be alive to use it. But the stupid cat was still stomping around on that noisy piece of ash, and seemed none the worse for his ordeal.

But a cat was only a cat. This was his cousin.

Jason Broadbent was a gentle boy, whose father had decided he needed toughening up, so had sent him to sea. Under Rob's charge and care, of course. Walter Broadbent wasn't stupid or unfeeling. He loved his son. Knew the perils of a ship's berth and had made damned sure Jason was protected as much as possible by entrusting him to Rob's care.

And Jason's first voyage at sea had turned into a series of disasters: A fierce battle with a French merchant vessel bound for Nova Scotia. Dead calm off the shores of Guadeloupe. The hurricane which chased them all the way up the eastern coast until they were caught in its fury just off Montauk Point. The fire on board causing a great deal of their magazine stores to blow—and he'd warned Captain Donahue that the magazine was too close to the galley and the open fires of the smithy, damn his eyes. Then the mast . . .

During the hurricane Rob had heard the guts being torn out of the strong main mast. He'd sent men to inspect it. They'd found deep cracks and splintered wood. But Donahue had insisted they had neither time nor money to replace it. So they'd left it there, wounded as badly as the men, ready to die. Rob sighed. He'd long ago realized his captain's frugality was furious penny pinching greed—and now it might cost Jason's life.

"Rob?"

"Ah, Emily . . . this is not Dragon's leg you're asking me to entrust to you."

"I know that better than you do, Rob. But if you don't entrust him to me, you'll be next entrusting him to reverend Mister Davies."

"You've gotten blunt in your years, Em."

"Get away with you!" she teased, trying to erase the tension in the room. "When have I ever been less than blunt?"

"Aye. I'll give you that."

"But will you give me Jason?"

Rob staggered tiredly to his feet. He faced Emily and asked the question that had been niggling at the back of his mind. "How much sleep have you had, Em?"

"More than Matthew."

"But not much."

"No. Not much." She didn't try to hide the condition of her clothing or the fatigue she felt. She untied the soiled apron she was wearing and tossed it in the corner. A fresh one lay on a shelf to her right and she put it on quickly. "There is one difference between Matthew Cox and me, Rob. I'm forty-two years younger than he is. And though I haven't amputated before, I've a steadier hand and a box of Hopeful Rose's remedies to supplement Matthew's medicine chest." She laid a hand on his arm and whispered, "Do you have a choice, Rob?"

If he had a choice, he'd pick her up, sling her over

his shoulder and take her to some spot where he could cover her with kisses, she was that delectable.

"No, I have no choice."

While Emily cleaned down the surgical table, Hopeful boiled the saw and other implements. Matthew took one look at what they were doing, gathered up his Turkey work bag, threw a few ointments and salves into it and stomped out of his house.

"He'll tell the whole damned island," Hopeful said.

Emily shrugged. "Let him. Everyone has so many problems they won't have time to stop me."

She examined her first real patient. Jason's calf was all but gone. But his knee and his thigh, thank God, was still in good shape, though cut in several places and splintered with pieces of the main mast. There was more than amputation to do but the cuts and splinters could wait. If she were to save the boy's life, she'd have little time to do it.

It took the three of them to remove Jason's breeches. Hopeful hastily covered Jason's hips while Emily replaced Rob's cloth tourniquet with a fillet-and-stick tourniquet, a fairly simple circular device made out of two-inch-wide leather and a strong oak stick that could be turned tighter and tighter as they needed it. Five inches above the worst of Jason's injuries, she measured off four finger widths below Jason's knee and added one more for good measure because her fingers were smaller than a man's. Then she secured several turns of tape around Jason's calf, just below what was to be the scalpel line. When all was ready, she said a quick prayer to God that her hand would be true and her skill guided by Him who had given it, took a deep breath and began the arduous, time consuming task.

It wasn't at all like Dragon's leg. But she was damned glad she had had the cat to practice on. From the books she'd read, and from the amputations she'd seen Matthew do, she did not miscalculate the skills needed to save Jason's life. She just hadn't realized how tiring it would be.

She stopped often to listen to Jason's chest. Beneath her ear, his heart wavered and fluttered but it still beat. She prayed she'd do naught to stop it.

"I'll need your help, Rob," she called to the lonely figure who sat by the door. His head had lolled back against the top of the chair and his eyes remained closed. "Rob!"

He jumped and the chair crashed to the floor. "Damn and blast!"

Emily almost laughed to see him sprawled in a heap; but jollity wasn't appropriate in the surgery. "I need you, please."

In Rob's dream Emily had been saying the same words—but with a much different meaning. Why was it that whenever he was around her she blocked out aught else, until he was filled with a throbbing ache that never seemed to go away?

God's blood, he had to get his mind out of his breeches and back where it belonged.

"What can I do, Em? I'm no doctor."

"But you're stronger than I am." Sheepishly, she admitted, "I haven't strength enough to finish the job."

When he saw what she was handing him and where her finger pointed, Rob jumped back from the table as if scalded. "You can't mean it!"

"God rot it, Robert Sears! Do you want your cousin to survive or not?"

"Of course I do."

"Then help me!"

It took another hour to tie the blood vessels together and fashion a flap for Jason's leg. Hopeful used almost all her Manissee herbs for sluicing liquids. The healing salve of boiled mullein leaves, heart leaf, and yarrow they divided into four large tin containers. One they used to dress Jason's leg. As they worked, Emily was shaken to the core when she thought Jason's heart had stopped beating but a vigorous shaking brought that familiar *tha-thump* back again. Weak, it was; but loud enough so Emily could start breathing normally again herself and continue her work.

A few cuts needed stitching but most only needed cleaning and covering with pledgets of lint smeared with the healing salve.

"I'll need Joe Pye tea, Hopeful."

"I made a full kettle while your First Mate was helping you. It should last the night."

Emily was worried. "Jason will need a clean bed and plenty of blankets." She frowned. "Matthew Cox is not going to like this and neither is Jack Donahue. But I can't send Jason back to the sloop in this condition. He'll need constant care, with someone in attendance at all hours. We'll have to keep watch." She made a decision and she was damned if anyone was going to stand in her way. "Rob, you'll have to stay ashore until Jason's ready to be moved."

"I could lose my commission."

"You'll get another one. Any captain would be glad to have you."

Rob smiled. "You think too highly of me, Em. But it's pleased, I am, that you do."

"I don't think anything but the truth. Now, go do whatever you have to to get out of Jack Donahue's service."

After getting an understanding nod from Hopeful, Robert took Emily's sticky hands and drew her into the front parlor. He sat her down on the wood settee, and dropped down beside her. "Em, sweetheart, it's not that simple. You may be able to avoid conventions but Jason and I cannot. We've both signed on to complete a voyage. Block Island isn't our last port of call. If Jack Donahue won't give Jason or me leave, and we take it anyway, we'll be mutineers. Jack will get a warrant for our arrest faster than you can say *Bob's your uncle.* And if the sergeants at arms find us, and they will if we're still here, then we will definitely end up in gaol. Now, they may let Jason off with a light sentence because I'll be making the decision; but if the justices are of a mind for it, I'll swing at the end of a rope."

"But these are unusual circumstances!"

"Aye. And I'll explain that to Jack. But knowing him as I do, I don't think it likely that he'll release either one of us."

Emily had never known such fury. "Damn his

eyes! Does he not know how important it is to give good doctoring?"

"Emily, you're talking about a man who didn't even bring a ship's doctor along on a four-month voyage."

Hopeful came to the parlor door, clucked her tongue and fairly spat out, "Fools! *Calumet* won't be going anywhere until she's repaired. How long will it take, Rob? A week? A month? And with you in charge . . . You will be in charge, won't you? . . . the work could be delayed on purpose. That's been done before, hasn't it?"

She spun on her heel and went to see to their patient, leaving Emily and Robert looking stupidly at each other.

"Fools," Emily said. "Ah, we are that." She giggled, more in relief and embarrassment than levity. Leaning her head against Rob's shoulder, she sighed. "So, we'll have some time and you can help us keep watch."

Rob couldn't believe his luck. He gathered Emily in closer and tucked the top of her head against his chin. "I have watches to keep on board *Calumet* and men to oversee as they repair the ship. I can't tell you how much time I can give or when I can give it."

"Just come. We'll be happy to have you anytime."

"Here?"

"No. Matthew would have apoplexy. If you could get some of your men to help, we'll take Jason to my house. We can put him in the garret room with John and Carter." She yawned and tucked her arms around Rob. "I'm so tired. But there's so much more to do." Her eyes closed and she slumped closer to the warmth of Rob's body.

When Rob was certain she was asleep, he eased himself away from Emily and settled her on the small wooden seat, tucking his rolled up waistcoat under her head. He gave her a quick kiss on her forehead—wishing it were more—and went to tell Hopeful what they had decided. Within an hour Jason was safely ensconced in Ned's old cot, pulled closer to the fireplace wall so the heat that radiated from the stones could warm his frail body.

Rob hadn't entrusted Emily to anyone else, and carried her in his own arms. She slept through it all, even when Rob laid her in her father's old bed in the large bedroom that the boys had allotted her when their father died.

She looked as close to an angel as Rob was sure he'd ever see on earth—regardless of the dirt and blood that stained her apron. Her blond plaits reminded him of a rag doll his sister had had. But the softness of her eyelashes as they lay in a half-moon against her cheek was nothing like the embroidered lashes of the clown-like doll. Emily's lashes were thick and looked softer than the down that filled her quilt. In sleep, her lips were full and slightly moist at the corners. When she opened them occasionally to sigh, he wanted to cover them with his own and taste their sweetness.

"Rob?"

"Aye, Hopeful." It seemed he was never to relive that moment they'd shared in the barn. Or if he was, he'd have to *make* the moment happen.

He left the woman who had endeared herself to him when she was only nine—and had haunted him for almost ten years—and went to help Hopeful make his cousin comfortable.

Hopeful eyed him speculatively. When he flushed, she smiled. "She's a handful."

"Aye."

"But you seem to be able to handle her."

"No one can handle Emily Gorton, Hopeful. You must know that by now."

"Oh, I do. I just wanted to know if you knew. Now that I know, I can rest easy. You'll find a way to her heart . . . if you want it, that is."

Robert chuckled. "Oh, aye, I want it. But if she ever finds out I want it, it's almost certain she won't give it up."

"You can but try, Robert Sears. You can but try."

Chapter Eight

The next morning Emily awoke to good smells coming from the kitchen—better than Tab had ever produced. She stumbled out of bed, shocked to find herself still in yesterday's clothes. Quickly, she stripped and was about to wash herself in the cold water left in her pitcher on the bedstand when a knock sounded on the door. Emily wrapped the quilt around herself and called, "Come in!"

Emily expected Hopeful or Tab to enter. The woman who carried in the black iron kettle was neither, however. She was short and dark like Emily's friends but she wasn't one of Hopeful's relatives, nor anyone Emily had seen in the Manissee village. Emily eyed the woman warily until she held up the kettle and offered the steaming water to Em.

"Hopeful said you liked a hot wash in the morning."

"I do. Thank you, Miss . . . ?"

"Rebeccah. Rebeccah Washington." She poured a good measure of hot water into the pitcher, handed Emily a clean towel and wash cloth, turned on her heel and left the room.

Rebeccah. Rebeccah Washington.

Emily knew that name. Had known it since she was old enough to understand why the mere mention of it got Delia Davies riled as a bull in season. Emily giggled at the suggestion and the pairing of the two women. Delia always said Rebeccah Washington's was a name to avoid, as was the woman herself. But it wasn't until the day she had become Matthew's apprentice that Emily had discovered why.

Rebeccah Washington owned the friendly house.

And here she was, in the doorway to Emily's bedroom, bringing in hot water and clean linens and doing God knew what else!

Faster than she had ever dressed before, Emily washed and got into a warm chemise Hopeful had had made for her—by one of Rebeccah Washington's charges, now Emily thought about it. It hung like an Indian's outer shift, but wasn't made of animal skins. Emily's was a smooth, soft cotton, made in two layers to keep in the warmth and allow plenty of room to move without restrictive gathers, waistbands, and those horrible, itchy petticoats Emily hated.

When she got to the keeping room table, Hopeful, John, and Carter were wolfing down griddle cakes and sausage. From the looks of them the griddle cakes were light and fluffy. Although Tab's cooking was miles better than Emily's, the young Indian girl had never made anything like this!

Emily coughed to get Hopeful's attention. She stared at her, then jerked her head toward Rebeccah. For answer, Hopeful pushed a trencher of griddle cakes toward Emily.

"Tab's upstairs with Jason," Hopeful said. "I sent

for Rebeccah because Tab is useless in a sick room for longer than ten minutes and we'll need more than you and me to stand round-the-clock watches over him. Rebeccah has been doctoring her charges for years, usually without the help of Matthew Cox. I taught her all I knew, just the way I did you. We'll need her help, Emily."

Rebeccah stood in the doorway to the kitchen. Her dress was as proper as any Delia Davies had ever worn. A blue and white flowered cambric, it covered her from neck to toes. And over it she wore a spotless white gossamer shawl that she'd pulled around her shoulders and pinned to her bodice with a simple cameo. A matching blue apron and plain black shoes completed her attire. She waited calmly as Emily inspected her, saying nothing until Emily's eyes came up to once more meet hers.

"I won't stay if you don't want me here, Miss Gorton."

Emily searched the older woman's face for any sign of animosity or fear. What she found surprised her. It couldn't have been pride; but it was close to it. Rebeccah Washington would bow to neither man nor woman. Nor would she force her presence on anyone who didn't accept her as she was. Emily made a quick decision—as she had most decisions in her life—and smiled at Rebeccah.

"If Hopeful says you're good at doctoring, you're welcome in my home."

"Then I'll take first watch," Rebeccah said. "Tab can do the washing up."

Carter's head snapped up and he frowned. "You mean you're not going to cook for us?"

"Breakfast, only," Rebeccah said. "The rest of the meals are Tab's job."

"Make double portions," Carter said plaintively. "Breakfast this good has to last us a looong time."

Rebeccah chuckled all the way up the center stairs.

If Tab was upset that the other woman had usurped her place in the kitchen for the morning meal, she said naught about it. She merely dropped onto the bench, shoveled the last of the griddle cakes into her trencher and ate them hurriedly. Then she picked up all the dirty trenchers, crockery, and cutlery and brought them to the wooden barrel on the shelf in the corner pantry. She dumped them in, added hot water to fill it and carried it into the kitchen.

Hopeful eased herself up from the table and for the first time Emily saw how tired her old friend was. Or was it more than that? The way Hopeful clutched her stomach, as if she were carrying it, gave Emily pause. "I want you in the bedroom this minute," she said sternly.

"That's where I intended to go."

But when Hopeful got to Emily's room, Em was right on her heels. "Sit on the edge of the bed and dangle your legs. I'm going to examine you."

"You'll do no such thing!"

"Hopeful . . ."

"Emily Gorton, have I ever not known when there's a problem?" When Emily shook her head, Hopeful said, simply, "Then there's no need for you to examine me. And you need not worry. I've known for some time. There's naught to be done."

"Hopeful!"

"Child of my heart. . . . I don't face the end of my

days with fear or regret. You will carry on the knowledge of my people and my work. There is none other that I trust or that has the gift. I chose you well. I'm proud of you. But there is one thing that you still haven't learned." She put her hand on her heart and then extended it to Emily, touching her head. "We are not the Great God. There is no magic in our hands, only simple healing. There are some ailments that we will never be able to cure, regardless of what we wish or hope. And I am an old woman who has lived out her days in comfort and peace and joy. It is enough. More than enough."

For the first time since her mother died, Emily's eyes burned with unshed tears. Though she turned her head aside, Hopeful saw.

"If you truly want to be a doctor then you have no time nor place in your life for tears, Emily. Have I not taught you to hide your feelings?"

"Mayhap that was not a good thing."

"But a necessary one . . . or you wouldn't be able to survive."

Knowing that the old woman did not want to prolong this moment any longer, Emily straightened her spine and blinked hard to clear her eyes. She bustled around Hopeful, pulling down the quilt and fluffing the pillows as Hopeful removed her moccasins and outside shift. Before Emily left the room, she closed the shutters to darken the interior so Hopeful could get a good sleep.

Hide your feelings. Hide your feelings. Hide your feelings. It became a refrain that thrummed in her head as Emily slipped up the stairs to check on Jason.

When had she not hidden her feelings? The only

times she could remember were those she'd spent with Robert Sears. Somehow, he managed to bring out the worst . . . and best . . . in her. Somehow he touched a place deep inside herself that she kept private, sometimes even from herself.

His teasing and easy friendship, when every other male on the island couldn't stand to look at her, had endeared him to Emily from the first. But there was more to it than that. There was a feeling she had for him that she couldn't recognize—something unfamiliar, yet demanding. She liked to be with him. She liked the way he looked at her, the way he touched her, the way he accepted her as his equal.

Humbuggery! She liked lots more than that.

She liked the way he made her feel when he kissed her. Rebeccah Washington could possibly tell her what that was all about, since she knew far more about men and women than anyone else on the island—certainly more than great-aunt Bella had, or Hopeful or Tab or Emily's closest female relative, her cousin Rachel. But she couldn't confide in Rebeccah! She couldn't admit that a woman who aspired to being a doctor didn't know the first thing about . . . about . . . good grief, she didn't know what it was that she didn't know!

When in the world was she ever going to find out, and how?

Rebeccah had removed the rest of Jason's clothing and covered him with a warm flannel sheet and two layers of blankets. When Emily felt his head, it was hot to the touch and when she removed the dressing it was stained.

"I want you to check on those dressings every two

hours, Rebeccah. If they look like this one, you must clean the entire area up to Jason's . . . uh . . . high up on his thigh. Wash it with warm water and Castile soap. Sluice it with witch hazel or vinegar. Then apply a good coating of salve and cover it with lint pledgets. We don't have many pledgets left, so have Tab tear up some clean cotton or linen homespun."

"What shall I do with the soiled pledgets?"

Emily hesitated. Matthew would have washed them and used them again. But he'd lost several patients to terrible infections. She wasn't sure how, but she had a feeling the pledgets and homespun strips didn't come clean enough . . . and might even bring the infection back to the site if they were used again. "Burn them."

Rebeccah gasped and Emily knew why. Cloth was not something people burned; it was so time consuming to make or expensive to buy. Which was why even lowly lint that was left from spinning was ground into fine felt and pressed between cheesecloth to be used as pledgets. To waste fabric as she had decided to do was tantamount to burning down a house because it was dirty!

"Burn them, Rebeccah. I can't take chances on this man's life."

"Man, huh! He's no more than a boy."

"And has a long life ahead of him. We will give him the best chance he has to live it all."

She and Rebeccah cleaned Jason's leg. While Emily smeared the salve and finished the bandaging, Rebeccah washed the rest of his body, and even combed his hair.

"He's a bonny lad," she said.

"Aye," Emily agreed. "Almost as bonny as his cousin."

"His fever seems to be rising."

"I noticed. I'll have Tab make a good pot of Joe Pye tea to sweat the fever out of him and some chicken and beef broth boiled with cattails and dandelions to give him strength. You'll have to force them down his throat. Hold his nose and he'll swallow." She picked up the soiled dressings and wrapped them in a page from the pile of Carter's ha'penny presses that he kept next to his cot. "I have to assist Dr. Cox this morning but I'll be home for midday meal."

"What if the patient wakes?"

"He won't wake until his fever breaks. And that's going to take a long time. He's still in a bad way—worse now than he was before the surgery."

Before she left, Emily fixed the older woman with a smile. "Thank you for your help, Rebeccah. There's not many who would do what you are doing."

"There's not many who would allow me in their house, Miss Gorton. Hopeful said you were different. She was right. I'm glad I came."

Funny, Emily thought as she hurried down the hill to Matthew's, Rebeccah wasn't half as glad to be helping as Emily was to have her. The friendly house was held in such fear and loathing by the women on the island that Emily had had occasion to meet only three any of its inhabitants. What she knew about Rebeccah was whispered by biting tongues inside heads which held small minds. Rebeccah might not be fit to marry any of the men on the island but she wasn't the devil she'd been made out to be. In fact, Emily liked her spirit and calm acceptance of her fate. Like Emily, she, too, had chosen different paths—or had them thrust upon her, it mattered naught which. And one of those choices had been to detach herself from society's expectations of what a woman could and couldn't do. She had survived. Certainly, it wasn't the kind of survival Emily wished for herself. But if she examined it closely, Emily had to admit it wasn't really that much different than what she already had, and seemed destined to have forever. Both were doing work no "decent" woman did. Both had friends—Hopeful Rose, for one—who were considered undesirable companions. Both were strangers in their own community. Both were unmarried. Both were condemned to live their lives alone. No, not much different at all.

On her walk to Matthew's surgery, Emily was shocked by the devastation around her. Because of the hurricane, the island looked like one of those straw villages with which the children played. Some of the houses and outbuildings had been leveled. Others . . . most others . . . were in such disrepair that Emily worried about whether her brothers and their families had survived intact. She made a round-about detour and satisfied herself that everyone had weathered the worst. Oh, they had some patching to do; but they had built their houses in protected hollows on the Gorton land. And they had built them strong enough to last forever. Emily's nieces and nephews clustered around her legs, and she had a hard time leaving them. But after a mug of tea with each family, she took her leave and hurried back the way she'd come.

On the path that led to the dirt track which served as a road, Emily passed close to John and Carter.

They waved and went on into the far North field, out toward Settler's Point and Polly Gibbs's farm. Startling alike, they were a happy pair, her two youngest brothers. Both tall and fair and sturdy, they had had girls vying for their attentions since they'd first started shaving. They wouldn't be with Emily long since both were engaged to village girls and were building their own small houses at the west end of the Gorton property. She would miss them.

When they were gone the house would be too empty, too large for only herself and Tab. She'd been thinking lately that she might have all her brothers build her a smaller place close to the village. If Matthew ever gave up his practice, or turned it over to her—and, Lord, wouldn't that rattle the villagers' bones—she'd need to be closer to the settlement and the town docks.

Deep in plans for a new house that would contain a surgery, waiting room, and simple family quarters, Emily was taken aback by the storm that waited inside Matthew's kitchen. As soon as Emily opened Matthew's back door she was met not only by Matthew's surly, disappointed expression but also by Delia Davies's wrath.

"No God-fearing Christian woman would have her house sullied by two Indian squaws and that doxy! What are you doing there with those depraved women? Are you practicing some devil's medicine . . . Indian magic . . . or worse? It's not bad enough that you flaunt your own indecent behavior. Must you sully your brothers' reputations, too? Can you not see what this is doing to their betrothed? Can you not feel the insult, the hurt, the heartache those lovely young women feel knowing the men they are soon to marry are sleeping under the same roof with one of the most notorious women on the island?"

"Rebeccah Washington is not sleeping at my house. She cooks breakfast for us, then takes a turn watching my patient. She will leave at three o'clock each day and return at six the next morning."

"She should not even be there!"

"Would you help, Mistress Davies?"

"Help what? A boy who's as good as dead?"

"But Jason Broadbent isn't dead, Mistress Davies. He's alive. Dreadfully ill, but still breathing. And while he's alive he's one of God's children. I haven't abandoned him. Hopeful and Tab haven't abandoned him. Rebeccah Washington hasn't abandoned him. Yet you God-fearing Christians refuse him succor." Her eyes flashed furiously at Matthew. "There doesn't seem to be any reason for me to continue as your assistant, Dr. Cox. I cannot ally myself with someone who gives up so easily." She spun and raced out the door.

Now she had done it. She had thrown it all away. All the work. All the heartache. "God rot it. God rot it. God rot it!"

She sought solitude in the one place she always felt peace—the dark, sweet-smelling barn. Tab had already milked Percival, the cow; but her low mooing lulled Emily. She sat on the ever present stool, laid her forehead on Percival's warm, soft side and tried to think.

She had gone too far—hadn't she?

But Matthew had stood there, mute, allowing Delia Davies to castigate—when he should have supported

Emily. No matter how he felt, she always thought they were in this together, battling the islanders as *doctors,* equals. Why hadn't he defended her? Why was it all right for him to do something untoward and not all right for her?

And had she done something so wrong?

No. She had needed help and Rebeccah had offered it. That's what neighbors did, especially on an island like theirs where isolation and loneliness was a tangible thing.

She heard the barn door open, but paid it no mind until Carter touched her on the shoulder. When she looked up, she was shocked to see the fear and melancholy in his usually happy face.

"What?"

"We went out to Settler's Point to see if Mistress Gibbs needed help. Em . . . everything is gone."

"What do you mean, *gone?*"

"Washed away in the hurricane. A great chunk of Settler's Point must have been weakened by the huge waves. It crashed into the sea and the house and outbuildings with it. There isn't a stick or stone left."

"But Polly and the children. . . ."

"Gone. John and I have been to every neighbor along the Point and called on most homes in the village where she might have sought shelter. No one has seen her. No one has seen any of them."

Whatever problems Emily had, they were naught when compared to what Polly must have endured in that lonely spot on the other side of the island. In the dark, alone, she and her children must have been frantic, battling winds that had finally defeated them. The terror she must have felt. And then to have it . . . Emily shuddered and got to her feet.

"We must tell reverend Mister Davies."

"John's on his way there, now."

When they came out of the darkness of the barn, Emily surveyed as much of the island she could see below them. Four ships lay at anchor off the town dock, one of them the bedraggled *Calumet*. Double-enders were strewn along the beaches, dragged . . . or more likely tossed by wind and ocean from place to place until the wind had worn itself out. Homes were smashed. Wagons snapped in two. Shutters hung off the windows, making some houses look as if they were crying black or red or blue tears.

Her neighbors walked along path and road with bowed heads and slumping shoulders. Her beloved island was in mourning, and there was naught she could do to help because Jason Broadbent needed her.

She tucked her arm through her brother's and drew him to the house with the admonition she always used with him, "We have work to do." He smiled and did her bidding.

Gradually, because of Carter's gentle teasing and true concern for everyone who passed, contentment replaced the anger and fear that had had her captive during the earlier part of the day. The difference was Carter.

He had always been her favorite. After all, she had taken on a good deal of his care when they were younger. He had been her playmate and her ear. She had bandaged him and splinted him and smeared him with all sorts of foul stuff in her attempt to play doctor. And he had borne it with laughter and good grace—and never once disparaged her as their other brothers had. If the hurricane had swept him away as cruelly as it had swept away the Gibbs's, she would have renounced her religion.

For two hours she worked beside Carter as they cleaned up the debris which had blown into the yard during the storm. Unlikely as it seemed, they filled three barrels with the flotsam.

"Set them at the back door," she ordered. "As soon as they dry out we can use the sticks for kindling."

Inside, Hopeful still slept and Emily took a few moments to put her feet up and have a hot mug of tea before she climbed the stairs to the garret. She was only a few steps up when she caught the wheezing sounds that signaled trouble. Hitching up her shift, she bounded up the stairs two at a time.

"How long has he been like this?" she demanded of Rebeccah.

"An hour."

"God's blood!"

"I made a mustard seed poultice."

"That's good." Emily examined Jason. His breathing was heavy and raspy, his heart fluttered, stuttered, then pounded hard. The site of infection, his leg, was clean, with no redness or puffiness. "You're a good nurse, Rebeccah."

"Had to be, over the years. That Matthew Cox will only come out to us if someone's dying."

Because of Hopeful's medicines, Emily's good surgery, and Rebeccah's unflagging nursing, Jason's leg, then, would heal. Now Emily had to worry about the catarrh—or worse, the pneumonia. She knew what

Hopeful would do if something like this had attacked one of the Manissees . . . their sweat house. But Jason couldn't be moved yet. How, then?

Poising herself on the side of the bed, she thought about the way the sweat house was constructed, a round opening cut into the cliff, its entrance sealed in, and water poured over stones kept red hot by a roaring fire. Above the center of the cave was a small outlet cut right through the earth . . . its purpose, to let in air and carry out evil spirits.

Damn near every evil disease-spirit was attacking Jason. There must be some way . . .

After several minutes, she snapped her fingers and began firing off orders to all around her.

"Rebeccah, comb through the house and garret. Get every piece of tinware there is in the house. And make damned sure it doesn't have any holes." She jumped to her feet and whirled on Tab. "Build up the fires in the fireplaces downstairs, then run to Ned's. Tell him and John to bring me canvas sails or any canvas cloth they have in their sailmaking room."

She jumped to her feet and streaked down the stairs to instruct a startled Carter about what he had to do. Two hours later Jason's cot was ensconced in front of the parlor fireplace, encased in a canvas tent-like shield. While Carter had helped her, Ned and John had hauled huge stones from the beach and heated them in the kitchen and parlor fireplaces, then wrestled them into a variety of tinware which had been placed around the cot. Emily, Rebeccah and Hopeful took turns building up steam under the canvas by dripping hot water over the rocks. When Rebeccah left, Tab helped out.

Robert Sears walked in to a scene straight out of any minister's description of hell. Eery lights flickered from behind the canvas wall and shadows flitted in and out of the steam. And the smell! The air was permeated with spicy and bitter odors, compounded by the steam. When he breathed, it bit into him, causing him to cough.

Emily stuck her head outside the canvas and laughed. "Just what we're trying to get Jason to do."

She was silhouetted there, against the lights, and Rob felt his heart constrict. Her shift was plastered to her body as if she had just stepped out of the sea. It left nothing to his imagination and he realized that everything he had ever dreamed at night about this woman was dross compared to the reality of her.

Her breasts were high and firm, their nipples large. Narrow didn't describe her waist. He knew if his hands spanned it, his fingers would overlap. Yet her hips flared and tapered to legs that seemed to go on forever. And her belly rounded slightly, enough to make his gaze skim over it to the shadowed triangle beneath. God's blood, she was beautiful! And so damned desirable.

"If I didn't see those golden plaits and sparkling dark brown eyes, I might think I'd died and gone to heaven."

"Humbuggery, Robert Sears!"

When she shivered and hugged her arms around her body, Robert wanted more than anything to hold her like that. To save himself, he backed into the front hall, retrieved Emily's cape, and draped it carefully over her. His fingers lingered for a moment, enjoying the feel of her, before he reluctantly dropped them and jerked his head toward the canvas cave she'd built in her parlor.

"Never expect the expected when dealing with Emily Gorton. A body is guaranteed to be surprised. What in the world have you got in there?"

"Jason. His breathing was bad . . ."

"He's dying."

"He is not!" With a bright smile on her face, she tugged him into the tent and pointed toward her patient. "He's breathing better since we added cloves and mint and mustard to the hot water. And his heart's a little stronger. He's not cured, yet; but I have more hope."

Under Emily's instructions, Robert tucked into the doctoring for a time, until Tab called them in to supper. Hopeful declared she'd be all right on her own and shooed them away. After the simple repast of codfish pie and apple dumplings, John and Carter offered to heat the stones once more before they headed to their fiancees' houses for their usual nightly visit. Emily announced that she was going to check the garden, the one thing she and Carter hadn't gotten to that morning.

"I'll help," Robert offered, taking the gathering basket from under her arm.

As they walked between the rows, straightening out the supports for the last of the pole beans and picking up the vegetables the hurricane had swept from their plants, Emily told him about the tragedy which had happened to the Gibbs's family.

"She was always so afraid of pirates or French marauders stealing her out of her bed. Yet she loved that place because of the bright orange and scarlet sunsets and the breezes that blew in off the ocean. Who could have guessed the wind would have been her worst enemy?"

"Anyone who has been to sea," Robert said quietly. "The wind powers our sails but it also whips up the waves to a life threatening froth. When you're out there in the middle of it and you know you only have a few inches of wood between you and the black depth of the water . . . well, you begin to know the true fragility of human life."

Chapter Nine

1772 —Aboard Patriot—June 13

The true fragility of human life. If Emily hadn't known what it was like before, she certainly knew it now.

Since that day almost nine years ago, many islanders had died. Matthew was first, only a few months after Jason had recovered. Some of her neighbors said he went so quickly because he had discovered something awful about himself during that hurricane. That he was mortal, that in his tiredness he could lose his surgical skills and positive attitude, or that during a crisis he had let down Emily and himself. Yes, Emily thought, it was surely one of those that he couldn't face, but he never let on which one.

However, to compensate for whatever he had discovered about himself, he did something wonderful which completely changed her life. In heated arguments at town meetings, he convinced the islanders that they no longer needed to petition the legislature in Providence to send them another doctor, that Emily could serve them well and faithfully.

It had taken another three months after his death before her practice included all the island residents—many in the Davies's ministry holding out. But once Delia had also been carried up the hill to the cemetery, Emily was firmly in place as the doctor of choice. The selectmen even awarded her a small wage. Half of what Matthew had received. But it didn't matter. Luckily, her father had included her in his will; so she shared in the income from the Gorton farmlands and was never at financial straits.

But then Hopeful died. Emily remembered the days her good friend had predicted she'd go quietly in her sleep. And when the time came, that was exactly what happened.

The Manissee ceremony for their last medicine woman was so beautiful it almost overcame the piercing ache in Emily's heart. Almost. But now, as she relived those days in her mind, Emily knew it had never been erased.

She'd mourned Hopeful more than she'd mourned anyone in her life. By then, of course, she had absorbed the Indian stoicism which was to stand her in good stead during the hard days every doctor had, when she lost patients she tried desperately to save. But losing Hopeful was the hardest.

Emily's hands stilled as she thought back over those days following Hopeful's death.

Block Island swarmed with Indians. Pequots, Narragansetts, Mohegans, Montauks, even the far flung New Hampshire Abnakis sent representatives from the remnants of their tribes. The colors, textures, and smells overwhelmed Emily. Roast fish and game, boiled samp—a corn and molasses mixture that was delicious—spicy pumpkin gruel, fried johnnycakes, steamed clams and lobsters, heady succotash. Emily woke to the smells and fell asleep filled to her chin with them. And the costumes! Soft beaded and fringed dresses hung from the shoulders of the women all the way to the tops of their wildly colored and embroidered moccasins. Loin clothes and rich, copper-flecked feathered mantles covered old and young men. Drums beat long into the night. Chants floated on the wind. Dancers circled fires along the coast and high on the cliffs where Hopeful's people had dug a ceremonial burial cave for this beloved and important woman.

Not for her an unmarked grave in the Indian cemetery. Hopeful was to be buried in the old custom. Most knew it would be the Manissee's last opportunity. All took great pride in the heritage it proclaimed.

The shift Tab brought out to dress Hopeful in was soft deerskin, dyed green for the trees and shrubs that lined mother earth, blue for the sky that gave sun and rain to grow crops, and red for the blood that made all peoples strong and powerful. It was lovingly embroidered with purple and white wampum beads, and was so deeply fringed at neck and ankle it looked as if Hopeful were floating in a bed of seaweed.

The elders of the tribe sprinkled her with burned clover blossoms, hyssop, marigolds, and colorful petals from all the wildflowers on the island. Then the women wound her body in leather strips, bound it to a wooden platform and painted it with red symbols that Tab said were prayers for Hopeful's journey into the great world beyond.

After the young men carried Hopeful's shrouded body to the cliffs, the great chief of the Narragansetts—the mother tribe which oversaw the affairs of the Manissees—gave Emily the tokens of Hopeful's order: Her medicine bags, gathering baskets, and the carved amulet Hopeful had always worn around her neck.

"You are her heritage," a tired, old, sad Miantonomi said. "You are now our sister. Do not forget our sister-mother who has gone before you."

It wasn't possible to forget. Hopeful's amulet was attached to the cover of Emily's medicine chest, a reminder each time she opened it that Emily owed all she knew—and all she loved—to the Manissee woman who had taken Emily to her heart and made Emily what she was. A doctor.

But even with all Emily's doctoring, four months after they had entombed Hopeful, Jeremiah Davies succumbed to the smallpox, refusing to the last to be vaccinated for the dread disease. Luckily, Emily convinced the rest of the islanders to accept the new procedure. Though they all got a case of the smallpox—and some were "rewarded" with small scars they would carry on their faces and upper torsos for the rest of their lives—Emily managed to bring each islander through it. Unlike their ancestors, none had to face the terrors of the pestilence house on the mainland, where no family member was allowed to visit, and plague and smallpox victims died in dirty quarters not fit for beasts.

Happily, the prolific Gorton family increased quickly. Emily's seven brothers and their wives birthed twenty-seven children but buried nine of them to childhood accidents and disease. It infuriated Emily that even her skills weren't enough to save them and she doubled her efforts to learn more from the books Robert and his friends brought her.

Rebeccah Washington fell from an apple tree while she was bringing in the meager harvest from the orchard behind the friendly house. As she fell, the ends of her apron caught on an old gnarled branch, wound round her neck and choked her. Emily and Rebeccah's "charges" were the only ones who attended her funeral, although Robert and Jason made periodic visits to her grave and left wildflowers for the woman who had given her time and energy to help a young man she had never seen before and was never to see again.

Eight men—three of them friends of the Gorton brothers—were lost at sea, mostly to freak squalls that took their double-enders and turned them into kindling. Two men who were catching a ride to the mainland drowned when their merchant sloop foundered off the coast of Newport and sunk with all hands. Another man and six women died together in a ferry accident as they were nearing Jerusalem.

Such was life on the island—perilously close to death at every turn.

But so was all life. Fragile. Transient.

Emily had known it all along. Every doctor did. And even during that time long ago—almost nine years, now—when Matthew and Delia had lined up against her, she had never doubted that she *was* a doctor. A good one.

Which was why, now, on *Patriot,* she left naught to others' skills but looked in on each of the men she had just treated, checked their bandages, adjusted their medications and diets, searched for anything that would negate the time and care she'd already given.

Finding nothing amiss, she gave in to her own problems. The guns boomed overhead, but Robert was obviously outrunning them since no more wounded had been brought below deck. She felt tired, suddenly, and stifled a yawn.

"You'd best get some victuals and some sleep, Emily," Jason said. "No telling when the next barrage will bring you down here again."

"Aye, Jason. I'll bunk down for a time." How easily she slipped into the cadences of the sea, even the language. "But be sure to call me if I'm needed."

Following Jason's directions to take her to the port cabin, the steward didn't escort her to the small box of a room with the hammock, but to more comfortable quarters, though not ostentatious. Several large wood and glass lanterns hung from the stays of the ship, but only one illuminated the darkness. Its yellow glow barely reached the door. As her eyes adjusted to the light, she saw that a table built into one corner held two water-filled pitchers and their matching washbowls. Underneath was a large thunder jug. A drop leaf desk took up much of the width of the room, standing just in front of a narrow, salt spray-crusted window set high in the wall. Two sea chests stood to either side of a comfortable wooden arm chair. A small pile of Turkish towels were pushed to the corner of one of the chests. And a table, with solid carved legs, held rolled up sea charts and several books, as well as navigational tools, not all of which Emily could recognize. In addition, three small worn but clean Turkey carpets—the only bright color in the room—covered the wide plank flooring.

But it was the bed that caught her eye. A deal wider than the cots her brothers had once had, it was set high and housed several brass-handled drawers underneath its deep boxlike frame. Two pillows were tossed into the corner at the end closest to the door. A faded patchwork and embroidered quilt covered it.

It looked like the sleighs of her childhood, where she had once snuggled, lulled to sleep by the swaying of the horse. God's blood, it looked inviting. But first, she had need of that vessel underneath the corner table.

Finished, she eyed the bed once more, remembering sleigh rides and warm brandy-laced tea. Patchwork wool quilts and fur hand warmers. Jingling bells and soft whinnies. Just a glance had brought back poignant memories. Poignant, because she was not tucked into a sleigh on her wonderful island but drifting along in the middle of the Atlantic. Kidnapped by a scurvy bag of potage! Oooh, when she got her hands on Robert Sears! But, for the moment, that wonderful bed offered warmth and sleep. Mayhap not exactly what would bring her everlasting peace of mind but enough of a remedy for what ailed her just now.

She was about to sink into its depths when a knock sounded and the door opened to admit the steward, who carried a wooden tray with high sides. In it was a medium sized crockery jug, a tin mug and a pewter plate piled high with bread, boiled beef and potatoes, and a handful of raisins. He pulled down the desk front and placed the tray there, bowing as he left the room.

Emily hadn't realized how hungry she was until she smelled the salty tang of the beef. Quickly, she poured water from one of the pitchers into a wash-bowl, rinsed her hands, drew the chair up to the desk, and sat down. Hardly stopping to breathe, she had the entire plate finished in less than five minutes. Then she quaffed the jug of sweet, hot rum punch. It was highly sugared and spiced with cloves and nutmeg. She allowed its potency to warm her body; but before it could cause her eyes to flutter closed, she quickly removed her borrowed shirt and washed her face and upper body, drying it with one of the Turkish towels. Even that small task exhausted her. Stumbling to the bed, she struggled to wash her-self as she removed the rest of her stained clothing. As she applied the wet cloth to her feet, she tossed the horrible smelling stockings of the steward into the farthest corner so their odor wouldn't spoil her nap.

She was asleep before her toes got warm.

After several hours of bombardment, there was a lull in the fighting.

"Looks like they're taking time to regroup," Almanzo Peters, the First Mate said, as he and Robert watched the British cutter tack off on a downwind course, bringing it outside the range of *Patriot*'s guns.

Robert dropped his spy glass and leaned against the wheel. "It will be full dark soon. If there are enough clouds to hide the moon, we may be able to slip away." He motioned his men down from the shrouds and away from the cannons, although he left one man in the crow's nest as lookout and posted a small armed watch. "Have the men eat and drink something while we have time," he ordered Almanzo. "Then have them set to, to mend the canvas and prime the guns. Post double watches. And get some rest. No telling what the damned British will do."

As he descended the ladder into the hold of his sharphulled schooner, Rob stopped a steward and told him to bring dinner to his cabin. "And retrieve my shaving gear from Jop."

Normally, he'd have Jop, an ablebodied seaman and the ship's barber, shave him. But Jop had been working as hard as any hand and a good meal and sleep would do the old man good.

More than a meal was needed before Rob could feel good, however. He rubbed his face to clear it from fatigue and felt the grease that was always there during battle. He needed to clean the grime of gunpowder and smoke and dying men off himself, if he was to feel fresh enough to face the British again. As if washing and eating were enough! Sleep was what he needed. A cat nap wouldn't do. He hoped to hell the British would back off with the dark. Orrin Mayotte was a good navigator and Almanzo Peters could maneuver through lines almost as stealthily as Rob himself. He could leave them to it for now. Someone would call if there were trouble.

As he strode down the port fore-and-aft gangway, Rob unbuckled his sword and pulled off his shirt. He dropped it in a ditty bag outside the door to his cabin. Once inside he dropped his sword on his old scarred and battered chart table—a gift from his friend, and now pirate, One-eyed Jack Saunders. One by one, he laid his pistols and rifle beside the sword. He needed them ready to hand, so he could dress quickly if need be.

He removed his belt and boots next and then peeled his breeches and stockings away. Splashing a generous amount of cold water into a large wooden wash basin—actually a small wide bucket with the top cut off—he cleaned himself with strong sandlewood soap and a hard Turkish washcloth. He didn't miss an inch, even raising his leg onto the table to tuck the cloth between his toes. It felt good, this kind of stretching. It would feel better if his hair was clean. As much as he yearned to call for Jop, he refrained.

"As if you couldn't do it for yourself, Robert Sears," he said aloud. "It's lazy you're getting."

The bucket was filled with dirty water but it would

do for the first rinse. Without hesitating because of the cold, he held his breath and stuck his head full into it, scrubbing vigorously with the sandlewood soap. Some got in his eyes and he swore violently.

Emily's head had snapped up when Rob's boots hit the floor. She started to call out to let him know she was there but he moved so quickly he was fully naked before a sound escaped her. When it did, it was a soft intake of breath as she peeked over the sides of the bed. Mesmerized by the sleekness of his body and the way his muscles moved, she watched him intently, ducking down into the bed only when a knock sounded on the door and the steward came in with a tray of food identical to the one he'd brought her. Just so the steward wouldn't get any ideas, she pretended sleep. But as soon as she heard the door close, her head bobbed up and she continued to watch the wonderful tableau being played out before her.

She had doctored men and wasn't unaware of what their bodies looked like; but she had never before seen a man washing or dressing himself. Such simple, routine action was beautiful. The scent of sandalwood when it drifted over to her was enticing. It spoke of exotic lands filled with mystery. She could picture Rob far across the sea, in the desert or a Turkish garden, the sun bronzing his face and body.

There was no sun inside the cabin. But the soft glow from the lantern made Rob's skin look as if it were dusted with gold where the light reflected off the hair on his chest and arms and legs. Inexplicably, her body began to heat and she longed to bury her nose against his skin to breathe in deeply of his scent. Her fingers itched to feel those hairs, to see if the gold would somehow be transferred to her. She forgot that she was angry at him for taking her away from her island. She forgot everything as she reveled in the thoughts that raced through her.

God, how she wanted to touch him!

Many times over the years he had warned her that someday she would feel like this. She hadn't believed him. And suddenly, now, at that moment she felt a desire for him so intense she could scarcely breathe.

Had it always been there? Had she been too blind to see? Or—as he had insisted—had she truly refused to acknowledge it?

Over the years she hadn't see Rob often. It sometimes took upwards of ten months to make the Southern Circuit or ply the trade routes to Europe and the exotic lands of Africa. Yet, at least once a year following Jason's recovery, he and Rob were among the crew of a ship which docked at Block Island. And each time Rob made it a point to seek her out.

She enjoyed their evenings together. She enjoyed the walks in the woods, the talks they had while sitting on the beach watching the tide come in. They were so much alike! He believed that everyone, male or female, should do and be what was their destiny.

He alone didn't ridicule her dreams to be the best doctor in New England. She had discovered that he boasted to his fellow sea captains about her skill and ability to cure because they brought their wounded to her on his recommendation. So ironic! Though the islanders accepted her doctoring, not once had they recommended her to their mainland friends. Her reputation grew because of Rob, and Rob, alone.

Now that she thought on it, her interest in literature and politics were nurtured by him—though she had always had a fierce fondness for anything that stoked the fires of independence.

He brought her medical books by European authors as well as British. But it was the literature that opened new worlds to her. Shakespeare. John Speed's *History of Great Britain*. Webster's *The Duchess of Malfi*. Homer's *Odyssey*—she couldn't help thinking about Rob as she read it, though she never once saw herself as the all-patient wife! She liked Beaumont and Fletcher's saucy tales. Corneille's *El Cid*. But Moliere? Pah! Only *Don Juan*. And Milton! She bogged down almost immediately in his hellish *paradise* and she cared not a fig for Samson's *Agonistes*. She hated to admit it but she liked the new novels. Marie de La Fayette's *The Princess of Cleves* was far more entertaining than anything Milton produced. She laughed at Congreve's *Way of the World* and Steele's *Grief a la Mode*. Robinson Crusoe and Friday had her clutching her quilt to her throat. And just the thought of Moll Flanders had her blushing for weeks. But *Don Quixote* was her favorite. The man tilting at imaginary windmills made her think of herself, aligned against the established society, always fighting for her independent spirit and her love of medicine.

While she read Shakespeare on her own, it only came alive when she and Rob were together. He would often read from the sonnets and they acted out parts from the plays. *The Taming of the Shrew* was his favorite. She decided he liked it best because it ended with a kiss.

And, oh! how he liked kissing her.

Often they had been together in the barn after playacting Shakespeare on the beach. Each time he had taken her in his arms, whispered a sonnet

—*Shall I compare thee to a summer's day? Thou art more lovely and more temperate*—and kissed her.

Or . . . *Not marble, nor the gilded monuments of princes shall outlive this powerful rhyme; But you shall shine more bright in these contents . . . So, till the judgment that yourself arise. You live in this, and dwell in lover's eyes*—and kissed her.

Or, from Hamlet that immortal line, *We know what we are, but know not what we may be.*—and kissed her.

Truth be told, she liked the kisses almost as much as he.

But knowing her as he did he had always broken it off, leaving her confused, with his stuttered excuses about not wanting to compromise her or having to get back to his ship her only succor.

Not that she would have allowed him any more than a kiss.

Rebeccah Washington had made very sure she got a good education in the ways of sailors and what they did with the women in the friendly house. Thus, Emily was well aware of what lay beyond if she wasn't careful.

But once she had been caught up in the beauty of the moment: the soft sounds of Rob's voice, the delightful chirping of a nesting robin, and the scent of sandlewood and sea air that always reminded her of Rob. She had basked in that day, remembered his words on the beach, nestled into his embrace.

Their kiss had gone far beyond anything that had come before. His hand had molded her breast and she'd welcomed it. His tongue had sought out tender spots on her neck and against the V of her bodice. She had liked it, the feelings Rob induced in her. She had liked it more than she feared it. And she often wondered what might have happened had Carter not ridden his horse into the yard and called out for her.

She had thought often about that dark, sweet time—and been shocked enough at her unbidden responses to be "too busy" to see Rob for almost a year.

But then he had brought his friends Jonathan Hobbs and Constance Proctor Sheffield to the island after they had been ambushed. Jonathan was weak and near death and Emily was truly busy most of the time until he came out of his unconscious state. When Constance took over the nursing, Emily had no more excuses.

And—as she always thought about it—it was then, when she had had some free time, that things took a turn she was not expecting . . . when inexplicably the friendly relationship Rob and she had developed over the years caught fire and got so hot it terrified her because she didn't know how to control it.

She should have expected it. Rob had shown her often enough that he desired her. But she had always shrugged it off, thinking that she was merely an interesting interlude until Rob once again went seafaring, where he might find enticing fare.

She couldn't have been more wrong.

Rob's friend, Jonathan Hobbs, got stronger and stronger each day. Soon, he and Constance were demonstrating their love for each other. That was natural, of course. But they were in Emily's bedroom and thrice Emily had almost walked in on them during moments of intimacy. Heavens, it was a wonder it hadn't happened more often. Emily's father had built the house so well she had to be next to the door before she heard the unmistakable sounds of lovemaking. When she did, she backed up, fleeing the heart-pounding things that were happening in her own bed.

Once—to her chagrin—Rob caught her racing away from the bedroom, her hands held over her burning cheeks. When he, too, heard the sounds coming from behind the closed door, he laughed until she wanted to throttle him.

When he caught her, she was halfway to her favorite hidey hole in the barn. He picked her up and whirled her in the air, setting her down with a great hoot.

"Doctor Emily Gorton, you have much to learn about men and women."

"Not so! I know all there is to know."

"Book learning."

"Not so!" she said, stumbling away from him so he wouldn't see the embarrassment she felt. "I've been to the friendly house."

"That, my love, isn't the best place to get your lessons."

"I suppose you have a better place."

"Aye." He came up behind her and steadied her with his hands on her shoulders. "Right here, where it all began between us, would be the perfect place."

She trembled beneath his touch but wouldn't give in to the feelings that had her so confused. "When what began between us? I swear, Robert Sears, you haven't made much sense lately."

"Whenever I'm with you I don't *have* much sense!" He turned her round to face him and cradled her head. "I've tried to show you how I feel but you'd have none of it. Now, it's time you heard it from my own lips. And if you cover your ears with your hands I'll have your liver for breakfast!"

Emily glared but she had respect for Rob's strength. She kept her mouth shut and her hands at her sides.

"Good. Now . . . how the hell to begin?" He stomped over to the wall of the stall and leaned against it. That didn't suit, apparently, because he swore and came back to pull out Emily's favorite stool and push her down on it. Then he hunkered back on his heels directly in front of her, put his hand under her chin to bring their eyes level and sighed. "Ah, Em . . . why can't I reach you? What is it you need to know to accept the fact that I'm besotted with you?"

"I will accept that you're besotted. But over *me?* That's a wicked and cruel thing to say when I know there isn't a man alive who finds me attractive."

"I do, Em. I've been all over the world and known all kinds of women. But they have no appeal. Wherever I am, whatever I'm doing, I count the minutes until I can see the silhouette of this damned craggy island of yours, drop anchor, and know you're only a few minutes away. There isn't another port that's home to me. Home because you're there. God's blood, Emily, I've waited eight years for you to grow up, to see how I feel about you. Why haven't you, Em? Why can't you see?"

She tried to turn her head away but he held it steady, his green and gold specked eyes boring into hers until she flushed at what she saw there. "I see, Rob. I see lust."

"Ah, Em. If that's all it was I would have taken you long ago."

"As if I would have let you!"

"As if you could have stopped me!"

One large hand held her head in place while the other dropped to her waist to pull her off the stool and on top of him. She struggled to get up—remembering that first day as she had tried to card wool and her skirts had settled round her head. As then, he held her firm.

His voice was hoarse as he said, "As strong as you

are—and I love that quality about you—you're no match for my strength, Em. You never were. You never will be. But it doesn't matter because what I want from you would be awful if you didn't want it, too."

"I don't."

"You don't know what you want, Em," he whispered seductively.

With little effort he surged to his feet, tugging her up to stand in front of him. If she thought she could back away, he showed her how much in command he was by circling her waist and drawing her into a net made by his arms.

"My beautiful Emily . . . You've lived so long believing Delia Davies's estimation of you that you don't know which end is up. Admit it, Em. You truly believe you aren't desirable to men, don't you?"

"I'm not."

"But you are. I desire you every minute of every day. And no one has dared call me less than I am, a man. Don't let Delia and the rest call you less than what you are, Em. Be a woman. Be what you were meant to be."

That time when he lowered his head it was no simple kiss he gave her. It blotted out the words she would have said, *I was meant to be a doctor,* and showed her a realm she had only suspected might be real.

Oh, his lips were soft! And strong, too. The pressure of them molded her own lips to the shape of his. The friction they made together forced her mouth open. She breathed in his breath. Tasted his taste. And felt a warmth creep over her all the way from her toes to the tips of her fingers and the roots of her hair.

Lassitude. She felt such lassitude. And something else that caused her to become unsteady.

She wanted to get closer to him.

As if he knew what she was thinking, he sighed deeply, then drew her arms up, to tuck them around his neck.

"Yes, Em," he sighed. "Yes."

His voice! She felt enveloped by it, as if it were a mist blotting out the rest of the world. It was scratchy, yet musical, and made her feel like a princess in a tower, enclosed in a special place he had made from a tone.

She sighed. He chuckled against her lips, then kissed her again.

His head moved from one side of her face to the other. Every time it did, her fingers brushed against his queue and the riband that held it. The hairs were soft to her touch, tantalizing her fingertips. She was curious to find out what the riband held and tugged it open. It fluttered to the straw as she combed through Rob's hair.

God, what a sensation!

The shape of his head next held her fascination. She learned it all, just from touch. She learned his neck had tiny curly hairs that felt springy; that the shape of his crown allowed her to pull his head down to hers, increasing the pressure of their lips; that his forehead was strong and sloped to arched brows that felt different, but as wonderful, as the hair on his neck; that his ears were wondrous places to outline and tug; that the cords in his neck hid a strong throbbing that increased when her fingers traced them from ear to collarbone.

It was nothing like examining a patient. It was an exploration of a man who treated her as she had never expected to be treated. An exploration of deep-seated dreams she had long denied.

Oh, yes, she had dreams of a man like Rob loving her. How could she not, when love and its mystery was in everything she read? But she never pictured herself as the heroine of a novel or play; so she had forced her dreams to the back of her mind, like unwanted baggage.

But she found out something wonderful—and awful—that day. She found out those dreams were not unwanted, simply stored away, waiting to be brought out and tested.

Rob was tugging them out of her as gently as he tugged her closer to him.

"Rob . . . I'm frightened."

"It's all right, Em. I won't hurt you. And we won't go any further than you want to go."

"I don't know where that is."

"When we get there, you'll know."

The ending wasn't when his lips feathered their way down her neck to send shivers down her spine. It didn't come when he ran his hands up her legs and hips and spanned her waist. Those touches were welcome. So welcome she wanted to know what his body felt like in the same places.

Following his lead, she learned his outline. He was

lean. His muscles were hard; but they jolted whenever her fingers brushed against them. It gave her a strange power over him that made her smile. She had felt many things in her life. Not once had she felt powerful. Yet there was power in the gentlest touch. His touch made her tremble. Her touch made him unsteady enough that he had to lean against the stall to stay upright. His touch heated her blood. Hers elicited guttural sounds and sighing groans from him. His touch drew her into him, to feel a strange hardness against her thigh. Hers caused the hardness to throb.

What was throbbing? The doctor in her wouldn't be put aside so easily. There was something there to explore, something new to learn.

She ran her hand down to find out what it was and Rob cried out brokenly, "God's blood, Emily!"

Fearing she had hurt him, she snatched her hand away, but he kissed her quickly and drew it back.

"Nay," he said. "Tis all right, love. Tis all right."

But it was not all right.

Suddenly, at that moment, she remembered Rebeccah's lessons. Vanished was the misty dream tower in which Rob had enveloped her. In its place was the interior of the friendly house.

This was what the women would be doing there.

This.

Emily cried out and pulled herself away from Rob. "Damn you, Robert Sears! Damn, damn you."

But Rob wouldn't let her go. His hands held hers captive.

"Emily . . . what are you thinking? Talk to me!"

"Delia said . . ." Emily choked and sputtered. "Delia said I'd be tainted if I associated with Rebeccah Washington and the women at the friendly house. She warned me. She said my doctoring would be guided by the devil to explore things a good woman was not meant to explore. And you . . . my friend! You prove it to me!"

"No, Emily! Delia was wrong. God's blood, she was an evil woman who saw sin in all things that didn't agree with her own narrow view of what was right and what was wrong. Haven't you ever wondered why she was the only woman on the island who never had children? And her husband, a minister. *Be ye fruitful and multiply.* Isn't that a commandment in the Bible? *Love one another. Cleave, husband and wife, together.* Yet, Delia described as sinful the only act that could make her fruitful. And she made you believe her poisonous thoughts.

"Think, Emily. Think! What you feel . . . what you just felt for me is what Constance and Jonathan feel for each other. What your brothers feel for their wives and their wives feel for them. It is not wrong. It is not tainted. It's a part of love, Emily. Not the only part. But a powerful part."

"For them, Rob. Not for me."

That had happened six years ago. Though he left her at her insistence, his eyes had held tender pity in them. She didn't want his pity; but she accepted it. She had accepted much worse.

Though she had never admitted it, however, she

did think about what he'd said. In her lonely bedroom at the top of the stairs in the new house her brothers had built her, she thought long and hard. It took her almost two years but she had come to understand what Rob had said in the barn that day. What he gently, yet continuously, explained each time they were together—that there would come a day when she would realize she was not set apart from other women, that she could feel as deeply as they did.

Well, it had taken longer for her than for most women. So long that she was well past marrying age. But the wait had been worth it. She now knew she felt deeply. She loved her nephews and nieces and brothers and their wives. She felt strongly about Rob. He was the only man about whom she felt strongly.

But strong wasn't the way she was feeling now. Weak-kneed and desperate more accurately described it. There was, burning inside her, a frantic yearning to know all there was to know about the mystery of the marriage bed.

Humbuggery! Who was she trying to flummox? That was *not* what she was feeling as she stared at Rob's naked body. The mystery of the marriage bed could hang! She wanted to know all about the mysteries of Robert Sears.

What would he do if this time, without reservation, she approached him?

Chapter Ten

Brrrr! The bloody water was cold. Rob scrubbed as much of the soap out of his hair as he could and reached out for a towel from the pile he always demanded be laid on his sea chest. Before his fingers found what he sought, he heard a coquettish laugh. He froze.

"Em?"

"Now, Captain Sears . . . you should know better than to try to wash your hair by yourself. You have enough soap left in it to do a month's worth of laundry. If you'll just lean down over the bucket, I'll finish the job you half started."

"Emily, you don't know what you ask."

"I didn't ask, Rob. I told you to lean over that bucket and let me finish the job."

He'd heard that commanding tone in her voice before, always when she was dealing with her patients. Damn, he didn't want to be treated as a patient by this woman! He was mad about her. And getting madder by the second as she leaned over his right side, lathered his head and worked her fingers over his scalp. Jop's touch was about as gentle as a bull-whip. Emily's, a whisper of velvet.

It wasn't surprising that his body responded to her. It was astounding that fury quickly followed.

Pushing her aside, he strode to his bed, grabbed up the quilt and wound it round his waist. Then he whirled to face her, oblivious of the water droplets that had struck her in the face or the rivulets of water that pooled at his feet. What he saw drained his face of all color.

"God's blood, Emily! Cover yourself!"

She looked down at her unclothed body and her eyes widened. She had felt no shame walking naked across the room to him. She still didn't. But it might be prudent, and warmer, to have something on.

With no hurry, she crossed to the bed—and Rob scuttled away, to press his back against the cabin door.

She giggled as she flipped a winding sheet off the bed and drew it across her shoulders. No, that wouldn't work. It was too short to cover all of her. Unless . . .

As she did when she had to bandage a chest wound, Emily tucked one end under her arm, then wrapped the other end behind her back and pulled it round in front. But she couldn't let the end dangle there like that. It would fall to the floor again. The doctor in her solved the problem by jamming the end of the winding sheet into the cleft between her breasts, hoping the fullness of them would hold it in place. The costume she had devised left her shoulders bare. Certainly, from the way it wrapped itself around her thighs, it didn't cover her derriere by half. But it was all she had unless she wanted to get back into those dirty, blood stained clothes. And she'd be skint if she'd do that.

Besides, she liked the way Rob's eyes sparked and darkened while he pretended not to watch her solve her little problem.

As soon as she was certain the sheet would stay safely wedged under her arm and between her breasts, she climbed into the bed, sat Indian style in the middle of it, and grinned at Rob.

By the way he squirmed and avoided her eye, and the giggly way she felt inside, it seemed there were some tortures even she could enjoy.

Rob was ready to explode. His upper lip had beaded with sweat at the sight of Emily climbing into his bed. She couldn't be aware that she had exposed the soft round bottom he'd once pushed down into the hay. God's blood, it was the most tantalizing sight he had ever seen! Giant pulses of energy throbbed through his body and he bit his lip to bring himself under the icy control that was his habit.

It didn't work. British and French and pirates had boarded his ship and he'd stood firm. None of their derring-do or escapades had unnerved him. But a mere slip of a woman? He was flummoxed. Emily Gorton shattered his composure merely by sitting there in the middle of his bed like an Indian princess, grinning. Damn her eyes, she was *baiting* him! After all these years of running the other way she'd found the perfect method to torment him—body and soul!

His teeth ground together as he growled, "Have you no sense? My steward will be here any minute with my supper."

She swallowed a grin and pointed to the tray on his desk.

He glared. "Don't be so smug. Anyone could walk in this door."

"Not without knocking, *Captain* Sears."

He raked his fingers through his hair, realized how wet it was and swore. "Damn, I need a towel." He started to move across the room when he realized the quilt which enveloped him had become wet clear through. It was molding itself around his arousal.

Lord, he thought, what else can go wrong?

He struggled to pull up more of the quilt to hide the all-too-obvious effect she was having on him. But his movement caught her eye and her gaze swooped down. Her grin got broader.

He turned his back.

"Em, if you could just toss a towel to me," he asked sweetly—but with a bite to it that any member of his crew could tell meant trouble. He hoped to hell she wouldn't push him beyond his limit—which wasn't too far away—because all he wanted to do at that minute was turn her over his knee and give her the paddling she deserved.

Or scoop her up in his arms and put her back in his bed where she belonged and make love to her until the British broke in his door. And even if they put him at sword point he wasn't sure he'd be able to stop.

* * *

Humbuggery! Emily wondered where her plan had gone awry. It had seemed so simple. But what did simplicity have to do with Robert Sears? From the moment they had met she had been walking a line between birthday devils and Delia's denouncements, Satan and Beelzebub. Certainly, she had never been on the side of the angels. Always, things took such unexpected and interesting turns! Things the doctor in her itched to explore.

Well, then, why not give this escapade one more twist and see where it led?

She hopped out of the bed. But instead of fetching Rob the towel he had requested, she slipped up to him and hooked her finger inside the bunched up quilt, which by this time was riding very low on his hip, so low her fingers skimmed the cleft between his hard, muscular buttocks. She felt his skin contract and laughed.

"Come on, Captain. Be a good boy. Sit in the chair and I'll dry your hair for you while you eat your supper. Then you can go play King of the Mountain with the British."

Emily knew from the way his shoulder muscles bunched into intriguing knots that he was about to resist her insistent pressure. But the quilt shifted precariously and nearly exposed his backside. It must have been an awful strain for him to keep his body just a hair's breadth away from her fingers! Somehow, however, he managed it. But, thank goodness, he allowed her to lead him on a backwards course across the cabin. It wasn't easy. Twice he stumbled until the chair seat came in contact with his calfs. With an oath, he sat. Then he looked up.

Emily was particularly pleased to see his throat contract not once, but twice.

"Ah, God, Em," he mumbled, "I'd be delighted to play King of the Mountain if I could only climb the soft twin peaks of Mount Gorton."

Pretending that she didn't hear him, Emily slapped a towel on Rob's head and rubbed vigorously. Soft twin peaks of Mount Gorton, indeed! If he had left her to handle the situation, that's exactly where he'd be right now. But, no. The great big man couldn't let the woman take point . . . She scrubbed until he yelped. The great big man wanted things his way or not at all.

"Em . . . leave some skin, I beg you."

She snapped the towel away and glared. "Where's your comb?"

"In the desk. Second cubbyhole on the right."

While she hunted through the assorted quills and ink blocks and buckles and ribands and papers in his desk, a knock sounded on the door. Automatically, she called, "Come in!"

"No!" Rob shouted.

Emily whirled, grabbing up a short, thick brass comb and blue riband before she turned. She couldn't believe her eyes. Thoroughly entertained by the spectacle, she watched as Rob jumped to his feet, tripped over the quilt, went sprawling, but somehow managed to slam the door before whoever was on the other side found them. She giggled, nervously. It *would* have been an embarrassing state they were found in.

"Ya shavin' things, Cap'n," a gruff voice called through the slammed door. "Ah thought ya sent for 'em."

Clutching the quilt as high up as he could get it, Rob struggled to his feet, shouting, "Put them on the floor outside, damn it! I'll fetch them when I'm ready, Jop."

"Aayah, sah."

They both heard stomping footfalls and Jop querulously wondering aloud about, ". . . wha' da blazes goin' on wid da cap'n! An us in peril o' da damnacious jackanapes what might strike in da night!"

For the first time Emily felt a tiny bit contrite. She had made Rob lash out at a faithful member of his crew, and he had become angry at himself for doing it. She could tell that much merely by the way his eyes narrowed and a white spot appeared in the redness of his cheeks. But he said not a word—although his jaw tightened perceptively as he eased open the door to retrieve his shaving gear and slammed it shut once more. Hopping and stumbling, he crossed the room, dropped the leather pouch on the sea chest and plopped back into the chair. His eyes flicked up at her and she gulped. She knew from that furious expression that if he said anything at all he'd probably scorch the walls. When he picked up his spoon and tucked into the boiled spiced beef and potatoes, she allowed him several minutes before she warily approached, comb and riband in hand.

Happy to find that he made no move to stop her,

she drew back a handful of Rob's hair and very gently pulled the comb through it. Wet, it was the color of walnut boards, dark with reddish highlights. A few grey hairs softened the color at his temples. Her fingers lingered to touch the mark of a man who—if her reckoning was correct—was on the downward side of thirty. Time had gotten away from her. He was thirty-two. She, almost twenty-seven. He was a bachelor, not a bad thing to be for a man of the sea. She was a spinster, an old maid, an eternal joke.

She swallowed back her bitterness and continued the task she'd started. She'd not dwell on the problems she faced on the island. She wasn't there. She might never get back—damn the eyes of all the British who had started this mess! But she had an important job to do here on *Patriot* and she'd do the best she was capable of doing.

Including combing Rob's hair.

It surprised her that it was thick and soft, even when wet. She liked the feel of it in her hands, sleek and clean. Since she had never had children—and Bella had always tended the younger Gorton boys—this was the first time she'd combed another person's hair.

There were snarls which took a bit of gentle teasing to allow the comb easy passage. And there was one hank which still had soap in it. As Bella and Tab had done to Emily's hair to rid it of soap, she dipped the comb in some clear water and pulled it through the soapy part, then toweled the majority of the soap away.

How good it smelled! Sweeter than cedar. Spicier than Castile chips. A smell that spoke of manly things. Nothing wrong with that. Rob was about the manliest man she'd ever known—if she ignored the fact that the hand that held his mug of hot ale wasn't as steady as a babe's.

"Do you want it plaited or left in a rattail?" she asked.

Rob's voice shook as much as his hands, though he said every word slowly and carefully. "What I want is for you to leave my hair alone and put your clothes on."

"I do not have any clothes, Robert. You haven't given them to me."

"The clothes Jason gave you!"

"They are dirty. And I have already washed. I will not wear them. Mayhap you have some old, *clean* clothes of yours that I could borrow for a time?"

The thought of her delightful body inside his breeches and shirt caused Rob to choke. Emily smacked his back and cautioned him to take small bites.

A vision came together in his mind of him taking one small bite of her earlobe. Or a tiny bite of her bottom lip. Or a nip of those white mounds to either side of the linen knot . . .

"God's blood, I cannot take anymore!" He slammed down his spoon and rose slowly. "I've been patient, Em. I've been so damned patient it astonishes even me. But you've gone too far . . ."

"Ah, but Rob . . . we haven't gone far enough."

Winding sheet dropped to the floor. Quilt followed.

His big hands shook as he framed her face and looked deeply into her eyes. "Em, do you know . . . do you have any idea . . . ?"

"I know that when I saw you there in the lantern light that I wanted . . . I wanted . . . I don't even know what I wanted. But there was something inside . . . an emptiness . . . a thirst . . . a fire. You warned me it would happen and it did. There's something that pulls us together. I don't know what it is but it's stronger than anything I've ever felt. Fill the emptiness, Rob. Stoke the fire. Quench the thirst."

He pressed himself against her and she felt his arousal rigid against her belly.

"Em . . . what you're asking . . ."

"I understand Rob." She smiled at him and reached to trace the brows that he'd drawn down to hood his eyes. "I want this. I want you. *Da damnacious jackanapes might strike in da night,* you know," she said, mimicking Jop. She smoothed the worry lines at the corners of Rob's eyes, traced down to their twins at his mouth, and ran her fingers over the softness of his lips. Her mouth missed not an inch of where her fingers had been.

"I'm not good at this, Rob," she whispered, brokenly—afraid, yet bold in her wanting. "You'll have to help me."

"You're doing fine, Emily."

He sucked her fingers into his mouth as he scooped her into his arms and carried her across to the bed. He sat her on the edge, steadying her so she wouldn't fall back, then knelt in front of her. With one hand on the small of her back, he kissed her left thigh, then her right. His other hand trailed up from her ankle to the spot where his lips had been. But he didn't stop there.

Feathers. It felt like feathers skimming her leg. She threw her head back at the ecstasy of his touch then jolted it forward when Rob's fingers found a spot so sensitive it made her gasp.

"Rob?"

"I'm only helping, Em."

A quick spasm shook her and she smiled. "Why haven't you helped me like this before?"

"*Before* wasn't the right time."

"And now is?"

When he felt the hot sleekness of her awaiting his gentle probe, he nodded. "The perfect time."

Yet he lingered to savor the lushness of her breasts with his fingers, hands and mouth. He burned the outline of her body into his brain, learning, as he touched, the places that made her smile, gasp, or writhe with pleasure.

The empty nights in hammock or bed, the dreams and fantasies he had conjured there, were nothing compared to the reality of the woman he loved. She was perfection now, as she had been perfection that first day in the barn. He had called her houri then, never realizing how true it was.

Emily Gorton had stolen his heart.

But then she had locked it away and kept it for seventeen years!

Suddenly, he was afraid. He knew his Emily. He

knew her strengths. He knew her one overwhelming weakness. It had been a barrier between them, nurtured by evil women and arbitrary societal rules. Regardless of how she was acting this night, the barrier was still there. One false move, one tiny misstep, and he might never have what he had planned almost every day of those maddening years. He loved her. But loving her physically wasn't the only thing he wanted or needed.

She had to want and need him as much as he wanted and needed her. She had to love him. She had to marry him.

He had one chance to show her what love and adoration was. One chance to prove to her that she was a woman in every sense of the word. One chance . . .

Emily's sensory track was running wild. She had never felt such opposing forces! Robert's breath was warm on her and smelled spicy sweet. His kiss shook her, sending heat throughout her body. His hands seemed to find every nerve ending, setting up a resonant thrumming in her body that was beyond pleasure. She gave herself up to it, loving the way he caressed her breasts, then molded them with his hands. More, she loved the way his eyes glowed, then darkened, as he brushed his hips and legs against hers. Instinct took over and she opened her legs to accommodate the hard, sinewy strength of him.

Rebeccah's lessons had told her what to expect; but they had never hinted at what she would *feel!*

One minute, like honey melting in the heat of the day. In Rob's heat, by Rob's hand. Another minute, breathless and jumpy, awaiting a feathery touch which always came, but then went, leaving an insistent tingling behind.

How could a body be tense and relaxed at the same time? How could one man's caresses call out to the deepest reaches within her? And how could her body answer with such overwhelming urgency that she didn't know where to look, what to touch, how to talk? She wanted . . . Ah, God! . . . how she *wanted!* There was a rhythm to it, this wanting. A rhythm that spread through her body and sent it cresting like waves along the shore. Her breasts ached and could only be soothed when she arched high enough to brush them against Rob's chest. As she had hoped, the hairs there were soft enough to soothe. But they were also rough enough to further excite her.

"Rob? Oh, Rob! It feels . . . it feels . . ."

"I know, love."

So good! It felt so good!

And when he took her nipple into his mouth to suckle as a babe did, she gasped. "Yes! Rob, please . . . the other . . . please . . ."

Pleasure followed sensation. Rapture. Ecstasy.

She had no more words to describe how she felt. She had only the feelings themselves . . . And what Rob was doing to draw them higher and higher and higher . . . until she was afraid the furious pounding of her heart would give a last convulsive shudder and die from such unbridled happiness.

But she was wrong. The shudder became a red hot fire when she felt Rob enter her. Her body accommodated the strength of Rob's arousal and wanted more. Rhythmically, she lifted her heat to his thrust. Obligingly, he fed her fire. Little by little it built, until she wrapped her legs around him and moved with him, melded with him into a white flame of pure sensation.

She was lost in his lovemaking, lost to the world around her. Only dimly did she hear the boom of guns over their heads. Only dimly did she hear Rob cry, "I love you, Emily. Ah, God, I love you!"

She didn't die. She exploded with such fierce joy she couldn't breathe . . . and didn't want to. Her heart, it seemed, could withstand a power greater than a hurricane.

But it couldn't withstand the insistent pounding on the door, nor the *kaboom* of cannons on deck. It shuddered painfully to a stop when Rob convulsed, drew out of her and leaped to the floor. He didn't bother with the quilt but opened the door a crack.

"Aye, Jason. Give me a minute."

He cursed the bloody British and rushed back to Emily's side. Giving her a quick kiss, he said, "I'm sorry." Pulling breeches and shirt out of his sea chest, he donned them quickly. "Get back into those dirty clothes you hate so much."

"Are you mad?"

He pulled on stockings and boots and stuffed his pistols and swords back into his belt. "If we're boarded and they find a woman here . . . I don't know what they'll do, Em."

"Surely even the British are gentlemen."

"I can't guarantee it . . ."

"Did you know this when you kidnapped me?"

"I had to take the chance."

"Damn. Damn your eyes, Robert Sears!"

"Dress, Emily! In men's clothes. With a cap to cover that gorgeous hair. I'll post a guard outside the door to this cabin; and I pray to God it will be enough."

A last pleading, frightened look, then he opened the door, closed it behind him, and was gone. And she sat there with her arms wrapped around herself. Furious at him. Terrified for him. Her body aching—from her muscles all the way to her soul.

They had left something unfinished. They had left *everything* unfinished!

Right daft he was if he thought she was going to sit here, in a hidey hole of a cabin, while he risked his life on deck . . . She shuddered, then edged her way off the bed. The breeches and shirt . . . No! Right daft by half, Rob was. To have those dirt crusted clothes on her body after getting clean . . . absolutely not.

She heard a clink and a grunt outside the door and realized Rob had been good as his word. She now had a guard . . . and a keeper . . . a warder . . . a gaoler. Damn his eyes! Damn this confounded British mess!

She had no time to think about what had just happened. No time to adjust—if that was possible. No time to bask in the warmth she had felt. No time to try to unravel the mystery that was no longer mysterious but yet unsolved. Her arms felt empty; she wanted so desperately to have them wrapped around Rob's body. And was more desperate to have his wrapped around her body. Or him inside her.

Amazing!

Amazed, she stumbled over to the sea chest from which Rob had pulled out his own clothes. Things were a jumble inside but she found a soft cotton shirt like the kind One-eyed Jack favored, with long full sleeves and dozens of tiny gathers at the shoulders. She couldn't hope to hide her figure in a normal shirt. But this one could be bloused out over breeches. It might hide some of the fullness of her breasts. The sleeves, of course, were too long; but rolled up they fit well enough to ease her mind.

Breeches that wouldn't fall over her hips or trip up her feet were her main concern. Rob was almost a head taller than she. His legs were long. His hips, lean. None of the breeches in the sea chest would do. She turned to the other chest and found herself foiled. No matter how hard she tried to push up the top it refused to budge.

Was there a key to the lock? If there was, it would be in the desk.

Four keys in hand, she tried each until a solid click told her she'd been successful. The top pried open and she stared down at the contents.

Dresses. Green. Blue. Peach. White dimity with tiny peach flowers and delicate lace trim. A purple wool of such fine weave it almost felt like linen. And, carefully packed between folds of cotton felt, was a cranberry satin with deep lace flounces at the low neckline, *pointelle francaise* broidery below it, and rich cream colored velvet swirls and whorls of trim.

Underneath the dresses were velvet and woolen capes, embroidered nightdresses of the sheerest cotton and silk, wildly exotic shawls with deep fringe, a box containing a shell and brass comb and brush set, and seven velvet pouches which held jewels too breathtaking to describe.

Dear God!

She knew without trying them on that the clothes would fit her perfectly. She knew the jewels would hang on her neck and fasten to her ears and that Rob had chosen them to compliment the dresses and her coloring. And she knew that the man she had just made love with had bought them all . . . for her.

Why, then, hadn't he given them to her?

Had he thought clothes and jewels as dainty and feminine as these not fit for her?

Then why buy them? Why keep them hidden behind a lock inside a chest in his cabin?

Hidden. Locked. Locked inside *his* chest. Not in his cabin but in his *bedroom*.

Emily sat back on her heels, a corner of the cranberry satin skirt in her hands. Absentmindedly, she brushed at the softness of it as she tried to digest this new image of Robert Sears.

No, not new. He had been trying to tell her for years. Trying to show her what he wanted from her. She simply hadn't credited it. Refused to acknowledge that a man like Rob . . . No! That Rob, himself, saw more to her than she saw to herself. These dresses and jewelry proved it.

The problem was that what he saw wasn't Emily Gorton but a woman of a substance unfamiliar to an island doctor, already eight years beyond the marrying age. Emily Gorton was a woman too familiar with men's bodies . . . yet not familiar enough. A woman who had long ago set aside womanly things and taken her place in a man's world. A woman who could no more give up that place than she could cut out her heart.

Because it was her heart.

Every hurt, every slur, every injustice she had suffered in her formative years had driven her further from a female perspective to a center of the universe she'd devised for herself.

Oh, she wasn't a *man!* The session in bed with Rob had proved that. Nor was she quite the woman these carefully preserved clothes indicated he hoped she'd become.

How sad. How painfully sad for them both.

Sighing, she carefully repacked the riot of colors and textures, closed the lid and turned the key in the lock.

The loud click it made was like the cocking of a pistol. Any moment she expected an explosion to rip through her. She waited for it, hoped for it . . . so the pain that would follow would block out the sorrow that overwhelmed her.

Chapter Eleven

In the end, she found a good clean pair of stockings, and an old pair of bell bottom short trousers that fit very snugly on her hips, so she had no fear of them falling down at every step. And though they would have been knee high on Rob, on her they skimmed the top of the boots she'd donned. A worn and patched pilot cloth vest, a green neckcloth, and a tri-cornered cocked hat completed her transformation from female surgeon to able bodied hand. The outfit would do naught to hide the delicacy of her features or the fineness of her bone structure; but she didn't intend for anyone to get close enough to see either.

She did, however, intend to get up on deck.

"You were wrong, Hamlet," she muttered. "Not frailty, but *curiosity,* thy name is woman."

She tucked her long blond plaits into the tri-corn, then opened the cabin door. The guard outside, a short, stout dark-skinned man, clicked to attention and eyed her warily.

"Wha' you be wantin', missus? Dare's a thunda jug inside."

"You're Jop, aren't you?"

"Ayuh."

With more authority than Emily felt, she demanded, "Get me a pistol, Jop. And a short sword."

"Now, missus . . . Da cap'm, he say fo me to keep you safe an' sound."

"From the noise topside, the captain has his hands full. He'll need both of us if he's boarded. So don't argue. Get me pistol and sword!"

She could see by his expression that he dearly wanted to get into the fray. But he'd had his orders and Emily surmised he wasn't sure if he wanted to pay the price for disobeying them.

"I'm ship's surgeon, Jop."

"Ayuh, I knows dat."

"Which makes me an officer, doesn't it?"

"I s'pose."

"Which means I can give you an order during battle, right?"

"I s'pose. But dat don' cut da cap'm's orders."

"I will take the responsibility, Jop. Captain Sears will understand."

"You sure, missus?"

"Positive." Positive Rob would pickle them both when he found out. "Now where is the weapons store?"

"You wait 'ere. Jop'll fetch wha you wan'."

He returned within moments with a pistol the size

of Emily's forearm, a short sword much like a carving knife, a powder horn, and a sack of bullets.

"You 'tatch da sack to yo belt. Put da powder in dis 'ole an' da bullet right 'ere, cock it . . ."

"I know how to shoot, Jop." When his eyes widened in surprise and disbelief, she snapped, "I've hunted with Indians and my brothers. I know rifle and breechloader and pistol and bow and arrow."

"We don' got no bow an' arrow on *Patriot* . . ."

"Perhaps you should." She stuck the pistol into her belt but kept the sword in her hand. "Lead the way."

She was grateful that Jop escorted her slowly through the gangways. As it was, she had to crawl over folded up canvas sails, duck as lines were lowered and raised, climb over ballast, wend her way around cannon and shot, and ignore the horrible smell and shouted curses of men soaked in black oily sweat, brine, and blood.

The noise below deck was deafening. Orders were shouted from above through several relays to men below. Lines snapped with an ear-splitting screech and a corresponding curse. Ballast wrenched out of its stays and crashed into crates and boxes. And, as each cannon was fired, it slammed backwards on its rollers. Before she heard the boom of the ball, the screech and scrawl of the rollers blasted her ears and set her nerves on edge. All of it reverberated from one deck to the other, echoing back, finally, from the deep cavernous hold.

It was Dante's hell come to earth. And Emily

shuddered to realize that it was repeated every hour of every day somewhere on the seven seas.

She was thankful they didn't ascend the quarter-deck ladder but the one near the fore hatch, far from Rob's position at the wheel. She had enough problems without adding to them Rob's fury when he discovered she hadn't stayed below deck.

Problems and more to spare.

The moment she popped her head over the top of the ladder, a black cast iron grenade lobbed past her. She ducked down and it fell to the deck and exploded, sending splinters of iron in every direction. Clutching the ladder below the hatch, she was choked by the grenade's sulphurous gases.

When she thought there was a lull in the battle, she stumbled onto the deck and took up a position behind the scuttlebutt near the center of the upper deck, tucking herself down so she could see, yet not be found out by Rob.

From the many conversations they'd had about his ships and the way to fight during battle, Rob had told Emily what positions were the most important to hold and win. Now, her eyes sought out *Patriot's* fighting tops—those platforms at the junction of the main and topmasts which housed the best marksmen. Even from her vantage point she could see that Rob had fitted his crew with the best smooth-bored rifles, a good quantity of grenades, four portable cohorns (used to lob grapeshot and shells accurately onto the enemy), swivel guns and their detached grips which were used for easier aiming, and a devilish number of stinkpots.

Emily grinned. Her brothers had loved to whip up a miniature version of this particular weapon and heave it into their enemies' yards. The stinkpot's evil concoction of saltpeter, brimstone, asafetida, and decayed fish was packed into molasses or whiskey jugs. A wick shaped like that of an oxtail—and called an oxtail wick—was inserted and lit. Then the jug was hurled in a high arc onto the deck of the enemy ship. The nauseating smoke it produced on impact was carried by the wind to every part of the deck and hold. It was a weapon of last resort—used only when the officers were about to board. But every sailor said it was truly effective. More than one enemy's recalcitrant crew had been overpowered by the noxious brew.

So she let out a cheer when she saw four stinkpots hurled over the side of Rob's fighting tops. Two headed for a British gunboat, *Cardiz*. The other two headed for the cutter, *Dover*.

Through the dense smoke of cannon fire, Emily saw that both ships were floundering in the water. The top of every one of their masts had been blasted away. A great gaping hole in the *Cardiz* was taking in seawater with each wave. The gunboat listed to starboard and showed no signs of righting itself. Already, there were scores of men in the rough sea, each trying desperately to keep his head above water and avoid being hit by bits of shot or falling debris.

It was a miracle there was no fire.

More of a miracle that the British flew their colors in surrender without Rob having to order his crew to board the other vessels and subdue them with hand-to-hand combat. Had the *Cardiz* been intact, Emily was confident Rob would have been in for a long, protracted battle. But if the British gave up now, they could take the gunboat to the nearest port—perhaps Block Island or Sandy Hook—repair her and be back on patrol in less than three days. If they didn't give up, they were likely going to lose the gunboat to the great hungry maw of the sea.

Whoever the captain in charge was, she had respect for his decision. He would lose this skirmish. But he wouldn't lose his vessel.

Emily crept closer to see and hear all that was going on. At a command from a tall, black-haired gentleman in red coat and blue breeches, both British crews laid down their arms. Then Rob and two of his senior officers walked a plank that had been secured from the *Cardiz* to *Patriot*. Though Jason was Second Mate (equal in rank to a Second Lieutenant in the British Navy), he did not accompany Rob.

Aboard the *Cardiz,* the captain bowed to Rob and extended his sword. Rob returned the bow, accepted the sword from the gunboat's British captain and the colors from a scowling officer.

"Ye put up a great fight, sire," the captain said.

"Thank you, Captain . . . ?"

"Douglass, sire. Donald Douglass of Devonshire."

"*Sir* Donald Douglass, Baronet," a harsh, deep voice spoke up.

Rob whirled to his left. A well dressed man had just ascended the ladder. He was of medium height, with a powdered wig that sat askew on his head of greying brown hair. His clothing was rich, if not sumptuous. Dark brown cock hat with silver cords, cambric neck cloth and fine ruffled linen shirt. An intricately patterned vest was bound with silver lace and from it hung two tasseled watch fobs. Over it, he wore the latest brown and white spotted frock coat. Brown breeches with silver buckles at the knee topped embroidered clocked stockings. His cane was a carved maple stick, with a silver cord which he tucked over his wrist. Shiny brown leather shoes with silver buckles finished his attire.

"Nathaniel?"

"Aye, Rob. At your service."

The man bowed and smiled but Emily thought his smile false for it wasn't accompanied by a corresponding glow of friendship in his eyes. On the contrary, his glance seemed almost hate filled.

"That's Nathaniel Appleton," Jason said.

Emily wasn't surprised that the young man had come to her side. She was astounded she hadn't heard the clomp of his wooden leg.

"Who," she asked, "is Nathaniel Appleton?"

"Merchant from Newport. He's one of the men who saved Rob and me from the noose."

Emily remembered.

How could she forget? It was her first surgical success. And nearly the last time she saw Rob.

Jason's leg had taken a long time to heal. He was still feverish and occasionally losing consciousness when Jack Donahue—blast his eyes!—had insisted Jason be taken back to *Calumet* and put in sick bay. Rob had consulted with Emily and Hopeful. They hadn't wanted to frighten Rob—and certainly not Jason—but they both feared that, without round-the-clock nursing of the sort they were giving, Jason's leg might fester or the dreadful congestion come back. If either happened, they were convinced Jason wouldn't survive more than a few days.

Nevertheless, Jack Donahue had sent four crewmen with a pallet to carry Jason back to *Calumet*. The ship left almost immediately, headed for Boston, then Newport. By the time they arrived in Newport, Emily had learned, Jason was almost as bad as he'd been on the morning following his surgery.

The rest of the story was pieced together by newspaper articles, other seamen who put into Block Island, islanders who traded on the mainland, and finally by Rob, himself.

One day, almost nine months after the hurricane, he and Jason came to the island, picked up a steaming kettle of cod and lobster and clams, and another of corn, and practically dragged Emily off to the beach for what they called a "picnic." They dug into the food and were nearly finished before

Rob brought up the terrible ordeal they'd undergone.

"It was hell, Em," Rob said. "But at least our necks are still attached to our shoulders."

The way he told it, Rob was furious that Jack Donahue wouldn't listen to reason and allow him and Jason to remain behind in Newport when *Calumet* sailed on its next long trip to Guadaloupe. He tried to buy out his and his cousin's commissions. He even hunted down two replacements who were highly recommended by several merchants in Newport, among them, Nathaniel Appleton.

But Jack was obdurate. Rob and Jason had signed on with him and they would work out their contract, come hell or high water.

"He was used to getting his own way. And he thought Jason was faking his illness to get out of hard work," Rob said. "He'd had too many others pull the same trick. This time, however, the whole crew knew it wasn't a trick. To a man, they liked Jason and they knew how hard you'd worked to pull him through his ordeal. Hell . . . Jack wouldn't have had Jason at all if it wasn't for you."

"And Hopeful," Emily said.

Rob grinned. "And Rebeccah, too."

"What Rob isn't saying, Emily," Jason said, "is that the crew hated Donahue and followed his orders only as long as Rob approved of them. It was Rob they respected. And Rob they thought of as their leader. When they discovered that Jack was willing to sacrifice my life for naught but his own pride and stubbornness, Jack Donahue found himself facing a furious band of men."

"But," Rob continued, "Jack had made a monumental mistake; and he knew it almost immediately. That's when fear took over. And a fearful captain is a careless captain."

"Aye," Jason said. "Now he had real trouble and it was the kind that wouldn't go away unless he did something drastic. I think he believed that if he didn't show the crew who was really the authority on his ship that he'd be facing the plank as soon as *Calumet* got a good league out to sea." Jason gulped. "I hate to say it, but he might not have been too far wrong—the men were that furious."

Emily swallowed her last bite of lobster and wiped her hands. "Which was when he had you arrested?"

"Aye," Rob said. "For conspiracy to foment mutiny, according to Donahue."

Jason picked up the empty shells, dropped them into the bucket and excused himself. He walked a good way down the beach and sat on the sand just at the water's edge. Over and over he lobbed the shells into the water, skimming them along the surface . . . four . . . five . . . six times. Emily knew he was remembering the horror of it all, just the way Rob remembered as he told her the rest of the story.

"I'd done nothing, Em. Nothing. *Calumet* was still in port. The crew were still repairing her and stowing the supplies. I still supervised the work.

And Jason still thrashed all day in sick bay. Where the hell was the mutiny?"

Where indeed?

Rob sighed and looked toward the horizon, where shadows darkened the outline of the mainland. Emily took his hand and held it in a gesture of friendship that wasn't enough, but would have to do.

Rob held tight to Emily's hand, tucked his arm around her and drew her head into the crook of his shoulder and neck. She knew he liked having her there, where, as he had told her, the sweet scent of her filled his nostrils. The story he told made Emily realize those were days he would not long forget. Surprised, she was, to hear his words laced with sadness—and that underlying anger he always showed when discussing Jack Donahue.

"I'd sailed with Jack for three years. He knew me. He knew the kind of man I was. Hell, he'd given me my officer's rank. And suddenly, because I wanted to protect my cousin, it meant nothing."

Rob was aboard ship, deep in the hold, supervising the last stowing away of the merchandise Jack was to carry to Guadeloupe when there was a tramp-tramp-tramp overhead.

"Tell them to hold it down." he ordered Jop Jefferson, Calumet's *man-o-work. "Every damn sound echoes like thunder down here."*

But the tramp-tramp-tramp got closer and Rob whipped around to yell his orders through a speaking trumpet. When his eyes caught sight of Jack Donahue and behind him the red-coated King's mi-

litia, with their insignia of rank around their necks, he was caught up short.

"Aye?" he said.

"Robert William Sears?"

"Aye, that's me."

Too late, he saw the fear in Jop's eyes and the triumphant gleam in Jack Donahue's. Instinctively Rob's hand went for his sword; but the captain of guards had his own out and at Rob's neck before Rob's sword drew an inch away from its scabbard.

"Your captain has issued a warrant for your arrest, sir."

The captain of guards waved his hand and the sergeant at arms unrolled a parchment and read from it. "Whereas this eighteenth day of October, in the year of our Lord seventeen-sixty-seven, Captain Jack Donahue of the sloop Calumet *has heretofore accused his second mate Robert William Sears of conspiracy to foment mutiny . . ."*

"Wot?"

"He never!"

Drawn swords and cocked pistols cut short the crew's indignant voices.

". . . such charge being a seditious act against the Crown, the Crown hereby orders Robert William Sears to be taken into custody. He will be held at the county gaol in the settlement of Newport in the colony of Rhode Island and Providence Plantations. Trial will be set. All persons having evidence to give will be called to come forward. Signed and sealed

this day by Horatio Paley, justice of the King's Court."

"Robert William Sears, I am here to carry out the orders of the court," the captain of guards said. "You will surrender your sword and pistols."

Rob wanted to say, There has been some mistake, but he knew it was useless. Once an arrest order was given, it would not be taken back—not in those days, when "seditious acts against the Crown" meant little more than stealing a chicken or simply delivering broadsides that dared to mention the hated British taxes. Everyone knew about young newsboys, their arms still wrapped around the editions they'd been trying to hawk, who were dragged through the streets to gaol.

Fury began to build inside Rob, a fury he never knew he possessed. "What of my cousin?" he asked Jack Donahue.

The captain of guards answered for him. "He's been charged, too, sir. He will be coming with you."

"For God's sake, man, he's ill, possibly dying!"

"Sir, we know that."

Rob's head snapped up and he looked the captain of guards in the eye. The man's tone had showed regret. His expressive green eyes showed something more: a deep embarrassment and anger that he had been chosen for such a distasteful task.

Rob gave him a short nod, acknowledging his feelings and asked, "Will I be allowed to retrieve my ditty bag?"

"Sir, you will not." The captain of guards stepped

back and two men came forward with leg and wrist irons.

"That won't be necessary," Rob said. "I will go with you willingly."

"Sir, the court so orders it in matters of this kind. I deeply regret it, sir."

As the wrist and leg irons were being screwed tight, Rob sought out his captain. Jack tried to avoid Rob's eyes, but the angry muttering of the crew gave him nowhere else to look. His head came up and he gasped. Rob stared him down, stared long and hard, until he sputtered, turned on his heel and made for the foreward ladder, tripping over almost everything in his path as he went.

"On the ship, Emily," Rob said, remembering. "On my ship. Leg and wrist irons! In front of my men!"

"Oh, Rob, I'm so sorry."

It had been bad, that. Having his men see him shackled was, perhaps, the worst experience of his life. But he was wrong. The worst experience was seeing Jason with his wrists and legs in iron, lashed down on a pallet.

"God's blood," he'd cried to the captain of guards. "You already have him lashed down. Where can he go? Take those irons off him, I beg you."

"Sir, I must not or I will answer for it."

"It's a sorry day for King George when he has to manacle a sick man who could not move if he willed it."

The walk to the gaol was long and hot, the hill

steep. Normally, there would have been jeering men and women. Jack seemed at a loss that the populace who came to watch the procession were quiet and respectful. Some women cried into their hands. Men removed their cocked hats. A few saluted Rob and Jason. As they got closer to the gaol, Rob spied the reason for this uncharacteristic show of respect: merchants under whose banner he'd sailed were lined up at the steps of the gaol. Each wore a red and blue ribbon on their watch chains, the ribbon Rob knew denoted them as part of the band that had burned the British naval vessel Maidstone in 1765. Sorrel and Appleton. Latour and Pavette. Duncan and Raleigh.

"They made that horrible walk bearable, Emily—*until* I saw the small figure in front of Nathaniel Appleton."

Rob had wanted to kill Jack Donahue, then. Wanted to strangle him with his bare hands.

"My sister . . . I can't forgive Jack for letting her see that, Em. I never will."

"Your sister?"

"Betsy. She'd come to Newport to visit Janet Appleton, a classmate from Mrs. Tysdale's Academy."

There Betsy had stood, a young girl dressed in flowered dimity with her long flaming red hair caught back in a blue ribbon. Tears streamed down her face but she smiled bravely as she blew a kiss to her brother and cousin.

They were in that gaol for three days before a doctor was called in to look Jason over. As soon as he did, Jedediah Montague demanded that Jason be removed to his house for treatment.

"Jedediah Montague." Rob chuckled. "Not only was his name a mouthful. So was he. He was as wide as he was tall, with big bushy eyebrows and a bald pate. But he was respected in the town. And his word had weight because of the people he knew. Em, he was physician to the governor, the crown minister, the chief officer at the garrison, every French merchant, and most legislators. Their wives and children, too. He gave testimony at the trial."

The trial.

Revelation was more like it. Of course Rob knew his crew would stand behind him. But he hadn't known he had so many friends in the small merchant settlement who would also give evidence. Newporters of note came; but so did legislators from Providence. Paines were there. As were Whipples and Browns and Lymans and Hazards. And from Shawomet came Greenes and descendants of Samuel Gorton, a compatriot of Roger Williams and perhaps an ancestor of Emily. To a man they gave testimony, affirming their belief that a man of such character and reputation would never disobey an order of his captain. But Nathaniel Greene was the most eloquent. A captain of his own vessel, he sneered at Jack Donahue as he spoke to the justices.

"Fomenting mutiny? A boy who could not move because he burned with fever? A second mate who kept order better than most captains? Absurd!

"Justices, the one who should be on trial here is the man who brought charges! I cannot even speak his name, it burns so in my gullet. He tarnishes his rank. And when he does not take into consideration the health and welfare of his crew, he gives a bad smell to all of us who carry the respected title, Captain.

"Sirs, were I, or any of my fellow Rhode Island captains, faced with such a problem as Robert Sears has presented, I . . . we . . . would, of course, have allowed the cousins to buy back their commissions. That, sirs, is the humane thing to do. But Jack Donahue knows nothing of humanity. By this damnable act, he shows himself to be unworthy of carrying bills of lading from any merchant in these waters."

Rob later learned that Jack's strangled cry could be heard by all, even those out on the lawn who could not get seats in the courthouse. Jack saw his future, and it was bleak. Nathaniel Greene had all but told him that all those wonderful bills of lading and his letters of marque to board ships and confiscate their goods would stop because of the action he had brought against Robert and Jason. He slumped in his seat, a defeated man.

"And you were acquitted," Emily said, linking her arms through Rob's and Jason's as they trudged up the hill away from the beach.

"Four months later," Jason said bitterly.

"But we didn't do so bad. We had invitations from all the best families in Newport. Nathaniel

Appleton insisted that since Betsy was already a guest in his house it was only right and proper that we accept his hospitality, too. So, we put up with him until we could find another commission."

Rob laughed. "Old Nathaniel was a wily fox. He wasn't merely being hospitable. He'd been a widower for a year and it was chaffing him. We soon found out that he wanted us under his roof because he was trying to convince Betsy to accept his proposal of marriage. Guess he figured if we were to hand and approved, she could do naught else but accept."

"And then she up and ran off with Lyle Latour, the son of an old friend of Rob's father and Nathaniel's best friend, one of the men who'd given evidence." Jason doubled over with laughter. "Ah, Em, you should have seen Nathaniel! For a week, first he harumphed about ungrateful young wenches who didn't know a good thing when they saw it; and then he muttered about being stabbed in the back by friends and those who should have been more grateful for his help. We ignored his barbs the best we could until we could secure new commissions. But then he began calling on Letitia Banbridge and their banns were announced. Our commissions came in, Nathaniel's wedding took place, and that was that."

But *that* was now standing on the deck of the gunboat *Cardiz* and Emily didn't like the looks of him. "What's he doing there with the British, Jason? Is he a sympathizer?"

"Not according to Newport gossip. He's supposed to be a member of the new secret organization called The Sons of Liberty, not the crown sympathizers' Newport Junto."

Suddenly, Emily said, "I want to go over there, Jason."

"Whatever for?"

"Look around you. There's wounded enough to choke the Atlantic. American and British. I want to make sure Rob lets me have the time to doctor them all."

"*All?* But, Em . . . that's the enemy."

"Not when they're wounded, they're not. They're patients."

Jason sighed. He'd seen that stubborn set to Emily's jaw before, in his sick room. He'd been glad, then, that she was as headstrong as his cousin. But now, he wondered how much trouble she'd get him in. He supposed if he didn't take her across to the negotiations, she'd go herself.

"Damned if I do and damned if I don't."

"Aye, Jason."

So, she could read his mind. Well, not all of it or she'd be as worried as he. Jason was just as anxious to get aboard the *Cardiz* as Emily. He wanted to know exactly what Nathaniel was doing in the company of a captain of a British warship, chasing down a licensed privateer, instead of helping out the Sons of Liberty back in Newport where he belonged. After all, the British might denounce Rob, or think him part of the conspiracy to burn the

Gaspee, but Nathaniel knew Rob carried letters of Marque from the Rhode Island governor, and a commission to ply the trade route from Narragansett Bay to Baltimore, Annapolis, Savannah, Guadeloupe, and the Mediterranean.

Before they could traverse the raging sea to the gunboat, however, Rob, his officers, and all the British officers came back to *Patriot.* Jason was amazed and proud of what Rob did next. He ordered some of his crew to help the British rig a double sail into a canvas sling and position it by ropes under the keel of the gunboat to cover up the hole in its side. Jason knew that as soon as the canvas became saturated, it would become almost watertight. Rob might not be able to stop the leak, but he could reduce it enough to get the *Cardiz* into port where permanent repairs could be made. Not many captains would have been that generous with any enemy, never mind one who was bombarding them for no reason.

As they headed to the ladder leading to the officer's boardroom, Rob, Nathaniel, Captain Donald Douglass, and the officers passed Emily and Jason. Rob's eyes flicked over Emily, but he gave no indication that she was anything more than one of his crew.

However, he couldn't ignore her when she blustered her way into the boardroom and sat at the table with the rest of the officers.

"Get below, doctor. The men need you."

"As soon as you agree to let me treat all

the wounded, including the British, I'll go."

Nathaniel and Captain Douglass leaned over the table and examined the man who had a woman's voice—and an imperious one, at that.

"Who do we have here, Captain Sears?" Captain Douglass asked.

Rob scowled; but when Emily dropped her pistol and sword on the table, crossed her arms over her chest and glared, he gave in. "Captain Douglass, may I introduce my ship's surgeon, Emily Gorton."

"Ah," Captain Douglass said. "I've heard of you, young lady. Your reputation among New England crews is legendary."

"Thank you, sire." She turned to Rob. "As you said, the men need me. Will you allow me to treat all the wounded or are you going to be pigheaded?"

"You may treat all the wounded," Rob said.

"Then I want to set up my surgery on the deck of the gunboat, where I'll have good air and plenty of cold sea water to clean out the wounds. The British can be billeted on deck or in the gunboat's sick bay and we can bring our own crew here to the *Patriot*'s quarters."

"We have to get the *Cardiz* to port for repairs as soon as possible," Captain Douglass said.

"What I propose shouldn't stop you, Captain." Looking to Rob so only he saw the pleading expression on her face, she asked, "Well?"

"You have your hospital ship, Emily."

Chapter Twelve

Emily might have her hospital ship but Jason had a problem only he and two others seemed to believe *was* a problem.

Rob had accepted Nathaniel Appleton's explanation that he was merely playing the part of a loyal Tory, while in *actuality* he was a spy for the Sons of Liberty; but Jason did not. He was afraid his cousin had too much else on his mind—Emily, the repairs that had to be made to *Patriot,* the prisoners they now had on their hands, and the danger that still lay out there on the sea. It was a danger called the British fleet . . . which could come creeping up on them in the dead of night or the morning fog. Rob, Jason feared, was too preoccupied to give heed to the underlying tone of Nathaniel's remarks.

Unctuous, they had been. Too silky smooth . . . as if they had been rehearsed for just such an occasion.

Jason remembered many times in Newport when he had chanced upon Nathaniel rehearsing what he wanted to say to Betsy. By the time Nathaniel actually spoke to Betsy, what he said and how he said it were letter perfect. As letter perfect as the things he said to Rob after the British officers had been dismissed and put under guard on deck.

In the boardroom, Nathaniel had unbuttoned his vest and waved a lace edged handkerchief toward one of Rob's officers, bo'sun Harry Lott. "Pour me a good measure of rum punch, my man. And mind you don't spill any." He reached out and took up a bone pipe wound round with blue cord and decorated with finely tied knots. He looked at it, blew on the opening a few times, then sniffed. When Harry Lott put the filled mug of spicy punch in front of Nathaniel, Nathaniel gave the pipe to the bo'sun and commanded, "Fill this and light it for me, too, while you're up."

He leaned back against a cannon that had permanent home in the middle of the boardroom, and gulped a healthy draught. "Yes, sir," he said, "this spy business is exciting. Although . . . for a time there, Rob, I thought I'd lose my head because of your bombardment. Why, that cannon ball came near to taking off my left ear." He patted his head and sent a fine mist of powder into the air. "The smoke and concussion blew off my wig."

Rob's attention wasn't on Nathaniel until he heard the damnable word *spy*. "Now here's something I need to know, Nathaniel. How in the hell did you expect to do any spying if you were stuck on a British gunboat?"

"Ah . . . but that's the best place for it, don't you see? I hear things. Things about the merchants they're investigating. Which ones will be trailed to be sure they aren't running illegal cargo. Who is to be brought up for seditious acts. All kinds of things. And as soon as I put into Newport I hurry home, contact my friends, and warn them." He accepted the lit pipe with a sniff at the tobacco to see if it suited. Although his nose wrinkled up, he puffed on it for a moment before waving bo'sun Lott away. "Rob, you do see my position, don't you?"

"I've known other men who have done something similar, so it sounds reasonable," Rob said, distracted by a thundering noise above his head. "Well, what are you going to do now? Will you go with Captain Douglass to repair the *Cardiz?*"

Nathaniel puffed out his chest as he puffed on the pipe. "I think not. Because Captain Douglass knows that you and I are good friends, my position may already be too much compromised. Might be best if I remain on *Patriot* until you dock someplace and I can get a ride on a friend's ship heading back to Newport. You *will* be putting into port soon, won't you?"

"Baltimore is our next port of call. Then possibly Savannah and finally Guadaloupe." Rob stared at the beams over his head. Things rumbled. Something heavy dropped with a crash. A man cursed and another shouted, *Look out!* "God's blood, Jason, what is going on up there?"

"Emily, I fear," Jason said. "I heard her give orders to Jop to bring barrels and boards over to the *Cardiz.*"

"Don't they have enough of their own?"

Jason grimaced. "You know Emily. She has her own reasons for everything she does."

"A fine looking woman," Nathaniel said, his head bent over his mug of rum but his eye on a distracted Rob. "Can't hide a figure like hers beneath seamen's clothes, eh, Rob?"

"No. Yes. Uh . . . excuse me, gentlemen."

As soon as Rob clomped out of the boardroom and up the ladder, Nathaniel laughed. "Yes, sir, a fine looking woman. Met her once when she was coming out of the friendly house on Block Island, though she probably doesn't recall. Seemed to be on more than speaking terms with the madam there . . . What was her name? Ah, yes. Rebeccah Washington. She ran a good house, did Rebeccah. Had some of the best looking harlots this side of the Atlantic. And her friend, the 'doctor,' seems to have our captain in a whirlwind. Mayhap he's having it on with her, eh? She'd be a right good piece of skirt, she would, seeing as how she knows so much about the workings of a man's body. No wonder our Rob can't keep his mind on the matters before us."

Jason stood up and stared Nathaniel down. "Sir, no gentleman would speak in that way of a lady who is unknown to him. Emily Gorton is a good woman, a friend and, for now, the ship's surgeon. She's also the only woman on board. Naturally Captain Sears is concerned for her safety. In these awful days we never know what man or woman to count as friend. Why, even Emily might hide the heart of a traitor beneath her surgeon's apron . . . but of course she doesn't. Or it might be Almanzo, here. Some first mates have been known to want their captain dead so's to step into his place . . . but of course he doesn't. Or it could even be you, Nathaniel, though you've known Rob and me for years . . . you could actually be traitor instead of spy . . . but of course you aren't."

"Well, I never! Course I'm no traitor. I've my family, business, and reputation to think about."

"Aye. Then think about them and not about the woman over your head." He called for the steward, who was helping prepare a meal for the officers. "Take Mr. Appleton to our officers' quarters and give him bedding, a wash basin, soap and towel. He'll take Cutter Hobbs's billet, since it's empty."

When Nathaniel rose, Jason warned, "I'd keep below deck if I were you, squire. There's those among the crew who consider you part of the enemy's contingent just because they saw you with the red coats. They're simple men, not used to the subtleties and intricacies of the job you do. They might get it into their heads that you're a danger to them. And in their minds a dead man can have no misguided loyalties to worry them, don't you know?"

"What are you implying, Broadbent?"

"What I'm saying, squire, is that you wouldn't want any *accidents* to happen, would you?"

Nathaniel's eyes skittered to the deadly pistol and short sword which Emily had discarded. His hand twitched, but he made no move to pick them up. His eyes, however, gleamed with fury. "Accidents. Yes, I see."

"I hope so, sir." Jason smiled and picked up Emily's weapons. He tucked them into his belt. "You'll be very comfortable in the officers' quarters. If you need something, seaman Jop will be right outside your door, available to you at all times."

"You're posting a guard on me, then?"

"Well, only for a short time. It's those accidents, sir. Best we don't take chances."

Nathaniel gave Jason a steely glare before he accompanied the young steward from the boardroom. Immediately, Jason dismissed all save Almanzo Peters and Orrin Mayotte.

Jason liked Almanzo and Orrin. Though entirely different in temperament and physical makeup, they were enough alike to make them representative of the breed of men newly called American.

Both had been born in England. Both their families had emigrated for economic reasons—because they believed they could advance in society in the colonies, where a man's worth was judged by what he did rather than to whom he was born.

Jason was especially fond of Almanzo. He was nominal head of the crew as first mate, but often deferred to Jason. Almanzo knew and respected the fact that the good fellowship which existed on *Patriot* came before petty bickering about who had precedence over whom. Besides, none would ever argue Almanzo's place. Though he was short and appeared to be stout, the man's body was as rock solid as the pig iron from which the cannon were made. Older than Rob by five years, he had been a blacksmith for fifteen years in Brixton, near the King's military prison. After he emigrated to America, he discovered that men with his skills were needed on privateers and that a good share of a year's voyages was more than thrice what he could earn as a farrier.

As soon as he signed on for his first voyage he discovered something that shocked him as much as it would have shocked the King: Almanzo Peters was a leader. Day to day, he was meek and mild, yet with an air about him that led better-born men to listen when he talked, and do what he bid. Five years fore the mast he rose quickly from armorer to master's mate. Four years aft the mast—as master and second mate—he led sorties or raids on enemy emplacements and managed to keep all his hands in one piece. But he was most indispensable when the crew found itself in a sea battle. From years of hauling and beating pig iron, his fists were almost as large as hams and had pounded many an unwary foe into unconsciousness during a boarding. Then, he was the bulwark behind which lesser men could find refuge.

But he had a softer side to him. He was also the best carver on board; and could produce the most delicate pins and beads by scratching tiny designs into carved bone and sea shells, then darkening the designs with lamp black. His purse jingled with the coppers he acquired from those crew members who wanted a memento to take home to wife or lover.

On the other hand, Orrin Mayotte, the third son of a Liverpool tavern keeper, was tall and thin and looked as if a gentle breeze would blow him over. He wasn't a crack shot, but was a good fighter. He was known up and down the trade route for the skinning knife he carried strapped to his calf—it was notched in five places, for the officers he'd personally killed in battle.

But his rock solid usefulness aboard a ship came

from something far more important than fighting skills.

From an avid childhood interest in the stars, he had chosen his profession. Books had begun his education. Apprenticeship to scores of sailing masters had honed it until his navigational skills were better than Rob's. He had quickly become *Patriot's* sailing master. During fog or storms, when other men saw naught but greyness, he seemed to have a sixth sense that told them where they were and how to get where they were headed.

After the lesser ranked *Patriot* officers had gone, but a minute passed when Almanzo slammed his fist on the table and hissed at Jason, "Slur me as traitor, dare ye, Jason?"

"Nay, Almanzo. I was but giving examples . . . and a little warning to the good squire Appleton. I'm not sure I believe his story. And I don't like the way he looked at Emily, or the way he judged her character. She's no doxy and I won't have anyone think she is."

"Aye," Orrin said. " 'e's slipp'ry, 'e is. D'ye note 'ow 'e talked wi'out lookin' ta the captain, 'cept for that sly peek from under 'is powdered curls? Been too many men on ships oy've sailed 'ad that look. Nay good's come from 'avin' 'em, ayther."

"And how he ordered the bo'sun around, as if he were the captain," Almanzo said. "Ye were right to post a guard on em, Jason. Old Harry looked like he'd be glad to slit the silly fop's throat. Don't think Harry's ever been ordered to start up a pipe for a body before—especially when it was *his* pipe!"

The men laughed.

"Funny, it is," Jason said. "But it's also deadly serious to have tension aboard ship."

"Aye," Almanzo said. He and the other two knew that on board a privateer, where officers and crew were from every rank in society and the crew shares in the profits, good fellowship was the order of the day. "Throw one rotten apple into this bunch—a body like that Appleton, who thinks every seaman, including us officers, are servants fit to do his bidding—and there's sure to be grumblings."

"And where you have grumblings, you're bound to have harsh words," Jason said.

"Fist foights," Orrin added. "Or knife foights. En we all know wot that means! The lash!"

Jason sighed. Orrin was right. If the crew couldn't get along, Rob would have to step in quickly to set the ship back in order.

"It's the lady what will give the most problems, if the silly fop's words give hint to his attitude," Almanzo said. "Every ship I've sailed has had women aboard. Captain's wives and daughters, mostly. Some female tars. Rare, it is, when it turns ugly. But with a man like that . . . who already sees Doctor Gorton as only a nice piece of skirt . . . well, if there's to be trouble it might come from that direction."

" 'e's roight. A cur sniffin' a'ter a bitch . . . Beg pardon, Jason. I know she's a lady. But on the *Wintersong* women aboard led to mutiny."

"Ah," Almanzo growled. "That were different. That were three women, all of them doxies, being transferred to new friendly houses. Every manjack wanted a piece of them. But their protector, that

Sheffield scum from the Naples group, wanted too high a price."

"I don't care the reason," Jason said. "I will not let anything cause grumblings among the crew or change the running of this ship. Are you with me?"

"Wot you want us to do," Orrin asked.

"I want the silly fop, as Almanzo calls him, under observation on every watch. I'll keep him below deck for the night. But Rob's going to want an explanation if Nathaniel is locked up tomorrow. I don't want to burden him with this. He has enough to do to get us out of this mess and safely into our next port. So, we have to divide up the day and night and put men near Nathaniel whom we can trust."

"There's not a manjack aboard we can't trust," Almanzo said.

"Let's hope so."

With Rob and Captain Douglass at her side, Emily inspected the carnage the two men had managed to inflict. The empty barrels and boards she had ordered onto the *Cardiz* were turned into waist high pallets. Twenty of them were jammed on the quarterdeck. Twenty more on the fore deck. Each supported a dreadfully wounded man in need of surgery. Those who had mere flesh wounds or lacerations were housed below, where they were being washed down and readied for needle and thread or simple poultices.

"I hope you have a ship's surgeon aboard, Captain Douglass," she said. "Without help, it will be impossible for me to save them all."

"I've a young whelp who's just finished his apprenticeship. He could assist you."

Emily looked over the toughest assignment she'd ever had and shook her head. "Send him below deck with two men Jason chooses. He probably knows enough to do simple doctoring. When he's finished, he can come and assist. But Jason's the best on board, Rob. I'll need him and three others."

"Whatever you need, Emily, you shall have."

"Before it sinks, I want all the medicine on the cutter brought over here to the *Cardiz.* And, of course, I'll need access to your stores, Captain Douglass. I promise not to use more than is absolutely necessary."

"If you send someone to the cutter, Captain Sears, he will find the medicine chest in the first mate's cabin," Captain Douglass said.

Emily had one last order. "It's almost noon. I want sails rigged to keep the sun off the patients. The last thing I need is for them to get sunstroke! And tow that cutter away from here. When she goes down, the force of the swell will put my patients in jeopardy."

"Would you like to captain *Patriot,* Em?" Rob teased.

"With all I have to do? Don't be daft!"

Laughter brought enemies closer and when the captains left Emily to carry out her bidding, they were chatting about the problems that faced them both.

As *Patriot* towed the fast-sinking cutter away and sailed back to anchor next to the *Cardiz,* for the next three hours Emily, Jason, and their assistants never left the quarterdeck. They soon ran out of vinegar and had to use sea water to clean the wounds. It stung worse than the vinegar but she knew the salt in it would help close up the kind of tear a bullet or shot made, where plain water would not. Every so often Jason ran below to check on the progress of the British assistant, Hapgood Lawson. Thrice Jason came back cursing the stupidity of men who still insisted on bloodletting for cure.

Just as Rob re-boarded the *Cardiz,* Emily took Captain Douglass aside and demanded that Hapgood Lawson stop the abominable practice. "Your men have already lost enough blood, Captain. Whatever humors Dr. Lawson thinks need to be loosed have been loosed during the fracas. Now they need simple suturing and clean bandaging. If he can't handle that, I'll have Jason do it."

Donald Douglass was not the only one to feel Emily's wrath. She fairly screamed at the cooks, who had brought steaming pots of pork stew on deck to be served to the patients. "Gruel, that's what they need! Oatmeal gruel. And chicken soup."

"Em," Rob said, trying to be patient, "we have no chickens. We've only salted beef and pork and great chunks of ham."

"Set the men to fish, then. Cod and tuna . . . anything they can get. It's better than that damnable mess of potage you're trying to force down their throats. For now, just bring kettles of tea, sifted loaf sugar and hardtack. I'll show the men what to do with them."

Rob took Emily to the aft rail on the port side, away from prying ears. He brushed back some wispy curls that had escaped her plaits and held her hands.

Just that small contact sent such heat through him that his voice cracked when he spoke.

"Emily, love . . . we can't stay here forever! The *Cardiz* has to get to port to be repaired. And we have to get the hell out of here before other patrol boats find us and blow us to bits."

"Just two days, Rob. I can save them all if I have two days."

"Impossible. It's too risky, Em."

"Overnight, then. And under half sail for two days?" She searched his eyes, pleading without putting her plea into words. But he looked so stubborn that she sighed and leaned against him. "Don't make me an undertaker, Rob. I don't want to see any of these men slipped over the side to a watery grave."

His breath fanned her hair and he encircled her with his arms. Her body felt so frail underneath his shirt and trousers. It was hard to believe that she was almost as tough as the men. In fact, it was impossible.

"Em, I'll give you overnight. But I want you to promise me something."

"It feels so good with you holding me up that I'd almost promise you anything . . ."

"I want you in my bed tonight."

Her breath caught and her heart thudded. "Rob . . . the patients."

"You need sleep, too."

"If I come to your bed, I won't get much sleep."

"Emily, I need you. I just fought a fierce battle. Men died. Good men. I need to hold you, make love to you. I need to blot out the screams with that delicious little sound you make when my fingers brush against you . . ." He brought his hand down to span her waist and sighed. "It's there, Em . . . down where my thumbs are . . . in that spot that's covered by the laces of my trousers. Remember the feeling? Remember?"

"Yes," she said brokenly. "It was . . ." She blushed and turned her head. "My patients . . ."

"God's blood, Em, don't use them as an excuse. After this day, you will need me as much as I need you."

Emily squirmed in his arms and buried her face against his shoulder. "All right. Yes. But, Rob . . . you can't touch me like this. Everyone can see . . ."

"Let them see. Let them know that I love you." Rob took one of the plaits in his hand and rubbed it with his fingers. It looked so sturdy, the softness astounded him. "Tonight we stay at anchor. Tonight we come together. If you're not in my cabin by three bells into the night watch, I'll come and get you."

She smiled at him and Rob thought the sun had come back to full measure. God, how he loved her!

"That won't be necessary, Captain. I need to blot out the screams, too. I can't think of a better place to do it than in your arms."

After Emily left him, Rob stayed at the rail, looking off toward the horizon. He couldn't turn immediately. His arousal would be too obvious. But the solitude afforded him a moment to think about what Emily was asking.

Douglass would take his gunboat and men now, if Rob would permit him leave. What Emily was asking, however, would expose *Patriot* to patrols—although they were far enough away from the ordinary patrol routes to be relatively safe. What he feared was a solitary British ship stumbling on them when they had their sails down. If that happened, they were vulnerable to attack because they wouldn't be able to maneuver at all until they got every sail hoisted.

And she had some of them as sun shades over the patients! Folly. Damned folly. Luckily, before he'd sunk her, he'd thought to take all the sails from the cutter that were still fairly intact. He had had his crew replace *Patriot's* sun shade sails with those from the cutter. Then the crew had stowed all that was left in the head, the only place that wasn't already being used. That way, he'd have the canvas ready to hand if anything untoward happened. And if *Cardiz* managed to get into port quickly and sent out another gunboat or three . . . it wouldn't matter a damn to him. The only thing that mattered was that Emily and *Patriot* survived.

It had been easier with Cutter Hobbs as ship's surgeon. Love wasn't involved, only duty and responsibility.

Rob shivered and his shoulders slumped. He hated the realization that crept into his thoughts; but it wouldn't leave.

Love wasn't involved for Emily.

Duty, aye. Responsibility for injured man or beast, since she'd been suckled. But love was a foreign word to her, one that had no correlation to what they'd done fourteen hours ago, and what he was planning to do in six more.

"How am I going to show her? How the hell am I going to show her?"

He felt a hand on his shoulder and didn't have to turn to know it was Jason.

"If the men hear you they'll be thinking you're seeing sea witches, cousin," Jason warned.

"If it were only sea witches, I wouldn't be talking to myself."

"Emily Gorton does that to all of us, Rob. But you'll tame her in the end. I've a silver sovereign under the mainmast to insure your success."

"That's for a successful voyage and a harbor filled with prizes."

"The first one, aye. But as soon as I saw the figurehead on this ship—that finely chiseled woman's head with golden braids and an Indian mantle—I decided you needed one more silver sovereign to convince the lady." He and Rob watched the sea darken before Jason said, "You know, I have never understood why you didn't name the vessel the *Emily.*"

"She would have had my liver for breakfast."

"She might, yet, cousin. She might, yet."

But Rob's liver wasn't what Emily had in mind when hours later she stumbled down to his empty cabin, to find it lit by three lanterns and smelling of lilacs. A wooden tub filled with hot soapy water sat square in the middle of the small space between bed and sea chests. Large Turkish towels were piled next to the tub. And wonder of wonders a scrub brush with a handle long enough to reach down her back!

Quickly, she stripped her dirty clothes off and

slipped into the hot water. Small slivers of soap bobbed up to the top as she settled herself against the sides of the tub. She grabbed a handful and lathered it in her hands until dozens of tiny bubbles broke away and floated up to tickle her nose. So that was where the lilac scent came from! French lilac soap. She had heard of it from Rebeccah. The women in the friendly house had gotten it as gifts from their admirers. Had Rob put them in her bath because he considered her like those women?

No . . . That was laughable. She would never be as free and easy in bed as she imagined they were. She was too aware of herself as unfeminine.

Yet Rob seemed to like her . . . and the things she'd done . . . they had done . . . Ah! What they had done.

Her eyes sought out Rob's bed, the place of such mysterious and wonderful feelings. There, they had explored each other's bodies. Not in a clinical way, though she had been as curious about Rob as she'd ever been about any of her patients. But for once, Emily had left the doctor part of her outside the bed and allowed herself to be what she thought Rob expected. And what she quickly realized she wanted to be.

No, she had not touched him in that clinical way that was expected of a doctor. She had touched him . . . he had touched her . . . with a hot rush of feelings. That was the difference.

Smiling happily, anticipating another exploration into worlds long denied her, she lathered every part of her and rinsed herself. As she stepped out of the tub, she wrapped one Turkish towel around herself and dried herself with another one. Then she knelt down, pulled her hair out of its braids, scooped up some more of the soap slivers, and washed and rinsed her hair three times until it squeaked. She would have braided it back again but decided it would dry quicker if she let it hang free. But when she drew her fingers through it, it felt so tangled she picked up Rob's comb and worked on her hair until she could draw the comb through without tugging.

Both towels were wet, so she draped them carefully over the chest in the corner. Chilled, she pulled down the quilt and winding sheet and discovered that a delicately embroidered nightshift had been folded on top of the pillow. She picked it up and let the hem drift down. It was softer than anything she'd ever slept in. It felt like liquid in her fingers, and shimmered in the lantern light. Tiny pink and green rosebuds covered the entire bodice—which had a low neckline—and several were embroidered here and there on the gathered skirt. There were no sleeves, just two inches of green lace to finish off the neck and the holes for her arms.

She ran her hands over it. It seemed a shame to wear something so beautiful to bed. But Rob had put it there for her. She couldn't disappoint him by refusing a gift, the like of which she'd never received.

When she slipped it over her head, she wished there were a large mirror in the room. Without one, she could only guess what a dress that hugged her breasts and waist and clung to her legs would make her look like.

She already knew what it made her feel like: A fairy princess. Tottel's Pygmalion. Snow White. No, the pricked fingers of her childhood made her closer to Rose Red.

Whatever . . . she felt beautiful, even if she couldn't see if it were so.

As she blew out two of the lanterns, leaving only the one next to the bed lit, she smiled toward the door and whispered, "Thank you, Rob. After this day, I needed all of what you gave me."

Rob was expecting her to wait for him. But she was so tired . . . just a short rest and she'd be ready for . . . for anything!

She eased herself into the box-like bed and stretched out, closing her eyes for naught but a moment.

Chapter Thirteen

When Rob closed the door to his cabin, the first thing he saw was spun gold cascading in tiny ripples down the side of his bed. He crossed and knelt. First, he merely reached out and allowed his fingertips to learn the texture of Emily's unplaited hair. It amazed him, the way the braids had made it dip and curve into generous waves. Then, his palm stroked the softness that rivaled the silk of the Orient, the satin of France, and the sable of Russia.

Pirates would have burned an arsenal of ships for less than this.

His heart hammered so hard he felt it in his throat and temples. It was beauty. More beauty than had ever invaded his dreams; and he nearly wept because of it.

For a few more minutes he stroked Emily's hair, watched the little changes in her face as she dreamed, and listened to her breathe with the heaviness of sleep. Then he hoisted his weary body up and stripped off his clothes. He tested the water in the tub, to find it cold and unwelcoming. But he had no time to have the tub dragged out, emptied and filled again with hot water. So he retrieved his sandlewood soap, climbed in, held down his shudders, and within minutes had cleaned the grime of battle off his body. A quick rinse of his hair with the soapy water that was left and a dousing in the bucket to remove the residue and he felt a thousand times better. As he stropped his razor and began scraping away at the stubble on his chin, he ruminated that it had been days since Jop had given him the luxury of a good shave. When they were well out of this mess the British had gotten them in, the first thing he'd do—after making love to Emily, of course—was to have Jop trim his hair and give him a leisurely shave.

Before crossing to the bed, he splashed his raw, scraped jaw with a spicy lemon water to close the pores and stop the sting of a dull razor. He smiled at the disorder of his cabin. Emily's clothes. His clothes. All were tossed hither and thither, as if they'd come in together and pulled each garment off the other.

That would have been exciting. But the sight he'd gotten when he came into the cabin was more soul satisfying. As he gathered up the bits and pieces of clothing to toss outside the door, he smiled to himself and his eyes sought her once more.

He had always known Emily was lovely. But it had been more than twelve years since he'd seen her with her hair down. With it spread out like that, her face took on the gentleness of a young girl's. Close to twenty-seven, she was. Yet there was no age in her.

She was as lovely now as she had been at eighteen, when she'd first become Matthew Cox's assistant. Or nineteen, when she'd saved Jason. Or twenty-two, when he had brought a dying Jonathan Hobbs to her and she had cured him. Twenty-two. She had been twenty-two when he had first touched the breasts now hidden by his quilt. More than four years ago.

So many years! So much wasted time!

She should have been his wife long ago. She should have borne his children, suckled them at her breast, tucked them into bed, and then welcomed him nightly into the soft, melting part of herself which he craved.

She should have been safe on shore.

But that was his doing. And hers. Her stubbornness had made her the best doctor on the eastern shore. His need had fueled him until he'd put her in harm's way.

Yet, something good had come of it. She had, at last, let the wall tumble down and become a woman. His woman. And if he had to hog-tie her, someday soon his wife. He hoped.

When he eased into the deep bed next to her, she smiled, sighed, and snuggled her body up to his. He wanted to wake her. God's blood, he *needed* to wake her. His body was burning with a fever that wasn't from sickness but from love. But a gentle shaking didn't rouse her. And whispered words brought naught but a tightening of her arms at his waist. He sighed and settled himself against the outside of the bed, encasing her in a protective cave with his body.

"Sleep, Emily. Sleep, love. We have all the time in the world."

All the time in the world—as long as the night hid them from other British vessels.

Nathaniel Appleton chafed under the guard outside his door. Though the cabin in which he was contained held all the officers' billets, not one man came in to have a word with him. He could hear them outside, though, in the ward room, where they took their meals. The smells floated in to him and he paced up and down, wondering if being under guard meant he was to be denied a ration.

Soon, however, the nigra seaman whom Rob had called Jop brought in a supper tray. Nathaniel sniffed at the spicy contents but didn't see the jug he wanted. "Where's the grog?"

"Mr. Broadbent'll bring it, sah. Mr. Broadbent, he say fa you ta eat hearty en ta ress easy, sah."

Without another word, Jop backed out of the room and shut the door.

Nathaniel sat at the small table to eat, furious that he hadn't been allowed liberties. Accidents, pah! That young cousin of Rob's had some nerve. No crew member would dare attack the person of a merchant such as he. The whole British fleet would be after him if he did. Impressment would follow. Yes, impressment.

He hadn't been aware he spoke until Jason snarled, "Impressment? Are you threatening impressment of this crew, squire?"

Nathaniel sputtered, "No, no, no, Jason. Not at all. I was merely . . . merely remembering the problems of other Rhode Island vessels . . . like the time *Maidstone* came into Newport . . . when was that, now?"

"Seventeen-sixty-five, I believe, squire."

"Yes. And the stupid captain sent a party into port to impress men from other ships to fill *Maidstone's* crew."

"As I recall, the captain got his comeuppance. *Maidstone* was burned by loyal Newporters when he refused the governor's demand to release the men."

"A mob, the British called us."

"You, squire? As I recall, you were in London at the time."

"No, no, no! I had just gotten back . . . yes, just gotten back. And lucky it was, for I was in time to help in the rescue of those poor men. Which is why, you see, you have naught to fear from me, Jason."

"Fear? Why should I fear you, squire? I've a half hundred armed men behind me. You have only yourself."

"Just so. Just so." Nathaniel took a long draught of the ale Jason had brought and wiped the suds off his mouth with the back of his hand. "But staying cooped up here in the bowels of the ship . . . well, I'm not used to it, you see. I need to move about. Go on deck. Exercise my legs. Fill my lungs with good salt air. Surely, you could allow me that privilege?"

God, how he hated the servile tone he had to take with this one-legged fool! More, he hated the man . . . and his cousin. Damn Rob's hide. Nathaniel was sure Rob had conspired to steal contracts from him and others in his circle of friends. Stealing or persuading others to bid lower, it was all the same. How else had a school teacher's son like Rob risen so fast in his field?

Of course, believing Rob had beaten him out in business by underhanded means was pure speculation. But Nathaniel *knew* Rob had scuttled his plans to marry Betsy, allowing that French bastard Latour to make off with her in the dead of night. Right under Nathaniel's nose, too! And after all Nathaniel had done. Giving testimony at the trial. Welcoming Rob into his home. Paying the best doctor on the mainland to treat Jason's illness.

After all that, wasn't he entitled to take that sweet girl to his bed as wife?

Nathaniel's groin still contracted when he thought of Betsy's slim waist and generous breasts. His hands had itched for weeks whenever he thought about touching those . . .

Damned that coquette smile! She was naught but a whore. She had to be. All the while she had been curtsying to him, she had been meeting young Latour in back alleys. And Nathaniel's own daughter Janet, the fool, had lied for Betsy so Betsy could toss her skirts and open her legs for that . . .

Nathaniel choked and Jason thumped him on the back.

"Down the wrong pipe, squire?"

"Wouldn't happen if I had some time on deck," Nathaniel muttered.

"Well, as it happens, squire, Rob said to put a guard on you and let you have the run of the ship until five bells into the night watch."

"What's that in regular time?"

"Ten-thirty, squire. Then your guard will escort you back to this billet."

"Least Rob has *some* sense."

"Aye. More than you think."

Nathaniel finished his ale and stood up. He patted his pockets to be sure everything he wanted was in there, scooped up the bone pipe he'd been using, lit it, and asked, "Who's to be my guard, then? You, Jason?"

"No, squire. I've work to do among the wounded." He opened the door to show Nathaniel an armed Almanzo Peters. "The first mate will be your guide."

Nathaniel made a mock bow and said, "Lead the way."

"Nay, sir. Couldna do that," Almanzo said. "We wouldna want anyone to come from behind and bash your head, now would we, sir? The ladder is just there ahead of you. I'll bring up the rear."

Moonless, the sky appeared to be made up of shifting patterns of blue and black, like that of a quilt which Letitia, Nathaniel's dumpy chit of a wife, had made. The gloom was punctuated with yellowish spots of light thrown out by wooden lanterns which had been lit and hung on the masts and along the side rails. But, Nathaniel was happy to note, they had been spaced too far apart. In between were great chunks of blackness.

Almost immediately after climbing on deck, however, Nathaniel saw he wasn't to be given much room to maneuver. As he'd hoped, Captain Douglass and his officers were also being allowed some liberties—

with guards posted every few feet. Liberty with guards? Pah! Wasn't much liberty at all. Damn Rob! But on thought, this was more that scalawag Broadbent's doings. It had his smell about it.

Jason had made it almost impossible . . .

Nathaniel knew he'd have to be quick as a pickpocket in Derbytown if he wanted the letter he'd written to get into Douglass's hands.

Lucky, that, finding pen and ink and a packet of paper in one of the trunks. Luckier, still, that Jason had been stupid enough to leave him inside, with his guard *outside!* Nathaniel had had plenty of time to pen a missive to Lord Dudley Douglass, the Vice Admiral in Sandy Hook and Captain Donald Douglass's father.

In it, Nathaniel declared his loyalty to King and England, offered to remain aboard the *Patriot,* sabotage it, and keep it foundered until reinforced gunboats could return to take their revenge for Rob's ignominy. In addition, Nathaniel requested that the Vice Admiral lead the gunboats and bring with him Nathaniel's crew (who were in Sandy Hook to sail to London).

In return for his loyalty and the danger he would put himself in, Nathaniel reminded the Admiral of his duty: To have every enemy of King George hanged for treason. Since they were on the high seas, Nathaniel expected to see Rob and Jason and the rest of their ilk hanged from the yardarms. Nathaniel also requested half *Patriot's* cargo. He really wanted it all; but by asking for only half, he thought to ingratiate himself and make the Admiral feel he was within his right to present such a bounty to Nathaniel . . . which, of course, he was. There were three other requests, which Nathaniel expected to get, and he'd fight all the way to the Newport Supreme Court if he were denied them: Captaincy of *Patriot*, letters of marque from the Vice Admiralty so Nathaniel and his crew could ply Robert's trade routes, and the girl doctor.

He hadn't been stupid. His request for Emily Gorton had been couched in such a way that it appeared once he had possession of *Patriot* his greatest need would be a ship's surgeon . . . and with one already to hand . . .

But Nathaniel had other plans for the wench. Warmer plans. Tastier plans. The kinds of plans he'd had for Rob's sister. And they would be all the sweeter being practiced on Rob's mistress.

But he'd get none of what he wanted unless he could get his message to Captain Douglass.

Mmm! Emily smiled. First lilacs. Now sandalwood, cinnamon and lemon. Rob's ship had such interesting scents!

And very interesting bed linens.

Long linens. Hard and sinewy. Hairy linens. Springy and soft. Linens with toes. Linens with knees. Linens with thighs and hips and chest and arms and hands.

Ah . . . such wonderful hands cupping her breasts. Such delightful fingers, teasing her nipples.

"Mmm," she breathed again. "If you're not awake,

Captain Sears, I'm going to wonder about the kinds of dreams you have."

"Interesting ones, Doctor Gorton. Especially with you in my bed."

His fingers traced around the perimeter of her nipples, then feathered over them and she felt a fiery rush of excitement. "Whatever you're doing right now, don't stop," she pleaded.

"Only to make it better, Em. Only," he drew her head up and kissed her, "to make it better."

She hadn't known that it could get better . . . better even than the first time . . . better than the wonders he'd opened to her the day before. She reveled in the way his mouth seemed to draw out every breath in her body, and then give it back again . . . with so much more. She loved the way he tasted, the way he smelled, the way he felt. His arousal was such perfection that she sought to draw herself closer to him, to wrap her legs around him, to feel his arousal nestled where her greatest fire was.

Suddenly, Rob thrust into her. And she welcomed him. The fullness inside her, and the way Rob fit her together with him, were altogether miraculous. She sighed and arched up into him, to bring him closer and deeper.

Suddenly, he pulled away.

"Rob?"

"Wait, Emily . . . wait . . . there's something . . ."

She was astounded when he kicked the quilt down and hopped out of the bed. Naked, he padded across the floor; but this time she had no time to appreciate his body because he acted the madman, first throwing up the covers of one chest, then pulling out the drawers under the bed. He rummaged deep inside, muttering all the while, "Where is it? Where the hell . . ."

He was Bedlam bound. The battle had overtaxed him. The wounded had etched madness into his brain. She gripped the quilt to her chin and edged closer to the wall of the cabin, all the while looking for a weapon to defend herself lest he go truly mad and try to kill her.

"Ah!" Rob said, and she trembled to hear that guttural sound. He appeared triumphant as he held up . . .

"A hammock? You left me . . . and scared me half out of my wits . . . for a *hammock?*"

"Not just any hammock, Emily. The natives in Guadeloupe weave this under a moonlit sky. They say this is the hammock of the angels. It's supposed to bring . . ." He looped the ends over two hooks in the ceiling and tightened the guide ropes until the hammock swayed gently about three feet off the floor.

Skeptically, she looked at the multicolored thing, with its red, yellow, green and blue pattern of diamonds and chevrons against an ecru background. It didn't look any different than the cotton and sisal rugs some ships's captains tried to hawk on the island's dock. In fact, because it had been stored in the chest, it looked more decrepit than the rugs, which were almost as mangy as some of the wild curs who roamed Block Island.

"What is *that* supposed to bring?"

He came to scoop her into his arms and whirl her

around in the air, "The natives say it can bring the happiness of the angels right down to earth. If we use it properly, of course."

"Aye, sir. But what's the proper way to use it?"

He laughed and waggled his arched brows and Emily felt herself blush from the tips of her toes to the roots of her hair.

"Humbuggery!"

"Not at all, Doctor Gorton. 'Tis true, the natives say."

Rob would have settled her in the center of the hammock immediately but when he held her up to do it, he realized something wasn't quite right. Chuckling, he instead set her on her feet. "Ah, but we can't sample the delights of the angels the way you're dressed, Emily."

"What's wrong with the way I'm dressed? The nightshift is beautiful, Rob. Thank you."

"You're welcome. But . . . ." His fingers plucked at the low neckline and skimmed over the deliciously firm globes inside. ". . . it has to come off, Em."

"Why?"

"There simply isn't any room to maneuver once we're settled inside that thing."

"How do you know?" she asked, and immediately the words were out of her mouth, she knew she did not want to hear the answer.

"Because I've had to sleep in it several times." When he saw her pretty mouth pucker into a pout and her sparkling dark eyes half close with unwarranted speculation, he laughed. "Alone, Emily, I give you my word—although I've dreamed of the two of us in this ever since I bought it. And because of the wonders that I've dreamed, I've saved it just for you. But it *is* tight for one . . . and it will be doubly tight for two. So . . ."

He slid the nightdress up her thigh, lingering to caress the softness that enclosed her womanhood. She kept his hand there and by herself pulled the silkiness over her head. He smiled and crushed her to him, his hand trapped between them.

"You *are* getting to be a wanton wench, my love. Thank the sea nymphs."

His fingers found a sensitive spot that made Emily gasp and shiver. Sliding over it in a rhythmic caress, he found heat and slickness; and he sighed because he didn't want to stop. But if they were to sample strange delights that night, he had to halt for a minute . . .

Once he had Emily settled in the center of the hammock, his hand returned to pleasure her. Her eyes became luminous and she sighed and gave him room to slip beside her. As his head lowered to kiss her, the sides of the hammock closed in around them.

Awed at the way it felt to have him over her, and the hammock close round them, enveloping them in an embrace that seemed timeless, Emily whispered, "It's like being in a world all of our own."

"The happiness of the angels, Em."

He kissed her long and deep and she tightened her arms around him, then crossed her legs over his hips, to hold him fast in the natural cradle of her pelvis. How good it felt! How wonderful to be here, with Rob, giving and taking the joys of their bodies.

The ship swayed and the hammock swung with it.

The pitch and roll of the sea seemed transported intact into the fibers of the hammock, and from the fibers of the hammock into the fibers of her body. The ship yawed and her hips undulated up in a timeless, eons old, innate movement that bound them more to eternity than themselves.

The dreams Rob had had were nothing compared to the reality of Emily cradling him within her body, her legs and arms wrapped around him like a quilt. He felt the soft mounds of her breasts brush against his chest, causing his nipples to harden. Sensitized, each rhythmic sway of the hammock sent furious jolts of power through his body. His arousal throbbed in unison with the jolts. God's blood, could any pleasure ever be greater than this? Greater than being one with the woman he'd waited half his lifetime for?

Hipbone to hipbone, they allowed the ship's movement to increase their arousal. It was slow, and easy, bringing Rob almost to the breaking point. But he was making love with Emily. Making love as they'd never known it—as he'd always hoped, but almost despaired of doing—and he wanted everything to be perfect and wonderful for her. He reined in his own passion to increase her own.

God's blood, Emily thought, was there *more?* Could there actually be nerves there? There must be. Yes! His gentle stroke had touched it again. And again. How? What?

The feeling was so delicious, she moved her hips only a fraction, enough to control Rob's thrust so it slid over an already aroused inner space. And instantaneously the wondrous feeling spread so sweetly that she sighed, her legs fell open and she arched up once more to meet him.

"You like that," he whispered.

"No. I love it."

Chuckling, he obliged her urgent body again. And again.

"More," she said.

"Much more."

There was so much more, she wondered if the natives who had woven their hammock had been angels come to earth. As her body rippled in tiny explosions, she marveled at the difference this loving was from the first and wondered what the next would be like. And the next. And the . . .

The long, drawn out playfulness had created a ferocious urgency inside her that could only be soothed by him. His mouth. His taste. His touch. His thrusting rhythm and her answering one.

Oh, God! It was happening. The heat suddenly ignited into roaring flames. Shivers and ripples were overcome by thunderous undulations. She couldn't breathe. She didn't want to. She wanted it to go on and on and on.

And it did, until it reached a crest, gave one last shuddering ascent and crashed over the edge. Her body tightened, tensed, shattered into a million sparks of light and feeling.

She screamed his name.

He cried hers; and then he couldn't breathe. He could only feel. As the cocoon of the hammock brought them to the gate of heaven, he thanked God for Emily, for this night, this love. Thanked Him for this human joy—being able to explode through the curtain of darkness, and over to the end of time.

Emily thought she saw a flash of light. She thought she felt an unwanted tug back to earth. But Rob's arms urged her on, higher and higher. His breathless kiss made her pulse race with the wind. His manhood thrust her into the clouds. And she flew with the spirits.

"Don't let me fall," she pleaded. "Don't send me back."

"You won't fall. But you must go back. You and your lover have other worlds to conquer, other heavens to explore."

When her heartbeat slowed and she could once again open her eyes, she looked up to find Rob searching her face for something inexplicable.

"Did you hear it, too?" she asked.

"The voice?"

She nodded.

"I thought it was you."

"And I thought it was you."

He smiled with such adoration that no matter who had said it—if anyone had said anything at all—she knew that she and Rob, her lover, did, indeed, have other heavens to explore.

"Take me back, Rob."

"To bed?"

"No. To heaven."

Nathaniel explored every damned inch of the quarterdeck, tipping his hat or calling out to the officers of the *Cardiz, A good evening to you, Captain* or *There seems to be a nip in the air.* But each round, he deliberately took an erratic course that brought him closer and closer to Captain Douglass. He prayed for a wildly pitching sea. He prayed for a fierce or howling wind that would send men scurrying to keep the ship from foundering under anchor. When none came, he had to improvise.

The shadows afforded him the greatest possibility. If he could just brush his cape against the captain's. If he could drop the letter near his boot so his step would feel it. If he could signal in some way . . .

In the end, he merely took the letter out of his pocket, strode up to Donald Douglass, held out his hand and bid him a good night. Startled, Donald's head jerked up to look at Nathaniel. But he gave no indication that else was wrong. So when Nathaniel took his hand away, spun on his heel and headed for the quarterdeck hatch and ladder, he left the letter behind in a confused captain's tight grasp.

At the bottom of the ladder, Nathaniel turned and took six steps before Almanzo Peters tugged him back the other way.

"That's the captain's quarters, squire. Officers's quarters are forward."

"Yes, of course. I got confused, is all."

But he was not confused. He knew damned well where captain's quarters were. After all, he had three ships in his own fleet. He had turned that way deliberately, hoping to hear exactly what he'd heard. No, he wasn't confused. He couldn't mistake the sounds coming from the captain's quarters.

So . . . the lady doctor was no lady, after all.

He'd bedded sufficient *obliging* females to be able to know when they were enjoying a blazing of passion . . . and when they were giving enough to earn a response that was equal or better than their own. And from Rob's response Emily Gorton was a very obliging female, indeed. Should his plan succeed, he'd taste a sample of that passion. More than a sample.

Without more bickering with Almanzo or Orrin or Jason, he tucked down for the night after another pint of ale. He intended to dream about the success of his plans and the complete destruction of his enemy.

And the King would help him do it.

"Well?" Jason asked, impatient with Almanzo for the first time in their many voyages together.

"As you guessed, he passed something to the British captain. Couldn't fathom what it was, but I'll bet a month's victuals it were a letter."

"So . . . he took the bait."

"Aye. What do we do now, search *Cardiz's* captain?"

"And bring down Rob's anger? No, I've something different in mind."

Jason explained what he wanted and Jop and Orrin scurried into officers's quarters. They were quiet as titmice but they soon discovered they needn't have bothered. Appleton snored so loud, the dead from the deep wouldn't be raised by Jop and Orrin's search. Within a few minutes they tossed a packet of parchment paper on the table in front of Jason. He held one piece after the other in front of a candle. When he found what he was looking for, he chuckled and drew over a cold lantern. He removed its glass top and wiped the inside with a soft cloth, then pulled the cloth out, being careful not to get any on his clothes.

"Lamp black," Jason said. "I read about this in one of Fielding's books. I hope the hell it works."

Gently, he brushed the cloth against the parchment. Soon there was a black background, with scraps of white letters set out against it. The three officers bent over it and studied its contents.

" 'ard to read," Orrin Mayotte complained.

"For us, aye. But for you, shouldn't be any harder than reading the ship's course from white stars against a black sky," Jason chided.

"Well, when ye put it like 'at. . . ." He adjusted his eyes to see like a navigator, studied the paper some more, and chuckled. "Got ta bugger."

When he explained what was there, Almanzo frowned. "But the letter breaks off. How are we to know the rest?"

Jason slammed his hand against the table in fury. He'd thought this the perfect way to trap the fly in the spider's web. But there were no other scratches against the rest of the paper. All they knew was that Nathaniel was loyal to the king, not a Son of Liberty, as he'd said. They knew he wanted to sabotage *Patriot*, so they'd have to be careful. And they knew he wanted certain conditions met once he'd carried out his plans. But what those conditions were, they could only guess.

"We have the bugger; but he has his secrets. So we've only half the puzzle."

"Aye," Almanzo said. "And only knowin' 'alf makes it damned 'ard to set up a defense."

"But not impossible," Jason said. "Not if we're careful. And damn me, we have to be careful!"

Chapter Fourteen

Rob thought to slip out of the hammock without waking Emily. But when he moved, she locked her legs around him and pulled his head round for a kiss.

"Where art thou going, sire? Has thee forgotten thy fair maid so soon that thee wants to quit her side without sampling more pleasures?"

Rob threw back his head and laughed and the chill of the morning was completely chased away for Emily. God, how she loved his laugh!

"Aye, fair maiden . . . ," Rob said, with a playful tug on her nose, " 'tis true we played the star-crossed lovers, Lancelot and Guinevere, last night. But in the light of morning that knight is gone. A ship's captain is in his place. And this captain would rather have the reality of a lovely female doctor than the illusion of a long dead queen."

"Lovely female doctor? Fie, captain! I'll have to check your eyes when next ye come to my surgery. You see things that aren't there."

"Nay, Emily. I see perfectly. Tis you who is blind for not seeing what I see. Or wanting what I want."

Suddenly, the cold came back and Emily shivered from it . . . or from something far more significant. She didn't try to determine which. "Don't, Rob. We've had this conversation before. We always end up shouting at each other. And I don't want to spoil the magic we had last night."

With sad eyes, he bent the hammock sides down and eased himself out of it. "Nor do I, Em. But it infuriates me that you always run away or change the subject when I profess my feelings to you. Why do you still do that? After all these years, you should know that I'm true and steady and will stay the course."

She marveled that neither of them were particularly embarrassed by their nakedness. "Ah . . . I know that. But what you ask is not for me. Never has been. Never will be. When have you heard me say aught?"

Rob glared at her, then began pulling clean clothes out of the chest. With his back turned, he managed to get his breeches on without tearing at that beautiful hair or screaming in that lovely face. When was she going to learn? What would it take? He had waited twelve years since the first day he'd realized he wanted none other as his wife. Aye, he had gotten her in his bed. But damn her eyes, it wasn't enough!

"You're angry," she said, plaintively.

"As you said, Em . . . let's not start it all again. We have enough problems without adding the circle-go-round of our differences about marriage!"

He jerked on his waistcoat, grabbed up his sword, and turned. She was still standing there in the middle of the room, her arms crossed under her breasts, her eyes darkened with unshed tears. Why wouldn't she cry? Many the time he'd seen her eyes sparkling, and she gulping back her sorrow. Never had any tears dripped over her thick lashes. There was so much control inside her! More than inside most men he knew. The barriers, then, had not come all the way down. He wondered if they ever would.

He picked up his pistols and tucked them into their holsters. He shouldered his sword, rather than strapping it on his waist. With a gentle smile, he crossed the room, bent and kissed Emily on the forehead. "Don't fret, love. My anger will cool quickly." At the door he turned and warned, "Don't be too long. I raise the sails as soon as the crew has been fed."

"But my patients!"

When Emily finally drew the quilt around herself Rob thought that regardless of her age, she looked a waif, like the ones he'd seen on the streets of London. He hated hurting her. But he had a ship to run and a half hundred men to protect, not to mention a valuable cargo to get to Guadeloupe.

"We agreed, Emily. I've given you a night. I dare not lay at anchor another day. Those who are in need of more doctoring on *Cardiz* will have to get it in the nearest port."

"We could keep them here."

"Seamen from the British navy? Are you daft?"

"They're wounded British seamen. What harm could they do you?"

He weighed her request. "All right." When she beamed, he cautioned, "Not all of them, Emily. I dare not risk that much enmity on my ship. Those who will stay will be for you and Jason to decide. Only those who would die without your help, Em. I'll explain to Captain Douglass that we aren't impressing his crew, but will drop them off in the nearest port as soon as they are well enough to leave your more than capable hands. But, Emily, if there are any among them who can wield a weapon and you decide to keep him, I'll have your pretty head locked in the stocks."

"Stocks are outdated."

"Not on a ship. Count on it, Emily . . . I will allow naught but those on the brink of death to stay behind. And to be sure you don't slip any past me, I'll have a wee word with Jason."

When the door closed, Emily fairly flew through her morning ablutions. Wee word with Jason, hah! There were ways she could make an illness appear worse than it was, if she needed to. But did she need to? Wasn't Rob right about not taking chances? Wasn't the safety of the entire crew more important than the life of only one or two men? It was a conundrum, what she faced, one she'd never had to tackle before. But if pushed, she was a surgeon. The welfare of her patient . . . one, two, or twenty . . . had to come first.

Jason tried to talk to Rob to tell him what he, Orrin and Almanzo had discovered. But Rob was in too much of a hurry, issuing orders left and right, to get *Cardiz*'s officers off *Patriot*, move *Patriot*'s wounded below deck, and get underway.

They were four leagues away from the *Cardiz*—by

Orrin's reckoning—when Rob decided he could at last breathe easy. He posted watch, had Almanzo Peters take the wheel, and went below in search of Emily.

She was in the mess-turned-into-hospital. Jop was beside her and they were busy tending to the wounded. She had naught but time to smile at him before she bent down to change dressings on a man whose right cheek was torn and bleeding.

Rob liked the way his old bell-bottom trousers fit over her hips. Gave a life to them they'd not seen before. And that shirt Rob had gotten from One-eyed Jack Saunders! Though covered by a drape to keep it as clean as possible, her breasts filled the fold to perfection. If One-eyed Jack ever saw her in that, he'd shanghai her without a blink of his only eye.

And speaking of eyes—Emily's lovely Black-eyed Susans of eyes drooped, though it was little past two bells into the midday watch. She had great courage and fortitude; but she was beginning to buckle.

"Have you had noon meal?" Rob asked.

Emily wiped the sweat off her brow and shook her head, which was once more tightly braided. "I've no time. I'll eat as soon as there's a break in this endless round of bandaging."

"If 'tis endless as you say, you'll find no break. Come, Em . . . give that swab to Jop and we'll rustle you up a light tea."

He saw the indecision in the way her body leaned toward the table, then away, then back again. He knew immediately he had to get her away from there. Though they had slept some the night before, if, between the lovemaking, he had strung all the cat naps together, he'd like as not be three hours short of seven. With the grueling day she'd put in yesterday and the morning she'd had, she needed food and rest. And this time, he'd leave her alone.

"Doctor Gorton, this is your captain speaking. Jop, take the swab and finish. Emily, come with me."

He grasped her elbow and walked her from the room into the officers's quarters. They passed Orrin Mayotte on their way and Rob sent him to fetch a pot of tea, a bit of boiled beans and bacon, and a bowl of the special sugared dates the cook always kept aside to satisfy Rob's sweet tooth.

Rob watched her take every single bite, lest the minute his back was turned she skittered away to her patients.

"Satisfied?" she said, licking at the last sugar crystals that clung to her lips. He grinned and she blushed. After last night she knew exactly how he reacted to that particular movement. "I've finished."

"Not by a league," Rob said, and his voice held a caress she could feel to her toes. "Tis only the beginning for us, Emily. That, I promise you."

For a moment neither of them spoke as they gazed into each other's eyes. Emily felt a tug toward Rob that was so strong she didn't know how she kept from leaping into his arms. In two nights he had become indispensable to her.

Humbuggery! It hadn't happened in two nights but in years that had flown by. Now, she wanted to savor every minute, slow down the world, so that she and Rob could wrap themselves into each other and shut problems and personalities out. She hadn't much.

What she asked for was so little.

Yet, it was the world.

"I love you, Emily."

Her head snapped up and she gaped at him.

"Don't worry. I'm not asking for you to love me. I know how damned hard it is for you to understand how I feel. But know this, love . . . you are the only woman in the world I want. The only woman I will ever want."

"I want you, too," she admitted gladly.

"I know. Satisfied, I am, that 'tis true."

He waited for more; but when no more came, he sighed, took her hand and kissed the inside of her wrist. "Get some rest, love. You didn't sleep enough last night to keep body and soul together."

"And whose fault was that?"

"Both of ours . . . or did I imagine the three times you woke me to satisfy some mysterious craving of yours?"

She pushed his hand away, rose from the table, and laughed. "Your memory is intact, Captain Sears, thank goodness." She turned at the cabin door and smiled at him. "I will take that rest. And I will take it *alone.*"

He was grinning happily when she stuck her head back and said, "Of course, I don't want to be alone too long."

"We'll have supper together."

She frowned. "That's all?"

Her forehead furrowed so delightfully, he had all he could do not to jump to her side, pick her up, and carry her all the way to the cabin . . . to have his way with her. Though, God knew, she'd probably have her way with him as much as he'd have with her, she was that lusty.

"All? Yes, I plan *all* for tonight," he said. "All the lovemaking in the world."

"Wonderful!"

Rob's jubilant mood lasted all the way to the quarterdeck, where Almanzo Peters was at the wheel. He smiled, gave Almanzo a salute and took up a position at the quarterdeck rail, allowing Almanzo to stay out the rest of the watch.

The deck was clear where Emily's patients had slept all night. They were below, now, being tended by the cabin boy and men hand-chosen by Emily for their compassion and ability to follow orders. Orders. Yes, Rob shook his head admiringly, Emily damned all at giving orders. Take the sails, for instance. Having outlived their usefulness as sun shades for her patients, she had finally allowed the crew to hoist some of them so Rob would have at least a half compliment when *Patriot* got underway. The rest she had jury-rigged below into large hammocks for those British she'd deemed on death's door. Sun shades, yesterday. Hammocks, last night. Today, taut sails—albeit fewer than they needed—filled with winds out of the Northeast, carrying them further and further away from *Cardiz* and closer to their destination.

Not fast enough, since they had but half the sails they needed to take them to their goal. Which wasn't Baltimore, of course. He had merely mentioned Baltimore and Savannah to throw off any British seaman who had been listening. He had learned long ago to keep clear of major ports where British patrol boats held strategic positions. And he had learned to give false information—to save his hide and the cargo he carried. He had learned the hard way that news traveled faster on land than sea. On land, fresh horses took circuit riders streaking down the coast, on the chase for escaping ships, crews, or prisoners of the British.

So Rob intended to round the point at night and put into a small inlet on Solomon's Island, at the tip of Chesapeake Bay. There, he had a safe house—with deep cellars beneath the barn and outbuildings. As he'd done dozens of time, the cargo he was carrying for merchants in Annapolis and Baltimore would be unloaded at the dock, transported to the safe house, and *Patriot* would be on her way before dawn. Chesapeake fishermen who were paid by the merchants would use their swift skipjacks to crisscross the bay, carrying messages informing those who were expecting him that their shipment had arrived. The merchants would pick up their supplies when the coast was clear of British patrol boats.

Thank God for the myriad irregularly shaped islands He'd scattered along the coast of the colonies! With them many a privateer had survived surprise attacks from French, Spanish, Dutch, or British—depending on the war in which they were engaged. Without them . . . Rob shuddered to think how many lives and livelihoods would have been lost.

But to get to Solomon's Island by dark meant

they'd have to increase sail. The fore-and-aft sails had to be augmented. And bowsprit rigging would help, but more would be needed.

"Hoist studding and spiritsails," he ordered Almanzo.

"Aye, sir."

The order was passed below, where Rob could hear seamen scurrying forward to retrieve the sails he had stored in the head. Several minutes passed without a sail being hauled on deck. Rob cursed.

"Send below, Mister Peters. Something's amiss."

"Aye, sir."

Almanzo ordered a seaman who looked no more than thirteen—and probably wasn't—to hurry up the crew. The boy hopped to his job and slid down the ladder, disregarding the rungs, to give him faster time. Almanzo and Rob chuckled at each other.

"He'll do," Rob said. "Any crew member who knows when speed is important will always find a place in a privat . . ."

The ashen face of the young boy as it topped the quarterdeck hatch told a tale neither Rob nor Almanzo wanted to hear. But hear it, they must.

"Tell, boy," Rob said.

The boy sputtered, "The sails . . . the sails . . . they be torn to ribbons, sirs. Ripped or cut. The second mate don't know which. They be tryin' to repair them, sirs. But Mister Broadbent, he say it be a week's work."

"All the sails?" Rob asked. He dreaded the answer because *Patriot*'s second set—their emergency sails, the ones they used when their primary sails were shot out in battle—had been stored in the head along with the rest.

"Aye, sirs. All o' them. Mister Broadbent, he say for Mister Peters to tell you about a natal . . . whate'er that is."

"Tis a traitor, is what 'tis," Almanzo growled. "Damn his hide. How'd he get a knife?"

Rob was stunned by the fury in Almanzo's usually cheerful face. "What are you talking about?"

Quickly, Almanzo told Rob what the three officers had learned.

Rob roared. "Why did you not tell me before this?!"

He whirled and made for the gangway. As the young sailor had done, he skidded down the ladder and stormed his way through the hold. Men shrank from him but he took no notice. His destination was the head, first. Nathaniel's neck, second.

True, the *Cardiz* was limping to port. But the canvas sling they'd patched her with would give her enough purchase to make it to Block Island . . . or, more likely, Sandy Hook in New Jersey, where there was a British garrison, with fresh British gunboats and fresh British crews. And Captain Douglass had every damned sail—and every incentive—he'd need to get there in record time! *Patriot* was hardly a sitting duck yet; but without a full compliment of sail she soon would be. And it was all due to Nathaniel Appleton.

No. Much as Rob hated to admit it, their predicament was due more to his own inattention. He had been uneasy seeing Nathaniel aboard the *Cardiz*, but

Emily had taken his mind elsewhere. Nathaniel had bamboozled him; but he'd not have been able to if Rob had had his mind on his ship, crew, and mission.

Damn the British! Damn their spies! Damn the whole stinking stewpot of politics! And damn the gnawing twelve-year ache in his guts put there by a flaxen-haired beauty who had no idea she was the cause of such tumult.

It had been folly to fetch Emily. Folly, to bring her aboard. Folly, to keep her. Folly, perhaps, to love her.

Love. What, in the end, had it gotten him? What had it cost him?

Jason's mute appeal when Rob burst into the head closed down Rob's vocal chords. What canvas Nathaniel hadn't managed to cut to ribbons, he had stuffed through the openings to the sea. It was soaking up water, becoming heavier than lead. If it hadn't already, soon the water-logged canvas would begin to act as an anchor, dragging through the waves, slowing *Patriot* down to a crawl.

"Can you get it aboard?"

Jason shook his head.

Rob whipped out his cutlass and sliced through the precious canvas. Jason helped. Sweating with fatigue, they managed to separate what was left in the head from what was already in the holes.

"Have the boys ram it out," Rob said. "Then come to Nathaniel's sleeping quarters. Keep me from murdering the bloody bastard."

As he moved down the gangway, Rob gave orders left and right. Every man had a job to do. They must prepare for battle and boarding. Without the sails to maneuver, they were crippled. And every last man-jack knew it.

When Rob entered the officers's wardroom, he was just in time to see Harry pull his pipe out of Nathaniel's mouth and begin to bring it down on Nathaniel's nose. "That'll do, Harry," he said.

Harry's arm still made the arc, but this time it veered off to the side and his pipe broke into a dozen pieces on the side of the table. Harry spit on the floor, turned, saluted his captain, and hurried out, leaving a smirking Nathaniel to face Rob alone.

"You always were a bit naive, Rob," Nathaniel said. He crossed his legs and smoothed down his waistcoat sleeves, drawing out the lace of his shirt so it brushed against the backs of his fingers. "But then . . . you were having it on with that piece of skirt who calls herself a doctor. I merely took advantage of your weakened position. You would have done the same if you were in my place."

"But I wouldn't be in your place, you slimy bag of potage. Using the head was just your style, wasn't it? The crapper for a piece of crap!"

He shook his hand in Nathaniel's face, only to find that he still had his cutlass in a grip so tight his bones showed through his skin.

Nathaniel eyed him but didn't move a muscle. "Will you run me through, Rob? You? A man of honor? A man of law?"

Rob cursed heaven and earth, the British, and Nathaniel. Because Nathaniel had him. His hand dropped to his side. "No, I'll not run you through. You will be tried in a civil court, by colonial judges, with a colonial jury. And you will be hanged for treason on the high seas."

Nathaniel giggled, then roared. From the way he puffed out his chest, he was enormously pleased with himself.

"Me? Tried for treason? Perhaps. But only if you get to land, Rob. And only if it isn't in British hands. And that's nigh impossible, isn't it?"

Rob knew if he didn't get out of Nathaniel's sight, he'd put his sword through the bastard. He staggered into the gangway and bumped blindly into Jason.

"Put him in leg irons."

"Aye."

"I'll be on the quarterdeck, with Almanzo."

"Aye."

"Jason?"

"Sir?"

"How bad is it?"

"Every sail that isn't already hoisted is gone, Rob."

"Will we have time to fix any of them?"

"I don't think so."

"Have the men try, Jason. It's our only chance."

"They know that. They're working as fast as they can."

"One more thing, Jason."

"Aye, Rob."

"If anything happens, I'll have to stay on deck. Emily is your responsibility. Guard her with your life."

"You didn't have to tell me, Rob. I owe her that much and I'll give it gladly."

"Let's pray we don't have to."

* * *

The tension aboard the *Patriot* was palpable. Though none told her what had happened, Emily caught snatches of conversation that apprised her of the danger they were in.

"No wonder you haven't left my side," she said to Jason as she changed the bandage on a man whose arm had been badly ripped up by exploding grapeshot. When Jason said nothing, confirming her fears, she stared off into the distance as she tied the final knot and dipped her hands into the cleaning solution. "How soon before we reach friendly territory?"

"There's no way to calculate. The wind has died down. With the reduced number of sails we have, we're barely moving. What should have taken us two days may take us four or five."

Emily voiced the concerns of an islander whose brothers had been caught in everything from rain showers to gales to hurricanes. "What if we run into foul weather?"

Jason would have preferred to keep Emily in the dark. But he knew this woman. If he lied to her, she'd not trust him again. "We won't be able to outrun it. We'll falter."

"Capsize?"

"No. But we'll be slowed." He shook his head. "Don't look like that. It isn't your worry. Rob has been in tight spots before. He'll do all he can to get us safe out of this one."

But Rob was no magician. He couldn't weave canvas from zephyrs. Consequently, *Patriot* limped through the waves, with every topman high in the shrouds, keeping a keen eye out for British ensigns and pennants, and every gunman below decks, readying the cannon or preparing grenades. Every contingency was gone over again and again, until each officer knew his station, what was expected of him, and what was required of the men in his charge.

On the quarterdeck Rob clapped his second mate and cousin on the shoulder, then turned to look down at his crew which had gathered round the scuttlebutt. The orders he had to give were brief.

"Fight with gallantry. But if you hear the captain's trump," Rob said, "you will lay down your arms. It's better to lose with dignity, save the ship, and have the possibility of fighting another day than to walk in front of grapeshot when no hope remains."

He looked into the gloom, trying to catch each man's gaze and hold it, so each would know his captain had made his decisions because every life aboard his ship was precious to him. When he was satisfied, he straightened his spine and saluted the crew. To a man, they saluted back.

"Treachery has brought us to this night," he said. "Let dignity and patriotism rule the day."

"Now we leave it in the hands of God," someone muttered in the dark. *Amens* whispered over the waves.

The attack came just before first light. And when it came, was fiercer than any Rob had ever seen—but only because he couldn't maneuver *Patriot* into a position to take advantage. He had been a crew member of eleven ships, had captained three ships in his own time, and engaged in dozens of sea battles. Never had he had to start out with a ship which was, to all intents and purposes, already dead in the water.

It was bitter gall for him to sound the trump; but he did. When the smoke cleared Rob saw that the ships which had bested him were Nathaniel Appleton's *Aquidneck* and a British gunboat, *Edgerton*. On deck of *Edgerton* a familiar red-coated figure saluted Rob. So . . . by covering that gaping hole in the *Cardiz* Captain Donald Douglass had managed to seize the initiative. Rob had expected naught else.

During the fray before the surrender, Emily found herself facing an obdurate Jason. She exploded with fury at what he was suggesting. "You are daft, Jason Broadbent. Too much fighting has addled your brains."

"Tis Rob's orders, Em. He wants you safe."

"I will not hide in a barrel in the hold amidst the cargo. I belong with the wounded."

Jason tightened his jaw and shook his head. "Not this time. Not with a man like Nathaniel roaming the deck. Now get out of those clothes and get into these."

"Why?"

"Because I'm going to put your clothes—the clothes Nathaniel has seen you wear—on a dead body. . . ."

"You wouldn't defile the dead."

"I'd do everything possible to keep you alive. Don't

fight me on this, Emily. It's the only way we have left."

"What will you do with the. . . ."

Jason sighed. He didn't like the situation any better than she did. But he, more than Rob, had seen the lascivious expressions on Nathaniel's face whenever Emily came near. "Nathaniel will find it floating away from the ship. There are men prepared to swear they saw you killed in the battle. We'll keep you out of his hands."

"But he's a merchant, not some white slaver! What. . . ."

"Don't ask me how I know, but I have a gut feeling that Nathaniel is more than most men, and less than a dog. He took too keen an interest in you."

"Humbuggery! I'm the only woman on this ship. Everyone takes too keen an interest in me."

"Not the kind he had." There was no other way round it, Jason decided. She wouldn't buy the truth. Mayhap she'd purchase a gambit. "He saw you once with Rebeccah Washington at the friendly house. He thinks you one of her harlots. If he got his hands on you what do you think he would do?"

Emily's bravado felt as if it had been punctured with a harpoon. She began tearing at her clothes. "Turn around, damn it!"

Jason dropped the clothes Rob had given him and bolted several feet away, keeping guard as the last booms of cannon went on over his head. "Hurry up!"

"I'm hurrying faster than ever I have," she croaked. The damned shirt was stubborn. Or mayhap it was her fingers. Shaking as they were, she had trouble doing anything right! "Done."

When Jason turned, he saw a cabin boy. A mite taller than the usual boy, but he and Rob hoped that once she was safe she would be overlooked.

The golden halo of her hair, however, was another matter. He whipped a soft woolen cap out of his pocket, the kind a baker's helper would wear in the winter as he delivered goods, and plopped it on her head. "Tuck your braids and any stray locks inside. And keep the damned thing on your head at all times."

"Aye," she said, rehearsing the role she'd have to play. "Will it do?"

"It had better." He rolled the large barrel close to Emily.

"One thing more," Emily said. She dug into her medicine bag and brought up the small box which Rob had given her two years after her ninth birthday. Large enough to hold her surgical tools, it was small enough to fit inside a pocket of her breeches. "Now I'm ready."

Jason didn't have to ask what was in the box. He'd seen it often enough during his convalescence and the myriad times he'd helped Emily do surgery. She was a wonder! Brave enough to face who-knew-what; but intelligent enough to arm herself.

He smiled at her as he held up the lid of a barrel and helped her climb in. "There are holes in the sides so you can breathe. But I have to nail the top back on or it will look out of place."

"How will I get out?"

"Let as much time go by as you can, Em. Then,

when you can't stand it any longer, bang on the sides. Rob and I would rather have you in the hands of the British than a 'guest' of Nathaniel Appleton."

Emily shuddered as the hammer hit its mark and brought five nails through to hold the top on. Small places. She'd always hated small places . . . unless they smelled of hay and the warm, wet muskiness of cows or sheep. Worse, she hated being vulnerable. She had always thought of herself as independent and strong. Now, after all she had done and after all the women had accused her of, she found herself in a barrel, hiding from a man . . . and simply because she was a woman.

To Nathaniel Appleton and to men like him, she was a woman. Not a doctor. A woman. And she would perform a woman's role whether she was suited to it or not.

Amazing.

And terrifying.

Lord Dudley Douglass stood beside his son as the captain of the *Patriot* waited for a boarding plank to be laid across the expanse of sea between the *Edgerton* and *Patriot*. He had been watching the way the tall, brown-haired captain had calmed his men, accepted the situation, and now saluted those who had bested him in battle—brief though it had been.

"He seems a valiant man," Dudley said to his son.

"Aye. He is, that. Captain Robert Sears saved *Cardiz* and his female doctor friend saved many of my men. A man such as he deserves naught less than our best form of justice, father."

"He shall get it. I like not the demands which that Appleton spy made in his letter."

"Nor do I; but we owe him something for his actions."

"He will get something. It won't be what he expects, however."

His words were cut short by a gleeful shout of triumph as *Patriot*'s rails were slung with grappling hooks by the crew of Nathaniel Appleton's *Aquidneck* and hauled closer to the merchant vessel. The shout escalated to a triumphant roar as dozens of *Aquidneck*'s crew members vaulted over the sides of *Patriot*, swinging cutlasses and swords, putting the point to the necks of men who were unarmed.

"Stop them!" an appalled Lord Douglass shouted to his officers. "Stop them or they, too, will be charged with sedition!"

Chaos reigned for several minutes until the King's officers restored order. Nevertheless, when Rob was accepted aboard the *Edgerton,* a rivulet of blood ran down the front of his captain's uniform from a wicked cut just under his jaw. Lord Douglass waved his surgeon over to tend it and extended his apologies.

"I gave no orders to board your ship, sir. Your surrender was sufficient for His Majesty's Navy."

"Aye, m'lord," Rob said, wincing from the sting of the salve the surgeon applied. He held out his hand to Donald Douglass, who took it gladly. "You have my compliments, sir. It took you less time than I reckoned for you to get to Sandy Hook and back. But, then, had we not been sabotaged I doubt not you would still be searching . . ."

"Without success, of course," Donald said with a smile.

"Of course."

"We will have your company with us back to Sandy Hook," Lord Douglass said. "Your ship will be towed. You will be put on trial. . . ."

"On trial?" Nathaniel strutted up to the threesome and dismissed Rob with a smirk and a wave of his lace-trimmed handkerchief. "On trial at Sandy Hook? What's wrong with right here? There are two ships. Two sets of officers. It will take less than ten minutes to commission a summary board of inquiry and issue a swift sentence. The traitors can be swinging from the yardarms before supper."

Lord Dudley Douglass thumped his walking stick on the deck. Its sound reverberated all the way to both fore and aft of the three ships. So did his words as he fairly shouted, "That may be how you colonials exact justice, Squire Appleton. It is not how His Majesty does."

"I am no colonial, m'Lord. I am a loyal British subject."

"Then act like one!"

Lord Douglass jerked his head to his son, to take Rob out of the way so the rest of the crew could be brought aboard and imprisoned below. When a man stumbled, Lord Douglass offered him his hand to steady him.

"Treat them easy," he warned his crew, "else you will feel the lash."

Nathaniel realized, suddenly, that the cards he thought he held were not being played the way he'd anticipated. It was best, he realized, not to antagonize this man, who could help fill Nathaniel's coffers, or destroy him with a patrician nod of his Lordship's head. So he smiled, put out his right foot, and swept a courtly bow.

"Beg your lordship's pardon. The heat of battle, you know. Sometimes it pushes a man to his limits."

Lord Douglass sniffed. Nathaniel Appleton wore powdered wig and unmarked clothing. If he'd been involved in the battle, then Maria Teresa was Queen of England. "We do have much to discuss, m'lord" Nathaniel said, his voice as genteel and ingratiating as he could make it. "First, there's transfer of the *Patriot* into my care. And its cargo . . ."

"Half the cargo," Lord Douglass amended. "But not the ship. His Majesty has need of it."

"Half, m'lord. Of course, half."

Although they were several feet away, Rob and Donald had heard every word. Rob turned furious eyes to his captor, who had the grace to look tortured with doubt. "It was promised Squire Appleton for his help. The King would get it all in any case.

"Better the King than his cur," Rob growled.

". . . and *Patriot's* surgeon, since I do not have one aboard . . . ?"

"He wants Emily?" Rob asked Donald. "God's blood! She's a free woman and never took part in battle. She cannot be impressed."

"She will not be impressed. My father will only accede if Nathaniel agrees to take her back to Block Island, her home I believe."

Rob's heart beat wildly. If Jason had managed his part of the scheme, then Emily was safely tucked inside a barrel . . . God's blood! What if she were to become part of the booty awarded Nathaniel? What if the fates had outsmarted them all?

Folly! Damned, damned folly!

Inwardly, Rob cursed himself. He cursed the night he'd sought her out and dragged her from her home. He cursed the Davies witch who had made her think herself unworthy of him. Cursed the British. The taxes. Friends-turned-traitors.

If they got out of this, he'd not take *no* for an answer from Emily. She would be his wife. God's blood on it. She would be his wife.

Chapter Fifteen

Nathaniel stormed all over the decks and sleeping quarters of the *Patriot*, muttering to himself, "Thought to pass off a man's body as hers, did they? Thought to keep her out of my hands? Wellaway, it didn't work! And someone will pay with their life for this!"

He had almost lost his mind when he'd seen Emily's clothes bobbing by him. He'd stomped his feet and swore under his breath, demanding that the grappling hook be used, then, when it wouldn't reach, throwing a man overboard to swim and turn it over.

Nathaniel smiled, remembering the relief and the quick fury which had washed over him when it was revealed that it wasn't Emily. The man who was directly in front of him shrank back. Good. A crew which feared its master and the crack of his lash was a sharp crew. He'd always kept his crews sharp. Lashed and sharp. Not blunt like Sears's crew, who were far too familiar with their captain.

Of course, there was one member of Rob's crew

with whom Nathaniel intended to become extremely familiar.

When he found her. And, damned the colonial traitors to hell, he *would* find her.

That cur Broadbent had been missing since the boarding. Nathaniel believed wherever Jason was, so would be Emily. Yet, unless there were a hidden closet in this damned ship, there was no place Nathaniel or his crew hadn't searched. Stymied for the moment, he went back on deck to watch as Rob's cargo was off-loaded, divided in half, and transferred to the *Aquidneck* and the *Edgerton*.

Nathaniel looked over to the *Edgerton* and laughed as he caught Rob's scowl. But his laugh cut off when he saw the intent way Rob watched barrel after barrel being brought up from the hold. Rob's body seemed poised for flight or battle. His eyes darted this way and that. His hands twitched. He bounced on the balls of his feet.

Had he never lost a cargo before? No, now that Nathaniel thought about it, Rob never had, which was why he was a trusted captain, whose wealth had been piling up because so many merchants trusted their shipments to his care.

So, what was in these barrels that was so important he appeared to be broken out in sweat?

Nathaniel could find nothing unusual. Meal and beans and salted meat. Calico and copperware. Silver flagons and sisal twine. Herbs and spices and medicines. Guadeloupe rum and Virginia tobacco. Molasses jugs and mustard jars. Beaver pelts and . . .

Wellaway. Wellaway! Nathaniel laughed. He laughed and laughed and laughed. Beaver pelts and Emily!

For a man who didn't like to get his hands dirty, Nathaniel did not hesitate to leap into the filthy hold where ballast and cargo and stores were kept. He shouldered aside the crew who were working in the hot, stinking hole, knowing she wouldn't be in the middle, in the barrels that would be off-loaded first. No, Jason would choose a shadowed corner, behind one of the ship's stays, hoping the most precious barrel of all would be overlooked. And he would be there, armed, no doubt, to protect the woman who had cut off his leg and saved his life.

Nathaniel kept his left hand tight to the handle of his cutlass. As he passed one of his crew he plucked his pistol out of his belt. Standing off to the side, Nathaniel primed and loaded it. He sighted down the barrel and tested it with one shot, scaring his crew and the British. He laughed. The pistol, while grimy and old, would do. As he made his way forward, he tucked the pistol into his belt; but kept his right hand on the grip. Now, he curled his finger round the trigger as he crept over the *Patriot*'s stores, searching for his quarry.

Rob hadn't missed a beat of what happened on *Patriot*. He had seen that look of jubilation, heard the sound of his laughter as Nathaniel snapped his fingers and patted a barrel on his way into the bowels of *Patriot*.

Nathaniel knew. Jason and Emily were over there, at his mercy. But Rob was helpless to stop Nathaniel. Helpless for the second time in his life. And both times had been brought about by an unscrupulous—perhaps evil—man and the damned bloody British!

Rob's only weapon was the British sense of honor and fair play. Lord Douglass had already shown it. His son had it to spare. Now, if Rob could use it . . .

"Donald, will you be accompanying Emily to Block Island," he asked.

"Nay, Rob. I've *Cardiz* being overhauled at Sandy Hook. I must supervise and be ready to put out to sea as soon as she's finished."

"Red-coat guards for her, then?"

Donald sighed. "I understand how you feel about Emily, Robert. The way you look at her; and the way she acts with you . . . well, 'tis easy to see you both love each other."

Would that it were true, Rob thought. "I fear for her in Appleton's hands, Donald."

"Squire Appleton may be a spy for us, Robert. But he has always been an honorable man. He does what he says. Always has. We have no reason to distrust him."

"But that's just it, don't you see? It's easy for him to put the face on, to play whatever part is expected of him. He ingratiates himself to you and pretends with us. How can you trust a two-faced man to carry out your father's orders?"

"He has no choice. If he doesn't, as my father said, he will be charged with disobeying a direct order of a

King's officer. A charge punishable by death, I must point out."

"In the real world I would agree with you. But I fear Nathaniel Appleton does not play in the real world."

"And I fear love has clouded your judgement." Donald smiled. "All will be well, Robert."

"How well, Donald? In your world Nathaniel Appleton is a gentleman, I am a traitor. Nathaniel will get rich on my labor. I will hang."

In the end, a rat gave Jason away. He had been trying so hard to remain still, to listen for approaching footfalls so he could kill anyone who came near Emily's hiding place, that he had allowed the ship's rats to run free over his pegleg and boot. He didn't notice when one began to gnaw on the leather until it had bitten all the way through. He yelped, kicked out at the cursed rat, tripped and sprawled on the slimy underbelly of the ship. As he tried to get up, he found himself with Nathaniel's pistol cocked against his temple. Nathaniel stamped his foot on Jason's cutlass and waved him to his feet, then kicked the cutlass far into the darkness of the hold.

"Which one is she in," Nathaniel asked.

"I don't know what you're talking about."

Nathaniel's cutlass came out and flicked at Jason's cheek, cutting him. "That's for you. The next time I use the cutlass I will jam it into every damned barrel around us until it finds a soft, bloody mark. It's your choice, *Mister* Broadbent."

Several seconds passed, all of which Emily used to decide whether Nathaniel meant what he said or not. When a hard thud sounded over to her left and she heard wood splintering, she knew he meant it. She wasn't going to die stuck inside a barrel.

"I'm in here," Emily called out and knocked on the side of the barrel.

"Em, no!"

"Jason, don't be silly. Mister Appleton won't hurt me." *Much*. "Now get me out of here."

"You heard the lady," Nathaniel said. "Get her out of there."

It took Jason less time to loosen the lid than it had to nail it on.

When Emily's head appeared over the top, Nathaniel held out his hand and helped her sit on the edge as she swung her legs over and down. He drew her up beside him to steady her and turned his head to Jason.

"So you thought to circumvent justice, Mister Broadbent? First doing battle with His Majesty's naval forces, then hiding a prisoner from His Majesty's naval commander? Do you know the penalty for such behavior?"

Jason nodded.

"Good." With one movement, Nathaniel clamped his hand over Emily's mouth as he rammed his cutlass into Jason's side, pulled it out and rammed it in again. "Tried, convicted, and sentence carried out."

Emily squirmed, kicked out, beat at Nathaniel with her hands. He punched her in the belly and she fell into his arms, unconscious. He picked her up and carried her back to the main hatch, laid her on a piece of torn canvas, and gave precise orders to one of his men. Then he wiped the bloody cutlass on the ill-fitting breeches Emily was wearing and climbed the ladder to the deck.

At first when Emily woke up, she thought she was on *Patriot* because the bunk she was in swayed as Rob's had done and she heard the snap and creak which she had become accustomed to hear when sails were in full hoist. But then Jason's face seemed to appear before her—surprise, pain, horror, etched on it. She had seen . . . Good God! He had been run through. Twice. His hand had gone to his side, where blood spurted, then to his belly, where it seeped. He had looked at her. Compassion. Fear. Apology. And then his eyes had closed. Almost immediately, a large brown rat had crept close to his body, the rat's nose twitching at the smell of blood.

"Jason! Ah, God, Jason!"

She sat up suddenly, and her head cracked on the wood of the bunk above her. She swore and swung her legs over the side.

Her belly hurt where Nathaniel Appleton had hit her. She looked down and sucked in her breath. She knew without being told that the brownish stain on her breeches was Jason's blood.

The bastard! Nathaniel Appleton would pay. Somehow . . .

Ah, yes, somehow.

She patted her breeches pocket and smiled.

If Nathaniel had seen that smile he might not have been so jubilant that he had spirited Emily aboard without the stupid British or Rob's crew knowing. Rolled in canvas, she had looked like any of the other sails he'd managed to include in his booty. And she was here on *Aquidneck,* in his officer's cabin, awaiting his "visit."

Good.

He would give her time to contemplate her fate. And time to remember what had happened in the hold of *Patriot*.

Nathaniel liked the feeling of power—a feeling he had each time he welcomed aboard a woman stolen by his crew for their captain's pleasure. That feeling of power didn't last long, however. Only a few nights, when the woman was still smoldering and their coupling was accompanied by struggles. As soon as she became used to her position and ceased to be his foe in bed, he would send out his special invitations to men who would pay good solid gold or silver for white women. Nathaniel didn't care which of the men who frequented his auctions bought the prize. Hareem, bordello, or whore house, what did it matter where she ended up? It only mattered where and how she began.

Nathaniel's captive, captive in Nathaniel's bed.

And this time it was all the sweeter because Emily

Gorton would stand in for Robert Sears's sister. Nathaniel would have the nights he should have had four years ago. But they would be better, tinged as they were with fear.

When the door opened, Emily was prepared to kill, if necessary, to avenge Jason's death and save herself from a fate worse than death. But it wasn't Nathaniel Appleton who wordlessly pulled her up out of the bunk and dragged her down the gangway toward the captain's quarters.

Inside, the room was shaped much as Rob's cabin had been. But that was all that was the same. This cabin looked more like the sumptuous room in which Rebeccah had slept than a room for a working ship's captain. It was a floating friendly house and Emily was almost positive she knew what it was meant for. She certainly knew it wasn't a captain's billet. No thunder jug stood in the corner, but a built-in commode with padded arms and a carved cover. No chart table with rolled up charts was jammed against the side wall, but a walnut sideboard with two drawers, on which stood cut crystal decanters filled to the brim with spirits. No rough captain's chair was pushed under the table, but a deeply upholstered wing back chair, with a needlepoint pillow tucked into one corner had been placed at an angle to the corner of the table. No desk took up the space beneath the porthole, but a small skirted table with a gilt-edged mirror above it and a woman-sized damask-covered slipper chair pushed up to it. On its surface were cut crystal bottles which looked as if they contained every kind of powder and perfume man had ever made and a large pitcher and ewer, not of stoneware but porcelain. No chests filled with gifts Rob had never given her and warm bits of clothing stood to either side of the chart table, but mahogany sets of drawers which were carved with pineapple motifs and topped with twisted finials. No squares of Turkish carpet were spread helter skelter over the wide pine boards, but an intricately designed tapestry of blues and golds and reds lay under her feet from wall to wall. No small sleigh bed sat under salt-darkened windows, but a huge carved four poster with a sumptuous tapestry coverlet and five plump satin covered pillows.

A friendly house on the open seas.

"You will put that on," the man said, pointing to a mass of red silk which lay across the bed. "And you will let down your hair. Squire Appleton does not like women in plaits."

Emily flicked a furious glare at the man, crossed the room, ran her hands over the softness of the dress, and picked it up. It was lush and scandalous, exactly what she'd expect in this situation.

"I will wear what I have on. And my hair stays as it is."

"You will put that on and take down your hair," the man repeated. When she crossed her arms against her chest, he glared, then smirked. "As you wish. My master would like nothing better than to rip those plaits apart, tear the clothes off your back, and dress you himself. I don't think . . . ," he enunciated carefully, so she couldn't mistake his meaning, "I don't think you will like that. My master enjoys the struggle, enjoys the pain he gives. Do you understand?"

Emily shivered. She nodded. "May I have a bath?"

"There is water in the pitcher. That's all we have."

He backed up and closed the door. She heard a key turn in the lock.

As she un-braided her hair, she wondered why he had bothered to lock her in. Where could she go? She was on a ship in the middle of the Atlantic Ocean. All she could do was throw herself overboard.

And if it came to that, she would do it. She wasn't afraid to die. As a doctor, she'd seen the peace death brought. The peace Jason now had. Ah, God, why?! Why had she been allowed to save Jason if the young man was only to be killed a few years later and left to die among the rats!

Her hands stopped stripping off her clothes. What would Rob be thinking right now? He would be frantic, she knew. His cousin, gone. She, gone. *Patriot*, a prize of the British. His world . . . all of their worlds . . . had crashed in one morning. And they hadn't had a chance to say good-bye. Or to say, *I love you*.

When she stepped out of the last bit of clothing, she bit her lip. No, that was wrong. Rob had said it. Jason had shown it. It was only Emily, herself, who had never voiced her feelings for either of them.

As she washed, she warred within herself; but there was no backing away from it. Her feelings for Rob went deeper than she'd ever dreamed possible. Had they not been in this horrible mess, she would never have acknowledged them; because she would never have let them come to the surface. But, finally, she faced them. And when she did, she smiled.

Regardless of the danger, something good had been revealed.

"Rob," she whispered as she scrabbled among the cast off clothes to find the small box which contained the tiny scalpels the man she loved had made so many years ago. When she found it, she asked, "Who would have thought they would be used for this?" She opened the box and retrieved the one which fit her hand best. She put it into the pocket of the red silk dress and hid the box under the bed.

"Rob, I'm all right. I'll be all right, don't you worry."

With a deep breath, she let the dress slide over her head. The attached stomacher was trimmed with intricate embroidery and she laced it quickly, sucking in as the boned stays cut into her flesh. As she'd suspected, the stomacher held her breasts high, so they were almost spilling out of the low cut neckline.

"Rob, I can feel you here, in this room. Help me, please."

Emily took a look at herself in the mirror and flushed at her reflection. She turned her back to the strumpet in the mirror and stood in the middle of the cabin, looking out the windows above the bed, wishing she could see Rob's ship, wishing with all her heart that he wasn't only in her mind, but truly close to her.

"Rob, if you can hear me . . . and even if you can't . . . I love you."

"Well, isn't that touching!"

Emily whirled. She had been too preoccupied to hear the key turn in the latch.

Nathaniel smiled with the feral smile of a fox and walked slowly around her, adjusting the dress's skirt, shaking out one of the triple layers of lace which ran from elbow to wrist, then standing back to admire his handiwork. "So touching, your little speech, and so meaningless."

"You killed Jason."

"Do you know, my dear, that he was the first man to feel my cutlass? He was. And killing him like that was . . . how can I put it? It was . . ." He reached out and traced the edge of the low neckline on the dress, letting his fingers linger on the swell of her breasts which were pushed high by the stomacher round her rib cage. "It was almost like cutting through a soft piece of pork. And nearly as satisfying."

Remembering the warning the man had given—that Nathaniel liked his women to fight him—Emily refused to give him the satisfaction and pleasure a good fight would bring. But she couldn't keep her mouth shut. "You are a slimy sack of potage."

Nathaniel grinned. "Yes. Welladay, you will be calling me worse things before this day is over, my dear." His hand grasped her breast and squeezed until she gasped from the pain.

"You bastard!"

"That's it." He squeezed harder and she bared her

teeth. "Anger. Hate. Rage. Good. Good. I like that. It's the fuel that will make our nights together most enjoyable for me."

She wanted to kick out at him, find that soft spot between his legs, claw his eyes out. But she would not, lest it brought any kind of pleasure to him.

A knock sounded at the door and Nathaniel called, "Come in."

The same man who had brought her to the cabin entered carrying a tray loaded down with food. He bustled about with his eyes downcast, setting the tray on the sideboard and removing dishes and cutlery. He poured two glasses of a ruby red wine, shook out two damask napkins and put them on the plate and drew up the slipper chair to the table.

And all the time he was there Nathaniel caressed Emily's body. He only stopped when the man left, and then only to cross the room to lock the door from the inside.

Emily's very soul cried out at the degradation Nathaniel Appleton had brought to her. It was an affirmation of the viciousness of Delia Davies, who saw her as naught but a wasted human being. But Emily was no longer the small girl who believed everything she was told. She had known the steadfastness of Robert and Jason, men whose boots Nathaniel wasn't fit to lick. She had known the gentleness of Rob's love, the wonder of his touch. And they were being defiled by this beast of a man who thought no more of Jason Broadbent, that good, true friend, than he did of a side of pork!

Nathaniel turned and tugged hard on Emily's hair. "We will eat later. Right now, I've better things to occupy my time."

His free hand went to the laces on the front of his breeches. As he pulled them free, his breath came faster and he smiled that awful smile she'd grown to hate. Without a word, he backed her up to the bed and pushed her down on it. He eased his breeches over his flabby flesh, then raised one leg and planted his boot right on her belly.

"Scream," he said. "I want you to, and my men expect it. They've heard screams coming from this cabin often enough, they've gotten so they can enjoy the experience along with me."

The heel of his boot ground into her but she refused him the satisfaction of a response.

"Scream, I said!"

Dear God, she could not stand it! By all that was holy, she could not be expected to allow Nathaniel to do this. She was a doctor. She gave life, she did not take it away. But no one, not even God, would condemn her for defending herself from sin.

And the only way to do it was to kill the sin-maker.

"The only scream you will ever hear will be your own," Emily said, her voice quavering.

Her hand sneaked into her pocket and she withdrew the small scalpel which had been her most precious possession.

With the speed she had learned in years of surgery, she slashed the tendon just above his boot.

He screamed.

Because his leg was now useless, she rolled away from him and slashed up and across the tendons of the hand that had held the cutlass. He roared and threw himself at her.

He was not strong, but he was big and heavy. His left hand grasped her wrist to hold the scalpel away and his bulk brought her easily to the floor. But he was blinded by his fury and gave not enough heed to the deadly scalpel just inches away from his head. As he fell, his face brushed against it. Honed every week, it was razor sharp. When Nathaniel raised his head, blood covered a long slash which split his upper lip, sliced his cheek, and cut off the tip of his ear.

"You will pay dearly for this!" Nathaniel shouted, his words slurred as he tried to use a useless mouth.

He wrestled the scalpel out of Emily's hand and almost brought it down to give her a face to match his own. But he caught sight of her hair spread out on the floor and he forced himself to a stop.

"No, no, no . . ."

He grinned, and Emily knew she was doomed.

It didn't even register when Nathaniel's men broke in the door. Didn't register when they bound her hands and, at his orders, dragged her up on deck. Didn't register when they pushed her down, forced her arms over her head and tied her to large stanchions that seemed to be placed there for just that purpose. She didn't move when her legs were forced apart and her ankles tied to large iron rings. She kept her mouth clamped shut, regardless of how tight the ropes bit into her flesh, or how long she lay there as the hot afternoon sun beat down on her.

She only smiled once; and that was when Nathaniel's yowls echoed through the ship as someone not as skilled as she tried to patch up the damage she had done. But that smile soon died when she became shamed by the joy that swept through her. No wonder the Bible said, "Vengeance is mine, saith the Lord." The triumph she felt at Nathaniel's misfortune—regardless of how well deserved—had twisted her soul.

From healer to maimer in less than a day.

How would she ever live with herself?

Chapter Sixteen

"Are you comfortable, Captain?" Lord Dudley Douglass asked Robert.

"I'd be more comfortable in my own cabin on *Patriot,*" Robert answered.

"I'm afraid that will never happen again, sir."

"Don't count on it."

Donald smiled at both Rob and his father as he poured them each another rum punch. "I told you he would not give in easily, Father. He is a man worthy of a British commission."

"God forbid," Rob said, absentmindedly, more concerned with what had not gone on than with what was.

Four hours ago, when Nathaniel had come up on deck without Jason and Emily, Rob had breathed easier. But when there had been no word, when Rob had seen no sign that they were free . . . when Emily had not kicked on the barrel to tell the British where she was, the visions in his head weren't of sweetmeats and sugarplums. God's blood! The late morning and early noon had been frittered away in a well-appointed cabin in which he'd probably worn a hole in the carpet worrying about the two of them.

Should he inquire? Should he ask Donald to send a search party to the *Patriot?* Or should he keep silent and hope that Jason and Emily had been overlooked and were now enjoying a free reign on *Patriot* as it was being towed behind the British gunboat?

Silence be damned! He had to know!

He was just about to voice his concerns when a cannon went off over their heads.

Donald jumped to his feet, spilling his wine on his spanking clean uniform. He bolted for the door and threw it open. His nose collided with the outstretched hand of his steward as he was about to knock on the door. Donald's eyes teared and he yelped, "Blast and hell!" Carefully, he felt his nose, which was now gushing blood.

"Who shot off that cannon," Lord Douglass demanded.

The steward seemed lost for words, then couldn't stop their spilling over. "Pirates off the starboard bow, m'Lord! Pirates! They came upon us as those damned Quaker ships, the ones disguised as merchant vessels which don't show any guns until the last minute . . . and they've already an advantage, sir, since we're to leeward . . ."

Rob recognized the maneuver, since he'd been engaged in many a rout that used the surreptitious "quakering" to fool the enemy. "What color are their hulls," he asked, although he already thought he knew the answer.

"Black, the big one, sir. Robin's blue, the littler."

Rob smiled for the first time since they'd discovered the sabotage aboard *Patriot*. He laughed outright. As one of his old friends might say—the very friends who were giving Donald and Dudley fits—it warmed the cockles of his heart to hear the rout on deck.

"You know these men?" Lord Douglass asked.

Rob tipped a lighthearted salute to the commander. "M'Lord, if I'm not mistaken, your men are engaged in battle with the fiercest pirates this side of the Mediterranean. One-eyed Jack Saunders and Dover Quince. And good luck to you. You're going to need it."

Lord Douglass rushed out after his steward.

As Donald buckled on his sword and finished wiping the blood from the nose his seaman had bashed, Rob warned, "Be careful up there, Donald. I've come to admire you. You're a man whose word can be trusted, even though he does some foolish things. Those are truly fine seamen you'll be facing. Finer fighters."

"Thank you, sir. I, too, have come to admire you, Captain Sears. But fear not. We red-coats, as you call us, have centuries of fighting behind us." Donald tucked his pistols in his belt and prepared to follow his father. "Do I need to lock the door or post a guard?"

"Nay. I'll not interfere. I've seen first hand the damage those two and their crew can do."

It took less time to subdue the *Edgerton*'s crew than it had taken Donald to overcome a half-rigged

Patriot. As soon as Rob heard the *Yeehaw* of One-eyed Jack, he figured his word to Donald was no longer in effect. He hastened on deck and was glad he did, for he was just in time to stop an eager Jack Saunders from running his cutlass through Donald.

When Jack finally realized that Rob wasn't going to allow him to do the red-coat in, he put away his sword. Thumping Rob on the back, he grinned his wicked grin, winked his lone piercing blue eye, and stepped back.

Jack's girth had increased in the years since Rob had found Emily in the back yard of Matthew Cox's house. He was now three hundred and fifty pounds, if he was an ounce. And he was more flamboyant, epitomizing the legend of the pirate rather than the truth.

Dover Quince, on the other hand, looked more the typical pirate of Rob's day. He was wiry yet short. Muscled and dark where the sun had toughened his skin. His clothes were dirty, blood splattered, remnants and odd pieces which he'd picked up from one raiding party or another. But they were serviceable for battle, not for prancing in society. His black bell bottoms and his grey shirt were cut loose, allowing plenty of room to maneuver. No lace, cloak, or vest. No feathered hat. No wild hair to blow across his eyes to blind him. He wore his blond hair cropped close, without even a rattail at his nape. No beard covered his chin because it was too easy to get a purchase on; it left a man vulnerable to a slit throat. His only affectation were silver buckles on his boots—and Rob knew they had come from a booty he'd gotten when his crew had taken one of the Earl of Halifax's merchant vessels. Dover liked to brag that the buckles were meant for the Earl, though he was not so stupid to believe it.

As usual, Jack was all bluster. "Rob, me lad! So ye *are* in one piece. When we saw *Patriot* in tow, I were not so sure. But I says to me first mate, I says, *If Rob was 'ere wot wod 'e do?* And I says, *'E'd board 'er, 'e wod. That's wot e'd do!* So that's wot we did. An' 'ere ye are!" He jerked his head toward Donald and his father. "Wot's wi' the red-coats ye want to save from the fishies? Ye've not joined the blasted Newport Junta or taken a Tory leanin'?"

"Nothing like that, Jack. But these red-coats are honorable men . . ."

"An' I'm the King's mistress," Jack roared. "Since when, Rob? Or are it jes' these two yer wantin' to be savin'? Ken we not take their crew an' all?"

"Beach the crew. Take the gunboat. You should have fun with it."

"Oh, aye! A gunboats a good toy, i'tis. But a crew, Rob. 'Ave ye not learned ennythin' I've taught ye? A crew ken live to fight another day. 'Tis best to run 'em through an' be done with it, or make 'em pirates."

Rob saw the agony in Donald's eyes at the thought of what a massacre could do to his brave men, and Rob made a "don't worry" gesture to the only British officer in the past few years he hadn't found pompous, arrogant, and downright vicious.

"They spared my crew, Jack. Every manjack of

them are below, locked in the forequarters. For that alone, I owe *these* red-coats their lives, at least."

"Ah, Rob . . . I cod niver refuse ye ennythin' . . . an' ye cod niver stomach our game once we turned pirate. So," Jack shrugged, " 'tis yer friendship I honor, if not yer weak stomach."

As Donald slumped against the rail with relief, Rob asked, "Jack, I need a favor."

"Another one? Yer goin' to use em all up, Rob, me lad."

"Jason and Emily are aboard *Patriot*. Hiding in the hold, I think. Send some men. Find them. And for God's sake get them over here as quick as you can. They've not had water or a meal in several hours."

"Emily Gorton? The lady doctor wot saved Jason's life?"

"Aye."

Jack gave orders to one of his men, who took a dozen others and lowered a dinghy to row across the small distance from the *Edgerton* to the *Patriot*.

"While they be gone," Jack said, "we cod talk o' booty fer Quince an' meself. There be ennythin' 'ere worthy o' our boarding?"

"The cargo's mine and the stores are mostly mine," Rob said. "I'll be needing them. Afraid this is one battle from which you won't come away with booty."

Jack shrugged. "The gunboat'll do, then."

"And which of you will get it?"

Jack's eye closed as he thought about the problem Rob had pointed out. When he opened it, Rob had to laugh at the mischief he revealed. "Mayhap we'll share it," Jack said, but Rob was sure Jack would find a way to shoulder Dover out of the bargain. Jack was stronger. Dover had depended on Jack's patronage many a time. There was no doubt who would be the proud possessor of the *Edgerton*.

"Ahoy, Cap'n!"

All men turned at the sound from *Patriot*. One of Jack's men held a limp body in his arms. A body with one wooden leg.

Rob felt cold fingers creep up his neck and his stomach knotted until he thought himself squeezed of all life. "Ask about Emily," he croaked.

Jack shouted over, "Did ye find a woman aboard?"

"Nay! And we searched the whole ship!"

Faced with his worst fears, Rob snapped back into cold, firm control. He whirled on Donald. "I warned you about Appleton's character. Damn your honor!" He pointed a finger toward a huge man who was Dover's right hand man and demanded of Donald, "Give him the key to the forequarters. I want my men on deck in three minutes!" He turned to Jack. "Beach these red-coats. Your word, Jack."

"Aye, Rob."

"Quince?"

Dover nodded and held up his hand to signify his word and bond to Rob.

"My stores and cargo are below. Bring them to Block Island," Rob asked of Jack. "Emily's brothers will hold them until I get back."

Jack and Dover exchanged glances. The eyebrow over Jack's patch raised in a questioning way. He pursed his lips and put his hand to his sword. Dover once again nodded.

Jack turned to Rob. "The beachin' ken wait an' so ken Block Isle. We be comin' with ye, Rob."

Rob gulped his thanks, then gasped and slapped his hand against the rail. "God's blood! I've no sails. Nathaniel Appleton ripped them to shreds."

" 'Ere's wot we'll do, then," Jack said. "We'll lock these red-coats below an' a quarter o' me men and a quarter o' Quince's ken take charge 'ere. Shouldna need more than that ta beach the red-coats on Montauk . . . or near abouts. Then they be takin' this 'ere toy for Block Isle to drop off ye stores an' cargo."

"Sound's good," Rob said.

" 'Tis good. An' as fer yer sails . . . 'Alf the sails from this tub, we'll use ta fill in the gaps on *Patriot*. An' I've extry ones on *Saber,* as 'as Quince on *Whirlwind*. Yer welcome ta what ye think ye'll need. Atween the three ships' sails and our eager crews, ye'll 'ave 'nuff man power an' wind power ta get where ye need ta go an' do what ye need to do when we get there." He stuck his grinning face nose to nose with Donald's. "An' yer King says there's no 'onor 'mong thieves. Pah! Seems 'tother way round ta me."

"So," Dover Quince spoke up for the first time, "where are we heading and whom are we chasing?"

None of Nathaniel's crew paid any attention to Emily and she wondered at the control that made them that afraid to touch Nathaniel's property . . . for that, she knew, was exactly what she was. By the reckoning of the setting sun, three hours the man had worked on patching up Nathaniel. It must have been a gruesome job, judging from the screams and curses that had blistered the air.

Three hours of that bellowing, then blessed quiet.

Another hour or so went by before the first crew member made a move toward her. Her skin contracted from the fingers that stroked the skin on the inside of her calf and she spit on him. He grinned and wiped the spittle off, but continued his pleasure. Then a boot came out and kicked him in the gut. He rolled away with a yelp and Emily heard the sounds of boots—several sets of boots—as their owners scuttled away.

The man who had warned her about Nathaniel and brought them the supper they had never eaten, knelt down beside Emily. He clucked his tongue at her and offered her a cold draught of water.

"The master is drunker than I've ever seen him. Sprawled on his bed, he is. When he wakes, I pity you. Why did you not heed my words?"

"I did. But the thought of staying quiet and allowing him to . . . I'd rather be dead."

"That's not what he has in mind."

"Do you know what he has in mind?"

The man—an average middle-aged man, of average height, with brown hair and brown eyes that were permanently glazed as if he had looked deep inside himself and found horror—sighed more plaintively than Emily had ever heard.

"Aye. I know what he has in mind. Do you think

you're the first woman who has been in this position? In this very spot?"

He looked off toward the horizon, away from the setting sun, as if seeing the bright red orb was too painful. His words, when they came, were as if torn from his guts. Emily was afraid he might be sick right there. Then, when she heard what he was saying, she was afraid she might be.

"After the women he shanghais spend a few days and nights in his cabin he always brings them here on deck and has them tied down the way you are. He lets the others do what that dog was doing to you. Touch them. No more. Just touches. It's what happens when the touches are finished that's the worst."

He shook himself and offered her a bite of hardtack. She chewed on the sour biscuit but couldn't swallow. *The worst*. What could be worse than spending days and nights with that monster? Death? Death would be a blessing.

She tried to force the man to look at her, to let him see the questions she had. She didn't want to ask them. She wanted him to volunteer. That way, she thought, she could take the knowing, chew it over in her mind, and find some way to accept it.

"There's no use in looking at me like that. I won't tell you," the man said. "I dare not. The last man who told a woman what she could expect had his tongue cut out."

"God's blood!" Emily spat the sour tack into a corner but quaffed the whole mug of water. "Why are you here?"

"To bring you something to eat."

"No, I mean, *here,* on this ship. You seem an educated man."

"Aye. Educated in ways I never dreamed possible when I was a lad. Educated in things I hope you never see. I was a school teacher, once. Even taught his son. Now, I'm a broken man. Not only am I in debt to Appleton but so are my four sons. Two years ago, just as I was sure the magistrates would take us all to gaol, Appleton agreed not to send us to debtor's prison if I served a term of seven years on his ship, did his bidding without question, and on land kept my mouth shut for the rest of my life. If you know anything about the British debtor's prison, you must understand why I would do anything to spare my family those horrors." He brought another cup to Emily's lips. "Ale. It's bitter but it will warm you for the night."

"Will you stay near me?"

"Aye. Unless he orders different."

"Where are we going and whom are we chasing?"

The two pirates and Rob were in Rob's cabin on *Patriot*, trying to plot a course with Orrin Mayotte, while Jack's apothecary worked on Jason's wounds.

It was a miracle the young man hadn't died. But it was due more to his constitution than the condition of his wounds, for they were reddened and swelling with poisons. Rob had hurled orders, the kind of orders he'd heard Emily give, hoping they were the right ones. To be sure Jason had the best chance to recover,

Rob had insisted Emily's medicines be used on him. Lucky they were that the giant surgical box which she'd filled for *Patriot*, and her own medicine cases which he'd kidnapped along with her, were still aboard. So they had all her herbs and the precious salves she had concocted.

Unlucky they were, for Rob didn't have the foggiest notion where to search for *Aquidneck*.

" 'E won't put into Newport," Jack said authoritatively. "Only a fool wod do that."

"Or Block Island, or Baltimore," Rob said. "There's too many Americans there."

Dover Quince exploded. "Newport! Block Island! Baltimore! Are you both tomfools? Do you know nothing of the man with whom you're dealing?"

"Appleton, the Tory," Rob spat.

"Oh, certainly that," Dover said. "But there's more to him than meets the eye, Rob. It seems to me I must know Nathaniel Appleton much better than either of you. Do you truly not know that he is more than a Newport merchant?"

"Out wi' it, man," Jack said impatiently. "Yer Oxford eddication makes ye slow an' it drives me crazy!"

Dover harumphed. "The man has a slave plantation on Guadeloupe, where he has three friendly houses."

Rob's head jerked up and he growled, "Appleton? Are you sure?"

"Positive. He probably owns more friendly houses and bordellos than any man on the Atlantic coast. Even the one on Block Island . . ."

"Rebeccah Washington owned that," Rob said.

"Owned, yes. But when she died Appleton added it to his stables. Have you naught heard of Naples?"

"It's a white slave group," Rob said, puzzled. "But what the hell does that have to do with a Newport merchant?"

"Take the first letter from Nathaniel and the first part of Appleton—without one of the *p*s, mind—and what do you get?"

"N. A. P. Drop a p. L. E." Rob groaned. "Naples." The name was the most hated on the slave route, not because slavers were particular; but because the group which called itself Naples kidnapped free white women and sold them into unspeakable slavery in Arabia, Europe, the Orient, and floating bordello ships. Some of the women who had been kidnapped from Block Island were said to have ended up in Naples's hands. "God's blood! If what you say is true, Emily is in worse danger than I imagined."

Dover nodded. "I've been following this scurrilous merchant's trail for years. I may be the only one who has put two and two together and come up with a full house. First, he makes frequent trips to the islands. Second, he cultivates impoverished widows who have no dower rights or family to support them and offers them financial help by taking their meager savings and offering them a percentage of the profits from his next cargo. Then he embezzles their money, telling them the ship and cargo was lost at sea. They rarely get suspicious. Too many ships do go down. But when the widows run out of ready cash and founder—and they will, especially with the taxes the British are imposing—he's ready with an unspeakable proposition. And as we all know, there are not many who can resist, for if they did they would starve. Rob, if you wish to rescue Emily from their fate, I would head due south toward the islands which he considers his safe harbor."

Why, Emily wondered, was the sunset that afternoon as beautiful as ever it had been? Though she couldn't see the horizon, she watched as the sky above her turned from a bright, clear blue to the palest of pastels, then a streak of crimson, then gold, then a creeping wash of indigo. How could such beauty be part of such an ugly world?

Though the night was still, the noises of the crew changing watch and the biting rawness of her bonds kept Emily awake. Occasionally, a man crept close to her; but a hiss from her school teacher protector sent him back into the blackness through which her eyes could not penetrate. And every so often a loud snore, followed by groans and mumbled curses, floated up through the hatch just outside the master's cabin.

The only bright light that horrible evening was Emily's fervent hope that Nathaniel Appleton might die from drunkenness.

The watch changed at midnight with the final ring of eight bells. The first time she had been aboard a true sailing ship, at the first complete peal of the time, she had thought a bit romantic the combined sounds of a tingling bell, waves lapping on the sides of the ship, and sails snapping in the wind. Now, it was but one more agony to add to her discomfort.

And at half after midnight it started again.

But so did a scuffle off to starboard.

Emily cocked her head to the side from where the scuffle—if that's what it was—had come, trying to catch more sounds, wondering what had happened, hoping her protector had not been overpowered by the lustful crew.

There it was again!

Her eyes ached from trying to penetrate the roiling fog and pitch but it was no use. She tried to see her protector but could not. "What's happening?" she called out. Her protector didn't answer.

Truly frightened, now, she began tugging on the ropes, letting them cut into her wrists, not caring, only desperate to be free to defend herself!

A grunt and a muffled oath sent her into a frenzy. The rope tore at her flesh as the fog parted and dark man-shapes closed in around her. She didn't know whether to scream or keep silent. But what would silence accomplish except her own debasement?

So, gathering all her strength, she opened her mouth to scream, only to have a large, spicy-sweet hand clamp itself over her mouth, and the loving, familiar voice of Rob whisper loving, familiar words in her ear, "Be still as stone, Emily, love. I'll have you clear of these ropes in just a minute."

When it took more than a minute for him to saw

through the ropes, Emily chided, "Remind me to sharpen your knife."

When at last she was free, Rob pulled her up into his arms and held her close. She tugged his head down for a kiss and reveled in the feel of the scratchy skin of his jaw against her cheeks, the softness of the underside of his lips, the crush of his hands on her back and bottom, the softness of his hair as her fingers relearned its texture.

"Oh, Rob! Rob! Jason's dead!"

"No, sweetheart. He's hurt bad—and needs your healing touch once more to make him whole—but he's alive. He's waiting for you on *Patriot*."

"An ocean away."

"No more than a half hundred yards. How did you think I got here?"

"How *did* you get here? The last I saw, you were a prisoner and *Patriot* had no sails."

"One-eyed Jack and Dover Quince. It's a long story, Em. Too long to tell now. We've overpowered Nathaniel's crew. Now, I only have to deal with the blackguard, himself.

"Too late," Emily giggled. "I took care of him."

"Em . . ."

"He's below. Nursing the wounds I gave him with one of those tiny scalpels you once made for me. He's in the only ship's cabin I've ever seen that has furbelows and lace instead of charts and deal tables."

"Speaking of furbelows," Rob said. "What is this I feel round your middle?" He struck a flint and lit a ship's lantern. Holding it high over her head, he took one look at what Emily was wearing and the most lascivious grin crossed his face. "Emily Gorton. I know I'm not supposed to appreciate that garment Nathaniel made you wear; but, damn, if it isn't . . . Wow!"

"Men! Show a little flesh and they get all kinds of ideas . . . Shut your mouth, Robert Sears, and follow me." She picked up her skirts and took two steps, but the ropes had bit too far into her ankles. Because of the pain, she dropped to her knees, cursing.

"Emily, love!" Rob quickly knelt and examined her ankles. They were red, raw, and bleeding. "That bastard! How long were you tied up," he asked, his voice a mixture of outrage and vengeance.

"Ever since I fought Nathaniel. About seven or eight hours." She jerked her head and looked around. "Oh, no! There was a man here, my protector. A former school teacher who was kind and wouldn't let the others . . . well, you know."

"Yes," Rob said, menacingly, "I know. And Appleton and his crew will pay for this."

"But, Rob! The man was kind. He must be saved. . . ."

"We'll find him, Em. But right now, I want to find Nathaniel." He sat her on the steps leading down from the quarterdeck and motioned over Orrin Mayotte to keep watch over Emily. When she tried to get up, he ordered, "Stay here, love. I'll take care of Nathaniel."

He found him in the master's cabin, and knew immediately what Emily had meant about laces and furbelows. "Damned fop! What a waste."

Jack and Quince poked their heads in as Rob was trying to rouse Nathaniel.

" 'Ere, now! Ain't 'e a pretty sight?!"

"Nothing more than he deserved," Quince said.

Rob sighed. He knew Emily must have been scared out of her wits or she would never have fought back as she had. He ached for her, knowing that when what she had done would finally sink into her, she would be desolate. But for now, he felt a supreme sense of justice.

"Emily's handiwork," he said.

Quince frowned. "She didn't do the stitching. She'd never let that kind of scar remain."

"Give a hand here," Rob asked. "He's so drunk, I can't rouse him."

Between the three of them they managed to hoist Nathaniel up the ladder and through the hatch. On deck, they dropped him like a sack of meal as they surveyed the *Aquidneck*.

Several of Nathaniel's crew had put up a half-hearted fight and were either dead or severely wounded. Already, Emily was busy tending to their wounds. Rob noticed that one man never left her side, but helped with whatever she asked. Her protector, she'd called him. He looked like the kind of man who deserved a second chance; and because of what he'd done to help Emily, Rob was determined to see that he got it.

"Well, you wanted booty . . . Here it is," Rob said to Jack and Dover, waving his hand around the ship. "Lots of what's below deck belongs to me. But the rest of the cargo . . . and the ship . . . is yours, with my thanks."

One-eyed Jack once again thumped Rob on the back. "Rob, me boy, yer most generous! Sure ye don't want ennythin' fer yerself?"

"Only Emily and that man who's helping her. Ah . . . and Nathaniel, of course. For what he has done and what he planned to do, he must face the combined justice of a real freeman's court. And I know just the place to hold the trial. . . ."

"Oh, I do admire the glint in your eye, Rob," Dover Quince said, bobbing up and down with glee. "If you could petition the authorities to declare an amnesty for the trial, I know several pirates—Jack and myself, included—who would dearly like to attend."

"I'm sure the selectmen on Block Island will be most willing. Especially when they find out what happened to Emily."

Chapter Seventeen

Once more Emily found herself working frantically to save Jason's life. This time, she was grateful for the expertise she'd gained over the years—and for the fact that Nathaniel's cutlass had gone clean through Jason's body, touching only muscle, not vital organs. No, it hadn't been Nathaniel's wound which put Jason in danger. It had been the muck and mire of the hold, and the foulness of its brown, furry inhabitants. For that, she needed every bit of skill and every herb, medicinal, and salve she had.

Her protector never left her side, acting as her assistant in all things, the way she had worked for Matthew Cox.

For two days they fought the infection with one brew or salve after the other. On the third day, Jason's fever broke, the swelling around the wounds went down, and there was no sign of disintegrating matter. Emily began to breathe easier and opened her surgery doors full time, instead of the limited hours she'd kept while nursing Jason.

The first three people to show up in the parlor were

the newly elected selectmen. George Briggs took his farmer's straw hat in hand and twisted it round and round as he stammered out their request.

"Daft, you are," Emily said, "if you think I'm going to doctor that *thing* you have behind bars."

"His screams and moans are something awful, Doctor Gorton," George said. "Keep us up day and night."

It was in a small lean-to attached to Briggs's house that the island had fashioned three barred cells; and it was his wife Dolly who cooked for the miscreants who were kept there, awaiting their trials or transport to the mainland.

Confrontations in Rhode Island and nearby Connecticut between the British and the Sons of Liberty took place daily. Tensions ran high. Usually the islanders would send their prisoners to the mainland for trial. Rarely would they hold court on their own.

But they were no longer in usual times. For the islanders to convict a British sympathizer was risky; but Nathaniel Appleton committed unspeakable acts against one of their neighbors. Because of the nature of the crime, and the fact that Block Islanders were independent enough to want to keep justice in their own hands, Nathaniel hadn't been transported to the mainland, even though his crimes were of sufficient severity to merit the colonial magistrates hearing the charges and passing judgement.

All across the small island, no one could talk of aught else. Nathaniel would be tried, convicted, and hanged on the scaffolding the islanders were building behind Briggs's barn. For everyone who knew the story, knew he deserved naught less than the severest penalty. Yet those same neighbors now wanted Emily to patch him up.

"It doesn't make sense," Emily said. "He's for the noose, regardless."

"But Dolly cannot stand the caterwauling. So we called a meeting and the freemen voted to pay you to treat the loyalist scum. We know he's already caused you much heartache; but if my goodwife doesn't get more rest she's going to cause *all* of us more headaches than we can stand."

Emily nodded her understanding of George Briggs's plight. Dolly was as vociferous as Delia had been, albeit of a much more pleasant nature. "I'll do it; but only if he's passed-out drunk and I don't have to listen to any poisonous venom spewing from his mouth."

Which was why, one day when Jason was resting comfortably, she and her protector stood beside a sweating, sleeping Nathaniel—trying for the seventh time to patch the God-awful repair job that had been done on his face. This was the final attempt, Emily decided. She had done all she could. The scar on Nathaniel's face—while far less noticeable than the one his apothecary had left—was there for good and all. Thanks to some fancy experimental surgery she'd done on his arm and leg, his pain had lessened. His arm would work, but with limited mobility, and his leg would straighten out. In fact, too much.

Nathaniel would always walk with a limp.

They worked silently for a time, until Emily couldn't stand the quiet any longer and had to voice the question that had been tearing at her for the past two weeks.

She led up to it slowly.

"Are you comfortable with us, yet?"

"Aye."

"No longer afraid?"

"I think I'll always be afraid, Mistress Gorton. But of you or your people, no."

"Then isn't it time you trusted me to know your name?"

He hesitated, more from habit than mistrust. "John Devere, they call me," he said.

"Well, John, and where are you from?"

"Portsmouth. Only a stone's throw from Newport."

"And your sons?"

"All of the Deveres are there. Mother, wife, sons, daughters-in-law, and four grandchildren."

She gave him her hand and he took it. "Welcome, John," she said. "Welcome back to freedom."

He had tears in his eyes when he whispered, brokenly, "Thank you, Emily. I never expected to see freedom short of the grave."

The next time Emily saw Rob, she told him the story of John Devere and asked that his family be brought to the island.

"Emily . . . you don't have room to house them, nor stores enough to feed the lot."

"There's Matthew's old house, the one he left me in his will. It's still vacant after all these years. They can stay there, if they'll fix it up. And I don't intend to feed them. I intend to find work for them. Surely the island can use a school teacher and some handymen."

"Shouldn't you consult John about this? He's the head of his household. Mayhap he won't want to be so close to the colony where he lost his reputation."

"And you have a better solution?"

"I might. My sister is a teacher in Savannah. I'll write to her. If there's a position open, and John wants it, I'll take him and his family to the new port. That way, they all get a fresh start."

Emily smiled and wrapped her arms around Rob's waist, hugging him to her. "I always knew there was something about you I admire."

"Admire. Well, that's a start."

But not enough, Emily knew. Not nearly enough for a man like Rob, who deserved everything—especially a woman who had something to give and would give it gladly. Since she'd come back to the island, she didn't know if she was that woman. She wanted to be. But something kept tugging her away from thoughts of marriage and wifehood.

It wasn't Delia Davies. Emily had shed that nightmare the first time she and Rob had made love. Rob had said she would discover her womanhood and she had. In fact, she reveled in it.

And that was what bothered her.

She was on edge every minute. Aware of Rob as a man, aware of herself as a woman. She felt drawn to him, like a doe to berry bushes. Her work kept her busy; but she wasn't as content with medicine as she'd once been—all because of Rob.

Each day, every minute, she kept one ear on her patient's complaint, one ear anxiously waiting to hear Rob's footfall. Most days he was busy repairing the damage to *Patriot*, sewing up new sails, restoring his cargo to the hold, or buying up enough stores to replenish those that had been lost or damaged during the three battles. And as if he hadn't enough problems, he had to change moorings almost every day, afraid a British patrol boat would discover *Patriot* and the whole thing would start over again.

And, of course, they had to be circumspect. Certainly, she wanted to continue the relationship that had started aboard ship and she was convinced by his actions that Rob did also. But Jason and Tab were in the house, John Devere walked in and out as if it were his own, patients came to Emily's door at any hour, and her brothers, their wives, and her nieces and nephews were wont to drop in at any time. In fact, the only place they seemed to have all to themselves was the stall where Emily kept her new cow, Jersey Bell.

But as much as she wanted to be alone with Rob, she balked at the thought of bedding down with a cow as companion!

Emily might be frustrated; Rob was at the breaking point. He had grown damned tired of the game they were playing. Cat and mouse, cat and mouse, with everyone watching their every move, and nary a mouse hole to hide in, certainly no bed to assuage their desire.

He was a man. He wanted his woman—Emily.

But pressing matters intervened until he could do something about it.

Once Nathaniel was completely mended, his trial was swift. Rob, Jason, Orrin, and Almanzo gave evidence of the sabotage. Emily gave evidence of her kidnapping. She omitted much of the description of what she had undergone; but—and for this Rob gave eternal thanks—the freemen hearing the evidence were worldly enough to fill in the missing pieces. As expected, Nathaniel was sentenced to hang. July twelfth was appointed as the day of his execution.

On July eleventh, a lookout spotted a boat near Sandy Point. He alerted a selectman but when Rob heard about it the area had already been searched and the boat was no longer there. The next morning they discovered why.

The door to the gaol was forced open from the outside and Nathaniel was gone. Inside, Rob found a British broadside in which Rob's piracy was prominently declared and a reward was offered for his capture. On the back of the broadside, Nathaniel had scrawled two sentences: *I will be back. And when I do, Doctor Emily Gorton shall pay the price for what she did to me.*

Though Rob couldn't keep Nathaniel's escape from Emily, he did ask everyone who had seen it to keep the contents of the broadside from reaching Emily's ears.

What Nathaniel had warned was the final shove Rob needed. He couldn't let anything happen to the woman he loved.

That evening after supper, he had Jop trim his hair, shave him, and polish his old boots until the black leather shone as new. Then Rob donned his best shirt, the one with the small ruffles at the wrist and a fall down the front, a green and cranberry tapestry-style vest, black linen breeches with silver trim at the knee, clocked white stockings, and his only tri-corn hat with a green feather at the cockade. He felt a fop, but he wanted to let Emily know his serious intent.

"If this doesn't work, I'll shanghai her again," he muttered as he trudged up the road from the dock—where he had gotten enough stares and snickers to last him a lifetime—and approached her house.

Why was he so nervous? This was Emily he was coming to see, not some British snob. Yet, before he knocked on her front door, he gulped twice to wet his suddenly dry throat.

When Emily opened it, she looked as if someone had poleaxed her. He noticed her chin wiggle, her shoulders shake, and her mouth purse from suppressed laughter.

"One word about how I look, Emily Gorton, and I'll turn right around," he warned.

"I couldn't think of a word if I tried." She gestured him into the front hall and looked first to the patients' waiting parlor, then to the keeping room, and back again.

He groaned. "I'm not sick."

"Did I say you were?"

"Em . . . . I warn you, I'm at the end of my

tether . . ."

"Obviously."

She preceded him into the keeping room, where a warm fire spread a golden glow on two upholstered settles which were drawn up on either side of the fireplace to ward off the evening's chill. She sat in one and gestured for him to sit in the other.

"Would you like some coffee or tea?"

"Brandy would be better."

"It's there on the mantel, where it always is. I'll fetch some glasses."

While she was gone, Rob paced back and forth from door to window and back again. He reached into his pocket and fingered the small box nestled there. Would it suit? His friend Jonathan Hobbs had sold it to him a year almost to the day after he and his wife Constance met Emily. It was a gold brooch shaped like a flower, with a large topaz stone and gold filigree to hold it in place. The topaz reminded Rob of Emily's eyes; it was almost the same color as the center of a Brown-eyed Susan daisy. A topaz that dark was rare, Jonathan had said. Almost as rare as Emily, herself. Rob had known immediately upon seeing it that it was the perfect choice for a betrothal gift.

"Jason is getting on well, I hear," Emily said as she came back with a tray containing two glasses and a plate of Tab's apple and raisin bread. "He wanted to get back to the ship so much, I didn't have the heart to deny him."

Rob added brandy to each glass—too much, he

saw, but in his nervousness, it was to be expected. Besides, they both needed the extra courage this visit was going to take.

Absentmindedly, he affirmed Emily's statement. "Aye. And the work seems to do him much good."

"I'm glad."

Emily looked at him over the edge of her glass, her dark eyes dancing with glee.

"God's blood, you're not making this easy, Em."

She put down the glass, smoothed down her ecru and peach striped shift, and sat ramrod straight, with only her head bent a slight bit forward—except for her breasts, Rob noted. They were thrust out, high and proud and oh, so enticing, that he almost choked on his brandy.

"Is that better?"

"No! Yes. It will have to do."

He gulped down the remainder of his drink, poured another, and took up a position near the fireplace, not daring to let his leg touch her or he was likely to scoop her up in his arms, drop to the floor, and make love to her right in front of the fireplace.

"Emily, I have something important to ask you."

"Yes?"

"Will you marry me?"

"Ah. . . ."

It was exactly what she feared since he walked in the door, so unlike himself it tickled something deep inside her. The solemnity of him, when he was the least solemn man she knew! The *appropriateness* of his clothing! The stiffness of his manner. Is this what marriage did to men and women . . . changed them completely? If it did, she wanted no part of it.

But she wanted him.

Each night, she ached with longing in her solitary bed, until the dull pain became her constant companion. She wanted what they had on the ship, what he had given her in the barn, what she dreamed in her dreams . . . Not this squire who sat in front of her but her Rob—her casual, disheveled, devil-may-care pirate of a man—kissing her, touching her, caressing her, entering her, loving her.

"I'm flattered, Rob."

"Why? You've known for years how I feel about you, what I want from you."

"But I fear you want more than I can give."

"You gave it on the ship, Em."

"And I would again . . . gladly."

"Then where's the problem?"

"Would you want me to wife and to doctor your crew?"

He looked puzzled for a moment. "To wife only me, Em. To doctor my crew, aye. You are a surgeon, after all."

"But I've a contract with the islanders, Rob. I have six years left to it."

"They would let you out of it, Emily."

"Aye, and therein is the rub . . . I don't want to get out of it, Rob."

"Nathaniel's threat . . ." He bit off, still not wanting her to know.

"Go ahead, say it. Nathaniel threatened me." At

his surprised, sour look, she laughed. "It's a small island, Rob. No secrets remain secret for long."

"Then that's all the more reason . . . ."

"No. What Nathaniel threatened isn't any reason for us to wed. And if you think it is, you're not the man who took me to such heights of joy that I can't imagine spending my nights without you. Ah, Rob, don't stand there like a Jack-a-Lent! Hold me! Love me!"

Rob groaned and pulled her up into his arms. His mouth ground down on hers and he drank of her, tasted her, as if he were starving and she his only succor. His hands skimmed over her and he cried out her name.

"Emily! How much I love you."

"And I love you." Smiling, she took his hand, plucked a lit lantern from the side table, and led him up the stairs. "Tab is at her sister's, helping birth their sixth baby. We have the house to ourselves."

When they got to her small bedroom, it was like a homecoming, Rob decided. A homecoming that had been more than fifteen years in the making. He loved her. She loved him. And they were to be wed. She hadn't said it; but by her admission of love, the question was answered to his satisfaction. After their lovemaking, after he brought her back to the ecstasy they'd shared on *Patriot*, he'd give her her betrothal gift. Now . . . now, he would merely love her.

"Tis convenient, these shifts of yours," he said as he slipped it up and over her head. "So easy to take off." His hands smoothed down her shoulders, and the length of her arms, until he came to her hands. Holding them in the warmth of his, he turned them up, then over, then up again. "These hands say so many things, Em. Strength. Tenderness. Skill."

"And clumsiness," she teased. "Mustn't forget the bruises of childhood."

Rob brought her hands to his mouth and kissed them, his eyes gazing deep into the darkness of hers as he tried to read the meaning behind her quavering voice. "Childhood is long past, Em. The bruises have healed. There is nothing now but skill . . ." He kissed one finger. ". . . goodness . . ." Another. ". . . tenderness . . ." And another. ". . . joy . . ." The last. ". . . love."

Emily shivered from the tingling that ran from her fingers clear up to her head, setting it all awhirl with feelings which had been put aside for three weeks. "My Lord, wilt thou do that to my other hand?"

Rob chuckled. "With pleasure, my Lady."

"Oh, yes," she whispered. "Please. With pleasure."

Rob didn't know how she managed it, but as he obliged her, she unbuttoned his vest and pushed it off his shoulders. It hung there on one arm as she tugged his shirt up and over his head. Before she completed the task, she held his hand to her mouth and kissed his fingers as he had done hers.

"Does it feel the same way for you as it does for me," she asked.

"If it feels wonderful for you, then, aye, that it does."

Her hands splayed across the muscles of his chest

and combed through the sprinkling of hairs. "I love how your muscles contract when I touch you," she said. "How your heart thuds under my fingertips. How you shiver . . . God, I love you!"

Within seconds he had her undershift off and he was pleasuring her, following her lead, going where she took him. Their hands and mouths covered every inch of their torsos.

He learned that her skin tasted salty-sweet beneath her chin. The essence of wild roses permeated her shoulder, her arm, the gentle swell of her breasts. But between them he tasted oranges, and lingered to savor the soft, melting flavor of her. Then his mouth swept over her breasts to find another taste. Her nipples were almonds, hard and suckling sweet. So sweet, he moaned in delight as he nibbled on her, sucked on her, molded the breasts that brought such delights.

In his head he knew all these sensations were from a rinse water she and Hopeful had once concocted but his heart preferred to believe that her body exuded such odors and tastes only for him when he aroused her.

Emily threaded one hand in Rob's hair, enjoying the springy texture of it; with the other hand, she took out her braids and finger-combed them until there was almost a tent of hair enveloping Rob's bowed head as he gently tugged at her breasts. God, how she loved him . . . how she loved to see him there, where no child had or would ever be. Her heart ached, and swelled with pride, that such a man loved her.

"Rob," she whispered, daring to break the spell she had initiated, "I want to make love with you in my bed."

No other words needed to be said as Rob picked her up and carried her to the small poster bed in the corner. As he lay her gently in the middle, his eyes, those beautiful many-hued eyes, smoldered with green and gold and grey dancing lights.

For several moments they stared at each other, until she broke the spell by raising her hand as she reached for the laces on his breeches.

"No, Em. Lie still. I want to look at you in the moonlight and the lantern glow. Your beautiful body looks as if it were made of silver and gold."

She smiled and held out her arms to him. Quickly, he kicked off his boots and peeled off his breeches. Both ended on the floor with the rest of their clothing. Then he eased himself onto her bed, felt a rush of heat envelop him as she wrapped her arms around him, and began a thorough loving of her. From forehead to nose to mouth to chin, his fingers traveled. Down, ever downward, to the soft, melting place that stirred his blood into white hot liquid. His manhood throbbed against her belly and he smiled as she let out a long, trembling moan of pleasure.

There was naught so wonderful as this, Emily thought. No one had traveled this road before. No one knew such ecstasy as she. And Rob had done it.

But the wondrous part was that in arousing her, he had become aroused himself. It amazed her, thrilled her, that he responded to her so ardently. But it was more thrilling to close her eyes and imagine what was going to happen next . . . imagine it and then make it happen.

Feathering her hands down his sides, she found his hip bones and the firm rise of his buttocks. Her legs opened, then wrapped themselves around him, as her fingers dug into him to urge him to that place where their bodies could be joined to become one breathless movement, one flesh, one eternal being.

He poised above her, his eyes telling her of his love, and then he slid inside and she convulsed around him, urging him deeper and deeper, until she thought she could feel him touching her heart. Only then did she raise her head until their lips nearly touched and said the words it had taken a lifetime to say, "Rob, I love you."

She kissed him and their journey began. She knew this step would end in a climax so wonderful, she would ache every minute of every day until they once more joined their bodies to climb another step. But where the sum of their steps led, she didn't know. She only knew she could no longer walk this earth alone.

Thus, she mated with the man she loved, giving every part of herself that she had to give, holding nothing back this night.

Their bodies slid together, retreated, slid back. She held him tight inside her, kissed his shoulder, learned every contour of his back, let her senses rule, and her lover lead. Her heart pounded in rhythm with his. She wondered if everyone in the village heard it . . .

and didn't care if they did. She gloried in this man and his love.

Arching up to meet his thrust, she saw herself for the first time as a woman. The realization made her heart race, her limbs strong, her insides tremble with joy. It burst out in a strangled cry as he thrust into her and her body contracted, expanded, shattered, repaired, and finally was soothed by several delicious tremors that brought on such lassitude, she decided she never wanted to leave such a delightful place.

Rob gathered her against him, tucking her under his shoulder in a protective gesture that was part husband, part lover. Soon, he hoped, the two parts would merge and their new lives together could begin. For now, however, he was content to cuddle her against him and listen to her breathing as it slowed down and sleep claimed her from him.

Chapter Eighteen

When Rob woke the following morning, the bed was empty. A slightly scorched smell drifted up from below and he smiled. Why had he thought she'd learned something about cooking in the past twelve years? But after their night together, even burned corn bread or biscuits would taste delicious. Everything else about Emily had.

His penis throbbed when he remembered the sweet things they'd done to each other after that first powerful coming together. She had not been afraid or embarrassed. No, she had been delightfully joyous in her explorations. And delightfully responsive to his. The first time her mouth had closed around him . . . . God's blood!

He needed some of Emily's god-awful cooking to calm him down, else he'd fly down those stairs and take her right there in the kitchen.

She was humming under her breath so she didn't hear him creep up behind her. When his arms encircled her waist, a tin plate of corn bread fell to the floor and she gave a half-hearted scream.

"Now look what you've done," she scolded. "Poor bread. We won't be able to eat it."

He laughed and swung her in the air. "Lucky us."

She batted at his hands until he put her down. Stooping, she picked up the only squares of the bread that hadn't crumbled on impact with the floor, brushed off a few strands of straw that clung to them, looked at the sorry things, then chucked them out the back door to the chickens which Tab allowed to run free. "I suppose we could have some of Tab's leftover strawberry pie and a tankard of buttermilk."

"Ah . . . now, *that's* a breakfast."

They ate in a companionable silence, although Rob noticed that Emily stole a glance at him about every ten seconds. When he finished off three pieces of pie and quaffed it down with two tankards of buttermilk, he wiped his mouth and smiled at her. "You're a bit skittish this morning."

Feelings were all muddled inside her. In the dark of night it was easy to focus on Rob and the way he made her feel. In the bright glare of morning . . . all right, the early haze of sunup . . . other things crowded out the delights of the night.

But one thing remained that hadn't been solved last night. Rob had asked her to marry him and she hadn't given him an answer.

"Um . . . about what you asked me last night. . . ."

Rob shushed her and dug into his pocket. "I have this to make it official."

She looked at the green velvet covered box and her heart nearly stopped dead. Oh, God . . . when it came down to it, she wasn't . . . she hadn't . . . he expected . . . she couldn't . . .

"Take it, Emily. It won't bite."

But it would destroy everything she'd worked so hard to achieve: the respect of her neighbors, the satisfying practice of medicine here on the island, the feeling that she was important, needed . . . not just to one man but to a whole community. If she took that box it wouldn't just bite. It would chew and swallow all of it whole.

"I can't, Rob."

Oh, God . . . she couldn't look at his face. The disbelief and disappointment etched there was too painful. It would haunt her.

She played with the edging on the linen nappery Tab had made from leftover pieces of cloth. Within seconds, Emily saw that she'd unraveled three edges. God rot it! She couldn't do anything right.

"Oh, please understand, Rob."

"I don't," he said, pocketing the gift which symbolized so many of his hopes. "Was I hearing things last night; or did you really say you love me?"

"I do."

"Then why don't you want me, Em?"

"I do."

"Then you need more time. Hell, I've already given you eighteen years. I can give you a few more weeks."

She shook her head. "You expect too much of me, Rob."

"Perhaps I don't expect enough."

"What's that supposed to mean?"

"I've let you rule me, Emily. All these years, I've

bowed to your needs, when I was burning up inside from wanting you."

"But you have me, now."

"I want you as my wife. And don't give me that swill about you not being wife material. I've heard it. It's not true. Last night proved it's not true. Who cares if you can't cook? I've got three cooks on *Patriot*. Who cares if you can't sew or spin or weave? I have enough money to buy a hundred years' worth of clothes. Who cares if you despise housework? We'll have stewards and cabin boys to fetch and carry and clean for us. So . . . there are no excuses, Emily. What Delia made you believe about yourself isn't true any longer. The world has changed. It will change even more in the near future, if our experience with the British last month is any measure. But what hasn't changed is the way I feel about you . . . and the way you feel about me."

"I know. It's taken me a long time to realize it, but I know it now. I do love you."

"Then, I repeat . . . why, Em?"

She dredged up the feelings that had overwhelmed her as soon as she saw his gift. Swallowing to take the ache away, she hung her head and whispered brokenly, "If I were to become your wife, you would want me to leave my island. If I did that, I'm afraid I'd die inside and very soon come to resent you and what you demand of me. I like myself, Rob. After all Delia and the others did to me, one thing good came out of it . . . I learned to rely on my best judgement. And right now, I cannot leave my neighbors or my practice. I'm important right here, where I am needed not only by you but by dozens of people whom I've come to love and whose respect I've worked hard to earn. If I become your wife, I'll lose all that." She braved the anger she knew would be in Rob's gentle eyes and looked up at him. "There is a solution, however."

"I'll listen to anything that will make you my wife."

"I'm afraid that's not what I had in mind."

"What ridiculous notion has been fermenting in your brain, Em?"

"We love each other, yes?"

"Yes."

"It's good, what we have together, yes?"

"More than good, Em."

"Why, then, do we need to complicate it with marriage?"

If Rob understood what she was getting to, he was a gun about to go off. "Emily, are you offering to become my mistress?"

"It makes sense, doesn't it?"

About as much sense as packing her off to a nunnery. "Suppose you tell me why you think so."

"Well . . . I can't become a pirate, Rob. And that's what you've become. We're compatible in . . ."

"In bed," he offered, although what she was suggesting was more crude than that "Yes. And I'll always be here, waiting for you when you finish your voyage . . . so not much will change, except we'll share . . ."

"A bed."

"Yes. And since I have such a good understanding of the human body, we need never fear pregnancy. And if you should find someone who would make you a good wife, I would be happy for you. But . . ." Her voice cracked, she swallowed and started again.

"But . . . I truly hope we can continue our arrangement, until we become too old to enjoy it."

"And what about Nathaniel and the threats he's made? I suppose you have an answer for that, too?"

"I will agree to a guard, if you will supply one. Two men, if need be. I don't want to die, Rob. I just want to stay here and be a doctor."

Rob's anger had bubbled beneath his surface calm; but now it erupted into controlled rage. "You want to be a doctor. Not a wife. Not a woman. A doctor. A shapeless, sexless thing like those shifts you wear."

"But we would have sex, Rob. . . ."

"I can get sex from a friendly house, Emily! I don't need sex. I need you."

"You would have me, Rob. I mean, there would never be any other man . . . surely you know that."

Rob once more brought out the box. He laid it squarely in the middle of the table, sat back, and scrutinized it as he reviewed everything Emily had said. But more important, how she had said it. So calm. So controlled. So sure that she was right, that what she needed was all important.

What she needed was a lesson on the realities of life. And he knew just the person to give it to her. Him.

He opened the box and pushed it toward her. She couldn't help herself—the brooch was so beautiful, so perfectly wrought, that she reached out and touched it, tracing its delicate golden lace-like edging, admiring the way the dark brown jewel gave off sparks from the light hitting the gold and bouncing off the facets of its face.

"It's beautiful," she whispered.

With a loud click that startled her, Rob closed the box. "That was meant for my wife, a betrothal gift. My mistress will have other kinds of things."

Emily's head snapped up. She felt a feather of fear in the pit of her stomach; but this was what she wanted, wasn't it? Rob agreeing to her proposition? It was, wasn't it?

"Then you agree."

"Absolutely. You will be my mistress. But, Emily . . . I don't think you realize what that means."

"Yes. I've thought about it all morning. I will be here, waiting for you. And when you need me, we will make love."

Rob shook his head and smiled, sad for the pitiful inexperience of his Emily, and joyous that she truly was so innocent. It would make his lesson all the easier to teach.

"There's more to it than that, love. I will be bringing you clothing more befitting my mistress. Jewels and gowns and nightdresses. Slippers and perfumes. Lace and silk and satins. I will also have a special bed brought here. Dover has one in his cargo that is large enough to accommodate both of us with comfort.

"Whenever I drop anchor, I will send you a card, telling you what to wear and what time to expect me. I will want the house empty. Even Tab must leave, so we may be together without interruption. Often, I will want a good meal waiting for me . . . cooked by Tab, of course. You will keep a well-stocked spirits pantry. I will supply the bottles and glasses to fill it. I will keep clothes here and will want a hot bath waiting. You, of course, will sponge me down with good sandlewood soap, to get the grime of the sea from my body. Then I will change into my clothes and we will spend a quiet evening together until we go to bed. In bed, I will set the pace and we will experience many delights. I will leave before first light.

"That is what is expected of my mistress. Do you have any questions?"

As Rob had outlined each expectation, Emily's fingers had curled into fists. Now, the nails bit into the palms of her hands. She hadn't counted on this! How could she have known?

It was her plan . . . and not her plan, at all. She had thought they would merely go on as they had. Since she wasn't willing to marry him and had proposed this damnable arrangement, she supposed Rob had a right to request that she conform to the way every other mistress acted.

He asked again, "Do you have any questions?"

Numbly, she shook her head.

"Oh, one other thing," Rob said. "I will want you to take your hair out of those infernal plaits and brush it until it feels like satin."

She nodded.

"Very good, then."

He pushed back his chair and rose. As he rounded the table, he pocketed the box with the beautiful brooch. When he got to Emily's side, he bent down, kissed the top of her head and caressed her breast, squeezing it gently.

"Look up, Emily," he said.

She gulped and raised her head. He didn't smile. He merely lowered his head and kissed her with an open mouth, his tongue delving deep inside as his hand still squeezed her breast. Abruptly, he stopped, turned, strode for the door.

As he picked up his tri-corn and positioned it jauntily on his head, he said, "You will hear from me."

The door closed. The black iron latch fell into place with a loud click, echoing the rending of Emily's heart.

The trunks began arriving two hours later. While she had a room filled with patients to care for, they were carried in by several of Rob's crew. If the crew or her patients were curious, they knew well enough to hold their tongues. Obviously, the crew had their orders from Rob because they knew exactly where to put the trunks. Two went bumping up the stairs and she heard them dropped into her bedroom. One went into the pantry. Thank goodness Tab was still at her sister's or Emily would have had her maid exploding in fury. The last, much smaller than the rest, the crew plunked down in the keeping room.

At ten-thirty, Emily's brother Carter announced the imminent arrival of the bed.

"It's the damnedest thing you ever saw, Em. Four carved posters, with a damask canopy trimmed in lace. It's already made up with sheets and pillows and a damask spread that rivals anything in the King's court. And six burly pirates are carrying it up the hill from the dock. Where the hell do you suppose they're going?"

"Here," she admitted, blushing madly. "Shut

your mouth Carter or gnats will be your next meal."

"But, Emily . . . it's going to take up most of your bedroom. Why did you order something that big? You don't need. . . ."

"Carter, that's enough! I don't pry into your affairs. Don't pry into mine."

Carter thought a minute, snapped his fingers, and said, "We can knock out the wall into the small storage room. That should do it." He hurried for the back door. "I'll just get my tools and be right back."

"Not today, Carter. I'll let you know when."

Getting the damned bed into the house and up the stairs took all the ingenuity of the pirates. One-eyed Jack and Dover Quince, of course, supervised their crewmen. Finally, they had to knock off the posters, take the bed up the stairs sideways, then put the posters back on.

Emily ate her midday meal—a ham sandwich—in silence as the pounding went on for forty minutes over her head. For their trouble, she had a half ham, two loaves of bread, and her brother Jasper's homemade ale waiting at the table.

But she didn't join them. From the looks she got from Jack and Dover, she knew they had some suspicion—if not the whole truth—about why Rob had purchased that monster of a bed from Dover and had them bring it to her little house. So she fled to the keeping room, where she buried herself in *Pamela* until Dover stuck his head in the door.

"Yes?"

"Rob said to tell you that John Devere has obtained a good post in Savannah, at a school near where Rob's sister teaches. Tomorrow we leave for Portsmouth to pick up John's family." Dover held out a folded piece of parchment. "Devere gave me this to give you."

Emily set aside her book and took the paper. She broke the seal and read it quickly. For the first time that day, she smiled. "He's going to be all right, isn't he?"

"Aye, Emily. And he owes it to you."

"That's what he says. But it wasn't me. It was fate that brought us together. And he was the kind of man he is. In fact, I owe him more than he owes me."

Dover nodded, turned on his heel, and left her. Jack took his place at the door.

"Rob says fer ye to empty the chests, missy. 'E wants things ship-shape when 'e gets 'ere."

"Do you know when that will be?"

"Nay, lass. But I suspects 'twill be in 'is good time."

"I suspect so," Emily said, surprised she wasn't more ill at ease. "Tell John Devere I said Godspeed."

"Aye, that I will. An' me men'll be back tomorry to fetch the trunks."

As soon as the house emptied out, Emily tackled the first trunk, the one in the keeping room. It contained a mantlepiece clock—probably intended to remind her of the time her new "master" would arrive, since when she wound it up it bonged every fifteen minutes; a footstool large enough for a man's feet; several books; a pewter tankard, which she put on the shelf above the mantle next to the clock; two pair of boots, one black, one brown; a riding crop; two pistols; a short sword; and three pair of slippers, green and red and blue wool. If he wanted them in the keeping room, he obviously liked them warmed for him, so she tucked them under the small table next to the chair opposite hers, where they would get the heat from the fire but not be scorched. It only took another twenty minutes to store the rest of Rob's things. When she was finished, she looked around. No more was hers a spinster's keeping room. A male presence had invaded and taken up residence.

The thought should have warmed her. Instead, she felt a terrible foreboding. What she had wanted had come home to roost and she had a dreadful fear that the fare wasn't going to be as appetizing as chicken.

But she had wanted it . . . nay, demanded it.

She gulped back her fear and squared her shoulders, preparing herself for the trunks upstairs.

The sight of the huge bed nearly did her in. Her old one had been placed in Tab's room, where it fit nicely under the eaves. Too bad she couldn't crawl in it, pull the covers over her head, sleep, and wake up to find this all only a dream.

Too bad.

She eyed the trunks, rather than having to deal with that furbelowed monster crowding her out of her own room. Sighing, she opened one, to discover it jammed with men's clothing. Luckily, she had demanded that her brothers install far more pegs for her clothes than she needed. Now, they held most of Rob's master-of-the-house clothing. The rest she began to put into the bottom drawer of her chest of drawers, but thought better of it and transferred her things down, leaving the top drawer for Rob's shirts and stockings and handkerchiefs and breeches.

When she finished with Rob's clothes, she gave all her attention to the other trunk, hoping to finally have the chance to feel the lovely things he'd bought her over the years, the ones she'd discovered in his cabin.

But when she lifted the top of the trunk, a riot of bright colors assaulted her eyes. These were not the gowns and cloaks and dresses and nightshifts that she'd seen on the ship. These were outrageously low-cut dresses of silks and satins, nightshifts and stockings of material so thin she could see through it, jewels of bright stones to match the dresses—not delicate like the brooch, but chunks of gems meant to impress some silly feather head rather than compliment the person who was wearing it.

So this was what a mistress wore.

All the fight went out of her when she realized what she had let herself in for.

And then she found the card tucked between the layers of dresses.

I will arrive at ten o'clock. Wear the green silk with white stockings and the green velvet slippers. Wear the emerald and diamond drops in your ears, your hair caught up with the green velvet ribbon. Bathe and perfume your skin with the essence in the black bottle. Have warm brandy waiting by the fire.

Emily plunked herself in the middle of the floor and dragged the large jewel box next to her. The emerald and diamond drops were in the first tier, right in the middle. But they were meant to hang from holes in a woman's ears!

Emily had never pierced her lobes and she wasn't

going to!

It was five o'clock, now, which meant she had five hours to empty all the trunks, store the goods, and get herself ready for Rob's first visit to his mistress. She gritted her teeth, determined to go through with this charade, since she had been the one to offer Rob this arrangement or nothing. If she turned her back on it now, she knew she would never see Rob again.

This was better than the living death such a life without Rob would be. Wasn't it?

Chapter Nineteen

So this was what a stuffed scarecrow felt like! Emily was more than prepared to hang herself on a board in the garden and chase the birds away. What she wasn't prepared for was the imminent arrival of her "master."

She had bathed—as ordered—in the strong-scented perfume in the black bottle. Now she was a stuffed scarecrow who smelled like a skunk!

The dress was worse than the one Nathaniel had forced her to wear. The stomacher, though trimmed with green and white crystals and lace, came up so high under her breasts she could hardly breathe. Of course, it performed its intended duty quite nicely. Her breasts nearly spilled out of the low, square neck-line. As for the dress itself, it wasn't silk, as Rob had said in his note, but heavy satin, with tiny white and green crystals adorning the lace around the neck and elbows—lace that fell in triple layers all the way to her wrists. The lace and gem treatment was repeated at the hem of the skirt, which was too short by three inches and showed off her ankle and a bit of stocking clad calf.

The only thing that saved the night for Emily was how clever she felt about the way she'd brushed her hair into a high topknot, tied it with the ribbon, and tucked the emerald and diamond ear bobs into the mass of curls that cascaded from the ribbon. With her hair hanging down as it did, it looked like a golden waterfall, sparkling with dew drops.

But her feet looked like great globs of dough rising above a loaf pan. The damned slippers were too tight! Her toes ached. Her arch screamed with pain whenever she tried to take a step. And the swelling was spreading up to Emily's ankles.

The doctor in her urged her to take the infernal things off and put on something that was more suitable for someone who usually wore naught but moccasins or comfortable boots. But the mistress she had made of herself tamped down the mutinous thoughts and sat in her slipper chair by the fire, waiting quietly for Rob's arrival.

The brandy was near to hand, warmed to perfection. She had shined the crystal glasses Rob had sent in the kitchen trunk and they now gleamed on a silver tray—also Rob's contribution. She'd already had three swallows of it—for luck as much as courage—and wondered if it wasn't time to have another. Glancing at the clock, which showed only five minutes until ten, she shook her head. Rob was always prompt. It would not do to appear tipsy on their first night of. . . .

Humbuggery! There must be some word for it other than *arrangement*. Something delicate, loving, suitable. In one of Rousseau's books he had described it as *L'affair d'amour*. At least it sounded better in French.

Ten o'clock came and Emily tensed, expecting Rob's footfall and the door to open under his hand. Ten-fifteen came and the silence was broken only by the infernal bong of the mantlepiece clock.

Ten-thirty.

Eleven.

At midnight a knock sounded on the door. Regardless that her feet now felt like encased sausages, Emily jumped up and ran to open it.

"Rob, you didn't have to knock," she said, throwing the door wide.

Three men stood in a semicircle around her granite front stoop, one of them Jason. He cleared his throat, stepped up on the stoop, all the while turning his hat round and round in his hands. His eyes brushed down the length of Emily's body; but no reaction showed on his face save pity.

"Rob sent your guard. He's made arrangements with Carter for them to sleep at shifts in Carter's house. *Patriot* sails at second bell. I came to say *thank you* and good-bye."

Emily couldn't breathe. Her mouth worked but no sound came out. Her grip on the door tightened; because if she loosened it, she'd surely collapse. Fighting for control, fighting to keep the pain deep inside from spilling over and shaming her more than she'd already shamed herself, she broke out in a sweat.

Finally, she managed a simple sentence. "No word from Rob?"

"No." Jason's eyes focused on a spot over Emily's left shoulder. "We're making for Savannah, to visit with Rob's sister Betsy, drop off the cargo and bring John Devere's household goods to him. Then we will swing down to the islands. Then back to Savannah for the holidays. Rob has decided to accept only Southern commissions for a time."

"How long?"

"At least until Spring."

Jason set his hat on his head and smiled a half-hearted smile. "I will miss you, Em. Be well."

"Go with God, Jason."

"Aye."

He backed down off the granite slab, hopped once, turned, and raced back down the hill. She watched until the gloom closed in around him and the dark made a solid wall beyond which Rob was preparing to sail out of her life.

Until Spring? No. The rupture was for good and all. That, she was sure of.

As Rob's guard made himself to home in her kitchen, Emily walked through her nightly ritual as if her body was numbed by ice. She stoked the fire, banked it, and put a large enough log in the center so it would warm the house all night. July, it might be; but on Block Island every night was chilled by the howling winds and salt-ladened air. She washed the glass she had used, dried it, and put it back on the shelf with the rest of the set. The brandy went into the stores. Satisfied that all was well belowstairs, she picked up the filled pitcher of water and trudged up to her room, where she poured half its contents into the ewer on the table in front of the fireplace wall. Leaving it to be warmed by the bricks—which were heated from the smoke and air coming up the chimney—she sat on the edge of the four poster bed and peeled off her slippers and stockings. The tingling started immediately, painful tingling which she ignored. There was already too much pain in her body to accommodate any more.

When the stomacher was unlaced, she could breathe easier but it didn't matter. Her breath was forced in great heaving sighs that didn't even register in her brain. She undid the back laces on the dress, stepped out of it, and hung it carefully on a peg next to a wild yellow brocade gown. The see-through chemise she folded carefully and put into her undergarments drawer. Naked, she stood in front of the mirror and pulled the ear bobs out of her hair. One stuck and she yanked, taking several strands along with it. As she dropped the emerald and diamond gems on the dresser, she stared at herself in the mirror.

It wasn't possible. It had never happened before. Reaching up, she touched a tiny tear as it spilled over her eyelids and dripped onto her cheek.

Another. And another. Then so many her fingers couldn't contain them all. And then suddenly all the feelings she had buried inside that day as she readied herself for Rob's "visit" came rushing into her heart and head. She gasped for breath, couldn't find any, and sank to the floor, crying loud, belly-tightening sobs for the first time since her mother's death.

She had asked for it. She had practically begged for it. Wives received good-bye notes. Mistresses could wait until the embers died and dawn crept in. And wait. And wait.

And she had told Rob that she hoped he'd find someone to marry some day and she would be happy for him.

Folly! No, she didn't want to use that word. That was Rob's word. She had no more right to his word than to the man.

Because her tears wouldn't stop flowing no matter what she did, it was a great struggle to get to her feet; but by grabbing hold of the top of the dresser, she managed to pull herself up. The water in the ewer was still cold but the cold felt good as she washed the awful essence off her body. Her old linen nightshift felt comfortable and familiar as she dropped it over her head. Comfortable and familiar, also, were with her as she took the ribbon out of her hair, brushed it, and braided it back into its usual style.

The four poster. It sat there, waiting for her. Huge. Empty. Mocking.

She almost crossed the hall to Tab's room, to her old bed under the eaves. But that would be total defeat and she had never allowed anything else to defeat her, ever. So, she climbed up into the wide bed, surprised to find it comfortable and the linens scented with roses. Snuggling down under the damask covering, she closed her eyes and willed herself to sleep.

But Rob's image intruded. The way his eyes had sparkled when he handed her his betrothal gift. The way they were dulled when he closed the box and put it back in his pocket after her proposition.

"Be careful what ye ask for," great-aunt Bella had been wont to say. "Be careful, lest ye get more than ye bargain for."

Emily knew she had gotten more . . . and far less. She was a doctor, what she wanted to be. She was no mistress, nor wife. Rob had given her a great lesson. She wondered if he had done it out of love or hate.

What did it matter? The result was the same.

She was alone. Again. As usual. But this time she couldn't look forward to his visits and the fun he brought with him. Nor could she anticipate his love-making. That would be reserved for his wife.

Ah, God, she had urged him to marry. Why, then, did it hurt so much?

She was still a doctor. She was still needed. She was still on her island.

Why, then, did it hurt so much?

Her pillow was soaked with tears by the time her eyes finally fluttered closed. She was in that realm between wakefulness and dreams when she bolted out of bed, awakened by a boom from a cannon. One boom, that was all. One boom, to say good-bye, to remind her, to haunt her.

Weeks went by when Emily didn't cry. Days, when

she didn't ache. She stitched so many cuts, she had to make more catgut from sheep's intestines. She set bones, cured ague, doled out cough syrups, salved insect bites and bee stings, pulled teeth, birthed babies, dug roots, gathered herbs and wildflowers to make concoctions and salves, dug bullets out of hunters who were bad shots, and treated infections at the friendly house.

Most nights she was so exhausted she went directly to bed. Other nights, while Tab finished up the housework or sat at the humming spinning wheel, Emily snuggled up by the fire, reading. Though she had dozens of books, during this time, her choices were few: Shakespeare, Chaucer, Cervantes. More and more she buried herself in the tale of *Don Quixote,* finding so many parallels to her own life, it was uncanny.

She, too, had tilted at windmills. She had had her own Sancho Panza in Hopeful Rose. She had been locked in a cage in which she didn't fit—the body of a woman. She had loved not wisely but too well . . . no, that was Othello . . . besides, she had not loved well enough.

But one night, after a particularly difficult lying-in for her brother Jasper's sixth child, where she barely managed to save both mother and baby, Don Quixote's adventures seemed unbearable.

A knight-errant tilting at windmills. Humbuggery! Was there nothing more pathetic, more absurd?

Suddenly in that night of terror when two lives had been held to life by a thread, Emily saw beneath the comic figure and began to comprehend the message of the book.

Don Quixote had for so long been her ideal, the image that she'd kept fixed in her mind to help her withstand the cruelty of Delia Davies, withstand and carry on with her life's ambition, that she had never really seen Sancho Panza as anything more than a foil for the great Quixote. Now, however, she read his words more carefully.

Mayhap it was because two people she loved had come so close to another death. Mayhap it was because the blasted tears had always been too close to the surface these days. Mayhap it was because the wind had shifted from west to east. All of these, none of them . . . there was something prodding her on to discover the truth behind the figure of Don Quixote. Mayhap to find the truth behind herself.

When she found it, Emily began to examine the lives of the people around her . . . and contrasted her life with theirs.

She had no more excuses for not marrying. Rob had blasted every last one of them that night she'd made her abominable suggestion. Yes, servants like Tab could clean rooms, cook meals, mend clothes, spin and weave. Itinerant farmers or indentured field hands could farm her lands. Lawyers could manage her household accounts. They already did.

But only a man and a woman who loved each other could, as her brothers and sisters-in-law had done, join two lives together to make a family.

Emily continued her doctoring. With at least one

of her guards beside her at all times, she went to church suppers, visited her brothers, nieces and nephews, made medicines for her surgery.

But every night when she closed her door, she came face to face with the reality of her life. Her meals were eaten alone. Alone, she dressed, read books, climbed the hills on her island. Alone she lay in her bed at night and woke in the morning . . . alone. She was almost twenty-seven years old. If she continued as healthy as she was and suffered no untoward accidents, she could expect to live another thirty or forty years.

Alone.

She would always be a doctor. Here, on the island, or. . . .

She set her thoughts aside because she didn't know what else to do.

The harvest was barely in the barn and storage when Thanksgiving was upon them. The Gorton clan that sat around two long board tables set on sawhorses in Henry's house now numbered forty-six, including Emily's two guards and Tab. Only Emily had no mate or offspring; but she was accorded full honors as the matriarch of the family and she took up position at the foot of the adults table, opposite Henry.

The Gorton lands were sweet and rich, their harvest more than ample, their coffers full, the table groaning with three kinds of fowl, a side of pork, and every special dish for which the women of the family prided themselves. Emily's contribution came from Tab: a creamy apple and bread pudding, with precious raisins saved from Dover Quince's largesse.

The men were lighting their pipes and the women sharing child-watching and clearing-up duty when a knock loud enough to shake a plate off the pantry shelf quieted down even Carter's newborn. When Henry opened the door, One-eyed Jack stamped into the room, leaving small mounds of snow which quickly melted from the fireplace's heat.

Jack smiled broadly and handed Henry two heavy sacks. "Oranges an' coffee from ta balmy isles an' tobaccy from Virginny. Them are from me. The raisins an' spices are from Quince. Won't be makin' our usual stop at Christmas, so I thought I'd best be bringin' it now." He spied Emily, swooped down on her and hugged her til she sputtered. "Yo, lass! Yer lookin' bonny as ever!"

"And you're getting fatter."

He patted his stomach, which growled almost immediately. Everybody laughed and Jack grinned. "Needs fillin', it does. Ennythin' left?"

Over three kinds of pie and a whole pot of fresh brewed coffee, he recounted his adventures in the south seas—though Emily was sure from the wink in his eye whenever he looked up at her that most of what he told was woven on the spot. Soon, she found herself alone with him, as the brothers and their families took their leave one by one.

"I've a wagon outside ta take ye ta yer door," Jack offered.

Emily thanked him and got her cloak, scarf, and mittens. When they left, the wind had picked up and the sky was blue-black, with only a hint of the orange setting sun.

Emily's guards and Tab hopped in back as Jack gave her a hand up to the driver's seat. Ruts in the road made it hard going but they arrived at Emily's door without a mishap. Jack followed Emily into the house and with his usual wink handed her two more full sacks, which exuded wonderful aromas.

"Coffee, tobaccy, raisins, and spices?" she asked.

"Oh, aye. An' sweet French lilac soap from Jason."

Emily's heart rate accelerated and she dropped into the nearest chair. "You've seen them . . . him, then?"

"Aye. In Guadeloupe. They . . . 'e's fine."

Emily was sure they were not talking about Jason, though neither of them gave any indication.

"Where are you off to next?"

"Chesapeake. Then Savanny. Always 'ed south fer ta winter, I do. Gettin' too old fer this cold an' wet."

Her decision was made in the space of a heartbeat; but she knew it was the best decision she'd ever made. "Will you take a passenger?"

"Oh, aye." Jack's dark weathered face beamed. " 'Ad ye no asked, I'd've shanghaied ye."

"I'll have to get a doctor from the mainland to take over for me. Could take a week or more."

"I'll leave me own surgeon behind. 'E cod use some quiet time an' some toughenin' up. Cod ye teach 'im what 'e'll need ta know in three days?"

"How long has he been doctoring?"

"Seven year."

"I'll do it in one!" She threw her arms around Jack and gave him a big kiss on the cheek. "Thank you!"

"Ah, lass . . . yer doin' me a favor. When a pirate gets careless, 'e's no good to ennybody."

"Rob is getting careless?"

"Aye. Feared, Quince and I are, that 'e's lost 'is edge. Flirtin' with death, 'e is. 'E needs ye, lass."

"Not as much as I need him."

Chapter Twenty

When Emily called on Betsy for the first time, she found the house nearly deserted, save for Betsy herself; Savannah Stewart, one of her fellow schoolteachers at Honesty Dunn's school for Young Ladies; and a student, Arabella Montgomery. Savannah, little more than five foot, three inches, stood tall at an easel, painting a portrait of Rob's sister and her sons. As soon as Emily explained who she was and why she was there, Betsy welcomed her as if Emily were already part of the family. And, after Betsy made sure Rob was not in the house, Savannah Stewart fairly ordered Emily to sit and tell everything which had precipitated such a courageous act.

The recitation of Emily and Rob's disastrous meetings and ill-fated love affairs led all the women from faint giggles to loud laughter. The turquoise-eyed schoolteacher clapped her hands and tossed a mass of curls so dark brown it was almost black. "But what a romantic adventure!" Savannah quickly cleaned her brushes and had her assistant, Arabella—a gay little miss, with delicate china doll features, wheat gold hair, and grey eyes—cover the half-finished portrait with a soft cotton cloth. "We shall all have to help you, and that's that!"

But that wasn't that, since Rob had been spirited away by One-eyed Jack and Jason, who were determined to get him back on track before he blundered into a battle with the red-coats from which there was no escape.

So, Emily was forced to wait to find out whether—or if she were to be successful in her quest to wed Rob Sears.

Betsy's house, large in comparison to Emily's but smaller than many of the plantations that dotted the surrounding plains, was filled to overflowing with holiday guests. Emily was delighted to discover that the Hobbs family had preceded her there by two days. Constance and Jonathan, Emily's old friends, had brought their children.

Emily was incredulous. "Five of them?"

Constance laughed. "You were right, Em. I was carrying twins. Patience and Patrick are now seven years old!"

"No. It can't have been that long ago when you brought Jean Louis to my door."

"Jonathan. And, yes, it was. And now we have Jason, Rachel, and Richard."

"They're all so well behaved and adorable. They fit right in with Betsy's two boys."

"Too well, at times," Betsy laughed. She ruffled the already unruly hair of her own sons, Davin and Lyle, then sent all the children out to play as she, Emily,

Constance, Savannah, and Arabella began to plan—as Betsy said, *a delicious, devilish, delightful drama,* with Rob as the central character.

When they had it all planned out, Savannah and Arabella went on a secret mission to find a wedding dress for Emily. Emily appealed to John Devere for temporary lodging. And Constance sought out a minister.

Emily was on her way to Savannah Stewart's school for a quick fitting of her dress when Jonathan Hobbs rode his horse up to her and jumped from the saddle. He drew her into an alley, out of sight and sound of any passing British sympathizer.

"What's wrong," Emily asked.

"Don't panic. Rob is all right. But only minutes after you left a half hour ago, British revenue agents stormed through Betsy's house looking for him. Luckily, Betsy and Rob had plans should something like this occur. She managed to get word to him and he got away safely."

"He's gone?"

"Yes. I'm sorry, Emily."

Emily thrust her basket at him and bolted for the horse. Without regard for the way her Indian-style shift rode halfway up her thighs, she vaulted into the saddle and called back, "I'm going to Jack's ship on the island. Get a preacher and follow me."

"Are you daft, woman?"

"There's only one ship that can outsail Rob's. Jack will find him. But I need a minister to marry us. So don't waste time arguing. I want to be Betsy's sister-in-law before sundown."

One-eyed Jack needed less persuasion than Jonathan had. He sent messengers scurrying to gather up his crew, many of whom were in town, buying up Christmas presents, or merely raising hell in the taverns. By the time a full complement was on board, Savannah Stewart had heard the news. She and Arabella bounded out of a carriage and up the gangplank, yards and yards of fabric in their hands.

"You can't leave without us!" Savannah said, glaring daggers at One-eyed Jack's crew as they raised the sails.

"We were so busy," Betsy bubbled, "that we didn't have time to worry about a wedding dress!"

Savannah's eyes danced with green highlights, like the water of the sound danced with green and blue and gold. "Good thing you have me." She bustled into the crowd which included Betsy's entire household—and the preacher they'd practically kidnapped. Everyone was at the rail, watching Savannah harbor recede in the distance. The children danced up and down with glee. This was an adventure they'd like as not ever forget!

But Jack Saunders was not celebrating with the landlubbers.

He cautioned Emily, "Rob'll 'ead fer safe anchor roun' Tybee Isle where pirates 'old sway an' red-coats dare no landin'."

"Can you overtake him," Emily asked.

Jack laughed. "Tis the sky blue?"

Jack held the ship so close to the wind, they fair flew through the waves. The lookout shouted as soon as he spotted the *Patriot* and Jack put a spyglass to his eye.

" 'E's spotted us; but 'e's no lookin' too close. 'E must think we be red-coats." He shook his head and muttered, "Careless. Much more o' that an' 'e'll be for it." He ordered his men to hoist his personal ensign and get them closer.

"Ahoy, Jack," Rob shouted through his captain's trump.

" 'Bout time ye recognized me, Rob, me lad!"

Rob caught sight of Betsy's flaming red hair and shouted. "Are the revenuers after the whole damn family?"

"Naught this time," Betsy told him. "We're here for a wedding."

"A what?"

"A wedding!"

Betsy pointed to Emily, who, now that the test had come, gave a weak smile and a tentative wave. Even from the hundred yards or so that separated the ships, Emily could see Rob's jaw tighten.

"Get him to anchor somewhere, can't you, Jack?" Emily asked the pirate.

Rob argued with Jack but finally both ships were drifting at anchor with their sails lowered, though no boarding plank had been set between them. The decks were crowded with crew. Every manjack of them had their eyes glued first to Rob, then to Emily, and back again. Jason waved and smiled, as did Orrin and Almanzo. But Rob stood silent and motionless at his wheel.

"Go on wi'ye," Jack urged Emily. " 'E won

make the first move so's it's up ta ye, lass."

Emily swallowed her pride, knowing that the prize would either be won or lost by her powers of persuasion—if she had any left. "Captain Sears, I ask permission to come aboard."

"Nay, Doctor Gorton. There's no place for you here."

"Tis not Doctor Gorton who's asking. Tis only Emily." She saw him scowl. It wasn't much; but she'd work with it. "If you won't let me come aboard, then will you answer a question?"

"Aye."

"Will you marry me?"

"Are you sure what you're saying?"

"Aye."

"You want me to husband?"

"Aye."

"You're not satisfied being my mistress?"

It stung, that did, him saying it aloud so it brought surprised gasps from Betsy, Savannah, and Constance and a wondering murmur from both crews. But Rob's pride was at stake; he needed to know she was serious.

"No, I am not satisfied being your mistress. I love you. I want to be your wife."

"And children. What of them, Emily?"

"Whatever God gives us, Robert."

He had won. He had risked it all, risked a life of terrible loneliness, misery, mayhap even death. But in the end her good common sense had won out. Or something like it. Rob felt like shouting and laughing with joy. And did.

He waved two of his seamen to lay the plank across the two ships. "Come aboard, Emily. No, on second thought, I'll come over there."

He fairly vaulted the space between them. A step in front of her, he stopped and stared into her beautiful dark eyes. "Please take down your hair."

She smiled and quickly and happily complied. But when she finished, he frowned. "What's wrong?"

Rob shouted to his cousin, "Jason, get the peach linen dress from the trunk in my cabin."

"The key is in the middle drawer of his desk," Emily called to Jason's back. She blushed at the shock and delight Rob showed. "I peeked one day while you were busy. They're beautiful gowns, Rob. So much better than those awful ones you sent in the trunks."

"Those were from Jack and Quince. Booty. Not meant to grace your back."

"But you sent them anyway."

"You had to see what you were asking of me, Em. What you had decided to become. God's blood, it was no more than what Appleton offered. Concubinage." His eyes twinkled. "I wish I had seen you in that gown."

"It was scandalous!"

"Exactly."

She put her palms to her flaming cheeks and groaned. "Oh, Rob!"

He laughed, held out the dress Jason had fetched, and bowed low. "Your wedding dress, Emily. I hope it suits."

"Oh, bother!" Savannah said. "And I had such

wonderful ruffles and lace all prepared."

"This is better," Emily said, holding the pristine peach frock up to her. "This is *me*."

In Jack's cabin, Constance, Savannah, Arabella and Betsy fussed over Emily, putting her hair in order with ribbons and water. Constance slipped the dress over her head. Betsy laced it up the back. Savannah and Arabella straightened the simple lace and gathers. Then all four gaped in the mirror at the transformation of Emily.

The dress had a round neck, with dainty lace trim and a row of seed pearls interspersed with topaz beads. The bodice nipped in under her breasts to hug her rib cage. A wide dark brown velvet ribbon accented the waist. The skirt fell straight to the floor in the front, but was gathered at the sides and back, adding just a bit more fullness to Emily's hips. More seed pearls and topaz beads embellished the skirt six inches above the hem in a pattern that resembled intertwined wild roses.

"It makes me look beautiful," Emily said. She was so shocked, she had to touch the image in the mirror to be sure it was her own.

Betsy hugged her. "You *are* beautiful."

When the women came up on deck, Rob was at the top of the hatch to greet Emily. He offered her his hand, bowed over hers, and kissed her fingertips. Skittery fire and ice skimmed over her body and she shivered in anticipation of the pleasures she could read in the depths of his eyes.

They lined up in front of the preacher. But before the man began the service, Rob reached into his vest pocket and brought out the topaz brooch. "I've carried it every day since I left the island." His fingers trembled as he tried to pin it at the center of her neckline. "God's blood, just touching you makes me clumsy."

She helped him. As their heads bent together, she whispered, "You were never clumsy when you touched me."

He took her face in his palms and kissed her nose. "I love you, Emily Gorton."

"And I love you, Robert Sears."

The deck erupted with loud cheers and huzzahs. They were repeated ten minutes later when the minister pronounced them man and wife and Rob kissed Emily as lustily as any man had ever kissed a woman.

"I'm givin' a weddin' celebration," One-eyed Jack said. "Ale, brandy, rum. An' some good fruitcake from Barbados." He whispered in an aside to Rob, "Me cabin's at yer service, Rob, me boy."

Rob took him at his word, scooped up his wife in his arms, and struggled down the ladder with her. When he slammed the door behind them, Emily laughed. "Everyone will know what we're doing."

"Aye. And wish they were doing it, too."

But seconds stretched out as they stood several feet from each other, gazing deeply into each other's eyes.

Emily felt a stirring that was always there when Rob was near her, a heat no one else produced, a warmth she welcomed because she knew it came from a deep, joyful love. "I made mistakes. I'm sorry, Rob."

"I caused you pain. I'm sorry, Emily."

Tears of joy spilled over her eyelids and washed her cheeks.

At such an unfamiliar sight, Rob crossed the room in one stride. "Emily, you're crying!"

"Yes. Isn't it wonderful?" She wrapped her arms around him and snuggled into the spot beneath his ear where she could breathe in the spicy scent of him and feel his hair rub against her forehead. "No more ghosts of Delia Davies, Rob. No more closed doors. When you took me at my word you shocked me out of my solitariness. I can't do everything on my own. I no longer want to. But I can have far more than I ever dreamed possible . . . as long as I have it with you. You're a part of me, the most important part because you make me whole. I love you for what you did. I bless you for it."

"Very nice. Very, very, very nice! But you're wrong, witch! You can't have everything. You will, however, have far more than you dreamed possible. I guarantee it."

The sarcastic, nasal, whiny voice sliced through Emily's heart and nearly drove her mad. She whirled, only to be thrust behind Rob as he tried to keep her away from Nathaniel Appleton.

"Move away, Rob," Nathaniel said, waving a cocked pistol to emphasize his words.

Rob watched the mad glitter in Nathaniel's eyes smolder and burn and felt helpless—again. He strained to hear noises from on deck but there was only silence.

"My men have guns pointed at your sister, two

other women, and the children. They are not my target. Nor are you."

Nathaniel fingered the scar on his cheek and Emily was horrified to hear herself whimper.

"That's right, my dear. I said I'd come for you and I have. Rob, stand aside."

"No."

Emily clutched at Rob's shoulders. "He'll hurt the children."

"Listen to your wife. She knows me better than you do."

There was a cutlass and some shaving gear on the small table to Rob's right. If he could only reach over and grasp the cutlass, he thought they had a chance.

With her hands on Rob's shoulders, Emily felt him tense and knew he was about to do something that might get him killed. When his right arm and leg tightened, she looked to her left and saw the cutlass and shaving gear. As soon as Rob jerked over toward the table, she shouted, *No,* and pulled him back. Nathaniel raised his arm and brought the heavy pistol down on Rob's head. In the instant when Rob collapsed and Nathaniel's attention was diverted, Emily grabbed up a straight razor, knelt to cradle her husband's bloody head, and slipped the razor in the bottom of her shoe.

Scalpels. Razors. After what she had gone through, they were all the same to her.

When Rob came to, he hurried up on deck. One-eyed Jack was swinging a cannon around, to point it at a sloop as it sailed away with Emily in the stern, her hands tied behind her back. The rope she was tied with was attached to the taffrail.

"No, Jack! One shot and Emily's dead."

" 'E caught us unawares, Rob, whilst we was drinkin' all that rot gut. . . ."

"We'll get him, old friend. Damn me, we have to get him. Raise your sails. And I'll get mine raised on *Patriot*. We'll both go after him."

"The women and children. . . ."

Rob scanned the small boat with his spyglass. "He's heading south. We've time to beach the women and children."

"But the British patrol boats," Betsy pointed out.

"Damn the British!"

Right after they dropped off the women and children, Rob wished the British damned for good. A patrol boat caught them only a few leagues out to sea. Although he knew he and Jack would prevail—How could any ship stand up to two pirate crews?—he cursed the whole British Navy for holding them back. To battle them meant Emily was getting further and further away from him.

His roar of fear, frustration, and rage spurred on the two crews. But it didn't stop the British.

Emily cringed at the salty words Nathaniel used when he described what he'd like to do to her. Although he touched her face and fingered her hair, he refrained—for now—from anything more.

"Petty Chow, my fine lady," he said, when they

pulled up to a shabby dock on a small island.

As he untied her from the taffrail, Emily noticed six boats—sloops, skipjacks, sailing dinghies—also docked at this isolated location. From each, a man stepped onto the dock. Every gaze was fixed on Emily as Nathaniel helped her from the sloop and onto the rickety wooden structure.

The closest man was short, old and fat, with almost pure white hair and dull greyish eyes. He chewed tobacco, which he spit into the water. His teeth were black from it. She was almost past him when she realized that this was Jack Donahue—changed, changed utterly. Not even his clothing proclaimed him as captain of a fine merchant vessel. Now, he was a rogue who dressed as a fop, with tobacco stained waistcoat, vest, and shirt.

The next man was tall, dark, and swarthy. His crooked smile when he doffed his tricorn never made it to his eyes, which were lifeless black embers. The fire, Emily thought, had gone out of them long ago. Flamboyant in dress, however. Flowing robes with fancy jewels pinned to them. Strange pleated trousers. Rings on every finger. And an ear bob in his left ear! As she passed him, he cackled and spoke in a tongue with which she was not familiar—and she had heard everything from visitors on the island from French to Dutch to German to Spanish to Italian. Since she had to treat many of them, she'd learned a few phrases in each of the foreign tongues.

The next two men bowed together. They were so much alike they had to be brothers. Short and dark, they smelled of pungent garlic and the exotic herb

Hopeful had liked so much, basil. They also smelle
of the crooked cigars they held in one hand as th
drank from short, fat green bottles.

The fifth man was taller, blond with mean gree
eyes and a close cropped beard. He smelled bett
than the others, as if he'd bathed in barrels of ro
water. And his clothes were close fitted, finely ex
cuted, with lots of delicate lace, gold, and silver trin
From his accent as he talked to the two brothers, sh
knew him to be Dutch, although he spoke in Italian

The last man could only be British. Supercilious
he took a position apart from the others. He wa
short, blond, blue eyed, and full mouthed, with a de
icate, upturned nose. His body was soft, with a fu
blown paunch. On his fingers were myriad golde
rings which flashed as his hands moved. His neck
cloth flowed with lace down and over his vest. A so
spring wool green frock coat sported a thin silve
braid at throat and wrists. His vest was overwrough
with a skilled needlewoman's art of *pointelle brode
rie,* worked into wildly colorful forest scenes. Roya
blue velvet breeches. Silk stockings, held at the kne
by satin garters, descended into shiny black leathe
shoes with large brass buckles.

"Lord Sheffield," Nathaniel said, jerking Emily t
a stop. "I trust your house is as you hoped it woul
be."

The Sheffield Lord sniffed and brushed a lac
edged handkerchief across his nose. "It needs but on
more blond beauty to make it perfect."

Nathaniel laughed. "Perfection is very expensive
My Lord."

"But if it's the right perfection, it can be very profitable as well as enjoyable."

House. The way Nathaniel had said the word, Emily knew he didn't mean *home*. She shuddered. Though this man was of the nobility, underneath his sartorial splendor, he was just as dangerous—or more dangerous—than the others.

"Shall we go up to the camp, gentlemen," Nathaniel asked. "There are comfortable chairs and room to maneuver."

The camp turned out to be a clearing behind a dune, where tents had been pitched, a fire circle dug, and, indeed, eight chairs placed in a semicircle around the fire. But there were also six palettes drawn up together to form a raised platform. The chairs faced the platform. And it was to this that Nathaniel pulled Emily.

He smoothed down her skirt, fluffing it at the hips, and fussed with the lace of her sleeves. She gritted her teeth at the nearness of him, at the way he stared at her and kept fingering the scar on his face. Though she had done everything she could to fix it, his smile was tortured into a grimace because of the scar.

"Nathaniel . . ."

"Shut up! Keep your mouth closed unless you're asked to open it. And then do it quickly or I will punish you with my whip." He brought his face nose-to-nose with hers. "Do you understand?"

She nodded, terrified by the hatred in his voice. He would enjoy hurting her. She knew that. Worse, he would enjoy doing it in front of these men. She closed her eyes, bowed her head, and prayed that somehow she could get free of him once again.

She hadn't finished her prayer before the first han
brushed across her cheek. Her head jerked up, sh
opened her eyes, and gasped. Each man was ther
ringed around her. They touched her. Turned her th
way and that, like a slave at auction.

God's blood! She *was* at auction. The men, no
knowing she could understand most of their lan
guage, talked of bidding for her!

Retribution. She had offered herself to Rob as
mistress. Now, unless she could get away or be res
cued, she would truly know what the women in th
friendly house felt when a slobbering, half-drun
stranger took them. Or, from the elated expression o
Nathaniel's face, she would know much worse.

Chapter Twenty-one

"Four hundred gold sovereigns."

"Four hundred?" Nathaniel roared with laughter. "She is a doctor. She knows men's bodies better than you know them yourself. She is worth four thousand. But I will accept one thousand to start."

Huddled in a small tent, Emily listened with disbelief to the men as they dispassionately set about buying her! They had spent almost an hour looking her over, even to the point of raising her skirt to see her legs. Hands had tested her flesh, her bones, the number of teeth in her mouth, the texture of her hair, the outline of her ear. Lord Sheffield had been angry that her nails were so short; but when Nathaniel chuckled and reminded him that indolent living would allow them to grow to the length Lord Sheffield required, the British fool had smiled, kissed her hand and continued his hateful examination of her body.

Now, bugs—gnats or sand fleas from the sound of them—were busy attacking those parts the men had missed. She couldn't even scratch them because her hands and feet were bound. The ropes chaffed, biting

into the same places that had been rubbed raw by N
thaniel's ropes the last time.

She could not stand it! Twice in less than s
months! No! Absolutely not.

Screwing up her courage, she fell over onto h
back and rolled to the edge of the tent. She kicked
it until the bottom gave and she could push it up wi
her feet enough to see beneath it.

The day had given way to night and the men we
huddled round a fire. Emily paid no attention
them. She knew too much about them already! I
stead, she strained her eyes to see beyond them, in
the distance. Clouds scudded across a dark, almo
black sky. But there was one spot . . .

There! A glow on the horizon. Then no light. The
light again.

A lighthouse.

Like all islanders, she knew every small rock alor
the coast from Florida to Nova Scotia. Because sh
and Nathaniel hadn't sailed long, and because of th
angle of the sun during the sail, she deduced the
were probably now off the island called Tybee—th
Indian word for salt—whose lighthouse was bui
forty years ago. So, the island she was on wasn't Pett
Chow. It was Petit Chou, French for little dog.

There were dozens of small outcroppings along th
coast and up the river near Savannah. Howeve
knowing where she was, wasn't going to do muc
good if she couldn't get away, or if Rob didn't kno
where to look for her.

"Two thousand of gold."

"Two thousand, one hundred."

"Two thousand of gold. Two thousand of silver."

A collective gasp from the other bidders made Emily's skin crawl—and not from the bugs that were biting her. It didn't matter whether Rob knew where she was or not. Soon, she would be a cipher in the Gordon family Bible, just like Patience Sands and the other women who had been kidnapped or simply disappeared from the island.

"Of course you have the gold and silver with you, sheik," Nathaniel asked.

"You question the word of Allah's servant?"

"If *you* are his servant, then I question Allah, himself!"

The man laughed with such malevolent glee that Emily conjured up old, faded images of the devil.

"You good bargainer, Naples. Better than most. I tell you what I do. I sell her for one hour to each of you for . . . oh . . . two hundred in gold for the hour. After I have my pleasure first, of course."

God's blood! Seven of them, counting Nathaniel! While the men described the delights they expected, Emily nearly snapped her spine getting to the razor in her shoe.

Rob watched the British patrol boat sink beneath the surface of the waves. He didn't stop to worry about the men in the water. One-eyed Jack would pick them up. They would either be impressed into his piracy or he'd drop them off on some island, where they would have to find their own way back to their navy. Although it hadn't yet been proclaimed, they were at war. And in war time, a captain had to worry about his ship first; his crew, second; his enemy, last.

But Rob had more on his mind than the British.

Jason came up beside him to give him the damag report. Luckily, because One-eyed Jack had bee with him and the British weren't able to attack bot ships at once, *Patriot* had sustained only minor dam age.

"But we have lost a mast, Rob."

"What we've lost in sail, we'll make up for i weight. A sloop may be fast but we can rig *Patriot* t plow through waves that would swamp a smalle boat."

"Let's hope to God that isn't what happened."

As the crew got underway, the four officers gath ered on the quarterdeck.

"Where ye think 'e's taken 'er," Orrin Mayott asked. "I'll fix enny course ye need."

Rob knew he had to follow his own instincts. "The left in a small sloop. Which means Nathaniel didn' plan to set out to sea . . ."

"So, 'e made fer one o' ta out islands," Orrin said

"Aye."

"Rob," Jason said, "need I remind you that yo aren't dealing with Appleton now, but Naples?"

"God's blood, Jason, I've thought of nothing else!"

"Then if he took a sloop and he's headed for th outer islands, chances are . . ."

"That he's heading for an auction. Aye, I know And the men he must have contacted are unscrupu lous. I know that, too!"

"But they aren't stupid, Rob. They'll want to ge away immediately after the auction. By ship, Rob."

"Jason, you're my level head in an emergency Thank you." He gave Orrin orders to hustle up th chart of the outer islands—but only those which had a dock and room to hide nefarious goings on. "Unless they're natives or have sailed these waters often, they'll need a point of reference."

"Need it, ennyway, at night," Orrin said. "Navigatin' in the ocean are easy. In shallows . . . lights from shore is best." He stabbed his finger at the only place on his charts that suited his reckoning. "Lighthouse. Tybee."

"He won't set down on Tybee," Rob said. "Too many people, including the damned British."

Jason offered, "There's St. Simons."

"Too big and in the wrong direction," Rob pointed out.

"Petit Chou," Almanzo said. "It's deserted, there's a dock, and enough deep water for any kind of draft bottom craft, including a sloop."

"Then get us there, dammit! Get us there!"

"Aye, Rob. We're already on the way."

Hold on Emily, Rob prayed. Hold on!

Emily knew her only way to freedom lay in the sea. As she ran into the shadows and over the dune toward the dock, she heard a wild shout and curses. She could slip out of there, but it would take too much time to hoist sails. Besides, each boat was guarded; she'd noticed that when Nathaniel had pulled her up the dock and away from the safety of his sloop, *Racer.*

Keeping the lighthouse in the center of her vision, she ran to the right, then left, then right again, trying to confuse the men by mixing up her footprints on the sand. Then she headed for the water. She didn't bother to remove her shoes. She simply ran along through the surf, allowing the retreating tide to cover up her footprints. When she was far enough away, she used the razor to cut all her bonds, removed her dress, rolled it up into a ball and lashed it to her back. It was irrational, she knew; but it was her wedding dress!

Her undershift she cut with the razor and pulled it up through her legs, the way she'd done as a girl, so it was more like men's breeches. She pulled off her boots but left on her stockings. With the razor clutched between her teeth, she slipped into the water.

She was a good, strong swimmer. Always had been. And though it was December, the water off Savannah was lukewarm compared to the icy chill of Block Island's surf. Enervated, she set a course for the beacon on the water, Tybee lighthouse.

She was hundreds of yards away when she heard the unmistakable snap of ropes and creek of a wooden boat. She looked up, hoping to see *Patriot*, but heard, instead, a loud voice at her back.

"There! There! Her golden head in the water!"

Something pinged into the water in front of her and then the boom of a gun splintered the night. A second shot. A strangled cry. The sound of a body falling into the water.

"No one harms my prize! But hundred gold pieces will I give to man who scoops her out safe."

Scoop out, be damned! Emily took a fix on the lighthouse, pulled the razor out of her mouth, drew in a deep breath, and dived under the water. No sun penetrated, so she couldn't see through the murky darkness. Within moments, her eyes stung from the salt; but they soon got used to it. She kicked, using her strong leg muscles more than her arms, to propel her. When she couldn't stand it any longer, she shot up to the surface, took another deep breath, and plunged downward once again. On the third surfacing, she found herself off course a little. As she was correcting it, a ship rounded Tybee's point. A ship with a familiar shape and size, and the outline of an Indian maiden as its figurehead.

Patriot!

With Rob in front and Nathaniel behind, Emily was caught in the middle. She could make better time underwater, so she dived beneath the surface once more. But this time she deliberately changed course and swam to her right—trying to draw Nathaniel away from Rob so he wouldn't see *Patriot*. Each time she crested the water it was in a different spot. And each time she was elated to hear one of Nathaniel's lookouts shout her position.

Still, with all she did, she could tell by the sound of the voices and the increased snap of the sails, that *Racer* was getting closer to her than *Patriot*.

She needed a diversion; but all she had was . . .

There was nothing she could do except use the razor to cut the ropes holding her beautiful wedding dress. Tears mingled with salt spray as she watched it float away. But she had no time to worry about it. Once more she dived into the water.

Jason clutched Rob's arm. "Ah, God, no."

Rob saw where his cousin's eyes stared and he, too, gave a strangled cry.

"No, no," Almanzo said. "Just her dress. See? No arms. No legs. No head."

Joy and hope filled Rob's heart. "She's the smartest damned wife any man could want. It's a signal, Jason." He turned and asked, "Who will volunteer to follow me into the water to find her?"

The words were hardly out of his mouth when six crewmen dived over the rail. Jason tossed cutlasses to all, and they put them between their teeth and stroked toward the peach colored dress. Rob took saber, cutlass, and short sword, all of which he tucked into his belt. As he jumped onto the rail, he ordered, "Fire on the damn boat. And don't let any shot drop short or I'll have your heads!"

He was several feet away when the first cannon ball went flying through the air. Jason's aim was true, as usual. The sloop lost its mainmast. The second cannon ball put a hole through its hull and set the deck on fire. Every man on the sloop dove or jumped into the water, more prepared to drown than burn to death.

On board *Patriot* the three officers who were left saw Emily's head pop up out of the water.

"Thank God," Jason said.

"Ye think Rob sees 'er," Orrin asked.

Almanzo was grim. He pulled a saber from the ones on the quarterdeck and tucked it into his belt. "He sees her. But he doesn't see *him*."

Jason turned his head to see what Almanzo meant, cursed when he recognized how close Nathaniel was to Emily, and shouted to Rob. But there was so much noise and so many men screaming death cries, Rob didn't look back. Jason leapt for the taffrail but Almanzo held him back. He said, sadly, "Ye'll get nowhere with that half-leg, Jason. Besides, I'm the best swimmer in the crew. But if that bastard gets too close, shoot him."

Kicking off his boots, Almanzo dove head first into the water.

When she came up for another lungful of air, Emily heard what the water had filtered out—the horrified cries of dying men. She smelled the burning wood of the ship, and saw the bay turn purple from red blood mingling with blue-green water.

But she was within a few hundred feet of *Patriot*. Stroking on the surface of the water, now, she closed the gap. Suddenly, a large hand grabbed a hank of her hair. She barely had time to breathe before it pulled her head underwater.

Though it was dark, she knew who held her captive beneath the waves. One hand held her. The other flopped loosely to the side. Nathaniel.

Emily held tight to the razor, trying to get an angle so she could use it. But Nathaniel was strong enough to keep her head at the level of his waist. His head was above water. Hers, below. She twisted and turned to break his grasp but his hold didn't loosen. Her lungs nearly burst from lack of air before she got in range and slashed out, not knowing if her aim was even close to the mark.

Suddenly, Nathaniel's body convulsed, jerking backwards as if skewered; and she felt an awful moment, wondering if she had hit a vital organ. But then her terror increased as Nathaniel's lifeless body began sinking—and she along with it!

She dropped the razor, kicked out, pulled up on Nathaniel's clenched hand, and almost got her hair out of his grasp, when her lungs couldn't stand another moment. As a doctor, she knew what was happening. As a human being, she despaired as her body automatically signalled her lungs to take in oxygen, when there was no oxygen to breathe.

She prayed to have it over quickly as a bright, white light burst in her brain.

Almanzo and Rob would argue later about whose saber hit the mark. They wouldn't argue about who dragged a nearly dead Emily up from the depths of the water near Tybee. Rob, himself, couldn't swim and still hold a lifeless wife. When Almanzo wrapped one of his huge smithy's arms around Rob and tugged him over to *Patriot*, he was more grateful than he could express.

It took them several minutes to tie a rope around Emily and lift her up the forty feet to the deck. Another several minutes before Rob and Almanzo were safe on board.

As soon as Rob hoisted himself over the taffrail, he rushed to Emily's side, shouting orders to get the ship underway before the British came to investigate the fire.

When Rob dropped to one knee beside Emily, Jason held a tin mug of brandy to her lips. "She needs its warmth, but her lips won't open."

Rob had seen such things before—too often. He bent and held his ear over her chest. "There's water in her lungs."

Jason dropped the mug. "God's blood! What . . ."

Rob turned Emily over, straddled her body, and pulled up on her waist. When nothing happened, he did it again. Then several times more. "Cough it out, Emily. God, please! Cough it out!"

Jason pounded on her back as Rob pulled up once more. A faint, kittenish sound came from Emily's chest, then stopped.

"Once more!" Rob shouted. "Pound on her, Jason. Don't hold back. She wouldn't hold back if it were you."

"Aye. I know, Rob. But it's hard to pound on a woman."

"Then pretend she's a sack of meal. But for her sake, pound away."

Rob pulled. Jason pounded. And all around them were sounds of toughened seamen hoarsely mumbling snatches of half-remembered childhood prayers.

Suddenly Emily gave a weak cough. Then a harder one. Dirty sea water gushed from her mouth. She sputtered, coughed, gagged.

And Rob's shouts of joy were drowned out by all the rest as one man after the other whooped with delight at the sight of Emily flaying her fists at her startled husband.

Rob turned her over, saw the way her shift clung to every hill and valley of her body, and gulped. Before she lost her modesty, he pulled a burlap sack over to cover her. "I'm taking her to my cabin," he told Jason. "Send warm ale, some bread, and whatever Jop can rustle up."

As soon as they were inside the cabin, Rob stripped off Emily's wet clothes, put her in the bed, and tucked the quilt all around her. Then he hastily threw off his own wet things, dried himself as best he could, and crawled in beside her. She was ice cold, more from shock of what had happened than the water, he guessed, since he was naught but a little chilled. Frantic to get life back into her, he chaffed her arms and legs, trying to turn her bluish skin back to her usually warm pink glow. Finally, he drew his wife close to his body to give her the warmth she needed.

Gradually, the choking breaths she had been taking began to slow into steady, quiet breathing. When Rob realized she was sleeping soundly, he smiled. Then his body shuddered, as he realized how close he had come to losing her, and only hours after getting her back.

Unashamed of how he felt at such a prospect, he allowed his tears to wash away the guilt he felt for what he'd done on Block Island and the months he had stayed away from her.

"It will never happen again, Emily," he whispered. "I promise you, we will be together always."

"I'm counting on that," she whispered back.

When he looked down, she was still asleep. Loving the way she had responded to him, even when she was sleeping, Rob chuckled. Then he, too, slipped into a quiet slumber.

Several hours later he woke to find the hot supper he had ordered was waiting on the chart table, stone cold. He slipped out of bed and padded across to quaff the ale. Stale as it was, it helped to chase the few lingering shivers away. When he heard sounds outside the door, he opened it to find Jop standing there.

"Master want breakfast?"

"The master does."

"So does the mistress," Emily said, stretching and smiling at her confused, startled, joyful husband.

"Two breakfasts," Rob ordered, then shut the door. He turned and took two strides toward the bed but stopped when Emily held up her hand.

"Stay there. Let me look at you. Umm . . . you are beautiful."

"Tolerable, maybe. But no man is beautiful."

"You are. Especially to a woman who slipped over to the eternal side of life and never thought she'd see you again."

He wanted to ask her what it was like, dying and then coming back; but he knew the answer already. He had died when she had. They both had come back from the depths. And he was determined to make every minute of life more precious than the last.

"Emily, love . . . stand up so I can look at you."

She smiled, slipped gracefully out of Rob's bed, and stood silently and proudly in front of him.

They were an arm's distance away; but neither made a move. Instead, their eyes sought out each wonderful part of the other's body, lingering long enough to whet an appetite already getting out of hand.

"Touch me," she said.

"And you touch me."

His hand touched her breast. Hers touched his

manhood. Caresses . . . gentle caresses warmed them both.

"I lost my wedding dress."

"I'll buy you another."

"But the brooch went with it."

"There are thousands of topazes. Only one Emily Gorton."

"Emily Sears."

"Oh, aye." One hand on her breast, one on the dark triangle beneath her belly. "Goodwife Sears, I want to make love to you."

"If you don't hurry up, I'm going to melt through the boards."

Instead, she melted when he entered her. She muffled her shout of pure joy against his shoulder so the crew wouldn't hear her. Then, as Rob took each nipple into his mouth she couldn't contain her sounds. She cried out and arched up into him, to bring him closer and closer, deeper and deeper, to sear her soul with him, so he would know that she held nothing back.

They had made love before; but not as man and wife. There was something more wondrous in it, a special give and take that she had almost closed out of her life, that Nathaniel's hatred had almost robbed her of.

With one fierce coupling, she threw away the years of denial and gave herself into the safekeeping of the man she loved. And he did everything right, everything wonderful, everything to let her know she was forgiven, cherished, loved.

Another meal got cold but they didn't care. They had a feast of their own, right there in the bed.

"Your skin is salty."

"Everywhere?"

Rob chuckled. "Not exactly."

"Where, exactly, isn't it salty?"

He showed her and she opened her legs wider as he drugged her into a deep, shuddering, wonderful release.

When she could get her voice back to normal, she pulled his head up and kissed him. "Unfortunately, you don't have a place like that."

"Would you care to make a wager on that?"

Fifteen minutes later, when they lay in each other's arms, she chided him, "You lied. It was most definitely salty."

"I didn't say it wasn't. I merely implied that I was not all that different from you."

"Different enough, thank God."

She had almost drifted off to sleep when he tugged her face up and said, "Wife . . ."

"Yes, husband?"

"After what happened today, I've decided there isn't a chance in hell that I'll allow you aboard this ship while the British are still after me."

"Then, where . . . ?"

"You will stay on Block Island, Emily."

"I truly don't mind coming with you."

"I know; and I love you even more for that. But there's too much tension. Even if the British didn't consider me a pirate, there's war coming, Em. Too many taxes. Too many men willing to die rather than be forced under the British yoke. You're going to be needed more on the island, where hundreds of ships can use your services, than you are here on *Patriot*.

And you said yourself that Jason is a born doctor. You could teach him what he'd need to be my ship's surgeon, couldn't you?"

"Yes."

"Why so sad?"

"We'll be apart for six months or more."

"Nay, love. I wouldn't do that to either of us. I couldn't stand it. I'll make sure to put into the island every couple of months."

"But how? Your runs are to Guadeloupe and Europe."

"Jack and Quince and I can split the runs into three parts. It will be safer for all of us. And, if war comes, we'll be close to hand to fight the British."

"You shooting them up. Me patching them up. Am I the only one who finds such behavior stupid and cruel?"

"Nay. It *is* stupid and cruel. But that's war, love. And war only comes when good men stop listening to each other."

"Then we must pray that good men will listen to each other and prevent this awful thing."

"Pray, but be vigilant. It's the only thing that might save us."

Rob sailed the *Patriot* on an easy cruise, taking seven days to reach Block Island. He and Emily never left the cabin.

When they arrived at the island, it was Sunday. All of them trudged up the hill to services; and Rob had the minister announce their marriage from the pulpit. In all Emily's memory, it was the first time cries of shock and surprise filled the church instead of joyous psalms.

But once the news settled in, Henry threw open his house, and she and Rob were feted by her family and all her neighbors.

As Rob tucked into a plate filled with scallop pie, boiled lobster, greens fried with salt pork, light and crispy corn johnnycakes, and peach conserve, he chuckled at the sideways glances they kept getting from the islanders, including Emily's brothers.

"We shocked them, wife."

"And delighted them," Emily said. "I don't think a one of them ever expected me to consent to be your wife."

"I'm very happy you found the courage to do it."

Emily's eyes filled with tears. "Oh, Rob. Only you would know how much courage it took to throw out all those images of myself that had ruled my life for twenty-six years."

"But I knew you could do it because you are the most courageous woman I know."

"Those feelings won't come back, Rob. I promise."

"Yes they will. Even you can't toss aside twenty-six years in only a few months. But when they do, we can ride them out together, Em. We can ride anything out together."

"Did I tell you today that I love you?"

"Aye. But go ahead and say it again. I can't get enough of hearing it."

"I love you, Rob."

"And I love you, Emily." He leaned closer and whispered seductively, "When can we get out of here?"

"Finish your wedding supper. We have a long nigh of lovemaking ahead of us."

Two days after the wedding feast, at Jason's insis tence, Rob gave in and allowed the crew to paint ou his ship's name and paint over it the one that shoul have been there in the first place. In only a day, a Rob was making love to his wife in the big four-poste bed in the bedroom of her small house, *Patrio* ceased to exist.

The *Emily* would ever after ride the waves unde Rob's captaincy, a fierce symbol of the courage, car ing, and commitment that would continue t strengthen them through the rest of their lives.